THE BOMBAY PRINCE

THE BOMBAY PRINCE

SUJATA MASSEY

THORNDIKE PRESS
A part of Gale, a Cengage Company

LIBRARY OF CONGRESS CIP DATA ON FILE.
CATALOGUING IN PUBLICATION FOR THIS BOOK
IS AVAILABLE FROM THE LIBRARY OF CONGRESS.

ISBN-13: 978-1-4328-9486-3 (hardcover alk. paper)

Published in 2022 by arrangement with Soho Press, Inc.

Printed in Mexico
Print Number: 01   Print Year: 2022

For Claire and Rekha
Dear sisters who taught me about
telling stories

1
A STUDENT VISIT

"Well done."

Perveen Mistry spoke aloud as she slid the signed contracts into envelopes. Lighting a candle against a wax stick, she allowed a scarlet drop to fall on the back of each envelope. The final touch was pressing down the brass stamp engraved MISTRY LAW.

It felt ridiculous to praise herself, but this rental contract had taken four months. Term sheets had passed back and forth between two men who seemed convinced that without yet another restriction, their respective honors would be stolen.

The truth was, the landlord and renter needed each other. Mistry Law's client, Mr. Shah, sought an occupant for a bungalow on Cumballa Hill. Mr. Ahmad, an administrator at a shipping firm, was a well-qualified renter. Perveen had composed an agreement based on her past contracts for the landlord's properties. But suddenly, her client wanted an amendment prohibiting the butchering of meat. Mr. Ahmad had crossed that out and written in capital letters that his wife had the right to cut and cook whatever she pleased. He also insisted that Mr. Shah replace a dying mango tree in the garden.

An adequate home was hard to find, especially a free-standing one. People from all across British India and the independent princely states were streaming into Bombay looking for good-paying work. The bungalows of the late nineteenth century were crumbling from decay, so the middle class made do with flats. Still, throughout the city most buildings stayed homogeneous in terms of religion, region, and language.

Perveen suspected that religious anxiety had infected her Parsi client and made the prospective Muslim renter react defensively. She'd sent each gentleman a polite letter reminding him that municipal taxes would rise in the new year, so he might wish to put a pause on all real estate activity until they saw the new rate.

The prospect of having an empty house when a tax bill was due led Mr. Shah to remove the butchering clause. Mr. Ahmad thanked him and removed his request for the landlord to replace the tree; however, he requested permission to make gardening improvements as the family saw fit. Perveen assured Mr. Shah that a tenant who made garden improvements at personal cost would improve property value and the landlord's reputation.

Now the contracts were signed, sealed, and almost delivered.

Taking the envelopes in hand, she went to find Mustafa. The silver-haired giant who served as Mistry Law's guard, butler, and receptionist was already coming upstairs. As he took the envelopes from her, he announced, "A young lady has come."

"Lily?" She'd been expecting a delivery of biscuits and cake from Yazdani's Café.

"No. She is named Miss Cuttingmaster." Mustafa's long, stiff mustache made an impressive show as he enunciated the name.

"What an unusual name. I suppose it is probably Muslim or Parsi," Perveen mused.

Mustafa nodded. "You are correct, and I think this one has the face of an Irani. She said that Miss Hobson-Jones referred her to you."

Perveen's interest was piqued. Alice Hobson-Jones, Perveen's best friend, was teaching mathematics at Woodburn College. Perhaps Miss Cuttingmaster was her student. "I'll be right down. Would you kindly bring us some tea?"

"Already on the table."

Perveen peeked through the half-open parlor door to observe her visitor. Miss Cuttingmaster sat on the edge of the plum velvet settee with a book in her lap. Her head was bent over it, showing a tumble of dark curls. Thin forearms peeped out from the sleeves of a crisp white cotton blouse worn under a drab tan sari. A khaki drill-cloth satchel rested against her legs.

"Kem cho." Perveen greeted her in the Gujarati that many Parsis spoke together.

Quickly, Freny Cuttingmaster closed her book. "Yes. Good morning, ma'am, how should I address you? Should it be 'esquire'?"

The young woman's use of English was surprising, given that she wore homespun cloth favored by independence activists. However, English was also the chief language of the academic world, so perhaps that was why she chose to use it.

The room had enough seating for four, but instead of taking one of the Queen Anne wing chairs, Perveen sat a few feet from the student on the settee itself. Her hope was to put the stiff-seeming girl at ease. "My name is Perveen Mistry. I feel a little too young for 'ma'am,' and 'esquire' is mainly used in the United States for lawyers. May I have your good name?"

"It is Freny." As she spoke, the girl edged away slightly. "I still don't know what to call you. 'Memsahib' is a term mostly used for the British, so I won't call you that. I don't like 'ma'am' much, either."

Perveen thought about the typical honorific used for Parsi women. "If you'd like, you may call me Perveen-bai."

Freny nodded. "Perveen-bai, I am representing Woodburn College's Student Union. We are seeking a legal consultation."

Activism was on an uptick throughout Bombay. In recent months the famous lawyer Mohandas Gandhi had been gaining adherents with his calls for protest against British rule. Perveen longed to assist freedom fighters, but she was a solicitor, so her work was mostly contracts. "I am honored you thought of Mistry Law. Would you like to tell me your concern?"

Freny looked intently at Perveen. "We want to know if we have the right to stay away from college without being punished."

Perveen mulled over the words. "I don't think I understand. Students are expected to attend classes as a condition of enrollment. Do you have a conflict with one of

11

the lecturers?"

"Not at all. I'm in my second year, and I love my college." She gave the book in her hands a squeeze. "Actually, we students would not be missing instruction on the day I'm thinking about, because classes that day are canceled."

For this, the girl had come to Mistry Law? Trying not to sound irritated, Perveen said, "In your case, I think you would be forgiven a day off. Students often miss college for reasons of illness and family matters."

"But it's not that. It is *political.*" She pronounced the last word carefully, stressing its importance. "We want to be absent from college on the day the Prince of Wales enters Bombay. Did you know that Gandhiji has called a hartal?"

"Yes. I've seen the placards advising people to boycott the prince." Perveen had noticed these renegade announcements next to the "Welcome Prince of Wales" signs posted by the government all over town. On Thursday, Edward would disembark at the Port of Bombay and begin a four-month tour of India. The arrival of the twenty-seven-year-old prince seemed like a promise of many more decades of British rule.

Freny leaned forward and spoke with hushed excitement. "We students put up

12

some of the placards. We don't want people attending the parade. However, the college principal said everyone must be present on the day of the prince's arrival. Workers are building a special viewing stand in front of the college. We're supposed to applaud that loathsome prince when he parades along the Kennedy Sea-Face."

Freny's passionate speech left no question of her conviction. But what would the consequences be if she held back from school? "Does your Student Union have a faculty advisor?"

"Yes. Mr. Terrence Grady." Freny's lips turned up at the corners.

Perveen hoped that Freny didn't have a crush. "Does Mr. Grady report about your club to the administration?"

"I don't think so," Freny answered after a moment. "He is an Irishman, and many Irish are not at all keen on being part of Britain. Mr. Grady confessed that because he's an employee, he must come to school that day. He knows about the Student Union's desire to stay back and urged us to follow our conscience."

Perveen's shoulders relaxed and she said, "He sounds like a fair man. What can you tell me about the college principal?"

"His name is Horace Virgil Atherton." She

13

spoke the name in staccato syllables, showing none of the warmth she'd had for Mr. Grady. "He's a temporary principal who joined in October. Our regular principal is away on furlough. During the Christian scripture hour, before the chaplain speaks, Mr. Atherton sometimes addresses us. I've only heard him say things like we must stop crowding and pushing past each other in the galleries and stairs. Nothing about philosophy or the nature of education."

Perveen snorted. "Your principal sounds better suited to supervising primary school. What reason does he have to talk about hallway behavior?"

Freny rewarded her with an appreciative smirk. "He thinks there is too much hustle and bustle, and someone could fall down. He said the college's females could be injured, which was very annoying to my friends and me. We aren't made of porcelain."

"No. Bombay women are at least as strong as coconuts!" After Freny laughed, Perveen added, "Why are you in a Christian scripture class?"

"It's not a mandatory course. However, roll call is taken at the start of that scripture class. So everyone goes, regardless of faith."

"Are you saying that in order to be marked

present, you must sit through a religious service?" Perveen paused, wondering if there were grounds for some kind of suit. "Woodburn College is a missionary institution, isn't it?"

"Indeed. It was founded by Reverend Andrew Woodburn, Church of Scotland, who came to Bombay in 1810."

"How do your parents feel about you having a Presbyterian college education?"

"My father says the college's name carries weight and I will benefit from the other coursework." Smiling wistfully, she added, "He's the head tailor at the Hawthorn Shop. He boasts to his customers that I'm studying at Woodburn College."

A tailor would be proud to send his daughter to one of the city's oldest colleges. And now she understood how perfectly suited his name was. "Your father must be a tolerant person."

"I would not say that." Freny pointed directly at one of the wing chairs and chuckled. "My father would be annoyed by that chair."

Perveen was mystified. "Why?"

"The red banding is torn. There, on the leg."

Perveen followed her gaze to the chair, which she hadn't ever inspected in such a close fashion. "Goodness, you're right. That's my father's favorite chair. Perhaps he snagged it with his shoe. He crosses his leg and taps his foot sometimes. Back to our topic — does your father know about your support of independence?"

Freny looked down at her book, as if the answer might lie within. When she raised her face, her expression was sober. "I wanted to tell him, but it was difficult. He thinks I'm too young to understand."

Perveen nodded in sympathy. "Fathers are like that. Are you saying that he doesn't know that you're one of the leaders in the group?"

Freny shook her head vehemently. "I'm not a leader. There are only two of us in the group who are female."

"You say you aren't a leader, but it's a significant responsibility to gather a legal opinion for the group," Perveen challenged. "Be proud of yourself."

"I can't. I only thought helping them was the right thing. I don't want anyone to be hurt." Straightening the book in her lap, Freny added, "And I think, just by visiting you, it might improve things."

Perveen didn't want Freny to consider her a miracle worker. "In what way could they improve?"

"Several of the boys have taunted me" — she took a deep breath — "about my father working on his knees for British and Anglo-Indians."

"Tailors must go on their knees to hem trousers!" Perveen felt great sympathy, because the Cuttingmasters were a working-class family who had surely overcome obstacles to send a daughter to college.

"Dinesh, who is the most outspoken boy in the Student Union, said that all Parsis love the English. He was quite friendly when Lalita and I joined, but now tries to keep me out of everything."

Perveen's stomach tightened. "What an ignorant thing to say about our faith. What about Dadabhai Naoroji, grand old man of the freedom movement, and Madame Bhikaji Cama, who is currently exiled in France? And we mustn't forget that a number of Parsi businessmen in South Africa and India have supported Gandhiji for years."

"Dinesh says Parsis are only thinking about money." Freny's rosebud mouth turned downward. "I'm sure they wanted me to speak with a lawyer so I'd be charged any bills."

"This is only a conversation, not a legal service. There will be no charge," Perveen

17

assured her.

"That's very kind." Freny's frown was starting to ease. "Miss Hobson-Jones talked about having a friend who is the first woman solicitor in Bombay. I was very excited for the chance to meet you."

Perveen found Freny's approval flattering. "I am glad we've met, too. Now, when you enrolled in the college, was there a handbook or a contract you and your parents signed? Documents like these might list information about grounds for suspension and expulsion."

"No handbook was given. I don't recall a contract, but if there is one, my father must have it." Wrinkling her forehead, she said, "I can't ask him for it."

Perveen didn't want to trigger a family argument. "Then ask another student if he or she has a contract. Read it yourself or bring it to me."

"I will do that, Perveen-bai." Freny accepted the business card that Perveen handed her from the crystal dish on the silver tea table.

"Taking a political stance is a serious matter. For many decades Indian students who protest have been beaten up, jailed, and some even executed." Observing Freny's eyes widen, Perveen added, "You would not

18

get a death sentence for missing a day's school, but please do not undertake a political action only for the sake of impressing your peers."

"Truly, I would vomit if I had to look at that prince. I would shame myself!" Freny declared. "I am just worried that we could have our lives changed for staying away. I was told that two years ago, some students were expelled for being Communists."

Perveen considered Freny's plight. How to avoid honoring the prince, yet not be punished by the authorities? "Did you ever think that you could stay in bed on Thursday with a stomachache, and neither your parents nor the school would know the reason?"

Freny shook her head. "That would not be truthful. You know about asha."

She was talking about the cornerstone of the Parsi theology: the principle of rightness. To be a good Parsi was to tell the truth. This was one of the reasons that Parsi lawyers were trusted by Indians of all faiths.

"Yes, I understand asha — and neither of us can guess how your body and spirit will be on Thursday. Illness is a solid reason for absence."

"Trouble comes after lies. I will not do it again."

After Freny's short declaration, Perveen sat in silence, hearing the gentle ticking of the grandfather clock in the room's corner. In the pause, she understood that she'd been trying to sway a young person who had a powerful conscience. "Freny, you must do what you believe — and each student should as well. Considering how the Student Union's leaders asked you to speak with a lawyer, at least some share the same worries as you."

"Yes. If we are thrown out, we might never get another college scholarship or money for education from our parents. We would ruin everything for them, and for ourselves." The words rushed out. "I thought if I came here, you would give me the answer. I was hoping you would say no, you will be safe and able to continue in your studies. But you haven't said that to me."

"I don't have enough information — and I cannot guess how Mr. Atherton will react." Perveen was sorry she didn't have something solid to tell Freny. "The prince doesn't come for three days. There's still time to discover if anyone has a contract. And I'll gladly look at it for you."

"Thank you." Freny turned over the book she'd been holding and moved it toward the satchel.

Glancing at the book, Perveen saw it was *Heart of Darkness* by Joseph Conrad. She had not read the popular novel, but Alice had said it was a scathing rebuke of European colonialism in Africa. "Is that for your literature class?"

Freny tucked the book tenderly into the bag. "No. This is for world history. Mr. Grady often assigns us novels and newspaper articles because he thinks they hold truths that history books don't. The thing is, there are so many different writers of these materials, which one is telling the trustworthy account?"

"That is an interesting observation. I would be happy to speak with you again — but send a note or make a telephone call first. I usually have several appointments a day, and sometimes I am out of the office."

Freny regarded her with admiring eyes. "Are you defending the innocent in the Bombay High Court?"

"Not yet. The Bombay High Court refuses to recognize women lawyers as advocates."

Freny's eyebrows went up. "Does that mean there is no court in India which allows women to speak on behalf of clients?"

"Outside of the high court, I'm not sure." Perveen saw the disappointment in her face and added, "Perhaps there will be a chance for me to find out."

"My brother was very, very good at arguing," Freny said after a silence.

"And he isn't anymore?"

"Darius has no way of speaking," she answered softly.

Perveen was perplexed. "What do you mean?"

"Darius died when he was thirteen and I was eleven. Pappa always hoped he would be the first in our family not to be a tradesman. I am going to Woodburn College with a partial scholarship. The rest comes from the bank account my parents had made for my brother's education."

The pieces were coming together. "That's very sad. You must miss him very much."

"I do. And if I'm thrown out of college, I shall dishonor my late brother as well as my parents." She blinked and straightened her shoulders. "How did you manage to get Mr. Mistry to let you become a solicitor?"

"Actually, he wished me to study law at Oxford because my brother would never have been admitted. I was the only way to fulfill my pappa's dream of a legal legacy possible."

"Your father could have done something else," Freny countered. "He could have hired men to be solicitors and barristers and

22

made a large important firm like Wadia Ghandy, or that of Mohammed Ali Jinnah."

Perveen nodded. "Those are important legal players in the city, yes, but my father chose to start with me. Probably he hoped he'd get a lawyer son-in-law, too, but that hasn't happened."

"He believed in you, all along. Yet it must have been strange to do your studies in the country that oppresses India." Freny shifted on the settee to look directly at her.

Catching judgment in the girl's eyes, Perveen answered, "In England, I encountered people who were prejudiced toward Indians. I also met a surprising number in favor of Indian independence. Among the most outspoken was Miss Hobson-Jones."

Freny choked, and then broke into a smile. "Lecturers are surprising! That's one of the best things about Woodburn College. Although I know for a fact some of them are hiding the truth about their pasts."

How many times had Freny mentioned truth? It seemed to be an obsession. "In principle, I agree that we should be truthful. The trouble is that my own understanding of earlier events could be very different from another person's impression of the same."

After a moment's reflection, Freny said,

"Yes. How can one say which truth is the important one?"

Perveen was intrigued by her reasoning. "That is the challenge of being an advocate: to convince a judge or jurors of one explanation when there are many theories flying about."

"I'm terrible at saying what I think." Freny's voice was rueful. "I speak out and it makes people very annoyed sometimes. Lalita says I'm turning myself into a marked person."

"I think you're very clear-spoken. By the way, if you are curious about legal education, go into the High Court during the school holidays. Sit among the public and observe. You will either be fascinated or repelled."

"Perhaps both," Freny said, and the two of them chuckled.

As Freny stood up, one of the stiff folds of her sari brushed the edge of the tea table, jiggling the china atop it. Perveen suddenly realized that she hadn't poured a cup of tea for her student visitor, nor had she offered any biscuits.

The rambling conversation had raised too many questions in Perveen's mind. At its end, it seemed like Freny was trying to say

something more but had been too cryptic
for Perveen to understand.

2
WALES ON PARADE

In the late nineteenth century, Arshan Kayan Mistry built a mansion in Bruce Street large enough to hold himself, his three sons, and their wives and children. As the owner of a profitable construction firm, he had superb architects at his disposal. The house was a triumph, built of golden Kurla stone and ornamented with carved crocodiles whose mouths spewed water when it rained. Inside, the high-ceilinged rooms had gas chandeliers that were later converted to electricity. Four bathrooms with marble fixtures were plumbed like those of the British elite. Grandfather Mistry treasured his house and mourned when his sons gradually departed to set up their own homes in neighborhoods with less crowding and better air.

Arshan had resigned himself to a life in a grand house with only his staff for company, and the occasional visitors. Therefore, he was pleasantly surprised in 1905 when his middle son, Jamshedji — a black sheep who'd preferred law to building — asked if he could base his fledgling practice at Mistry House. Having an office so close to the Bombay High Court was a wonderful advantage.

The house-cum-office was a mutually beneficial arrangement. Father and son communed over lunch or afternoon tea for twelve years until the elderly gentleman's death in 1917.

His presence was still felt in a huge portrait hung in the entrance hall. In the painting, Grandfather Mistry was sixty years old and dressed in a European suit with a tall black fetah on his head. His right hand rested on a table holding a religious book, a fountain pen, and a construction ruler. The artist, Pestonjee Bomanjee, had painted his stern dark brown eyes in a way that allowed his gaze to track anyone looking at the painting, just like da Vinci's *Mona Lisa.*

No matter where Perveen stood in Mistry House on Thursday, November 17, she felt under observation. The sensation started with her father's reaction that morning when she'd suggested stopping by the freedom fighters' bonfire. Her father had snapped that she'd done enough pro bono work for the year. And why would she go all the way north to the mill district, when she'd declared herself too busy to celebrate the prince's arrival at the Gateway of India?

Perveen had been annoyed, but she knew better than to disobey outright. And surely her late grandfather would have agreed with Jamshedji. Sighing to herself, she turned her back on Grandfather Mistry's portrait and trudged up the grand polished stairway and along the second floor to its end, where a small cast-iron staircase led to the roof.

The short trapdoor opened with a creak and she stepped out carefully to the flat limestone surface. The roof was like most others on the street, with a laundry line and several tall clay pots for collecting rainwater. When she was little, she had thrown a ball back and forth with her brother over the line — until Grandfather's angry face had appeared in the trapdoor space, warning them to come back down or suffer the consequences. Mistry House was taller than most buildings on the street, and a child's careless step could have been deadly. But now was not the time for wistful memories.

Perveen looked toward the port, where a hulking gray ship dwarfed the vessels around. She didn't need binoculars to recognize it was a military destroyer. She'd seen such giant ships off the coast of England during the Great War.

The trapdoor creaked, and she turned to see Mustafa. The tall, dignified Pathan looked incongruous with a laundry basket in his arms.

"And why are you on the roof?" he asked as he began pinning up wet napkins and towels.

"Just checking if the prince arrived. And laundry is not your job, Mustafa," she added.

"What to do? The dhobi is not coming today." As he caught sight of the destroyer, his eyes softened. "The HMS *Renown!*"

"A pompous name to match its passenger," Perveen commented.

"We should not show prejudice against the prince. What if he carries great news?" Mustafa flung a dish towel with the expert aim of a former Indian Army sergeant. The pension he'd received upon retiring was so pitiful he'd had to start a second career working at Mistry House.

"Fifty more years of British rule is not great news to me."

Mustafa pinned up the dish towel and smoothed it before answering. "Perhaps the government decided to grant India dominion status. Who better to announce it than our crown prince?"

Perveen rolled her eyes. "I understand that you are interested in Edward, but let's remember he's still the Prince of Wales, not the Prince of Bombay."

"You seem in a bad temper, Perveen-memsahib."

"It's the wrong time for parties and flag-waving. As you know, many are staying home to boycott, and Gandhiji's followers are building a bonfire today. The prince's arrival will simply fan flames."

"That fire has already started." Mustafa pointed north, where a thin wisp of black smoke was visible. "I am troubled that people would burn clothes when so many need them. Fortunately, the bonfire is distant, and His Royal Highness will not travel in that direction. I feel jubilant that his first steps into India will be through a structure built by your brother." Mustafa's voice had lowered, as if afraid of being overheard boasting. "If your honorable grandfather was alive, he'd be very proud."

"Yes, he would. But the Gateway of India isn't complete. Grandfather would say that too many contractors were involved, and that makes delay."

As if he hadn't heard, Mustafa continued,

"Prince Edward will come through the Gateway and then give remarks to his audience. He will be welcomed by our viceroy, the governor, and the mayor. Finally he will take a carriage ride through the city and up Malabar Hill to Government House, where he will be residing."

"You memorized his itinerary?" A sharp gust of wind tore a small piece of white cloth that was not yet fully pinned from the line. As it dropped, Perveen caught it: one of her father's linen handkerchiefs, his monogram embroidered in the same curving script as the law firm's seal.

"Shukriya," Mustafa said in gratitude as she fixed the handkerchief on the line. "Yes, I read the schedule in the newspaper. Your father gave me leave to attend the assembly of military veterans on the Maidan next week."

This reminded her of Freny Cuttingmaster, who hadn't come back. Perveen regretted counseling her to feign illness; that was hardly the example an idealistic Parsi lawyer should set for a younger person. Would Freny show up to college, or not?

Why should it matter so much? Perveen had a tight, anxious feeling in her body. Checking her watch, she saw it would be forty-five minutes until the prince took his

31

first steps through the Gateway. She spoke impulsively. "I will go out after all. Have you seen my opera glasses? I mislaid them."

Mustafa's silver brows drew together. "What is your scheme this time?"

The plan was coming together in her mind. She would ride the train from Churchgate to Charni Station. From there, she'd walk the short stretch to Woodburn College.

"You and my father think this is a once-in-a-lifetime opportunity. It's true. I will watch the prince's procession." She spoke casually, hoping this would be enough to satisfy him.

"But you missed your chance to go to the amphitheater at Apollo Bunder. Arman is remaining there with the car," he said, referring to the family chauffeur.

"I'm going to Woodburn College, where there is another viewing stand."

Mustafa tucked the empty basket under his arm. "Really? Will Miss Hobson-Jones be there?"

"Yes, of course." Perveen knew that Mustafa was fond of Alice. Before the English-woman landed the position of assistant mathematics lecturer, she'd assisted the firm on a part-time basis, employing her special knowledge of local government as well as mathematical skills.

"But how will you reach the college?" Mustafa's expression was still wary.

"The Western Line train. I promise I'll be fine." Dryly she added, "I'm sure every compartment will be crowded with admirers of the prince."

Perveen set off with the opera glasses in her briefcase, as well as her business card case, pens, and a legal notebook. Carrying the briefcase made her feel more like a worker than a celebrant. And while others were bedecked in holiday finery, she'd worn an everyday, peach-and-red silk bandhej sari with a white cotton blouse underneath. Today, she wished the blouse were not so distinctively European. Activists would make assumptions about her, and so would the crown loyalists. Nobody would know that the reason she was out had nothing to do with adulation or destruction. She was on a mission to observe the city's reaction to Edward — and to discover what action Freny had chosen.

On the way to Churchgate Station, she had to pass through Elphinstone Circle: a round road ringed with some of the city's most elegant and important office buildings.

Two Mistry stonemasons helped build

Elphinstone Circle in the 1870s. Later on, the family's contracting business prospered to the point that Grandfather Mistry bought one of the spacious Elphinstone Circle buildings for his own business use. Today, Union Jacks fluttered from the top stories of Mistry and Sons Construction and its neighbors.

The circular roadway lacked the usual morning bustle of carts, buses, and cars. A Bombay Police sign on the circle proclaimed no traffic was allowed due to the Prince of Wales's procession. Indian Army soldiers and Bombay City police stood at stiff attention, each positioned five feet from the next. As Perveen tried to walk across the circle to Church Gate Street, a young constable with a bayonet spoke sharply.

"That side only."

Perveen followed his gaze toward the stands, where small clusters of Indians and Anglo-Indians in holiday finery were seated. The stands were occupied, but not crowded. "Can't I please cross quickly to get to Churchgate Station? The procession is not in sight."

"No exceptions."

"Perveen-bai! Perveen-bai!"

Perveen gazed upward and spotted thirteen-year-old Lily Yazdani seated with her family in the stands.

"Come up here!" Lily squealed. "Please do, Perveen-bai! We have biscuits and puffs just baked!"

Lily's parents, Firoze and Ruxshin, were also beckoning. Perveen abandoned her plan to cross the circle and went up to visit with the Yazdanis.

"I don't know how you managed all this baking and still made it to the parade," Perveen said as she selected a crisp curry puff from the assortment of baked goods the Yazdanis offered her.

"Easy. I have good helpers, and we start at four o'clock." Firoze was in his early forties and had a pleasant round face surrounded by a halo of dark curly hair. Today was the first time she'd seen it without its usual faint dusting of flour. "We baked because our customers would expect us to be open today."

"It is hardly crowded here — not like I expected." Ruxshin shrugged as if trying to show she didn't care. "More room for all of us, I suppose."

"The railway station nearby was more crowded than here," Firoze added. "Many young men are going to the mills. A protest can be held any day. It's silly to do it on the day of our future emperor's arrival!"

Perveen shook her head. "That is the point — to protest *because* he is here."

Firoze's cheeks pinkened, as if he were gathering the words for an argument.

Ruxshin spoke swiftly. "Come, come, tell us what is going on at your house. When will your brother and sister-in-law have a baby?"

Perveen understood Ruxshin was trying to avoid trapping her in a political conversation. "Rustom and Gulnaz would really like to have a child, but man proposes, and God disposes. Anyway, Rustom is very busy these days."

"A little bird told me he is putting the last touch on the Gateway!" Ruxshin beamed.

"Yes. He's sure the prince and viceroy will have firm footing."

"Perveen, please take your family some mixed pastries as our congratulations on Rustom-ji's role today." With a flourish, Firoze pulled an unopened box from the picnic basket.

Perveen took it and smiled her thanks. "I'm sure he will enjoy it. Now, I beg your pardon, but I must get on to Churchgate Station."

The local train was running on time, and as she waited to board, many well-dressed

Parsi families disembarked, bound for El-phinstone Circle. Perveen exchanged pleas-antries with a few people from her fire temple. Nobody asked her if she was excited to set eyes on the prince. Their mutual pres-ence implied support.

Coming out of Charni Station, she walked along the Kennedy Sea-Face, where the viewing stands had larger crowds than at Elphinstone Circle. Woodburn College was a wide two-story building with three levels of long, open galleries that faced the road and seaside. The college's galleries could have made excellent parade viewing, but they weren't wide enough to hold all the students. Therefore, a series of viewing stands were placed right in front of the col-lege's fence, so the community was outside and close to the street. The stand's wooden benches were mostly filled with male stu-dents and older people she guessed were faculty and staff. The girls numbered less than a dozen and were dressed in saris, like all the other Indian women nearby. Perveen didn't see Freny.

On the other hand, with a dark day dress and black boater on her head, Alice Hobson-Jones was swiftly recognizable. An Indian woman was offering her an oversized handkerchief, which Alice smilingly rejected. Finally, the lady simply flung the handkerchief over Alice's knees. Finally understanding that her modish dress had risen to an indecorous level, Alice clapped a hand to her mouth.

Perveen laughed, although with the noise of the chatting students, nobody would have heard. She made a quick scan of the single row of girls sitting alongside Alice and the other lady. Had she missed identifying Freny?

No. She wasn't there.

Perveen's attention was diverted by the sight of a slender Indian gentleman in his fifties escorting a stocky European man of similar age wearing a brown woolen suit unsuitable for the weather. The European was approaching the first row, which appeared designated for male faculty. From the way that the teachers in this row all arose, she guessed the man was the college principal. Mr. Atherton settled down as if his bones hurt, and the Indian quickly ascended the edges of the risers to seat himself in the empty back row.

Had the Indian lecturers been instructed to sit away from the Europeans? Perveen suddenly realized that they were seated with the students, rather than in the front row. Her friend Alice was the only white sitting amidst the student body.

Perhaps the tense-looking fellow had chosen to sit in the very back instead of alongside students because he was trying to keep as distant from the sight of the prince as he could. Probably, many students and staff didn't want Prince Edward in India. At least a dozen male students had white Congress Party caps atop their heads.

Her thoughts were interrupted by a Parsi boy of about twenty in a formal white coat and trousers who was pushing his way along the riser edge with a camera on a strap swinging from his right shoulder. The Parsi was good-looking, with a strong jaw and aquiline nose, but his appearance was undercut by smudges of dirt on his clothing. The slightly unkempt appearance reminded her of a young Rustom. Her brother could never make it to the agiary in pristine whites.

The young photographer made his way up the staggered rows of benches, calling out and aiming his camera at various classmates. Some of the students smiled and posed, but those wearing Congress caps grimaced or made shooing motions with their hands.

"Come. Over. Here!" Alice cupped her hands around her mouth as she called out.

"Miss Mistry, we have room for you!"

Perveen approached the risers but paused at the first one, not wanting to cause disturbance to anyone already seated. She saw the principal looking her over with an anxious expression, as if he should know who she was. She hesitated, not knowing whether his noticing her meant she should walk on. After all, she wasn't part of the college.

To her surprise, he nodded at her. In a thick Northern accent, he said, "Go ahead. You may join the ladies' section."

She uttered a quick thank-you and stepped along to the second row of seating, where the females were.

"Good morning, dear!" Alice's voice was merry. "You came just in the nick, and I see you've got your favorite opera glasses. Bully for you."

Perveen winked at her. "We can share."

Alice gestured with her hand to her neighbor, the woman who'd covered up her knees with the handkerchief. "May I introduce you to Miss Roshan Daboo? She's a lecturer who's been here five years. Miss Daboo, this is my old friend Perveen Mistry."

Through thick spectacles, Miss Daboo gave Perveen a penetrating stare. "I know your name. Miss Mistry, aren't you the lady

40

solicitor I've read about?"

"Guilty as charged," Perveen joked.

"Miss Mistry, I should like to hear all about your work!" a girl chirped from a few seats away.

"Lalita Acharya, may I inform you that you cannot practice law with a Woodburn degree?" Miss Daboo reproved. "You are going to become a teacher."

Perveen wondered if this Lalita was the one Freny had mentioned. She was irritated by the dismissal of student curiosity, but she couldn't present herself as an antagonist. Softly, she said, "Miss Daboo, you must have overcome many obstacles to gain a teaching position in a co-educational college."

"That is true," Miss Daboo agreed. "I expected I'd teach high school girls. And here I am — lecturer of English poetry to college students, both male and female. How the world has changed!"

Turning her head to directly address Lalita, Perveen said, "By the way, a graduate of Woodburn could get a post-graduate degree in law, if she wanted. I'll tell you about it, but first this!" She opened the Yazdanis' pastry box to a chorus of excited comments.

After Miss Daboo and Alice had chosen

between pistachio biscuits and curry puffs, Perveen handed the box and some of her own business cards to Lalita to dispense. Everything was divided up neatly; the whole row of girls had something to enjoy.

"Where are our sweets, madam?" the student photographer called from close behind her.

"No rudeness toward ladies, Naval Hotel-wala!" barked a stern male voice from an upper row.

Perveen turned her head to see the same Indian man with gold-rimmed glasses who'd climbed up shortly after her arrival. She asked Alice, "Is that gentleman an administrator?"

"Mr. Brajesh Gupta is in the mathematics department, but he's also the dean in charge of students," Alice said. "Never mind him. It's such a nice surprise that you're here. I thought you might be at the bonfire!"

Perveen saw the students nearby had leaned in closer. In a low voice, she said to Alice, "I hoped to say hello to Freny Cuttingmaster."

Alice's eyebrows rose. "You've met? She didn't say anything about it."

From a few seats away, Lalita waved to catch their attention. When Miss Daboo nodded her permission, she spoke. "Freny

42

came to college today. She was in the chapel for roll call. She did not walk over with me, though."

Lalita Acharya must have known Freny didn't want to see the prince but probably didn't want to bring that up with a row of white male teachers nearby. Perveen held back the questions she wanted to ask. The evidence seemed to be that Freny was sitting out the prince's parade. She turned to Alice and spoke brightly. "How is that new puppy of yours? Did you name her yet?"

"Yes, indeed. I'm calling her Diana, because she's quite a little hunter. She's taken full charge of the house even though it's just six days ago that I found her. It's become dreadfully sad saying goodbye to her when I get in the car each morning." As if realizing she sounded immature, Alice hastily added, "Of course, I am so very happy to be teaching here. I only wish dogs were also allowed."

This comment created a flood of laughter from both the girls around them and some of the boys behind.

Perveen asked, "What time is it? The prince should be coming by now."

"Surely your fine watch is in working order?" Miss Daboo cut in.

Perveen blushed and glanced at the

43

Longines timepiece on her left wrist. "That's right. My watch says five minutes to eleven."

"Look at the way the soldiers have changed position!" Naval Hotelwala called out from the row behind them. "The cortege is approaching!"

Perveen turned to the row directly behind to look into his flushed, excited face. "Are you photographing all of this for the student paper?"

He nodded enthusiastically. "I'm doing it for our student literary magazine, the *Woodburnian*. Whatever one's feelings are about the Prince of Wales, my photographs of him will make it an edition to remember."

"You have an excellent camera. The college must have a good photography department," she said.

"It's my own! It's the new Kodak 2C Autographic." He angled it so she could see the manufacturer's insignia. "I also manage the cost of developing pictures, even though it's for the college magazine."

"Do you ever do portraits?" Perveen had the sudden idea that Naval could make some pocket money doing a photo session for her father, but she had no chance to continue her query.

"Hotelwala, stop jabbering. Now is the

time to get your fancy camera in focus," Dean Gupta bellowed from the top row. "The prince is nearby. Stand up!"

"Stand up, stand up!" the call was repeated all along the viewing stand by teachers and students.

Perveen stood, too. Rising was an acknowledgment of the importance of the occasion, and participating would avoid bringing potential controversy for Alice with her employer. However, she didn't take out her handkerchief to wave, because that gesture seemed too adoring.

She glanced at Alice, who was painstakingly focusing the opera glasses Perveen had handed her. Alice said, "There they are! The Prince of Wales, and Lord Reading, and Sir George Lloyd. Who else wants a look?"

Perveen did not need the opera glasses to notice the young royal, who seemed more intent on chatting with the viceroy and governor than waving back at the spectators.

The crown prince was only twenty-seven years old. Perhaps he felt cowed by the viceroy and governor, who were much older, and felt he had to give them his full attention rather than interacting with the public. But it reminded her of what she'd said to Mustafa: Edward was no Prince of Bombay.

"May I?" Miss Daboo eagerly took the binoculars. As she focused, her mouth gaped. "I see him! Our future king-emperor. He has the loveliest smile. He looks near enough to —"

"To kiss!" a mischievous boy shouted from the row behind them, and there was uproarious laughter.

"Stop it! You are undisciplined and rude!" thundered Mr. Gupta.

In the next moment, above the cheers, a new male voice shouted.

"Empire must die! Empire must die!"

3
THE START OF CHAOS

The screaming was in front of her — down on the road.

A short young man dressed in a blindingly white kurta rushed behind the prince's carriage, hands outstretched as if to grab it. Shouts arose from viewers in the stands and police along the road. *Where had he come from?* Perveen wondered. Just as quickly as he'd appeared, he vanished inside a thicket of soldiers and police.

The prince's carriage moved along, with none of the important men inside looking behind them. It was as if they hadn't noticed the man who'd tried to stop the prince's journey.

In the Woodburn College viewing stand, all decorum was gone. Most of the male students were scrambling to get down to ground level, Mr. Gupta right behind. As Perveen glanced into the teacher's face, she thought she saw tears behind his glasses.

He understood the gravity of the situation and probably knew the young man involved.

On the street, Principal Atherton was standing up, and the teachers near him closed in to make a tight circle, keeping their conversation private. This reaction, combined with those of Mr. Gupta and the other students, made it apparent the protestor was known to them.

"Dear God." Alice put her face in her hands.

"Why would Dinesh do that? He could be expelled!" said a girl on Perveen's left.

"Expulsion is nothing compared to what the police will do to him!" Lalita shot back. "Oh, he shouldn't have. The prince and viceroy didn't even notice."

Dinesh. Perveen felt a shock of recognition. Freny had confided that someone named Dinesh was the most outspoken member of the Student Union.

Perveen elbowed Alice. "Do you know who this Dinesh is?"

"Dinesh Apte is a third-year student, one of the best in advanced geometry." Alice stood up, using the advantage of the platform and her height to look over the crowd. "What are those brutes doing to him? Miss Daboo, I need the binoculars!"

Alice focused the binoculars, and Perveen

climbed higher in the empty stand to obtain her own view. Her stomach clenched as she saw police waving lathis at the students trying to break into their knot. But then, the crowd parted. Perveen saw Dinesh in the grip of three soldiers who held firm to his thin arms and the back of his neck. Blood stained the boy's face, but he held it high as he was propelled along the edge of the parade route.

Kennedy Sea-Face was wide open, because most of the photographers and reporters had kept pace with the slow-moving royal carriage. This made Perveen even more worried. Not only had the newspapermen missed the student's protest, they also hadn't seen the instant, savage takedown by the soldiers and police. Dinesh could disappear, and nobody would be held accountable.

"This is unforgivable." Miss Daboo had retrieved her handkerchief and was using it to wipe her perspiring face. "Our college has disrespected the Crown Prince. And what a tragedy that the boy is local! His family's reputation will be ruined."

Perveen's mind was not on reputation; it was on what would happen next for Dinesh. She remembered Freny complaining about the boy's mockery. It had sounded like he had been absolutely horrible to her. But would it create a conflict of interest to offer him assistance?

Perveen ran through the arguments. Freny had not signed any contract; she wasn't a Mistry Law client. She decided to get close enough to Dinesh Apte to witness his treatment by the police and caution him not to answer questions without a lawyer present. She could ask if he wanted a referral.

Her dilemma resolved, she came down from the high bench to stand next to Alice, who handed back the binoculars. "What a horrible thing to witness. Here you go."

"Thank you." She fitted the binoculars back into her legal briefcase. "I must leave."

Alice's face was anxious. "You're going to try to intervene, aren't you?"

Perveen nodded. "I want to make sure they don't kill him."

"I'd go with you if I could — but Mr. Atherton has called for teachers to guide the students back into the college. Will you please be careful?"

"Very careful. I'm only going to observe."

Perveen made her way down the spectators' stand. Walking as rapidly as her sari would allow, she tried to forget what her father had said about not becoming involved with protestors. She was certain that if Jamshedji had seen the intensity of the police reaction, he would have done what she was about to attempt.

As Perveen approached the knot of soldiers, an Indian constable moved in front of her. Gruffly, he said, "This area is closed."

Affecting an innocent tone, she said, "But the prince is far away. I'm not encroaching on his passage, am I?"

"The prince does not matter." Glowering down from a foot higher than her, the man added, "This is police business!"

"Oh, is that so? I am only wishing to walk along." As she set another foot forward, the constable squarely blocked her, waving his lathi in front of her face.

Perveen's heartbeat thundered, but she did not move. If he struck her, the crowd might react. But his emotion was high. She could be badly injured, blinded, even killed.

"What is this woman's business?" a man demanded.

Perveen glanced at the interloper, a furious-looking Anglo-Indian with a badge that said SERGEANT T. L. WILLIAMS on the breast of his uniform. Quickly, she said, "I have no complaint, sir. I am Perveen Mistry, a solicitor at law wishing to see the arrested person."

"Bombay's *lady* solicitor." The police officer wrinkled his nose, as if he'd smelled something bad. "Never mind, the rabble-rouser is already gone."

Perveen caught Sergeant Williams's gloating tone and was filled with fear. "Do you mean you killed him?"

"No. The boy's going to lockup at Gamdevi Station. And I think it's vile of you to want to represent him. Positively vile." He stared down at her, as if daring her to cause a commotion so she, too, could be arrested.

"Sergeant Williams, may I please have a word with you?" a commanding female voice rang out, and Perveen realized that Alice Hobson-Jones was not with her students, but right behind her.

"Is something wrong, madam? Is someone bothering you?" The police sergeant's manner became more compliant, now that he was talking to an Englishwoman with a posh accent.

Alice used every one of her seventy-two inches to glare down at the officer. "I am extremely bothered to see you harassing Miss Mistry, the noted solicitor and community philanthropist who assists my father. Perhaps you've heard of him — Sir David Hobson-Jones?"

Sergeant Williams's face flushed. "Madam, we mean no disrespect and there was no harassment. We have arrested a person for a threat against His Royal Highness. He never said he had an advocate."

Dinesh had only shouted three words, but unfortunately, one of them had been "death."

"Very well. Let's go, Perveen." Alice's hand was on her arm, and the police didn't protest as the two of them walked back in the direction of the college.

"I don't need to be saved by an English-woman's intervention. And I don't work for your father!" Now that Perveen was safe, she was conscious of feeling nauseous — first from fear, and now from shame at being rescued like a child.

"But you have worked for him! You accepted the request to go to Satapur," Alice said defiantly. "I said what I did because the police were all around you. I got the most panicked feeling. I didn't know if —"

What Alice would have explained was interrupted by one of the female Woodburn students. Perveen recognized the heart-shaped face of Lalita Acharya. Her expression was anguished. "Miss Hobson-Jones, please. You and Miss Mistry must come with me!"

Lalita sounded anguished, making Perveen think that someone at the college was angry about Alice's brief absence. Alice's deep blue eyes were stricken as she regarded Lalita, and Perveen realized that though Alice had no fear of the police and military, she was terrified of losing her hard-won job.

"What are they saying?" Alice asked.

"It's Freny Cuttingmaster!"

Perveen felt her stomach drop. "Where is Freny? Is she —"

"Let me speak. I was walking through the gate back into school ahead of the others, and I saw Freny lying in the garden!" Lalita's voice was panicked. "She didn't answer me and won't look up."

As Perveen felt herself becoming dizzy, Alice jerked her arm. In a controlled voice, Alice said, "Are there responsible people around her? Has a doctor been called?"

"Yes, there are loads of teachers trying to keep the students from seeing her. Miss Daboo told me that I needed to fetch Miss Mistry. Miss Daboo said only Parsis should be around Freny right now. I don't understand it —"

"It's a religious custom. I'll go." Perveen felt terror rising inside her. The rule was that deceased Parsis could only be touched by those of the same religion. Miss Daboo must have feared a mortal injury but couldn't say that.

"Don't worry, Lalita. We'll come with you." Alice's voice was reassuringly confident, though her face was still tight with worry.

As the two of them followed Lalita, Perveen recalled her premonition that the day would bring trouble. It had, but in a far worse manner than she'd imagined. One student had been beaten by the police and arrested; the other was . . . no. She could not think ahead to the worst. "Miss Hobson-Jones, what is the plan for the rest of the school day?"

"You mean, after the procession? There's going to be a celebration lunch followed by early dismissal. The student body was proceeding to the canteen when I cut out to look for you."

Perveen kept her eyes focused on Lalita's bright red sari as they struggled against the crowd, which was slowly dispersing in the wake of the vanished procession. It seemed like a hundred people were between them and the college fence.

"She's with me!" Alice said to the college's chowkidar, pulling Perveen along without bothering to sign the logbook at the guard station. Perveen took a close look at the guard, a short man in his twenties wearing a dark blue uniform that had no nameplate. He was twisting his hands in a helpless motion as he stared into the college garden.

Lalita had told them about Freny's condition, but Perveen felt unprepared for the surge of horror that filled her.

Freny's body was on its side with the head jerked back, the curly hair that had been tightly bound before now loose and half-hiding the right side of her face. Two rivulets of blood ran out from underneath her head. Her arms lay askew and her legs, underneath the loosened sari, were stacked one on top of the other. There was something odd about the position, although Perveen couldn't figure out why.

Professor Daboo was kneeling beside Freny. The poetry lecturer had placed one hand on the student's wrist and the other on her heart. Her lips were moving, and Perveen recognized that the teacher was silently intoning Ashem Vohu, the prayer that every Parsi was supposed to recite before death.

Miss Daboo was worried that Freny was hurt so badly that she might die. And in the heat of midday, Perveen had never felt colder. If only she'd said when she first saw Alice: *Excuse me, but can we please go inside the college for a moment?* They might have found Freny in this garden and convinced her to come to the stands with them.

Alice's grip dug painfully into Perveen's hand. Her friend was clinging to her like she was a lifeline cast from a boat into the sea. If only that lifeline could have reached Freny.

"Miss Daboo, please tell us what happened." Perveen struggled to sound composed, although she felt like she was collapsing.

"I don't know anything except that she was lying here, perhaps as if she'd fallen." Miss Daboo's voice trembled.

Perveen looked at Freny lying so silently, and maybe close to death. Panicked, she scanned the crowd of teachers and students standing ten feet back and noticed Naval, the boy with the camera. He had it on his shoulder and was standing stock-still, his mouth agape. She asked the crowd if anyone had called for a doctor.

Mr. Gupta stepped forward to answer. "Yes. Reverend Sullivan is in the principal's office making a call to the European Hospital."

"What? The European Hospital won't admit Indian patients and it doesn't have . . ." Perveen suddenly realized she was about to say, "a morgue," and was grateful for a swift interruption from Miss Daboo.

"Because of our religious laws, it would be better if a Parsi doctor came. Surely one is near!"

But would they still be in the stands? Perveen thought about what else was nearby, and then had an idea. Her eyes returned to Naval, who hadn't taken his eyes off Freny. "Mr. Hotelwala, may I ask you something?"

His mouth twisted in anxiety. "What, madam?"

"Will you please summon a Parsi doctor? Ask in the street, and if nobody answers, go across to the Orient Club." Perveen turned her attention back to Freny, who hadn't changed position.

"Yes. But what kind of doctor? A surgeon, or —"

"Any kind will do!" Alice interrupted. "Tell them there's been a very serious occurrence at Woodburn College."

"Yes, madam."

Perveen watched Naval speed off. The camera was over his shoulder again and bumped against his hip. She thought of calling out that he could leave the camera with her in order to move faster, but it was too late.

Everything she'd done was too late.

4

UPON CLOSER EXAMINATION

"Miss Mistry, come down here," Miss Daboo beseeched.

Perveen knelt down and, feeling queasy, reached out to touch Freny's wrist. It was still warm, yet the veins on the inside of her wrist seemed deflated. She could not detect a pulse.

Perveen's mother, Camellia, and sister-in-law, Gulnaz, were the kind of women brave enough to volunteer in hospitals. They might know another spot to look for a pulse. All Perveen could think of was the heartbeat.

Freny had fallen on her right side, so it was possible for Perveen to slide her hand under the khadi cloth and over the left side of Freny's white cotton blouse.

"Don't be obscene!" Miss Daboo muttered in Gujarati, and Perveen belatedly realized there were men watching her. Having felt no sign of life, she pulled back her hand.

"We must pray. God can work miracles." Another Englishman had appeared. He looked to be in his fifties, with a long face made even paler by its contrast with his black robe. Right behind him was a breathless Principal Atherton.

The principal and the college chaplain had taken long enough to arrive at a scene of crucial emergency. But perhaps the police had occupied Principal Atherton's time getting details about Dinesh Apte. And why weren't they with him now?

The answer came: *The college's leadership didn't know Freny was dead.* Only she and Miss Daboo knew the truth. Or maybe — Lalita also did. *Surely she would have tried to help her friend sit up. Surely —*

Mr. Atherton spoke between gasps. "I've just heard — about the accident — from the reverend." Two more breaths. "Who is she?"

"Her name is Freny Cuttingmaster," Alice said. "She's a second-year student."

"And what about you? Are you a nurse?" Mr. Atherton's face was reddened, no doubt from agitation and heat.

"Sorry, I am not." Perveen looked away from him and back at Freny. She thought of saying she was a lawyer, but it didn't seem the right place.

"Miss Perveen Mistry, my old friend from Oxford, is here at my invitation," Alice said quickly. "Miss Mistry, this is Mr. Atherton, our principal, and our chaplain, Reverend Sullivan."

Principal Atherton pressed his lips together disapprovingly. "I am not — entertaining interviews for women faculty. This is an emergency —"

"I'm not a teacher; I'm a solicitor with a practice nearby." Having honestly admitted her field, Perveen didn't know how long the college administrator would allow her to linger.

"Miss Acharya, is it correct that you were first on the scene?" Atherton had turned his attention to the student, who was clutching Alice.

"Yes. I was a few yards ahead of the others," Lalita said in a choked voice. "Miss Daboo was with me as well."

Atherton's eyebrows drew together. "And where was Miss Cuttingmaster during the procession?"

"Actually, we realized midway through the proceedings she wasn't in the stands with us." Lalita's voice was hesitant, as if she didn't want to admit she'd known all along the girl hadn't showed up.

"Yes. She must have had her accident

while we were turned watching the prince!" Miss Daboo said.

The excitement of the parade could have masked any cries, even though the college and its garden were just a few dozen yards behind the viewing stand.

"Maybe she fell down. I only hope . . ." Lalita's voice trailed off.

"What is it you are hoping, my dear?" Reverend Sullivan prompted.

"I hope she's going to wake up." Lalita was clenching and unclenching her hands. "Why can't the nurse come from the infirmary? Didn't anyone call for her?"

"Leave the response to faculty," said the reverend.

"I think someone should fetch the police." As Perveen said it, she couldn't believe the words had even come from her mouth. The police! The men who'd so recently challenged her were needed to secure the scene and take note of details.

"The police?" Mr. Atherton's voice faltered. "But Miss Daboo says this is an accident." He shook his head as he looked at the smooth path and neat green lawn. "I wonder what caused her to fall?"

"It could be that she jumped. This was going to be a day of protest for some." Reverend Sullivan turned to grimace at the mass of students standing a respectful distance behind. "I know some of you are in the resistance club. If you were aware that she was planning self-destruction, you must tell us now."

Did the chaplain understand Freny's life was gone? Perveen looked at his stern, unmoving face until he glared at her.

One of the boys in a Gandhi cap raised a hand and spoke when the chaplain acknowledged him. "Reverend, nobody heard any such talk in the Student Union meetings."

A blond man in his twenties, who had a shaken expression, put a hand on the shoulder of the student who'd spoken. "That is my impression as well. Arjun, thank you for coming forward."

"I'll go for the police," a student voice said from within the crowd, and three boys took off through the gate.

Very soon, the area would be cleared of people. Now was the time to remember details. Perveen turned her gaze upward. The college had a spacious ground floor and two stories above. Both the first and second floor had a stone half-wall that bordered the upper porches. The walls appeared too tall to allow for an accidental fall.

Though they would have made good

perches, if someone intended to jump.

Freny might have given up her life to bring attention to Indian independence. But if that was her plan, why had she bothered consulting Perveen about how to protest without getting into academic trouble?

"Miss Hobson-Jones, I know nothing about this student." Atherton's querulous voice interrupted Perveen's internal monologue. "Is she of sound mind?"

"Yes, indeed. There is no trouble with her thinking at all — no unhappiness that I knew of. Miss Cuttingmaster is taking Introduction to Mathematical Logic. She is so sharp that I encouraged her to explore more in the field of mathematics, but she said she preferred history." Like the principal, Alice spoke of Freny in the present tense — as if willing Freny to be alive.

History students made excellent lawyers. Perveen felt sorrowful, remembering the conversation about women and court. Freny would never have the chance to observe trials or go to law school or apprentice as a clerk or get her first week's pay. She had died at eighteen with a destiny unfulfilled.

"She answered roll today in the chapel." As he spoke, Reverend Sullivan bent his head toward Miss Daboo. "Now we are hearing she was not outside with the others.

Yet you didn't report her missing. Why was that?"

"It is not just Miss Daboo who had responsibility for the girls." Alice's voice shook slightly as she spoke. "Any one of the faculty could have counted up girls — and boys, for that matter. But no specific instruction to take roll again was given."

Reverend Sullivan's eyebrows rose and he shook his head very slowly, as if to issue a warning of insubordination.

Alice was the same height as Reverend Sullivan, but she seemed to draw herself up, and even in the rumpled dark linen, she looked more dynamic and powerful than him.

Perveen looked away from them. As she surveyed the college building she saw, on the far corner of the ground-floor gallery, two barefoot young men wearing lungis. Perveen assumed that they were servants, wracked with fear. Because they'd been inside the college when the death occurred, they'd be questioned; and the police were automatically distrustful of guards, servants, and cleaners.

"This is a very bad situation. You are right, Reverend Sullivan." Atherton was breathing normally now, but Perveen noted that the white shirt underneath his heavy suit was

66

drenched in sweat. "Nobody was authorized to be inside the college during the parade. For this to happen was a violation of rules. She could not expect assistance or protection alone. We have very strict rules about the comportment of our lady students."

"Is there a handbook, then?" Perveen asked.

Atherton's answering frown told her that if there was, he didn't know about it.

By now, even more students had come to see what had happened and were pressing in to get a look at Freny. Many of the girls were crying. Perveen counted silently and thought, *Just eleven.* Had the college decided a dozen was the right number to show they supported women's education, but not so many that they'd cause trouble?

Reverend Sullivan took this as his opportunity. Moving forward, he spoke in a somber voice. "Let's have the student body assemble in the chapel. I can lead prayers for Miss Cuttingmaster."

"The perfect idea," Atherton said. "I want all of you teachers to assemble the students in lines and proceed into the chapel. You can begin without me."

"And me," said Miss Daboo in a shaky voice. "I will stay close to Freny."

A few students began moving into lines, and the teachers came alive, directing them.

Moments after Alice and the other teachers and students departed toward a wide Gothic-arched wooden door at the end of the gallery, Naval was back in the garden with a doctor. Both of them were slightly breathless, as if they'd been running. The doctor wore a fetah and spoke Gujarati to Miss Daboo, who declared to Atherton that this was Dr. Boman Pandey, a general practitioner.

The doctor produced a stethoscope from his bag and held it to Freny's chest; this time, Miss Daboo didn't complain. He only listened for a few seconds before taking the stethoscope away. Looking at Principal Atherton, he asked, "Are you the principal?"

"Yes, temporary principal for this year only. I am not — I don't have experience with this type of, ah, accident. It was very good of you to come."

Pandey looked hard at him. "Yes. I regret to tell you that this young woman has died."

Atherton bowed his head, and so did Perveen. She had known Freny was dead, but now she did not have to hide the tears that had welled in her eyes. Miss Daboo raised her voice as she continued chanting the prayers.

The small, mournful assembly was shattered as three constables came hustling through the college gates behind Mr. Gupta.

"What's happened? Is an ambulance needed?" asked the tallest of the three policemen.

Dr. Pandey had stood up and was dusting off his hands with his own handkerchief. "Sadly, this child is no longer alive. She should be transported to the morgue at Sir J. J. Hospital."

The constable who'd spoken for the group cleared his throat and addressed Dr. Pandey in a subdued voice. "Doctor-ji, will you make a death certificate?"

"Yes. I only need clean paper and a pen." Dr. Pandey had changed to English and was looking at Mr. Atherton. "I'll make a formal declaration as the constable has requested."

"Gupta, please fetch what's needed," Atherton directed. Then he turned back to Dr. Pandey with a harried expression. "It's an accident, isn't it? What will you report?"

"I shall detail all medical facts as I see them. The police surgeon will determine cause of death during an autopsy at the morgue." Pandey switched back to Marathi and told the chief constable that a detective inspector and sub-inspector should be called, as well as a municipal cart to take

69

Freny to the morgue.

"We will collect evidence first," the constable insisted. "Will you please turn her body, Doctor?"

"There is no need to turn her. I have observed what I need to know she is dead!" Pandey said, but the constable bent down and, putting a hand on Freny's shoulder, turned her.

"Parsi only, please!" squeaked Miss Daboo, making a shooing motion with her hand. "Sir, you must not touch her."

"I also think a forensics officer would wish the scene untouched —" Perveen stopped speaking when she saw what they'd revealed. The right underside of Freny's face was smashed, with bits of bone protruding. She had fallen very hard indeed — or been struck.

It was a horrifying sight that she wished she hadn't seen. Somehow, Perveen found her voice again. "We must all be careful not to disturb the scene. Please."

At Perveen's words, Atherton turned and said, "I shall manage that, Miss Mistry. And now I am requesting you vacate the premises."

Perveen was not surprised he was trying to close ranks, but she was anxious about leaving after the constables had been so careless about a scene that would later be described in coroner's court. "Might I stay a bit longer? I'm not obstructing anything or anyone. I am only staying to give my witness report when the detective inspector arrives."

"The college has its own lawyer, Mr. Alistair Johnson. Can you be on your way?"

Atherton's voice was sharp, and his mention of Johnson by name made it seem he thought she was angling to defend the college. Clearly, he felt she was an invader.

"I know Mr. Johnson," she said coolly. The solicitor had a reputation for drunkenness, but she would let Atherton discover this for himself. "I will leave, but I'd be most grateful for the chance to pray with everyone first."

As she'd expected, the principal of a missionary college could hardly refuse someone prayer. He pointed in the direction Alice had gone. "Certainly, Miss Mistry. The chapel is at the corridor's end."

Perveen walked slowly down the gallery, her eyes moving along the black and yellow encaustic tiles, looking for something that might have fallen along with Freny. The corridor looked fairly clean around the edges, as if it had been scrubbed earlier in the morning, but there was a heavy pattern of

71

many footprints going over it — these would be from the students who'd all been sent to the chapel. There was a stairway in the corridor's north end, but she felt the gaze of the principal on her back. She could not get away with such a detour.

She opened the heavy wooden chapel door and closed it softly behind herself to find a long room filled with teak pews. Light streamed red, gold, and green through the stained glass windows. She could not see the windows' biblical depictions, because they all stood open, allowing air to circulate.

Reverend Sullivan stood at the pulpit with his head bowed.

"Almighty and immortal God, giver of life and health, we beseech thee to hear thy prayers for thy servant Freny, for whom we implore thy mercy, that by thy blessing she may be restored if it be thy gracious will, to be of body and mind . . ."

It was frustrating to hear Reverend Sullivan speaking as if there were hope. The students would feel even worse, later. But his role, as chaplain, was to comfort.

Perveen saw Alice sitting in the very back, with space on either side of her. Perveen sidled in next to her and took her friend's hand. It was ice cold. Perveen fell into silent prayer, letting the old Avestan words of the

Zoroastrian faith fill her head, drowning out the English.

After some time, Alice whispered, "It was good of you to come in. I can't stop crying."

"I'm so sorry, Alice," Perveen whispered back.

"Don't worry about me. What about Freny's parents?" There was a catch in Alice's voice. "They need to hear how much she was valued in this school. I want to tell them how much I liked her."

Perveen remembered Freny saying her older brother was dead. This meant that the parents had now lost both children; a horrific fate.

She thought about the ruin of Freny's smashed face and her drab sari, loosely wound. In death, Freny appeared the opposite of the alert and tidy young scholar with a satchel full of books.

The satchel. It had not been anywhere near her body. Wouldn't she have brought it to school?

Tilting her head up to whisper in her friend's ear, Perveen asked, "After the service, will you please go up to the third floor? Freny has a brown drill-cloth satchel. We didn't see it near her."

"Yes. But why?"

The female students sitting a few feet away, Lalita included, were starting to listen to them, rather than the reverend's droning. Perveen shook her head. "Just telephone me tonight."

5
ACTS OF VIOLENCE

Emerging from the darkness of the chapel, Perveen blinked to adjust her eyes to the light. Many police had filled the garden. She walked along the gallery perpendicular to the grass and was interrupted midway by the blond British man who'd responded to the chaplain earlier.

"Sorry, madam. This area is secured," he said, a light Irish accent giving a pleasant roll to his Rs. She wondered if this was Mr. Grady, the teacher Freny liked.

Playing dumb, she said, "Sorry, I was just leaving. Are you with the police?"

"No!" He scowled, as if she'd insulted him. "I'm just dispersing anyone who doesn't teach or study here."

"And do you work here?"

"Of course I do." His voice shook with outrage. "I'm Terrence Grady. History department."

Mr. Grady was one of Freny's favorite

teachers, the advisor for the Student Union.

With curiosity rising, Perveen looked him over. He had a most ordinary-looking face; wide-set, questioning blue eyes over a short, straight nose. Despite the blond hair, he did not have the typically burnt complexion to go with it; his skin was lightly tanned, as if he'd been in India for a while and adjusted. Mr. Grady wore a gray cotton suit, white shirt, and red silk tie that appeared locally made. The only thing striking her as odd was his battered brown portmanteau. It looked like a traveler's suitcase.

"And who are you?" Grady sounded indignant. "Why did you come to our campus?"

Suddenly, the tables were turned. In this teacher's eyes, a stranger had appeared in the stands, then taken charge of the death scene.

"My name is Perveen Mistry. I am a solicitor who's acquainted with Miss Hobson-Jones." Hopefully, this wouldn't lead to trouble for Alice. "I came onto the campus because Miss Daboo requested Lalita fetch me — for reasons of religion."

"Religion. Without it, we wouldn't have wars and colonialism." His voice shook again, and Perveen suddenly wondered why his emotion was so high.

If he was going to speak of ideology, she could forge on. "Did I hear you are the Student Union advisor?"

As if he'd read her mind, his eyes narrowed, and when he answered, his voice was defensive. "Yes. Who told you?"

"I saw you vouch for one of the Student Union boys in front of the reverend. Freny was in the Student Union. You must have known her well."

He opened his mouth, then closed it abruptly. The open vulnerability on his face was gone. His eyes had narrowed, as if to match his pressed lips.

The awkward stillness was broken by the sound of fast footsteps. Mr. Gupta, the slender Indian teacher Alice had said was a dean, was approaching.

"Mr. Grady, I've been looking for you." He was panting between breaths. "The chaplain wants you to perform the final Bible reading in the chapel service."

"He wants me to read?" snapped Grady. "What could that do to change this situation? A promising young person has died. No deity can change that fact."

Dean Gupta regarded the shorter teacher with a pitying gaze. "He thinks it will calm the students. Principal Atherton wishes for all the school to be together — and for

Christian teachers to read verses to the students."

"You can tell him I'm unable to attend. Sorry." Not sounding penitent at all, Mr. Grady hefted his portmanteau and departed. Bypassing the crowd of police, he headed toward the college gate; then they could no longer see him.

"I thought he was on duty to guard the school property," Perveen said in Marathi to Mr. Gupta.

He looked startled, as if he hadn't expected to switch to the city's dominant language. He muttered, "That is most unlikely. But as you just saw, our European faculty does as it likes."

"How long have you been here, Dean Gupta?"

"Seventeen years. I was hired after matriculating from the University of Bombay. Terrence Grady joined us two years ago. He has no college degree, but once wrote for a newspaper." A smirk made his opinion clear.

Movement caught her eye. A European man in a black bowler hat and a black-and-gray suit was marching briskly toward them. He stopped so close she could see his auburn eyebrows drawn disapprovingly over cold gray eyes. "Who are you, and what are you doing?"

Mr. Gupta's expression shifted from condescension to alarm. Quickly, he bowed his head. Sensing the interloper was in the mood to throw weight around, Perveen tried to defuse the situation. "We are just parting ways."

"Answer my questions."

"My name is Brajesh Gupta, and I am a dean." Mr. Gupta's gaze flittered nervously toward Perveen. "I am bringing people over to the chapel."

"What about you?" The man wagged a finger at Perveen. "Why are you on our college grounds?"

"I was an invited guest in the viewing stand. And then, I was summoned to assist with the crisis." Perveen tried not to sound defensive.

"Highly doubtful," he snapped. "I met the doctor and the first witness to arrive at the scene."

He'd said "witness," not "witnesses," so she corrected him. "There were two, I believe. Lalita Acharya and the lecturer Roshan Daboo arrived together."

"Enough! You admitted you have no business in this place. We are dealing with a security crisis. Go out that way." He pointed toward the length of the gallery that Mr. Grady had said was closed.

There was no point in contradicting him. If he was an Imperial Police officer, he would not be managing the investigation. She felt fortunate he hadn't pressed further for her name.

As Mr. Gupta fled back to the chapel, Perveen walked swiftly along the gallery toward the college exit. Mr. Grady had lied about being charged with keeping certain areas cleared. Was it because he'd feared she'd go up the stairway and see something there?

As she proceeded toward the college gate, she saw that individual constables were kneeling throughout the grounds, making close inspection of the grass and paths. As it should be, with such a mysterious death.

Outside the gate, a horse-drawn municipal cart was parked. A woman wearing a pink-and-apricot sari was throwing herself against the cart, and a short man wearing a well-tailored European suit with a fetah hat was striving to pull her away.

Briefly, Perveen hesitated, not wanting to intrude. But they might know Freny, or even be related to her. She hurried toward them. "Do you know Miss Cuttingmaster?"

The man jerked his head sharply and looked at her through horn-rimmed glasses smeared with tears. Righting his fetah with his hand, he answered her Gujarati question in the same language. "We are her parents!"

The hard moment Alice was worrying about had arrived. "Mr. Cuttingmaster, I'm so very sorry. Did the college staff find you?"

Moving closer to her, he lowered his voice. "No. We were watching the procession from the Orient Club. We heard that Dr. Pandey was going to an emergency at the college. We decided to follow because my wife here" — he gestured toward the weeping lady — "wanted to bring Freny away from any trouble."

"They are not even letting us see her! How can we know she is the one in that cart?" Mrs. Cuttingmaster had stepped away from the cart, revealing her anguished face to Perveen. She was a pint-sized but plump lady of about forty, with golden-brown eyes like Freny's. "That person's sari is brown. Freny wore green today."

Seeing their grief, Perveen felt tears rising in her own eyes. "I'm sure it is Freny."

"You are a teacher, then? You know her? How could you allow this to happen?" Mr. Cuttingmaster gripped his abdomen and bent slightly, making himself seem even smaller.

"I'm a solicitor. My name is Perveen Mistry. Your daughter visited my office earlier in the week." Perveen slipped her hand into her briefcase and pulled out her business card for Freny's father. He took it with trembling fingers and slid it into his jacket pocket. His suit was beautifully tailored — his shoes were gleaming. It was clear he'd dressed for a celebration.

The driver for the cart, a thin man with a nervous expression, stood at a respectful distance and gestured to get Perveen's attention. She asked, "What's going on?"

"Tell them I am taking her to the morgue at Sir J. J. I tried to say earlier, but they are still wishing for her not to go." The driver looked back at Mrs. Cuttingmaster, who had returned to the side of the cart and was loudly chanting the prayer for the dead.

"They are the deceased's parents. If you allow them to see her, you will have a firm identification for the morgue staff, and you will give these poor people a moment of clarity."

With reluctance, the driver returned to the cart and pulled the cloth from Freny. The Cuttingmasters, both short, had to stretch to look over the cart's edge.

"Our Freny." Moaning, Mrs. Cuttingmaster fell back, and her husband stepped behind her to break her fall.

"How?" Mr. Cuttingmaster gazed upward, as the driver put the cloth over Freny again.

"God, how could you allow this for our beautiful child?"

"It's terrible," Perveen said, the words catching in her throat.

"Freny cannot — go into a morgue! She cannot be lying among — every diseased dead person in Bombay!" Mrs. Cuttingmaster gasped between her words. "I cannot go through this again."

Perveen guessed she was referring to her son Darius's death. "I'm sorry to say that an autopsy is required by law when there is a sudden, unnatural death. We all need to know why this happened. After the coroner rules on her cause of death, Freny will be allowed to go."

Mr. Cuttingmaster pointed a finger at the driver. "She must have funeral rites as soon as possible to avoid the devil taking hold."

The driver's face was beginning to darken with frustration. "I'm going now. Enough of this delay!"

"Would you like me to see if I can arrange for priests to begin prayers?" Perveen asked.

"Can you?" Mr. Cuttingmaster's expression was anxious.

"Certainly," Perveen assured him. "I'll send an urgent note to Doongerwadi once I've left this place."

The driver had gotten back in his seat and

cracked his whip. The horses started to move.

As Mrs. Cuttingmaster stumbled after the carriage, an Anglo-Indian police officer stepped in, pushing her aside. Perveen rushed forward and caught her, just in time.

"You again!" the officer was grimacing at Perveen.

Now she recognized his tone; he was the sergeant who'd kept her from looking for Dinesh Apte. Trying to steady her breath, she said, "Yes. There has been a death, and I'm ensuring the family's right to identify their deceased."

Unhooking the lathi at his belt, he scowled at her. "There is too much weeping and wailing going on. The scene must be cleared. And you go, too. No more inciting civil unrest."

Just like the officious Englishman on the Woodburn campus, this was not someone she could argue with. If she were arrested, she couldn't help Freny's family.

As Perveen backed up, she saw anger in Mr. Cuttingmaster's eyes.

"Let me assist you with getting home." She made the offer, not knowing where they lived, or how she could help without having Arman and the car.

"No. You are helping us with the agiary.

We will find our way." Mr. Cuttingmaster's voice was sober as he took his wife by the arm and gently led her away.

Perveen wished she'd been brave enough to stand up to the officer, but she'd been in trouble with the authorities three times within the space of a few hours. Actually, it was five times, if she counted Mr. Atherton and Grady.

Her thoughts were so turbulent that she walked slightly off course, and the side street that she believed was a shortcut to Charni Station ended. As she reversed course, she noticed three men outside a fancy-looking shop. One man with a Congress Party cap was yanking hard at the door, and two others were wielding lathis. Before she could call out, she heard glass shatter. Shards flew, sparkling like diamonds. As she drew closer, she read the golden letters painted on the building's lintel. THE HAWTHORN SHOP, A FINE HABERDASHERY, ESTABLISHED 1905.

She'd never been inside, but she knew the name. This was the place where Freny's father worked.

The sorrow and fear she'd felt before were turning to anger. Perhaps in the vandals' minds, they were part of Gandhiji's movement; but orders to destroy were inconsistent with his beliefs.

That afternoon, she'd been unable to speak up to the British, but she wouldn't be afraid to raise her voice to fellow Indians. Drawing in her diaphragm, she yelled, "Stop that right now! This is the business place of hardworking people. Indians just like us!"

One of the men turned; stepping back, he looked ashamed. But the younger fellow beside him, who had a stocky build, righted the Congress Party cap on his head and looked defiantly at her. Then a third man hefted his lathi in Perveen's direction.

They knew they'd been caught, so they should run off. Only they didn't run.

Perveen felt her heart pounding as the three young men deserted the haberdashery and rushed along the street toward her with weapons in hand. As she tried to step back, her sandal's heel caught on the hem of her sari and she stumbled. In an instant, she was surrounded. The threesome smelled of smoke and sweat, and two of them were grinning.

She counted silently to three, mustering her courage. "My brothers, did you hear that Gandhiji's orders are to be peaceful in all that we do?"

The largest man spat at her. "I am no

brother to you. True patriots resist colonization. This is a British shop."

"You Parsis love the British!" His compatriot spat. "Are you going home to have cake and tea?"

"I am speaking to you as an Indian first and a Parsi second. Many of us fight for freedom. Remember Dadabhai Naoroji and Bhikaji Cama!" Perveen had hoped the names of famous Parsis in the movement might lead to a more reasonable discussion, but the leader of the pack advanced so he was inches from her face, and looked down with a sneer.

"If you were a patriot, you would have gone to the bonfire. Aren't you a pretty lady? Let us see where your sari comes from." The man reached out and flicked the length of sari fabric from her head. "Chutiya."

He had called her the curse word for a woman's private part. But that profanity paled next to the fact that he'd touched her sari. Stepping back, she said, "Good men don't harass women. And my sari was woven by women in Gujarat. It is Indian-made — just like khadi cloth."

He was so close she could smell his breath — hot and reeking of toddy. "You can afford anything you like. What is in that briefcase you carry? Your husband's money?"

She had known they meant harm from the time they'd looked at her. There was little inside of value, but the briefcase meant everything to her — it was the symbol of her education, her work, her status as something more than a daughter from a good family.

"Leave me alone," she pleaded, and she saw reluctance in the eyes of the youngest. But the other two moved forward and batted away her hands to start pulling the front of the sari out of its secured place in her waistband. She screamed, finally understanding that their intention was to unclothe her.

As terror settled in, she was pushed violently to one side. Her palm smarted as she struggled to keep hold of her briefcase. The push had come from a Parsi man — a group of them, wearing formal white suits but shouting curse words as they battled her assailants.

"Go!" one of them called to her. Clutching her sari around her upper body again, Perveen sped away. The footsteps she expected to follow did not — the men behind her were all embroiled in battle.

Perveen ran, trying to hold up the lower

section of her sari to clear her sandals, and clutching her briefcase across her front. Her breath felt like it was being torn from her chest.

Not until she'd rounded the corner to safety did she slow down. There were tears at the edges of her eyes. She was crying for herself and for Bombay.

Charni Station was closed. A constable and a line of wooden barriers told her this. The police were breaking up fights around the gate.

She walked shakily, her eyes moving constantly as she tried to avoid groups of people who appeared to be arguing or close to blows. Some people were fleeing, but she knew she hadn't the strength to run the mile-and-a-half to Mistry House.

Hope surged when she recognized Nawaz Wadia, a solicitor in his seventies who lived in a neighboring building on Bruce Street. He was being assisted by a driver into a horse-drawn taxi.

"Mr. Wadia!" she cried out, hurrying toward him.

"Miss Mistry. Good to see you on this fine day. Where is your family?" he called out, smiling.

"They're not here. And I'm trying to get to Bruce Street. Please, would you —" She stopped, realizing she was close to tears.

"Please come in the taxi with me." Mr. Wadia waved her up. "Hurry, because the driver is saying there's trouble in some areas. And trouble can spread!"

"I am so grateful." Perveen would have said more if she hadn't been so breathless. She settled into the carriage, doing her best to tuck her sari back together without allowing the gentleman to notice the disarray.

Mr. Wadia was craning his head, looking out at the road. "It is still fine here. But look at the police. They are swarming like ants! Good thing they are so plentiful."

Fifteen minutes later, as they disembarked on Bruce Street, Mr. Wadia said, "There, your durwan is standing outside. Mustafa is quite vigilant."

"Yes. He is quite protective." Perveen thanked Mr. Wadia again for his kindness and walked up the front steps to meet Mustafa in the house's portico.

"You are returned, Alhamdulillah!" As Mustafa invoked thanks to Allah, his voice cracked with emotion. "Violence has swept the city. Mistry-sahib telephoned from the construction company office and was so worried to learn you were on the streets."

She could not bring herself to explain the details. "I am so glad to be here. Charni

Station was closed, but Mr. Wadia shared his taxi with me."

"I see." Taking a long look at her, he said, "Your sari is torn. What happened?"

Perveen pulled the sari closer around her. "There were so many people. I was rushing in the street, and it must have happened then."

Mustafa shook his head. "As your father said, the city is dangerous. The roads past the mill area are not safe tonight. You will join your father and brother at the Taj Hotel to stay overnight."

All she wanted was to wash herself at home, to erase the memory of the brutal men. And hide under her own covers. "I don't want to be there. The Taj Hotel is going to be full of visitors. Probably a lot of British people —"

Mustafa's voice was firm. "Your father said on no account will you go anywhere but that hotel. And I'm coming in the car with you for protection."

6
A CHANGE OF PLANS

Perveen would give it one last try. She picked up the telephone in the hall and placed a call to Mistry and Sons Construction.

The construction company receptionist picked up and called her father to the telephone.

"Perveen, thank God. Nobody knew where you were."

"At the parade, just like you." This was not the time to explain how frightening the day had been. "Pappa, I'm exhausted. I can't imagine staying at a hotel tonight. Aren't there some byways Arman could take to get home?"

"Fires are burning all around the mills, and men are racing through town with their own incendiary passions. It's too risky." His voice was heavy.

Perveen's mind flew to where the rioters were headed. "What about Mamma and

Gulnaz?"

"Arman drove them home right after the amphitheater ceremonies. I reached Mamma by telephone and told her about the unrest. Both will stay with the Bankers until our return."

Her sister-in-law, Gulnaz, hailed from a family whose financial service roots stretched back to seventeenth-century Persia — so they'd chosen the name Banker, in English, upon arrival. It continued to fit well. In the eighty years these particular Bankers had been in India, they'd established the Apollo Bank with branches in Bombay and Poona. Gulnaz could have married into a far grander family than the Mistrys, but her friendship with Perveen had brought her into the Mistry home as a child — and that was where she'd set eyes on Rustom, who even at eight years old was good-looking, with a genial disposition. Gulnaz had seen him grow into the shrewd executive officer of Mistry Construction. Their arranged marriage was approved of by both families, and more importantly, was a happy union.

"Why shouldn't we stay away from the city, if this is where the trouble is?" Perveen pressed.

"I've spoken with a police superintendent.

At this point, it is not safe to drive out of the European Quarter. The police believe the violence is only beginning. Fortunately, the city has extra military presence to assist because of the prince's visit."

"I see." She knew her father was right. And he couldn't know about what had happened near the Hawthorn Shop, for it could have a lasting effect on whether she was allowed unescorted through the city again.

Jamshedji's voice boomed into her ear. "Tell Mustafa to open my almirah on the second floor and pack up several day suits and a dinner suit with the patent pumps. Also, my nightclothes and toiletries. Are you able to pack for yourself?"

"Yes, of course." Like her father, Perveen kept a cupboard of clean and pressed clothes at Mistry House.

"Now that you are back, I'm off to check in at the hotel. Then Arman will fetch you at Mistry House. Mustafa already knows he must ride along as added protection."

Perveen said goodbye to her father. Remembering what she'd promised the Cuttingmasters about notifying a priest, she dashed off a short letter, put it in an envelope, and handed it to Mustafa. "It's dangerous out, but do you think anyone would be willing to go to Doongerwadi? Priestly

94

prayers are needed for a family who's just lost their daughter."

"A daughter?"

Looking sadly at him, she said the name they'd gossiped about so recently. "Freny Cuttingmaster."

"The girl who came to see you on Monday. How can it be?" The creases around his eyes deepened.

"I don't know very much," Perveen interrupted, to save them both. "I'll be able to say more after the autopsy. In the meantime, her family needs priests to pray."

Mustafa nodded. "Ervard Framji works around the corner, and his home is up Malabar Hill, near those funeral grounds. I'll see if he can bring the message. If not, I'll go myself."

Mustafa could be overprotective, but he was also a steadfast, trustworthy solver of problems. Perveen thanked him and went upstairs, feeling that at least one thing was as good as done.

She proceeded to the pretty green-tiled bathroom that she used exclusively and took a bucket bath; the cool water and soap were bracing. It felt like she was sluicing off the very touch of the men, although she could not forget what they'd done. Coming so closely after Freny's death, the two traumas mingled; some parts were fuzzy, others starkly detailed.

"Time to go, Perveen-memsahib," Mustafa called to her as she came downstairs wearing a sari meant for social functions: a lustrous purple Paithani weave, with a border of gilded palm trees.

Arman, the family's chauffeur, opened the door of the Daimler for her but he was not smiling as he usually did. Either he'd seen the city's unrest or gotten an earful from her father. She settled in the back seat with her briefcase and valise and the luggage for her father. Mustafa, carrying his rifle, went up front to sit next to Arman. Looking over his shoulder at Perveen, he sighed. "I wish that I could stay at the hotel to assist with any needs. But your father thought it better to keep an eye on Mistry House."

The Daimler passed through the city's main avenues, now devoid of spectators. Union Jacks littered the street like chestnuts after a storm.

"It is surprising nobody has snatched up all those flags. They could be sold for this and that," Arman said, taking a hand off the wheel to point at the flags still hanging on lampposts and buildings.

"I don't know how many people would

feel safe carrying the British flag," Perveen said.

"Unless to a bonfire!" Mustafa said darkly.

Arman drove swiftly, and they soon turned into Apollo Bunder, a hive of activity, with horse-drawn taxis and motorcars lined up outside the Bombay Yacht Club Residency and the Taj Mahal Palace Hotel.

"I'll get out now," Perveen suggested, because she never liked waiting in lines.

"I don't see your father or brother," Mustafa protested. "We should wait —"

"They'll never see the car — there must be a dozen ahead of us. This is perfectly fine!" Perveen stepped out of the car, keeping hold of her valise, and walked around a cluster of Europeans chattering and embracing each other. As she made her way to the hotel's open front door, she passed well-dressed Parsis and some royal-looking children in jeweled turbans and formal achkan coats.

As Mustafa followed, giving two suitcases to a hotel bellman in livery, he spoke in a subdued voice. "Are you certain my service is not needed?"

"Yes. I promise you I won't run away. And be very careful going home." She tried to communicate with her eyes what she could not say here; that he was far more than a servant, and she worried for his safety, despite his strength.

By the time Perveen got to the long desk to check in, she had been shoved twice by English wanting to get ahead of her. The first time, she had been so surprised she had no words, but when someone tried again, she nudged the edge of her valise against him and remained in place.

What a hubbub, she thought; not just English, but Indian trinket-sellers, Indian royalty, and even a greyhound dog stretched out in front of a massive pile of suitcases stamped with a maharaja's coat of arms.

It was a half hour until she reached the polished wood desk and the Anglo-Indian behind it. After she gave her name, the clerk nodded. "No need to check in. Your father has already taken the key to your suite. Rooms three-one-five and three-one-six."

"He's upstairs, then?"

"I cannot say." The clerk was already looking past her to the next guest in line. "A bellman will bring you there and admit you if he is not inside. Is that all you have?"

"My steward already gave the suitcases to the bellman," Perveen said, feeling somewhat affronted at his reaction to her trim Vuitton valise. "In any case, we are only staying the night."

"The reservation is longer than a night," he said crisply. "That is required, when booking a suite during this city holiday."

To some, it was a holiday. They were the people with dozens of cases holding elegant clothing and hats and necessities for a half week's worth of parties. She only hoped the unrest wouldn't continue, and she could go home.

Perveen moved on to join the queue at the lift, which was said to be the first electric-powered one in the city. The elevator had been manufactured in Germany; the late Mr. Tata had an appreciation for German technology. Germany was the country where India's most famous businessman had been visiting when he'd died in 1904.

How had his family managed, having him die so far away? This thought reminded her of the Cuttingmasters, who had been very close when their daughter died. If anything, this had added to their grief. Perveen's irritation about staying in the hotel faded. After all, her brother, father, and she were safely together — and she didn't have to worry about her mother and Gulnaz if they were in the Banker family fortress.

A bell sounded the lift's arrival and its

handsome engraved brass doors opened. A throng of well-dressed Europeans streamed out. She waited to the side for the last person to emerge and was caught by surprise when he addressed her.

"Miss Mistry?"

With shock, she recognized the tall young man with wire-rimmed glasses and dark brown hair that was just a bit longer than was acceptable. "Mr. Sandringham."

Colin Wythe Sandringham was the ICS political agent assigned to the princely state of Satapur. Outside of Alice's father, she knew very few men in government, but she'd been sent to the mountains to assist him with an assignment he could not succeed at by himself. Colin was an unusual Englishman, enthralled by his posting on an isolated mountain where he lived in an old-fashioned bungalow. The Taj Mahal Palace in bustling Bombay was not where she'd picture him staying by choice.

The appearance of Colin was so unnerving she felt fixed to the ground. The man who'd been waiting behind Perveen for the lift stepped around her and carelessly knocked against Colin's right leg. Colin was caught off-balance and Perveen gripped his arm in the second it took him to right himself.

"Never mind!" Colin said, shrugging off her touch. Instantly, she was sorry; she'd reminded him of his prosthesis, and he felt embarrassed.

Perveen motioned him to follow her out of the congested area and toward the reception hall's central table, which was dominated by an arrangement of lilies and birds of paradise. It was tall enough that it would screen them from the people waiting for the lift.

As Colin joined her, she saw from his warm expression that he had forgiven her physical assistance. Softly, he said, "What luck to see you here."

Perveen's day had been the opposite of lucky. A tragedy had occurred. But this chance meeting would give her a moment to think of something else.

Colin continued speaking in a rushed, low voice. "I expected you'd come back to Satapur for the installation of the regent. When you didn't attend, I worried something was very wrong."

The weight in her chest made it difficult to speak. Somehow, she found a way to make her mouth move. And at least her excuse was the truth. "I had to cancel at the last moment. My father was caught up in a big trial and that meant twice the usual workload for me at the firm."

Colin's hand strayed to the arrangement, and he righted a tall bird-of-paradise flower that someone had knocked askew. "I see — work interferes with the best-laid plans. Tell me, then, why are you in this hotel?"

"Due to the riots, my father, brother, and I are bunking here for the night."

Colin's eyes widened. "What rioting? I only knew there was a protest near the mills."

"It has spread. And while we may not have trouble here, the danger is spreading, according to my father."

"I'm quite sorry to hear this. You probably don't want to be here at all." His voice was heavy.

How well he understood her, Perveen thought. "Yes. It's so crowded, and everyone seems ready for a week of parties."

After a pause, he said in a low voice, "Might we speak for a few minutes with a bit more privacy than these flowers can offer?"

She hesitated. She would welcome a more personal conversation without eavesdroppers. But where? One side of the reception area opened to a narrow hall that contained some tourist shops and at the far end, a beauty salon. In a low voice, she said, "Fol-

low me along that corridor. But not too
closely, please."

7
PRINCE EDWARD'S PLEDGE

With senses on edge, Perveen traveled down the corridor, trying to look like a sedate woman unaware an Englishman was trailing. She passed the beauty salon and stepped back into an alcove that was large enough for two. But Colin hung back, staying in the hall. He said, "I don't want to crowd you."

"Thank you." She smiled at him. "As I said before, my father and brother are in the hotel. And the city's only female solicitor must conduct herself above reproach. Now, tell me. Are you here to celebrate the prince's arrival?"

He paused before answering. "Not exactly."

"Have you any business meetings in Bombay?" Perveen was curious because Colin, a civil service employee, was responsible for maintaining relationships with several princely states deep in mountainous western India.

"Nothing for the Kolhapur Agency." Lowering his voice, he added, "I've got temporary orders to assist with the prince's travels."

"Why you?" The question sounded rude once it was out, but Colin didn't seem to react.

"Eddie was at Magdalen College and we knew each other slightly during that year we studied before the war. When he saw my name on a list of civil service officers, he asked his equerry to contact our agency head. He wanted someone close in age on the tour."

"And you both are twenty-eight." Perveen tried to imagine the two of them at college. "He was at Magdalen, and you were at Brasenose. Did you meet at a lecture?"

"It was at a party," Colin said. "He heard someone call me by my last name. Apparently the royal family has a place in the village of Sandringham." His speech sounded stilted, as if he'd caught Perveen's apprehension about the prince. "When he asked, I told him I was a lifelong Londoner, although there might have been ancestors in that village."

"Many Parsis have also adopted surnames related to place," Perveen said. "So, that shared origin was what made you friends?"

Colin shook his head. "It's not really a friendship. But we saw each other again in France, when he was touring a field hospital. We were both glad to have a moment to laugh about Oxford days. He pledged that we'd meet in a happier place after the war was done. He might have remembered that promise when he requested that I join him — but I don't know, because we haven't spoken yet."

Perveen paused, thinking things through. She could not put all the wrongs of colonialism on Edward's shoulders. The evil started much earlier, among a host of countries in Europe, and England was not the only player. "Even if it's not a friendship, it could become one. In any case, you could help make a difficult situation better."

Colin looked intently at her. "I had no idea that this trip would cause us to meet again. To think, we are even under the same roof. And I'm glad for a few days in Bombay. I've got business of my own at the Asiatic Society of Bombay."

"Yes, that's right. You are an out-of-town member," Perveen said. "How is your work on maps coming along?"

A clock chimed far away, making them both jump.

"It must be half-five." Colin glanced over her head and down the hall. "I'm supposed to be checking in with the others billeted here. We're riding up to a reception in Malabar Hill tonight. I could ask if I might bring a guest."

Perveen did not feel like going to any kind of party. "I don't think it would be a good idea."

"Because of your family?" His expression was wary.

Roughly, she said, "Not just that. Too much is going on in the city. A girl was killed today. I cannot go about smiling and bowing as if everything is fine."

He was silent for a moment. Sounding strained, he said, "I can't go out without hearing more about that. Do you know who? Why?"

"Freny Cuttingmaster was a Parsi girl, just eighteen and a tremendously promising college student. She came to my office on Monday with a question I tried to answer. I liked her very much." She could have said more, but there was an ache in her throat, and she did not want to weep in front of Colin.

Colin exhaled heavily. "I'm so very sorry, Perveen. And was she a victim of the riots?"

"No." Perveen looked back at him, seeing

the sympathy in his eyes. "Freny was found in the garden at Woodburn College. Very few were around because everyone was in the viewing stands."

"Was it murder?" Instantly, he'd lowered his voice.

"Murder, suicide, who knows? She looked dreadful. There will be a formal inquest by the Coroner of Bombay. However, with the violence unfolding in the city, I fear there will be more work for the morgue technicians than usual."

Stepping back, he looked at her soberly. "I'll keep my ears open at the reception tonight, in case I hear anything about this case."

"Thank you very much." She knew he would do it. He was loyal to her, and his concern over Freny's death was a reminder that it wasn't all the people of Britain who were wretched, it was the government's policy toward their colonies.

She also needed to remember that because Colin was open and attractive, he was more of a danger to her than typical clients. She could not let any evidence of her feelings lead him toward wanting more. So when he casually asked for her room number, she shook her head.

"I can't tell you. I'm staying in a suite with

my father and brother. They'd both be aggrieved if an Englishman came by wishing to chat."

Colin's face flushed. "Sorry. You were different in the mountains."

Behind the plate glass window, Perveen saw that a client with her hair wrapped in a towel was watching them. Perveen glared at her, and the woman's eyes slid away. Turning back to Colin, Perveen murmured, "I am the same as always. And I must check into my room."

He moved away a few paces. "Of course. Good afternoon, then."

Perveen knew she'd injured his feelings, but to linger and reveal her own confusion about her emotions wouldn't improve the situation. She answered in a tone as starched as her sari. "Good afternoon, Mr. Sandringham."

The waiting crowd for the lift was just as dense as before, so she decided to take the grand spiral staircase. It was quite a climb, and when she arrived on the third floor, she was slightly breathless. As she turned down a hallway, a white man in a black tuxedo approached.

"Are you Miss Mistry?" The gentleman had a soft European accent that she could not place.

"May I ask how you recognized me?" She hoped her tête-à-tête with Colin was not already hotel gossip.

"A bellman came with your valise quite a while ago. I shall open room three-one-five for you. It's a very pleasant suite with a sea view."

The butler opened up the door to reveal a small parlor with a settee crowded with tapestry cushions and some lounging chairs in coral velvet, and a Regency-style writing desk with a caned chair. Two doors opened to the bedrooms, one of which had twin beds and Rustom and her father's luggage, and the other bedroom, a single bed and her own valise.

"It was kind of you to wait for me," she said, thinking about how busy the hotel was. "Did you see my family at all?"

"Yes, madam. Your father told me they were going downstairs for tea."

As he finished the declaration, a slim woman with blonde hair swept into a tight chignon entered the room. She wore a black uniform with a lacy white apron. Bowing slightly, she said, "May I assist with your unpacking?"

Perveen spoke clearly, because she had detected the woman's accent came from somewhere other than Britain. "There is no need, thank you. Actually, I would like to rest undisturbed."

"But the others?" The maidservant glanced toward the opened bedroom door revealing Rustom and Jamshedji's luggage.

"They prefer to unpack themselves." Her voice came out more sharply than she wished, but the last thing she wanted was a European going through their things. Her father carried all manner of confidential papers in his briefcase, and possibly the suitcase, too.

Appearing nonplussed, the lady smiled and departed with the butler.

Perveen had grown up with servants of many religions, but they were all Indian. Having Europeans and British catering to her felt odd. She could not help wondering, did a European resent being in service to an Indian? It had seemed that way with the Anglo-Indian desk clerk when she'd checked in. Or was she pushing her own anxiety onto people who were merely trying to do a day's work with honesty and conviction?

Feeling restless, she walked back to the parlor. It was the first time since the morning that she'd been alone; the ideal moment to do some writing.

Perveen went to the desk and filled the

pen in the stand with ink. She opened a leather folio embossed with a crown and took out a piece of stationery. She intended to write a record of what came to pass at Woodburn College.

She dated the top of the page and began writing down her memories, beginning with Dinesh's cries and subsequent arrest, and ending with her departure from the college under the direction of the man with the bowler hat. She was so focused that she hadn't realized her father had entered the suite until she heard his familiar cough.

"Ah. You reached us safely," he said with satisfaction. "But where is your brother?"

"I haven't seen him. The butler said you were together?"

Placing his fetah on a hat rack near the door, he said, "We started out together, but he departed. He wanted to speak with some people who'd just arrived and were talking about an attack on the Byculla Club. All over the city, Parsis are being attacked on accusation of being loyalists."

"And how does that make you feel?"

"I was not eager to see the Prince of Wales." His voice was measured and unemotional. "Yet it was very important to celebrate Rustom's accomplishment of the Gateway to India. His business is different than ours, as you know."

Perveen nodded. During Rustom's childhood, Jamshedji had been frustrated with his only son's lack of academic interests, which had made a career in law impossible. But Rustom was handy at making things, so it was natural for him to begin working under Grandfather Mistry's careful guidance.

With a wry smile, Jamshedji added, "So I applauded the prince, even though I donated to the Congress Party last month."

"What?" Perveen was stunned. "Why did you decide to give to them?"

"I didn't think one hundred rupees would cause our country to be torn asunder," he answered with a casual shrug. "But if these people are killing others, I cannot be a part of it."

"It's been very frightening today." She spoke slowly and moved into one of the easy chairs. She needed the rest. Without bidding, Jamshedji followed and sat across from her. He waited in expectant silence.

Taking a deep breath, she said, "A young Parsi woman I met died today. Freny Cuttingmaster was her name."

He leaned forward, searching her face. "That is terrible news. Are you sure it's true?"

"I am sure because I was there. It happened close to the procession route."

Jamshedji stiffened. After a pause, he said, "Mustafa told me you went out into the city. And now I'm guessing that you went to the procession alone, when you could have gone to its starting point with your whole family?"

Not meeting his eyes, Perveen explained how she'd had the sudden urge to join the viewing group at Woodburn College, and how Dinesh Apte had run after the prince's carriage, and how she and Alice had rushed onto the campus to find Freny's body.

"What, exactly, did you see?" Jamshedji's voice was calm, as if he were in a courtroom questioning a witness.

"Freny was lying on the stone path, as if she'd fallen. Part of her face was shattered." Perveen swallowed, trying to suppress her nausea. "One student went for the police and I asked another to find a Parsi doctor. Dr. Pandey arrived from the Orient Club."

Jamshedji nodded. "I know Boman Pandey. He's good."

"He told the police he would sign a death certificate. I went to sit with Alice in the chapel, and after I left the campus I met Freny's parents."

"Oh? So they were nearby?"

"Yes. They were celebrating the prince's procession from the vantage point of the Orient Club. They were naturally overcome with grief. I told them I'd make sure prayers began at Doongerwadi, and I also gave them my card."

As she'd continued talking, Jamshedji's thick salt-and-pepper brows had drawn together. He did not look aggrieved anymore. "I feel as if I know this name, Cuttingmaster. How many could there be in our city?"

She had to tell him sooner or later. "Freny came for a consultation at the start of the week."

"I see." Studying her, he said, "Perhaps I spotted the name in our logbook, but I don't recall whether there's a signed client agreement."

"I didn't make one because it was just a brief consultation," Perveen explained. "She only asked my opinion on whether Woodburn College could expel her if she stayed away from school to protest the prince."

"And what did you tell her?"

"I said she should check if her family had received a contract or if she could locate any college rules regarding student attendance. I also mentioned that if she stayed home due to illness, that would be a safe

115

way to avoid conflict." Feeling a rush of sorrow, she added, "How I wish she had done that."

Jamshedji was toying with his monocle. "The college is one of the Sea-Face Road's premier landmarks. I wouldn't expect it to be in disrepair."

Perveen leaned forward. "Are you thinking of the family's right to sue the college for an accidental death caused by building neglect?"

Putting his monocle away, he shrugged. "Even if there was a fault in the building, I don't think a suit would succeed. The courts rule very favorably toward institutions and companies rather than the plaintiff. And Woodburn's principal, Mr. McHugh, is a popular gentleman in Bombay."

This was a rare situation where she had social news that her father hadn't yet learned. "Actually, a temporary principal is in charge while Mr. McHugh is on furlough. His name is H. V. Atherton, and he seems fresh off the boat — didn't even have proper clothing for India yet," Perveen added, remembering the woolen suit. "I never saw such sweat. It must be very nerve-wracking to have a tragedy occur on one's watch when one is new at the college."

Jamshedji looked past Perveen to the open

windows and the seaside view. He was quiet for a few moments, and when he spoke, his voice was pensive. "Because Mr. Atherton is a newcomer, he won't know the story about the University of Bombay."

"Oh? What story do you mean?"

Her father paused, rubbing his chin. "There was a death — two actually. Female students falling one after the other from the Rajabai clock tower inside the University of Bombay in the 1890s. A most unusual pair of deaths, and nobody was convicted in either case."

Perveen's attention was jolted. "Why?"

With a deep storyteller's sigh, Jamshedji began. "I was a fledgling lawyer when this happened; and it was all we talked about at the Ripon Club for a year. As I said, both girls fell from a great height to their death within minutes of each other. One theory was that the women had thrown themselves off the main hall's clock tower due to shame at being accosted by some unknown man or men in the tower. Others believed that they were the victims of a premeditated murder. Many young men were questioned, both students and workers in the area, and there were two trials, but nobody was convicted." Then a curious look came into his eyes. "Come to think of it, this is the thirty-year anniversary of their deaths."

Perveen spoke slowly. "It's odd for Freny to die the same way. Truth be told, people fall, jump, and are pushed off buildings every month. Based on the prior case, it seems this could be a very difficult verdict for the coroner to argue."

Jamshedji nodded. "Did the parents ask for your assistance?"

"Not exactly," she admitted. "I introduced myself and gave my card, because I felt . . . some responsibility, having met with their daughter earlier in the week."

His vision snapped back from the window to her. "Do they know that?"

"I said she'd seen me at the office. No further details."

Jamshedji sucked in his breath. "By doing that, you might have given them a chance to blame you for something."

"But I didn't tell her to *go* to the college. I specifically suggested the idea of staying in her home and feigning illness. She reacted strongly against the idea, saying it was not truthful."

Jamshedji looked soberly at Perveen. "You should document this. Is that what you were doing when I came in?"

"I should have taken notes that day. I was documenting events from my arrival at the

Woodburn College stand. Just in case we need to assist the Cuttingmasters. I feel a responsibility." She paused. "I don't want her to suffer the same lack of justice as those girls who fell from the clock tower."

"Agreed." Jamshedji frowned. "If the inquest or resulting police investigation goes astray, we can help push a case for them to be heard in another court."

She was grateful for his turnabout in mood. "You would help me?"

"Normally, I'd be eager to represent such a family. But so much is unknown at this point." Jamshedji rose to his feet. "With respect to the Cuttingmasters, I will be watching over your shoulder from now on. Agreed?"

"Yes, of course. Should I send a message to the Cuttingmasters tomorrow?"

"Let's not think of tomorrow today. You have been sitting alone up here worrying. Better have something to eat."

8

CONFESSIONS AT DAWN

An hour later, a waiter delivered a plate of chicken and chutney sandwiches, a pineapple tart, and a pot of Darjeeling. Perveen found herself suddenly very hungry, despite the troubles on her mind — her grief for Freny, and her worry for her mother and Gulnaz. She couldn't bear the thought of them facing down hoodlums like she had. She was thankful they weren't staying alone, but with Gulnaz's family.

Her dinner finished, Perveen went downstairs. The lobby was just as crowded as before, and there was a queue for the three private telephone booths in an adjoining hallway. When she finally got inside one after thirty minutes, she picked up the receiver and asked the hotel operator to dial the residence of Mr. L. M. Banker. A servant answered and went to fetch Perveen's mother.

As Camellia Mistry spoke into the receiver, her voice sounded calm as ever. "Hello, my darling. Where are you?"

"The Taj Mahal Hotel. Pappa didn't want us to come home because of having to travel past the mills."

"Yes, he rang me earlier and I agreed with his decision. Better to stay put in the European Quarter until the goondas settle down."

"How is it at the Bankers'?"

"They've been spoiling me with good food and such a lovely room; and of course they are happy to have Gulnaz home for a night. I am certain I'd be fine in our house without Pappa, but Gulnaz was so excited, I could not deny her."

Perveen wanted to feel settled, but she knew that Dadar Parsi Colony was perhaps the only Zoroastrian community in Bombay not guarded by walls. "Have any trouble-makers been seen in the neighborhood?"

"No, and they could not possibly enter. There are police and some of our strongest young men patrolling the streets. You should enjoy the Taj and not think about us," her mother soothed.

"This is the most crowded I've ever seen it. What a miracle that Pappa found room for us."

"In the old days, I'd say it was because of

Grandfather's friendship with Mr. Tata, but now that he is gone it must be Rustom and his connections. After all, he is building the Gateway nearby, so he's had many business lunches and teas at that hotel. How does Rustom like the suite?"

"I haven't seen him yet."

"Up to expensive fun, I suppose." Camellia chuckled indulgently.

A businessman was standing with his face pressed up to the glass of the telephone booth. She got the message. Perveen bade her mother a sweet good night and exited the booth.

It was ten o'clock, and Perveen cast an eye around the lobby as she waited again for the lift. The crowd was about half the size it had been at check-in; perhaps many of the guests were at Government House along with Colin. She imagined that if the police learned things were difficult on the road, everyone would stay at Government House's grounds until it was safe.

She should not worry about Colin; but still, she did.

The English-style four-poster bed with large soft pillows and a thick mattress was quite different from her bed at home. And instead of mosquito netting around the bed, there was mosquito wire covering the tall arched windows, just the same as in the Hobson-Jones home. It was the European way, designed to make the whole room free of the pests. But despite the screening, an insect had entered the room, and Perveen fell asleep very slowly as it whined.

And then, she was dreaming. It was the morning again, and she was strolling along Kennedy Sea-Face. The viewing stands lined the road but nobody was in them. Why was this, when the prince was coming? Perveen looked again and she saw just one person sitting there. Freny, dressed all in white, the color for religious observances. She was calling out to Perveen, and Perveen was trying to run to her, but her sari was hampering her progress. Freny was holding up a book for her to see, and though there was distance between them, Perveen knew it was a rule book for Woodburn College. But while Perveen was walking toward Freny, her view was obfuscated by Professor Gupta, Mr. Grady, Reverend Sullivan, and Mr. Atherton. The man in the gray suit, and the police sergeant who'd been by the cart.

How could she counsel Freny in front of them?

And then the Prince of Wales was coming

along in a car, not a carriage, and he was driving it himself. The car picked up speed, and Perveen saw to her shock that the prince was laughing uproariously as he drove. The car was going faster and faster, and Perveen realized the prince was gunning for her. She could not move from her spot.

"Hey, hey! Stop that crying."

A hand was shaking her shoulder, bringing her out of the nightmare and back to the present. She was in a hotel, and light was coming in, a bluish gray that meant dawn.

Rustom was sitting at the edge of the bed, his hand still on her shoulder. The room was filled with the scent of whiskey.

"You're just dreaming. Stop that crying, or Pappa will think someone's broken in!" Rustom's voice was very slightly slurred.

She let out a gusty breath. "It was a terrible dream. The Prince of Wales was about to hit me with his car."

Patting her shoulder again, he joked, "I thought I was the only one who dreamed about cars. Never mind, you're safe and it's almost morning."

Perveen fumbled for the switch on the bedside lamp to see him better. "You're a sight! There's dried blood on your cheek —

oh, and your hand, too!" She shrugged away from him. "Did you attack someone?"

"Sssh!" Rustom hissed. "It's not your business. I wouldn't even have come to you if you hadn't been crying!"

Perveen couldn't let it go. "Did you go home to defend Dadar Parsi Colony?"

"No. The colony's not suffered any trouble. Gulnaz told me. There's no need for worrying, I tell you."

"Then why are you looking like you went down to the docks and fought with sailors?"

Rustom narrowed his eyes, then got up to check that the door between the rooms was fully closed. When he returned, he stood at the bedside, shifting from one foot to the other.

"I don't know if I should tell you."

It had been years since Rustom had confided in her — though when they were children, they had been close. She realized now that she wanted to have this intimacy again. "I won't tell anyone."

"All right." He gave a shuddering breath. "I'll start at the beginning, when we were waiting for the prince to arrive. Journalists from all over the world were hammering me with questions about the monument. Somebody joked that Indians should not finish the Gateway before we gain independence, and I had words for him. Some hours later, I ran into the same American newsman in the hotel dining room: Mr. Jay Peter Singer — he goes by J.P."

"I didn't know Americans would think the prince's visit would be important enough to attend. After all, they went to great lengths to end British rule."

"That's true," Rustom admitted. "But it was a long time ago, that war. J.P. is my age and comes from California and writes for a paper called the *San Francisco Chronicle.*"

"Just as we have the *Bombay Chronicle*!" Perveen said.

"Yes, but I don't see stories in our newspaper with the critical opinions he's thinking of expressing. By the time I saw him at the hotel, he'd learned something about the riots and wanted advice on how to get around the city to report on the unrest. He said he couldn't find a taxi."

"Since public transport is halted, there was a high demand on cabs," Perveen said.

"That's right," Rustom said. "The only driver I could think of was Arman."

Now Perveen realized why Rustom had been reluctant to tell her what had happened. "But Pappa doesn't allow him to drive for others."

Rustom hiccupped. "This is the reason I

went along with Jay; the driving orders to the main police headquarters came from me. And Arman knows many routes to police headquarters because of Pappa's work. He did not complain."

"Only because we are his employers — and he is obliged to do what we want." Perveen remembered Arman's nervousness driving her to the hotel.

"It was seven when we left, and I was certain we'd be back by suppertime. It was difficult to get information at the police headquarters — the top brass had gone up to Government House for a party." Rustom lowered his voice, as if he was afraid their father might be able to hear through the closed door. "J.P. was trying to find out if it was true that a female student had been killed, and the men on duty said that they couldn't give a name. J.P. told me that when police don't give names it's because something very bad occurred."

"Or because the family wasn't yet notified," Perveen pointed out, not wanting to talk about Freny. "Did he learn all that he wanted?"

Rustom shook his head. "J.P. could not get confirmation of any murders, so he asked about arrests in general. The corporal admitted there was trouble in the city and said if we wanted to know more, to go to the Carnac Street station."

"Did you go there?"

"I couldn't stop him!" Rustom said defensively. "By that time, Jay was giving Arman orders where to go next."

Perveen thought this was an exaggeration. Her brother probably wanted to have his own story to tell his friends about touring the city with an American newsman.

"Along the driving route, so many businesses selling European wares had been smashed up. Badmashes and goondas running everywhere. One of the bands caught sight of us. They must have seen Jay's foreign face peering from the window."

Or Rustom's — he was obviously a wealthy Parsi. "You turned back, then?"

"No, Arman drove like a demon, and we made it to the police station. Other reporters were already there, and the building was packed with men in handcuffs."

"Rioters?" Perveen wondered if the men who'd been smashing the shop had been arrested.

"From the way they were shouting, I think it was a mix of rioters and thieves. We finally managed to get the station's superintendent for a brief interview. Outside, we found a very talkative constable, and I translated his

Marathi to English for Jay."

She was impressed by her brother's efforts. "Could the police say how much of the city was in danger?"

"At least four had died and many more people were injured. Jay was pleased and wished to get back to the hotel to file his story. We left — but we got caught up with another mob. We were the only car on the road, and they rushed toward us, throwing stones."

"And this is how you were hurt. I'm so sorry, Rustom. How did Mr. Singer and Arman fare?"

"Arman has a cut on his arm, but he was much more concerned about the cracked windshield. I made J.P. lie flat on the floor — he didn't have a scratch on him, but he was very demanding that I give him descriptions of all that transpired."

"You were prudent," Perveen said. She didn't add that having a Westerner in the car — someone who could have been assumed to be English — had been highly dangerous.

"When we made it back to the hotel, J.P. rushed to his room to begin typing. He was going to send the report by telegraph. It will appear in tomorrow's paper."

"And did Arman have to drive out in the

midst of this again? You put him at terrible risk."

"He was quite shaken," Rustom said. "I gave him enough money to get a hotel room in the area, but he said Mustafa would let him stay inside Mistry House."

Where Perveen had wanted to stay put. "Have you spoken to Pappa yet about the damage?"

He shook his head. "He's sleeping like a log. I'd rather not wake him with bad news."

"You were doing a good deed. He won't hold it against you —"

"Even if he doesn't shout to high heaven, which I think he will, he's certain to be very tight on my use of the car in the future."

"He's bound to learn about the windshield," Perveen said.

"Arman said he'd do his best for me." He paused. "I think I'd better wash up before the morning."

Perveen thought a moment. "Don't you go. You'll frighten someone with your appearance."

The washrooms for men and lady guests were at the corners of the guest room hallways, and with a full-length wrapper tied over her nightgown for modesty, Perveen hastened toward them with a pair of clean towels. Hampering her progress were bodies

— scores of servants, lying fast asleep on mats outside their employers' rooms. Some had blankets, others did not.

Perveen had always understood that very wealthy people traveled with servants, but she hadn't realized that they would literally be prostrated in the hotel's hallways. She was glad Mustafa hadn't come; she could not bear for the dignified retainer to be put in such a position, when he was accustomed to sleeping with great comfort on an extra-long rope bed.

The ladies' lavatory was spotless and lit with soft electric lighting; Perveen used the facilities, had a drink of water, and returned with damp washcloths to clean up her brother.

"Thank you," Rustom said as Perveen dabbed at the smudges of blood on his face. "Better not tell Gulnaz any of this. She's so delicate now."

Perveen mulled over his comment; she saw Gulnaz daily and hadn't thought she seemed any different. "Does that mean she's with child?"

Rustom caught his breath, as if she'd shocked him. After a moment he said, "After all these years of trying — finally, our dream is coming true."

Perveen felt happiness, both for the news

and the proof her intuition was right. "I knew it would come to be! How many months along?"

"About five. Our baby is coming in April."

"I can hardly wait to be an aunt." Perveen smiled at him in the darkness, understanding this was another very good reason for Gulnaz and Camellia to have stayed in place at the colony that night.

After Rustom tiptoed back to his room, Perveen lay down again, unable to sleep. Her happy-go-lucky brother was almost a father; Gulnaz would be a mother; and she would become an aunt.

Nineteen twenty-two would be the year a new generation started. And the night's conversation seemed to hint at a new beginning for her relationship with Rustom: one that was friendlier and more accepting, despite their political differences.

Yet her happiness at the thought of the long-awaited child was mixed with sadness. The violence in the city was a harbinger of the future. How dangerous and divided would this new Mistry child's world be?

9

BATTLE OF WILLS

Just before seven o'clock, Perveen awoke to an unpleasant cawing. She realized she'd fallen asleep after Rustom's visit. The crows wouldn't stop, so she climbed out of the magnificent bed and went to the tall windows to shoo them away.

Watching the fat black birds fly off to visit crows at a neighboring balcony, she wondered if they were all one family. She'd learned from reading novels that a flock of crows could also be called a murder, which was gruesome. Still, the birds were known to devour anything from fish to mice and food scraps. Bombay's rodents and crows had played a role in spreading the bubonic plague that had been rampant in the late 1890s.

Disease was why those who could afford it left the historic city center to settle on higher ground. This created an architectural boom for new neighborhoods like Cuffe

Parade and Kemps Corner, Cumballa Hill and Malabar Hill.

In 1915, Mistry and Sons Construction had landed the contract to build some homes on the land north of the city that was allocated for an exclusive Parsi colony. Sensing this would become the ultimate neighborhood, her brother had convinced their father to co-invest with him on a plot that would become their family's duplex.

Rustom's residence was on the duplex's right side and boasted four bedrooms. Perveen's parents were on the left with the same square footage and layout, but one bedroom was used as a library. No extra bedroom was needed, because there would be no more children.

Looking out at the Arabian Sea, Perveen thought about the four years that had passed since she'd been granted a legal separation from Cyrus Sodawalla, whom she'd impulsively married against her parents' wishes at age eighteen. After six dreadful months she'd fled from him, grateful that her parents allowed her home and didn't protest her resuming her maiden name.

The Parsi family court would never grant her a divorce, so this had put her into the same kind of limbo as the circling crows.

She could live comfortably as an adult daughter to her parents, and she could be an aunt to Rustom and Gulnaz's children, but she could never remarry and build her own family.

Perveen's estranged husband had an incurable disease and had been nursed by his parents in Calcutta for several years. Perveen knew that the Sodawallas and everyone in their social circle considered her a heartless woman to have left. After all, she had chosen to marry him. Very few people knew about the abuse and infidelity that had wracked her brief marriage.

The twin scandals of her love marriage followed by a marital separation were enough for the Mistry family. This was why she had to be excessively careful about socialization with any male. While accepting a ride from an elder like Mr. Wadia was permissible because of his age and friendship with her family, chatting with an Englishman in a hotel could create harmful gossip.

Why would she risk this? She had never been happier than as a solicitor. Whether she was working on a rental contract or a business settlement, she was building Bombay. Her sense of duty to the city was almost as strong as to her family.

Gazing down from the window at the promenade along the harbor, she saw a few early morning walkers. The area was clearly safe, and when would she ever have such a time to stroll so closely to the Arabian Sea?

Perveen dressed quickly, washed her face, and left a note on her desk saying she'd gone out but would appear for breakfast at eight-thirty.

She rode the lift downstairs by herself, relishing her independence.

As she passed the front desk, the same Anglo-Indian clerk who'd checked her in cleared his throat. "Madam, may I ask where you are going?"

She was affronted by his inquisitiveness. "Just taking a walk."

"Alone?" he asked pointedly.

She released her irritation with an equally sharp rejoinder. "Do you ask your male guests such questions?"

Squaring his shoulders, he looked disdainfully at her. "We are warning guests that only the area near the hotel can be seen by our durwans. With the current conditions in the city, we do not recommend anyone going out of their eyesight."

This reminded her of what had happened yesterday: the men who'd watched her, then rushed forward to attack. Tilting her face up to look levelly at the desk clerk, she said, "I will only go down to the promenade to look at the sea."

"If you stay where the benches are, you will be safe."

How much violence had occurred in the night? She looked at a stack of newspapers on the counter. There was quite an array — not just the *Times of India,* but the *International Herald.* "Are these papers gratis?"

"Yes. A boy will bring one to your father's suite in the next half hour."

"Actually — might I have one myself right now?"

He raised his eyebrows, as if the thought of a woman reading a newspaper was something untoward. But then, as if remembering the hotel's motto — Guest Is God — he nodded. "Of course, madam."

Perveen picked up that morning's *Times of India* and the *International Herald* and walked out the doors toward the sea.

It had been so busy when she'd checked in that she hadn't looked around, but now she had a full view of Front Bay, sparkling in the early morning light. Boats of all sizes were heading out, mostly to bring back fish. The Gateway to India, the welcoming monument where the prince had set foot, was still decorated with streamers and garlands, but some of them were detached and flapping in the wind.

Perveen walked a few feet south and settled herself on a bench overlooking Front Bay. If she craned her neck, she could see the *Renown.* The destroyer was a hulking, ominous presence. She wondered if it would stay all four months of the prince's sojourn in India, or if he'd sail aboard it from Bombay for Calcutta. Mustafa probably already knew.

Perveen picked up the *International Herald* first and saw that it carried news from two days earlier. She put it aside for later and inspected the front page of the *Times.* The most important articles were always in the center, just below the fold. The story was a glowing account of the grand spectacle of the prince's arrival; it named all the princes who had come to pay respects, and described his immaculate military dress and medals, the welcoming speech by Mayor Sassoon, and the remarks by the King that Edward had read aloud. The article contained no mention of rioting, nor the fact that people had died.

She thought the American reporter who'd been with Rustom would tell a more dramatic story. He had seen the fury of everyday Indians. And while it was important for the truth to be told, she knew that a vivid description of riots could also cause the greater world to see the freedom fighters as troublemakers.

Everyone was capable of happiness or rage, kindness or evil. The question was, how much violence was within her? She knew that if Freny had been murdered, she would wish the perpetrator to lose his right to walk freely in India.

Perveen finished the article and refolded the newspaper. She heard the sound of footsteps and turned sharply. She saw the color first; one man wearing flaming crimson and his companion in peacock blue. Two prosperous-looking Indian men, walking slowly along the promenade. As they came closer, the sunlight glinted off the jeweled brooches on their stiff turbans. She felt a sudden rush of nausea, even though her stomach was empty. What might they do if they noticed her?

The men, quite likely nobility of some sort, ambled along, one gentleman pointing toward the *Renown,* and the other man shaking his head and looking grim. They probably hadn't wanted to come into Bombay but had been forced to by their government minders. They had no interest in troubling a young woman sitting alone: her mind was playing tricks on her, bringing back the same flash of panic she'd had near the Hawthorn Shop.

"You're still an early riser."

She turned her head, having recognized the voice of Colin Sandringham, sounding slightly hoarse. He must have been out all night, she guessed from the black tuxedo and satin top hat.

"It's not very early. In your case, I'd say it's rather late," she teased.

"May I join you?"

Perveen knew how improper their association could appear. Yet they weren't inside the hotel, and she longed to hear about the events at Government House. Hesitantly, she said, "Why don't you take the bench that's just to the right of me? We can still talk."

"So we are like spies reporting to each other." Colin seated himself on the bench she'd suggested, carefully moving his right leg so it was at ease.

"Well, you sought me out. You might as well tell me about the party." Perveen refolded the newspaper she'd been reading and smiled at him.

"It was massive," he said, gesturing with outspread arms. "An estimated three thousand people. I was mad to leave within an hour, but I wasn't able to depart until six-thirty because the hordes of guests outnumbered the official cars."

"That's a very long wait. And I imagine the prince must be exhausted, especially after just ending a sea voyage."

"His Royal Highness left us before midnight. He was scheduled to play polo this morning. You know that I dislike it when people assume my leg prevents me from doing what everyone else does." Perveen nodded, surprised by his candor. "This morning is one of the rare times I don't mind having an excuse. No polo for me."

"Fiddlesticks. I've seen you ride a horse for hours," Perveen said sarcastically.

"But I'm dead tired this morning." He delivered a giant yawn. "And why would I want to play a game of mock jousting? I've seen horses fall in the line of battle, and also at polo. There's no reason for either."

"You are so tenderhearted toward animals." Perveen changed the topic. "At the party, did you meet my friend Miss Alice Hobson-Jones?"

"Yes." Colin grinned mischievously. "I recognized her immediately — she is still the tallest woman in the room. She was quite proud to have become a mathematics lecturer. She said she would never have had such an opportunity to teach male students in Britain."

"Male and female students. Woodburn College was founded as co-educational," Perveen clarified.

Nodding, he continued. "She asked me how the two of us met, and I was about halfway through our adventure in Satapur when her mother, Lady Hobson-Jones, joined us and took over the conversation. She thinks teaching is too taxing for her daughter."

Perveen snorted. "Lady Hobson-Jones wants Alice to have more time for teas and dinners at the Bombay Club and Government House. Those are likelier halls to find eligible bachelors than a missionary college."

"Oh, is that it?" Looking amused, he shook his head. "Mummy dearest had scores of questions about me, starting with my ICS rank and ending with how I was chosen to accompany the prince on his tour."

"Or she was assessing you for eligibility as a son-in-law." Perveen had to admit that Colin would be an especially appealing match for Alice, in Lady Hobson-Jones's eyes. However, she knew that Alice could not be tempted toward the handsomest or most brilliant of men.

"Oh, dear. Really? She invited me for tea, but I pleaded that there will be very little time. Miss Hobson-Jones barely seemed to hear. When her mother arrived, seemed like the electricity shut off."

"Alice is in the same kind of gloom as me. The young woman who'd died — the one I mentioned yesterday, Miss Freny Cutting-master — was a student she knew well."

Colin bit his lip. "I wish you had told me in advance. I would have given my condolences and not made so many jokes about Oxford."

"It's all right. Alice probably would not wish to discuss it with you, especially if her mother was present. Lady Hobson-Jones would adore to have a good reason to stop Alice from being a college lecturer." As she spoke, she looked over her shoulder. She had a feeling someone was watching them. But the promenade was still quite empty.

"There was a bit of talk about the death at the party."

Perveen turned quickly back to him. "By whom?"

"A man who seemed high up in the police was chatting to someone in the prince's entourage. He said the worst part of the riots so far was the death of a lady student.

He was boasting about being first on the scene. I was listening over my shoulder, mind you, not part of the conversation."

"Did this man wear a bowler hat?" Perveen asked.

"We all checked hats upon entering Government House, though the maharajas and nawabs naturally kept their turbans. Why? Do you know who he is?"

"I've no idea. There were likely hundreds of Imperial and Bombay City Police officers involved with the prince's procession. Did the man speak of her death as murder?"

Colin was silent for a moment. "No, but I'd guess that his mentioning her death in the context of the riots means he suspects this."

It would be easy to attribute Freny's death to angry nationalists. But Freny had been inside the school, not on the street. Wasn't this being taken into consideration?

"What's wrong, Perveen?"

"Nothing." She unclenched her jaw and affected a normal expression. "Please tell me what is on your calendar today."

"I have freedom until about noon. I'll get a rest and then try to do something about my military trousers."

She felt a laugh coming and put a hand over her mouth. "What's wrong with your trousers?"

"There's a ball tonight." Glumly, he added, "Qualifying ICS officers are supposed to wear military dress, but the trousers are not long enough on the right anymore. They were measured and sewn for me before."

She understood he meant before the amputation. "There are plenty of haberdasheries in town. I'm not sure if the Hawthorn Shop — the place where Freny's father works — is open today. You could ring —" She cut herself off, realizing that as an Englishman, he would be vulnerable to the same kind of attack that she'd suffered. "Actually, that may be too far to go! The hotel surely has a tailor on call."

"The latter sounds better to me, as I am dead tired." As if to prove it, he yawned widely. Recovering, he muttered, "Fussing about wardrobe seems like a terrific waste of time and money for a party I'd rather miss. But it's part and parcel of being in the entourage."

"Yes. You do need proper clothing for the prince's tour." Just as she'd had to bring her better saris — like this dotted green-and-blue Kanchipuram silk she was wearing — because she was in high-class company at the Taj. "Anyhow, aren't your colleagues in the Kolhapur Agency envying you the friendship with the prince?"

"It's not a friendship. He did not even recognize me until someone reminded him he'd requested that I join the entourage." Colin's lips drew into a thin line. "And then he seemed rather annoyed that I wouldn't play polo this morning."

"You told me you didn't want to play," Perveen reminded him.

"Of course, I don't. But I don't believe he's comfortable being close to imperfection. It disgusts him." He looked away from her to the sea, where two fishermen were rowing a small boat. How companionable they looked.

"How can you know the prince's thoughts?"

"His younger brother, Prince John, had some kind of disability. It wasn't talked about much in England, but word got out that Prince Edward said it was better that he died. That was two years ago," he added. "Apparently our crown prince was said to live as if his little brother didn't exist."

Perveen had chosen to live as if Cyrus didn't exist. But she wasn't going to bring that up with Colin — it would only bring about an argument.

"Anyhow there are plenty of Brits who are

eager to speak with the prince. Do you recall the lady who was gawking at us from the beauty salon?"

Perveen winced. "Seeing her made me realize we'd better go off separately, lest we get a reputation."

"You wouldn't have believed what was done to Miss Hortense Bingham's hair. A short style, utterly frizzled and frazzled. As if she'd been electrocuted." He demonstrated by contracting his fingers.

Perveen could not resist laughing. "That hairstyle is called a permanent wave."

"Miss Bingham did not explain. But she does say she's an assistant at the Secretariat and there's a position opening in an office near hers for someone of my rank."

"Did you tell her that you love the countryside and don't care to work in Bombay?"

"No. I don't think Bombay's all bad, Perveen. I'm hoping to go all over the city this week, because of the prince's agenda."

Perveen wondered if Miss Bingham had asked Colin to ring her. She made a point of glancing at her watch. "It's already a little past eight. My family will be waiting for me to go to breakfast."

"I hope I didn't delay you."

Of course he had — but she hadn't wanted to leave. Who knew how many months or years it might be until they met again? It should not matter to her — after all, she had been doing her best not to speak publicly to him. He did not understand that their association could be poison to his career, just as he was to hers.

Rising from her bench, she said, "I erred by not watching the time. I wish you all the best with your activities today."

Colin handed her the two newspapers she'd forgotten. "I know you're not much for parties, but would you consider a geography lecture at the Asiatic Society Friday evening?"

Her answer was automatic. "Sorry, I don't think that I'm available."

He gave her a resigned look. "No need to apologize. I won't keep inviting you."

"I'm sorry," she said again, but he had already stood up and walked away.

Perveen let out a sigh as heavy as the net the fishermen were now lugging onto shore. She knew she needed to explain that to sit inside a lecture hall, chatting with Colin, would be as scandalous as walking outdoors with her hair uncovered. That was the part she could tell. The thing she could not express was that the more she saw him, the more agitated she became. And now was hardly the time for such feelings.

■ ■ ■ ■

Returning to the hotel, Perveen headed straight to the dining room, where she saw her father and brother conferring with the maître d'.

Jamshedji folded his arms and glared at her. "It's perturbing to wake up and find one's daughter has vanished."

Perveen was annoyed. "I left a note on my desk about taking a walk. And I'm on time for breakfast."

"I did see the note." Jamshedji looked accusingly at her. "Then I went outside. I did not see any Indian women walking on the promenade excepting for the one lady from behind, but it could not have been you. She was on a bench with an Englishman."

Perveen almost said they were on separate benches, but that would have meant admitting to a conversation with Colin. She would not take the bait.

"I've half an hour only," Rustom said. "Let's eat."

"Be sure to have eggs," Jamshedji advised. "You need strength today."

Perveen glanced at Rustom, whose cheek showed a thin line of dried red blood. He looked back impassively. She wondered if their father had said something about it to him. Probably.

Without the cheerful companionship of Camellia and Gulnaz, they were as pleasant as a murder of crows.

Not wanting any more arguments, Perveen ordered the standard fried eggs with rashers on the side and toast. The Taj was reputed to have its English-style bread baked in the early hours each day by a French chef, so she wanted to taste this. To her pleasure, the meal was perfectly prepared. She said, "With the dining room this busy, it's a marvel the food is coming in such a timely manner."

"Yes. They run this place like a Swiss clock," Rustom said, happily munching on bacon.

"Your brother was in a fight yesterday evening," Jamshedji said as he tucked into his eggs Benedict. "The car was attacked while driving back here. Arman is getting the glass fixed. This means that we might need to take taxis today."

So Rustom had confessed. Perveen raised her eyebrows at him, signaling surprised admiration.

"I'm very sorry, Pappa," Rustom said, giving Perveen a warning look. She stayed quiet.

Their breakfasts finished, they proceeded toward the elevators.

"The line is too long. Shall we take the stairs instead?" Jamshedji suggested.

Rustom grimaced, leading Perveen to think that he was perhaps more sore or tired than he was letting them believe.

The Taj's stairwell was cantilevered, which meant that although it was a grand, winding structure that rose four stories, it did not have a thick base. It seemed to float, wide and elegant. A middle-aged Marwari lady stepped behind her, cutting off her brother and father, who waited out of respect before joining the upward procession. Perveen glanced back at the lady and was startled by the extent of her finery; not just a sari heavily embroidered in gold, but arms laden with ruby and diamond bangles.

Perveen was distracted by the sound of men shouting angrily in English.

"Don't tell me I can't go!"

Perveen noted the American accent and looked up sharply. Two men were standing chest-to-chest on the third-floor landing. One of them was quite tall and wearing a fedora, and the other slightly shorter and wider.

"It's J.P. Singer!" Rustom blurted.

"Which one?" Perveen asked. The elegant

lady on the stair had followed her gaze and had stopped climbing up.

"The tall one with the hat. Look, he keeps a pencil in the hat band — that's where he had it last night!" Rustom was chattering at breakneck speed, in an excited pitch. "My God, he's arguing with Mr. Daventry. He's the governor's press attaché."

"Not a good one to argue with," commented Jamshedji dourly. "Is this Mr. Singer the same one you were with yesterday?"

Rustom answered, "Yes, Pappa. Sssh, let's listen!"

It was hard to make out all the words, but Perveen could hear Daventry roaring ". . . not part of the official press pool."

"Hell if I'm not! Keep me out, and you'll be the story!" Mr. Singer bellowed.

"You damned darkie!" Daventry snarled. The Englishman was using his bulk to crowd the American journalist toward the edge of the staircase. Perveen gasped, because Singer couldn't see how close he was to losing his footing.

By now, Daventry had his hands on the lapels of Singer's jacket, and the man's hat tumbled off his head, revealing a head of sleek dark hair. The American dropped his notepad and was reaching for something in his pocket.

Rustom cupped his hand around his mouth. "Jay, never mind about him!"

Perveen raised her own voice. "Watch out! You're about to fall!"

"No, no, sirs! Not in our hotel!" shouted a solidly built man who raced up the stairs with two waiters in tow. But by the time these men reached the landing, Mr. Singer had broken away and fled down the hallway.

"He vanished on our floor!" Perveen's mind raced with possibilities. Would he flee down a back staircase or lock himself into his guest room?

"Good thing they stopped, or we might have been witnesses at a trial for manslaughter," Jamshedji commented as the Mistry family continued up the stairs and past the scene of the trouble. The security chief was questioning Daventry, still blustering about "American interlopers."

Perveen's pulse was racing. Moments earlier, she'd believed they were all going to see a terrible fall over the third-story railing. And although the stairs were carpeted, this balcony was even higher than the Woodburn College gallery.

She kept a skeptical eye on Mr. Daventry. It seemed unwise for a man charged with press relations to be obstructive to a journalist.

And not just that.

The Englishman had called Mr. Singer "darkie," even though he was an American.

10
A Father's Request

The fight inside the Taj made Perveen anxious. An hour later, she was sitting alongside her father in the back of the car, keeping her eye out for signs of wreckage and ominous men. However, the European Quarter was placid. The High Court was closed, and there were no buses or street-cars. Only a handful of men were visible at ten-thirty, a time the streets were usually thronging with advocates and merchants, the Fort's regulars.

It was an irregular day.

"You are returned, Mashallah." Mustafa's voice came through the crack of the door as he undid bolts and locks. "There was no trouble here, sahib — I stayed awake the entire time, to make certain. And Mr. Franji brought the request for the Cuttingmasters to the agiary," he added for Perveen's benefit. "Today, we only have tinned milk because the dairy-wallah didn't come. Your chai will be extremely sweet."

"Tinned milk gives me a headache," Jamshedji grumbled. "I would rather take coffee."

Perveen followed her father up the staircase to the first floor and the office where they shared a partners' desk. Jamshedji's side was uncluttered; Perveen had a more scattered way of working, but she noted that Mustafa had straightened the papers she'd worked on, for a semblance of propriety.

Jamshedji peered at the green leather book set on his blotter. "Looking at my diary, I don't see much for today," he said. "How about you?"

"I've got a few things."

"How many hours billed this week?"

"Fifteen."

He sighed. "We are not doing well at all. Perhaps we should begin distributing cards."

"I met a young man who might be able to photograph us for a fair price," Perveen said. "Then we can run an advertisement in some newspapers."

He shook his head. "It's just an end-of-the-year slowdown. We will manage without having to put our faces in an advertisement. Cards are cheaper."

Perveen's joining her father's firm should have meant close to double the revenue. But too many people who were offered her services decided they'd rather not trust a female. An advertisement featuring her wouldn't help; what had she been thinking?

Feeling unsettled, she leafed through a short pile of letters and some messages Mustafa had kept for her. Alice had already called that morning. There was also a message from the Parsi Ladies' Society asking for her RSVP to an audience with the Prince of Wales at Government House on Monday afternoon. She had probably been selected to represent the Modern Parsi Woman Lawyer. People liked to talk about knowing a Parsi woman lawyer; they just didn't want to hire her. She imagined what the other women in attendance would represent. Perhaps "Outstanding Parsi School Principal." Or "Admirable Lady Philanthropist." Surely, there would be many Perfect Parsi Wives.

She made an aeroplane out of the invitation and sailed it into the wastebasket as Mustafa came back into the room carrying a tray with their coffee. As he set it down, he told Perveen, "Miss Hobson-Jones is ringing again. Will you speak to her now or after your coffee?"

"I'll take it now." She was not in the mood to stay in close quarters with her father. She went downstairs to the telephone in the hall and answered. "Hello, Alice."

"Where have you been? Nobody's answering at your house, and with the riots, I was worried."

"Sorry. I just arrived. We weren't staying at home, because as you said, the roads were dangerous. So Pappa booked himself, Rustom, and me into a suite at the Taj."

"Oooh, lovely. What did you eat? Did you sleep extra soundly on their famous bed linens?" Alice's voice had a forced cheer.

"Not at all," Perveen said. "Any other time, I might have enjoyed it — but not now."

"I understand." Alice's false gaiety dropped. "Today's a day of mourning for the college. And there are no buses or trains running, so it would have been very difficult for the students to attend. Some teachers were griping about the closing. It's payday, and now they won't get their checks till Saturday morning. The banks will be closed then."

"Perhaps a few will be open." Perveen wanted to get off the telephone. She sensed Alice was ready for a long conversation.

"Although Fort and the European Quarter are safe, things are bad north of Carnac Street and between Lamington and Parel

Roads," Alice said. "My father said that rioters are targeting anyone dressed like a European or with Parsi clothing."

Perveen could have told Alice what had happened to her in Carnac Street but didn't want to speak about it in a place where Mustafa might overhear. Ignoring her rapid heartbeat, she said, "You must be terrified. How is Malabar Hill?"

"No, I'm not frightened. Soldiers are stationed on almost every corner because His Royal Highness is here, my mother keeps reminding me. She seems to hope that we are going to see him strolling by, and then she will strong-arm him for tea."

Perveen thought Alice was putting on a brave front. "If only the prince would quit Bombay. There would be nothing more to fight about."

"I don't think he will — that would make him look cowardly, my father says. Gandhi tried to cancel his hartal, but nobody's listening to him anymore."

"Not at the moment." Perveen could not stand the idea that Mohandas Gandhi's role as an influential freedom fighter had ended.

"Father said that hundreds have been arrested today for assault and arson and vandalism and suspicion of murder. I tried to find out if anyone specifically was arrested on suspicion of killing Freny, but he said not."

"They may be thinking it's an accident, or suicide," Perveen reminded her. "We have to hear from the coroner. Did anything more come to light at the college?"

"I never managed to get upstairs. The police closed the area." Alice's voice was dull. "It's so hard not to think about what Freny must have suffered. Lying in pain, dying, with nobody hearing her crying for help."

"It shouldn't have happened." Perveen tried to swallow the ache in her throat. "So many times I've wished I'd said something that could have changed her mind."

"What do you mean?" Alice's voice rose. "You still haven't told me how you met Freny!"

"She came to see me in my office on Monday. We spent about an hour's time together. I thought you'd sent her."

"Not at all." Alice's sigh crackled over the telephone line. "I mentioned you in passing during a conversation about professional careers for women. What did she ask you? Was it more than career advice?"

Perveen hesitated. "I don't know if I should say. At least, not over the phone."

Alice was silent for a moment. "Very well.

I'm thinking of going back to the college today to look around. Join me?"

Perveen was surprised at Alice's daring. "If college is officially closed, doesn't that mean it's locked up?"

"Maybe, but I'm a full-time lecturer known to the guards. They will surely allow me inside to get whatever I've left in my classroom."

Going to the college still seemed a rash idea. "Think it through, Alice. Such a visit could hurt you later if the principal finds out."

"Mr. Atherton does not have any suspicions of trouble." Alice's sarcastic tone made her opinion of him clear.

"He gave me orders to leave the campus less than twenty-four hours ago; so I am definitely staying off. Besides, we are not doing very well with billable hours at the moment. I've got to find something to do or my father will be sorry he ever hired me." Perveen would have said more, but she felt the judgmental eyes of her grandfather watching from his oil portrait.

"Oh, very well." Alice sighed. "Before you cut me off, I met someone at the reception last night who holds you in the highest esteem."

Despite the distance from Alice, Perveen

felt her face flush. "I'm not sure I need to hear about this now. I'm quite busy —"

"Apparently, a Mr. Colin Sandringham, ICS, was an undergraduate reading geography at Brasenose when we were at St. Hilda's. He recalls meeting us both during a card game, although I have no memory of the occasion. It's hard for a man to make an impression on me, I confess."

Perveen laughed. "Such a shame!"

"I thought I was your only British friend in India. And now it turns out you have a handsome young Englishman in your pocket."

"Saris don't have pockets," Perveen retorted. "Besides, I only associated with Col — Mr. Sandringham — during my assignment to Satapur."

"Why didn't you tell me about him when you returned, then? It's been more than a month," Alice chided. "Mr. Sandringham seemed almost smitten. Does he know anything about . . ."

"No need to talk about it!" Perveen interrupted. "He knows the basic legalities of that situation — and to not bring it up in conversation, which I hope you can remember as well. My reputation in this city is dangling on the thinnest rope."

"A rope of spun gold," Alice said with a

laugh. "Don't worry, dear. I didn't gossip about you. Mummy was so close by. She invited him for tea but he said he had a full program of activities following the prince. Wise man, because she would never have let him go."

Perveen smiled, imagining it. "She wanted him for you, didn't she?"

"I think her main motivation was befriending someone in the prince's entourage. She's angling to have more time with the prince than the handshake yesterday evening."

Was it because Gwendolyn Hobson-Jones was starstruck? Could she be one of the middle-aged socialites who dreamed of a royal flirtation?

Her musings were smashed by a sharp knocking at the front door. Perveen looked around for Mustafa to answer it before remembering he was upstairs with her father. She would answer the door herself.

Begging pardon of Alice, she hung up and approached the entrance to peek through the stained glass windows flanking the door. Just in sight was a middle-aged Parsi man, on the small side, dressed in a formal white coat and trousers. This was the attire that Parsi men wore for weddings, funerals, and important events; its simple, elegant uniformity sometimes made men hard to recognize. But his sorrowful face revealed the visitor as Freny's father, Firdosh Cuttingmaster.

11
A FATHER'S GRIEF

Mr. Cuttingmaster recognized her as she opened the door. "Kem cho, Miss Mistry. I came to see your father."

Perveen was surprised to see him this soon, because it was customary for families to mourn alongside the priests. He should have been at Doongerwadi. The fact he'd come could only mean he was very concerned about something relating to Freny's death.

She nodded and said, "Welcome. Please come inside."

As she brought him through the hall and into the parlor, her eyes went to the chair where Freny had pointed out the torn piping. If Mr. Cuttingmaster noticed, he didn't say anything. He went straight to the farthest chair from the door, the one in the corner by the grandfather clock. It was as if he wanted protection.

Perveen, sympathetic, told him she'd be a

minute. She needed to alert Mustafa. She spotted him coming downstairs with a tray and its two empty cups.

"I think I've got a new client. Mr. Cuttingmaster is in the parlor," she said in a half whisper.

He gave her an approving nod. "The father of the girl from Monday. Will he take coffee or tea?"

Perveen poked her head back into the parlor. "What do you prefer, Mr. Cuttingmaster, coffee or tea?"

"How can I eat and drink?" He grimaced as he spoke.

"Sir, please keep your strength," Perveen coaxed. "If you collapse, you will not be able to pray at the ceremonies."

"True." Shaking slightly, he said, "I'll take tea."

Mustafa murmured, "I'll put milk on the side because of mourning."

Mr. Cuttingmaster stayed quiet, his eyes on the Agra carpet as if he were studying the path of every vine and tree. He reminded her of Freny waiting nervously on the settee. Perveen sat down on it, leaving empty the side where Freny had nestled.

"Freny came to see me on Monday. She made such an impression of honesty and wisdom, even at her age. I will do anything

I can to help."

He remained mute, so she tried again. "You can tell a lawyer anything in confidence. Our conversation is protected."

His eyes flashed at her. "You speak as if I'm a criminal. I am here for my daughter's sake, only!"

"I'm sorry. Nothing negative was implied —"

"You will not be my advocate!" he barked. "I will speak to your father."

Perveen had done the work of reaching out to him; she had counseled his daughter. And still, her services were being rejected because of her gender. She needed to step away to catch her breath, lest her frustration show. Rising, she spoke in a level voice. "Very well. I'm going upstairs to see whether he's on his way."

Jamshedji was putting away his papers when she stepped into the office, slightly out of breath from her climb and her emotions. She went to her briefcase and withdrew her notes about Freny.

"Mustafa told me we have company. What type of service will Mr. Cuttingmaster need?"

"He hasn't explained yet. He wishes to consult only with you." She could not keep the disappointment from her voice.

"In that case, you should take notes during the conference. Later we will explain to him the way we work together." Her father could be officious and strict — but he was also her champion.

As Perveen and Jamshedji entered the parlor, she saw her father's eyes soften as he regarded the visitor slumped in the wing chair. His compassion was real; it was why so many clients came to him, time and again.

"May God be with you, sir." Jamshedji took a seat in his favorite chair, the one with the torn piping. "I am Jamshedji Mistry, and I've been practicing here since 1893. Perveen already told me about your family tragedy. There are no words profound enough to express the injustice of losing your daughter."

The sharp lines leading down to Mr. Cuttingmaster's lips softened, and he spoke in a subdued tone. "My name is Firdosh Cuttingmaster. And you are blessed to have a daughter who was able to finish her studies."

Perveen hoped the statement was a peace offering toward her. She exhaled audibly and, taking her pen and notebook, went to seat herself on the settee.

"Yes, I am fortunate. And although Perveen is a young solicitor, she is quite hard-working — as your own daughter was." Leaning toward his client, Jamshedji added, "Ahura Mazda knows that you did all you could for your daughter. And we will endeavor to assist as well."

Firdosh Cuttingmaster gave Perveen a curt nod and returned his attention to Jamshedji. "Freny should have been properly bathed and had her funeral yesterday. I am afraid that with this unrest and the delays, she will be forgotten by the coroner."

"God understands," Jamshedji soothed. "I have seen such situations many times, and while it seems insurmountable, your daughter will be released within days."

"Days?" blurted Firdosh. "It is best for a Parsi to be consigned as soon as possible. She has already been held twenty-four hours."

"Yes, we have our religious ideal," Perveen agreed. "The trouble is that British Indian law takes precedence."

"How can that be?" Firdosh sounded bewildered.

Perveen realized she'd spoken, despite her promise to her father; however, Jamshedji was nodding at her, so she ventured on. "The British government has given us all a law requiring we adhere to their process for an inquest for sudden deaths where there's not an obvious natural cause. A police surgeon must present the results of a physical examination known as an autopsy in a public court hearing organized by the coroner. This process can take time, as my father was saying."

"I know that already. I've only said she has been at the morgue almost twenty-four hours!" Mr. Cuttingmaster's red eyes darted wildly from her to Jamshedji. "Mr. Mistry, you must understand this is unacceptable."

"There is a chance a physician is making the examination now — or maybe later today," Jamshedji reassured. "Did anyone tell you a day and time for the inquest?"

Firdosh Cuttingmaster shook his head. "No. I don't have the time today to find out. The haberdashery where I work was attacked yesterday. I've got orders to be there now — in fact, I'm going in late. I should be at Doongerwadi praying, but I am not."

Jamshedji's eyebrows rose. "I'm appalled to hear this about your workplace. What is it called?"

Perveen already knew, but she stayed quiet.

"The Hawthorn Shop. At least ten suits were taken. His losses are mine, too." Firdosh closed his eyes.

"That is the shop where my son had his first English suit made," Jamshedji said in an approving voice. "He still goes there for his shirts."

"How blessed you are to have a son and daughter live to adulthood." Firdosh Cuttingmaster had dropped his gaze, as Perveen had seen him do before. It was as if he could not bear to look in another's face. Or perhaps he found strength in the ground. "I once had both son and daughter. Both are dead. We will grow old with no weddings to see; no grandchildren to enjoy; nobody to assist in our years of weakness."

Mustafa stepped into the room, carefully balancing the silver tea tray loaded with the Minton tea service. Perveen poured tea into a cup and placed it before Mr. Cuttingmaster. There was a plate of bhakras, sweet doughnuts that were made daily at Yazdani's. She offered them to him, but he shook his head.

How could she eat before a man who was denying himself food while in mourning? She didn't take a doughnut, although her father did.

With a cup of tea for herself, Perveen returned to the settee and took up her notebook again. "Won't you try the tea, Mr. Cuttingmaster?"

Mr. Cuttingmaster picked up the cup and took a sip. "It has been a terrible morning. I woke with knowledge that my daughter was forever gone. Then Khushru — a neighbor boy — arrived to tell me of the destruction at the shop."

Perveen didn't reveal that she'd witnessed the vandalism; it could lead to uncomfortable questions from her father. She was supposed to be taking notes, anyway.

"That is more hard news."

Placing the cup back on its saucer, Mr. Cuttingmaster shook his head. "Our city has gone mad. I wonder if Freny could have been killed by such rioters, but the college principal told me it was an accident."

"When did you speak with Mr. Atherton?" Jamshedji passed the plate of doughnuts toward the man, and Mr. Cuttingmaster waved it away.

"We came late, when she was being placed in the cart. Mr. Atherton came briefly to speak with us. He said he believes Freny was leaning over the edge of the gallery because she wished to have a better view of the prince, and she fell."

"Did Principal Atherton say that someone witnessed this?" Perveen asked.

"No," Mr. Cuttingmaster answered. "He only said the police found a patch of khadi cloth in the branches of a bush just under the railing. That is the sari she was wearing when she was found — although she did not leave our house looking that way. She left our home in a green sari, as my wife told Miss Mistry yesterday. I'm thinking now that rioters could have put that brown sari on her — just as they are trying to force men to wear Indian clothes only."

It was a convoluted idea, but it brought up something Perveen wanted to discuss — something her father wouldn't think to ask about. Hesitantly, she said, "Sir, I know you don't wish me to interview you, but I have a question about clothing."

He looked sharply at her. "Go on, Miss Mistry. You are as loudmouthed as Freny was."

The word he'd used was jarring, especially since his daughter was dead. But she would not allow him to silence her, and her question was a simple one. "Did you ever see Freny wear a khadi cloth sari?"

He squinted at her. "I don't understand."

Perveen repeated the question.

"I would never allow it. Such rough, poor cloth, when I'm a tailor! Why would I let her make me a laughingstock?"

So Freny must have changed her sari outside the home — perhaps in a train station lounge, or the ladies' lounge at school. "I saw her lying on the path. Her sari was not caught up in a tree. I can't imagine why there would be a piece of khadi cloth there."

His brows knit together. "You did?"

"Yes. Others saw her lying there, too: the first ones were a student called Lalita Acharya and a lady teacher, Miss Roshan Daboo." Thinking about the khadi cloth brought another question to mind. "Do you recall if your daughter carried her satchel to school that morning?"

"I'm not certain. I was satisfied with her sari — it looked suitable for the parade. My mind is . . . confused."

Of course, Perveen thought sympathetically. Freny's father was in the midst of a shocking tragedy. Perhaps mental dissonance was the reason he'd called his deceased daughter a loudmouth.

Perveen's father asked, "Did the principal tell you anything else?"

"He told me that she'd appeared for roll call that morning, but she wasn't in the stands. That surely should have been noted!" He swung his gaze from Jamshedji to Perveen. Fiercely, he said, "You told me she had come to see you. I am asking, what would a young girl need with a solicitor?"

Perveen was surprised he had taken this

long to reach the question that surely had been on his mind. "Whether the college had the authority to expel her."

Behind the thick glasses, his eyes blinked. "But why? Her marks were excellent."

"That's true," Perveen reassured him. "Freny studied hard, and she also belonged to an extracurricular organization called the Student Union that advocates for Indian independence. She said that in the past school year, a few members had been expelled for various protest actions. She wanted to avoid that."

"First the clothing. And now this?" His face had flushed with emotion. "The policeman who came to our home said students are the city's worst troublemakers. But I know my daughter. She is not one of them."

"She was a shining light," Perveen assured him. "She didn't want to make trouble and cause you the shame of her expulsion. All she was trying to do was avoid the celebration for the prince."

Firdosh was silent for a moment. "She wished to stay away from the parade? I never knew that."

Of course, he wouldn't know. Because Firdosh Cuttingmaster was a strict father who was also against independence; Freny wouldn't have brought up such a matter

175

with him.

"Yesterday morning, she told us that she felt ill. I said nonsense, she was only tired from staying up too late. I said that she must go to the college." His voice cracked. "I'll regret my insistence for the rest of my life."

"Please, sir. Don't fault yourself. You did not know your daughter's internal agony." Jamshedji had crossed his leg and was tapping it against the same place where the banding was loose.

Seeing her father's habitual movement brought back Freny's sharp observation about the chair. And it almost felt like Freny was there, raising questions in Perveen's mind.

According to Parsi faith, a soul lingered on earth for seventy-two hours after death. It could be that Freny knew what was transpiring in the room. And she would want Perveen to know the truth about her death.

"I am wondering about something," Perveen mused aloud. "If Freny abhorred the prince, and tried to stay at home, she wouldn't have leaned over the railing to gaze at him."

"That is supposition," Jamshedji said crisply. "Maybe she was watching something else."

Perveen turned back to Mr. Cuttingmaster, whose expression was wary. "A male student ran out to try to disrupt the prince's parade. His name is Dinesh Apte. Did she ever mention him to you?"

Mr. Cuttingmaster drew himself up in the soft chair. "Absolutely not! My daughter did not socialize with boys."

"We are not impugning your daughter's character," Jamshedji said, shooting a warning look at Perveen.

"Agreed," Perveen said hastily. "The possibility may arise, though, that someone — stranger, student, or faculty — was involved in Freny's death. Sir, can you think of anyone who was angry with Freny? Or someone she disliked or feared?"

"She had no unkind word for anyone and was loved by all who knew her. That girl you mentioned, Lalita Acharya? They were very good friends. They studied together sometimes at the Asiatic Library after school." For a moment, he closed his eyes. "I am sure she must be very sad."

"Yes, indeed," said Jamshedji. He had uncrossed his leg, a signal that he wished to draw the meeting to a close. "Now, back to our offer of service. You are on your way to work. It would be a straightforward matter for us to go to Sir J. J. Hospital for you and investigate the status of the autopsy. That would be the obvious step in moving toward her release for consignment."

"I would be grateful, but how much is your fee?" The man's eyes shone with anxiety. "I am only a tailor."

Jamshedji assured him, "Just as you tailor clothes, we fit services to the specific client. Perveen will draw up a contract with a . . ." He hesitated. "No, I would rather not do that. Mr. Cuttingmaster, I will not charge you anything. How can I take money from a man who's lost his child?"

Perveen's heart warmed. Usually she was the one who did pro bono work; it was wonderful to see her father step into the same role, knowing help must be given without remuneration.

But Mr. Cuttingmaster didn't look pleased. Rising from his chair, he spoke stiffly. "You are speaking to the head tailor of the Hawthorn Shop. I am not a charity case."

"Of course not," Perveen said swiftly. "But would you kindly allow us not to charge you for our assistance today? If there is something more you wish done in upcoming days, we could discuss hourly rates as my father first offered. Time is of the essence, isn't it?"

After a pause, Mr. Cuttingmaster nodded. "Very well."

Jamshedji's glance toward her was evidence of his gratitude.

"Mr. Cuttingmaster, may I have all the names of close relatives living in your home, and your home address?"

"My wife is Mithan, and my mother, Bapsi. She lives in a flat above ours. We live in Vakil Baug, building G, flat one."

Vakil was an Urdu-origin word that meant "guardian" or "personal representative"; it had come to mean "lawyer." Perhaps Freny, growing up hearing the name Vakil every day, had taken it into her heart.

"Does your mother live with someone else?" Jamshedji asked.

"She is alone now since my father passed fifteen years ago. When they moved in, my older brother and his wife were also in that flat. They shifted to a different colony in Kemps Corner. She could have gone, but she wanted to stay close to Freny."

"Is this the full sum of relatives in Bombay?" Perveen asked once he had given their names and address.

"Yes. We come from Surat. We moved here twenty-three years ago. Our children were born here."

It had been a family pilgrimage. Firdosh

and Mithan had dreamed of a prosperous life in Bombay. But what had the city given them?

A tailoring job for the English and a home in a colony.

And two children, now both gone.

12
FOUNTAIN OF KNOWLEDGE

The district where Sir J. J. Hospital was sited was called Byculla; and like many places inside Bombay, its name contained a few unanswered questions.

The spelling was created by the British and might have been a corruption of bhaya and khaala — Marathi words for "ground" and "low." On the other hand, the area might have had a grove of bhaya trees, or the name might have something to do with grain. In any case, it had been the site where East India Company men built grand homes in the eighteenth and early nineteenth centuries. Naturally, the area had also appealed to Sir Jamsetjee Jeejeebhoy, the successful shipping merchant turned philanthropist. In the 1840s, he had provided the seed money for a quality hospital with a medical college attached. In the succeeding decades, the hospital grew to have many buildings on more than forty acres that remained parklike, with plenty of tall trees, green lawns, and shrubs.

Getting to the hospital required a long ride through a normally bustling area that today was full of smashed windows. Here and there police walked, lathis in hand, ready for the next onslaught.

"Look at the damage to the Byculla Club doors," Jamshedji tut-tutted as the car passed by the historic English-only venue. "The Prince of Wales is supposed to visit tonight. I would not be surprised if he's given a full military escort."

They'd reached the hospital campus, a myriad of small stone and stucco buildings. Arman parked the Daimler close to a two-story building with tall Gothic windows, the coroner's court and morgue building. "The proximity is sensible," Jamshedji explained. "One wall inside the courtroom has a window that allows a limited view inside the morgue. In that manner, a corpse on a gurney can be viewed without jurors going into the morgue itself."

Perveen felt nauseated thinking about it. "Could Freny's body be at the window now?"

"Surely not. There are many cases on the docket — just look," Jamshedji said, pointing to a notice close to the coroner's courtroom door. "Try to find out if her inquest is scheduled. While you do that, I'll check with the morgue officers about how the postmortems are proceeding."

Walking up to the court, Perveen passed through a veranda crowded with anxious-looking people. From their dress, she could see that they had grouped themselves by faith; Parsis in one corner, Anglo-Indian Christians in another, and most benches filled with Hindus and Muslims. If there hadn't been a riot, would there be this separation, and the accusatory glances?

She looked at the docket, which had a majority of Hindu and Muslim names, although there was an English name and two Parsi names. All the names were male. This made Perveen wonder: perhaps Freny's name was being left out because she was female?

That didn't make sense, but the way to know for certain was to inquire. Perveen proceeded to a booth close to the courtroom door. A sour-looking man in his thirties was seated at a desk in the booth, along with a policeman. When she asked about whether Freny's inquest was scheduled, he answered her curtly.

"If his name is not on the docket, not today," he said sharply. "Come again."

She caught his mistake about gender. "Miss Cuttingmaster is female and eighteen years old. Is she recorded as such?"

"I have no time to check. Please move along, as you can see the veranda is terribly crowded with people attending inquests today."

"Miss Mistry?"

Perveen turned around to see, just below the veranda in the garden, a young woman had called out to her. She recognized the strong features of the Woodburn student Lalita Acharya. Behind Lalita, a stout woman of about forty years was scrutinizing Perveen.

"Miss Mistry! Did the coroner also wish to speak to you?" Lalita asked loudly.

Perveen stepped down from the veranda so she wouldn't have to shout her answer back. "Hello, Lalita. No, I don't think I'm being called as a witness."

Lalita inclined her head toward the woman with her. "My mother came with me. She did not trust conditions were safe enough for me to travel alone."

"There are no buses. We had to take a taxi; it was most expensive," Mrs. Acharya grumbled. "We live on Opera Road. But that area was also beset with hooligans of all faiths. Today the police are guarding — but I am sure it is for the sake of the Opera House, not for us."

Perveen focused on Lalita. "Will you need to testify at the inquest?"

"No, the inquest is tomorrow. He wished to get my testimony to put into his report. I am so glad to be done with it," Lalita said, casting an eye back at the court building. "Mr. King is a very stern gentleman. He spoke so quickly it was hard to understand."

Perveen wondered how much more Lalita would share with her. "May we speak somewhere a bit more private?"

"There is a small park with a fountain on the other side of the garden," Mrs. Acharya said. "It would be good for me and Lalita to wash our faces and hands."

The three ladies went to the other side, where a group of young men in white doctor's coats were passing.

"My nephew is a student in Grant Medical College," Mrs. Acharya said, following her gaze. "He lives in a hostel on these grounds. It has very small rooms, but he says it is better to be close to the hospital than to travel from home."

At the center of the green was a fountain with a statue of two ladies with Indian features but draped in Grecian robes. Water shot up around them like a protective shield.

Noticing Perveen's inspection, Lalita said, "My cousin says that one of the women is the goddess of a healthy body, and the other the goddess of a strong mind."

"Lovely," Perveen said.

From their perch on the edge of the fountain, the fine spray was pleasant. But as the women turned away from the fountain, Mrs. Acharya's expression was tense. "What is it you are wishing to know from my daughter, Miss Mistry?"

"I wondered if the coroner was pursuing any particular line of questioning," Perveen hedged. "But I don't work for the coroner's office or for the college. If you speak with me, it's completely voluntary."

"I will speak to her, Ma," Lalita said, patting her mother's arm. "I know her. Mr. King was very stern, and the other man had such cold eyes," she told Perveen. "Mr. King asked why I was walking around the school instead of being in the stands. It made me feel like he thought I was the bad one."

Perveen caught a hint of defensiveness in the girl's words. "Attention is always paid to the person who discovers a deceased person. You might have seen someone else out of the corner of your eye who would be gone by the time others came. Do you think the other gentleman was a police detective?"

"He was not introduced to us," Mrs. Acharya cut in. "He was another Britisher who seemed most unfriendly. He had his head uncovered. Red hair. That is quite unlucky."

"I don't suppose you saw the kind of hat he brought with him?" Perveen asked. The mention of red hair made her think of the gentleman with the bowler hat who'd been so officious with her after Freny's death.

Lalita hesitated. "I think . . . it wasn't a pith helmet like most of them wear. It was a black bowler."

Perveen caught her breath, realizing her suspicions were right. Most likely, the man was a plainclothes detective trying to gather information from Lalita without identifying himself. She'd heard of government agents who specialized in spying on students. Motioning toward a wrought iron bench, she said, "Could we sit for a few minutes? I'm still confused about what happened yesterday."

Lalita hesitated again, and Mrs. Acharya spoke sternly. "Just repeat what you told Mr. King."

Lalita sat stiffly next to her mother. There wasn't room for three, so Perveen stayed on her feet. Standing in front of them, she felt a bit like a teacher with wary pupils.

"After Dinesh was taken away, we students made lines to walk back into the college. We'd been told there would be a special celebratory luncheon." With a furtive glance at Perveen, Lalita added, "I thought if I arrived early, I could get a good seat and the other girls would be able to join me — and we'd be close enough to the food so we'd get enough on our plates before the boys tucked in."

"That was selfish of you," Mrs. Acharya chided.

"There's another way of looking at it," Perveen said, seeing the flush on Lalita's cheeks. "Men and boys are always given priority at meals — why should it be so? We have the same need to fill our stomachs. Please go on, Lalita."

"Well, then, I asked Miss Daboo if I might go to the lavatory. She agreed but said she'd walk me into the college garden before returning to oversee the line of girl students. She was anxious because of what happened with Dinesh being arrested."

"So you were not alone." Perveen had not known this.

"That's right. We went back into the college, passing the guard, who recognized us so there was no need for signing in. In the next minute, we saw Freny. I called out and we both hurried over to her, but she didn't hear us or move any part of her body. Miss Daboo told me she would begin praying and that I should summon a Parsi lady."

"And then?"

"I ran for help. When I saw Miss Hobson-Jones's head standing tall above the others, I thought that you might still be with her. And I was right." Her voice held a note of satisfaction.

"What else did the coroner talk about with you?"

"He asked me what kind of girl Freny was."

Perveen felt her ire rising. "What kind of a girl? Did he attempt to blame her?"

"I don't think so. He meant, what was her character like." Blinking back tears, Lalita said, "I told him the truth: she was the most admirable girl I ever knew. I wished that I had her brains."

"Freny scored higher than Lalita on many examinations. A few times Lalita prevailed." Mrs. Acharya's heavy bosom fell with the weight of her sigh. "Competition is good, I told my daughter. Now she has none."

"Male students are competition," Perveen pointed out.

Lalita's eyes widened. "We don't pay attention to them. When the coroner asked if Freny had any friendships with boys, I said she didn't. She was just like me — eyes on the work. She was as quiet in class as any other girl."

Perveen wondered if Lalita had spoken those particular words for her mother's benefit. It was proving impossible to ask difficult questions when Mrs. Acharya was tucked snugly against the witness.

"Mr. King asked if Freny had any great worries or was very sad. I said no. He asked if there was any reason she might wish to kill herself. I said I didn't know." Lalita's voice shook as she continued. "You see, she worried about the same things all of us do, but her marks were so high, and she had said to me just on Tuesday she wished to try for a scholarship to study law at Oxford."

Freny had been inspired by the conversation on Monday. And Perveen could have helped her. Lalita's distress was making her own misery deepen.

"Mr. King asked about Dinesh Apte, the boy who ran in front of the crowd," Mrs. Acharya prompted. "He was wanting to learn about everything."

"How strange. I wonder why?" Perveen had also asked Freny's father about Dinesh, but that was because she knew Freny had felt bullied.

"Mr. King asked if I saw Dinesh any other times that morning. I remembered then that Dinesh didn't answer his name at roll call. I was certain of this because his surname is always called shortly after mine. Maybe he came to college late."

Had the coroner asked about Dinesh on behalf of the other man in the room? The government might be afraid that Freny's death was an act of protest. News of such an act could go around the country, soiling the prince's tour.

"I heard Dinesh is in the Student Union." Perveen made the statement because it was an opening that Lalita might want to follow, if she had knowledge of the group.

"Yes, he is." Lalita's cheeks were pink.

Mrs. Acharya looked solemnly at Perveen. "I have told Lalita that she must refrain from that group. And no studying at the college library or the Asiatic Society after classes are over."

"She found out two weeks ago." Lalita cast a reproachful glance at her mother, who scowled back. "The last meeting I went to was about that time. Freny was upset to have to continue as the only girl in the group without me. I'm so sorry I abandoned her."

Quickly, Perveen said, "You can't blame yourself for her death."

"But I *knew* she was going to stay out as a protest." Lalita's voice rose. "If I'd been with her, she wouldn't have been alone. Nobody would have dared come near to hurt her!"

"You are wrong. Both of you could have been hurt!" Mrs. Acharya turned to address Perveen. "Miss Mistry, the coroner did not ask Lalita about the Student Union. Do you think that was wrong of us not to mention it?"

Perveen shook her head. "If the coroner wants to know more about the Student Union, all he has to do is ask the principal or the group's faculty advisor."

"Mr. Grady," Lalita said. "He's not very talkative, though."

"Is he a good teacher?"

Casting a furtive glance at her mother, she said, "He has unusual ideas and he is lively. He thought highly of Freny."

Perveen wanted to ask more but she thought Mrs. Acharya didn't need to hear. She'd also caught sight of a familiar straight-backed figure on the coroner's court veranda. She walked a few steps closer to the building and waved so Jamshedji would see her. He waved back, and upon reaching the fountain, washed his face and hands before approaching her and the Acharyas.

"Mrs. Acharya and Miss Acharya, may I introduce my father, Jamshedji Mistry?" Perveen said as he walked over to them, patting his cheeks with his fresh handkerchief.

"I'm glad you also came here with family." Mrs. Acharya smoothed her sari's pallu a bit closer to her face and motioned for Lalita to do the same.

"My honored ladies, it is a pleasure to meet you." Jamshedji gave a respectful nod to each of them.

"Miss Acharya was a close college friend to Freny Cuttingmaster," Perveen explained.

Soberly, Jamshedji said, "I am very sad about your friend's passing. I heard from Perveen, who had the privilege of meeting her, that she was both a bright and highly moral young lady."

Lalita's mouth tightened slightly before she answered, "Everyone thought so."

And there it is, Perveen thought: *hidden resentment.*

"Challo, we are going," said Mrs. Acharya. Her brisk tone made Perveen wonder if Jamshedji's praise had also annoyed her.

"Would you like us to drive you? We have our car," Jamshedji offered.

"That is most kind of you, but we will take a taxi," said Mrs. Acharya.

Perveen added, "It is no trouble, really."

"We will be fine." Mrs. Acharya's answer was firm.

Perveen considered the possibilities. Mrs. Acharya might be refusing the hospitality because she didn't want to trouble them.

Or was it because the Mistrys were Parsis, who had become a lightning rod for the city's anger?

They made polite goodbyes. After they had gone out to the street, Jamshedji asked Perveen what she had learned. Then he said, "Miss Cuttingmaster's postmortem was completed today. The Cuttingmasters may wish to have an advocate during the inquest tomorrow." Jamshedji stretched, preparing to move.

"What value is our continued service?" Perveen asked, trying to think of how this could be presented to the grieving parents.

"It's a chance to make sure the cause of death sounds correct. The jury, the public, and the deceased's relatives are all allowed to ask questions of the police and coroner and witnesses. The only person involved in the inquest who does not answer questions is the police surgeon. His report is stated as fact."

"But he's the key part of a medical investigation!" Remembering her training, Perveen added, "In Britain, the public can question the police surgeon."

Jamshedji raised a cautionary finger. "*British Indian* law insulates the civil surgeon as a supreme authority. They want to establish that European medical understanding cannot be contradicted by ayurvedic medical knowledge or other local beliefs."

"But there are aspects to this rule that are so troublesome!" Perveen remembered what she'd worried about at the procession. "What if a protestor died after a kick in the head from a policeman? Can we trust the civil surgeon to be honest about the kick being fatal, or might he claim the man died due to a pre-existing condition? I have read some newspaper articles about protestors dying from falls and blows that would have been minor were it not for a pre-existing condition."

"Naturally, corruption sometimes occurs. But we must go forward with the expectation that in this case, the police and doctors have no reason to be dishonest." Jamshedji studied her tense face and added, "Most Indians are relieved to have a medical cause given that can't be overturned. This allows for immediate burial or cremation."

Perveen didn't agree with his assumption. She sensed it was in the city's interest to have a college girl's death ruled accidental. A suicide would heighten political unrest, as would a verdict like homicide.

"I'll go across the street for a little bit; I have some business at Magen David synagogue. After that, I'll see you in the office," Jamshedji said. "You take the car. Arrange for someone to deliver a message to the Cuttingmasters about our willingness to assist with the coroner's court tomorrow."

"Should this message be delivered to Mr. Cuttingmaster at the haberdashery?"

Waving Perveen into the car, Jamshedji issued his opinion. "Send the message to their home, for reasons of privacy. Surely his wife will be there. Do you know their address?"

"Yes. Remember, this morning he told us it was Vakil Colony. It's not far from Carnac Street."

"Have a safe journey home," Jamshedji said, stepping back from the car. "We have spent an hour here for which we are not charging, but which we must record for our own purposes as two hours' work between us. I am finished with the Cuttingmasters at the moment. Now you will clock your own time."

13

INSIDE VAKIL COLONY

As she waved goodbye to her father, Perveen's mind was turning. She'd been asked to find someone to carry a complicated message to the Cuttingmaster household.

It made sense for her to be the firm's messenger. And she was already in the car with Arman, so they'd get word to Mrs. Cuttingmaster more quickly.

Arman was familiar with Vakil Baug. He said, "It is like most of the city's old colonies: a variety of people of all ages and means living close together."

The colonies were a joint effort of the Parsi Panchayat and Bombay Presidency; a conscious plan to make it possible for Parsis to always have a safe place to live, regardless of income. The communities stayed homogenous because a flat or house owner could only rent or sell to another Parsi.

If the British left, would these religious enclaves expand or vanish?

■ ■ ■ ■

On the way to Vakil Baug, she felt depressed to see so many damaged storefronts and shuttered businesses. Her spirits lifted briefly when she observed a splash of bright colors: a section of pavement covered by baskets overflowing with jasmine, roses, marigolds, and orchids. A Hindu flower-seller had organized his wares as if this were any other day. He even had two young men sitting cross-legged stringing jasmine garlands.

An elderly Parsi lady was supervising the teenage boy who was gathering flowers for her purchase. Perveen's inner tension softened at the sight of the customer and merchants engaged in the beauty of ordinary life. Very likely the man's business had survived the night because it was portable, not confined to a shop.

Arman's voice interrupted her thoughts. "This is the place."

She couldn't see much of the colony at first because of the limestone brick wall surrounding it. A wide wrought iron gate was closed, but two elderly Parsi men sat behind it on a pair of garden chairs, sharing a newspaper. One was tall and the other quite petite, so the *Bombay Chronicle* was set at a tilt, allowing both a chance to read. She called out, "Good morning!"

Both gentlemen peered around the newspaper without putting it down.

Perveen pointed at the metal sign that included the colony's name and building date, 1906. "Excuse me, but is this Vakil Baug?"

"Who is asking?" demanded the taller man.

She was relieved to have an opening. "My name is Perveen Mistry. I've come to see the Cuttingmasters."

"He is out. She is in mourning," he said curtly.

"Yes, I am also grieving their daughter's death. That is why I've come." Mourning was a community event. This restrictive behavior at the gate was strange, especially since she was clearly of the same faith.

The elderly man gave her a sorrowful look. "The colony has rules to keep people away who don't live here. For safety."

It would be improper to reveal that she was their lawyer; that could raise all kinds of gossip. Touching her softly draped sari, she said, "Do you understand that I'm also a Parsi?"

The smaller man let go of his side of the

newspaper. "Are you a relative?"

"Freny saw me as an older sister."

He nudged his companion. "They do look alike, don't they?"

Stubbornly, the taller man shook his head.

Perveen reached into her purse and extracted two quarter-anna coins. Putting a coin in each palm, she looked deep in their eyes. "This is for your kindness in allowing my driver a safe place to wait. I will explain to anyone who asks that I am only going quickly to the Cuttingmaster flat."

The men exchanged glances and the taller man stood up. He began to pull the gate open. He gestured to Arman, who was sitting in the car, to drive forward.

Arman parked the car where they suggested, in a shady spot under some trees, while Perveen walked through. She saw several blocks of low-rise buildings painted a variety of colors; some were fresh, and others faded and colored by mildew. This was what happened when some flat owners had funds and others were just surviving.

The tiny man said, "Building G is the white one on the far end of the courtyard."

As she walked across the cobblestones, she passed a fountain of carved stone. A weak stream of water dribbled from a large fish's gaping mouth. Two children knelt at the fountain's edge, pushing toy boats, while their ayah, a young Hindu woman, sat a few feet away. She was watching Perveen with a frown, making Perveen wonder if the tensions of the outside had permeated this woman's life.

It could be that in a small colony, any visitor would be inspected. Perveen saw many faces peering at her from windows. Her arrival might be commented on later. So she kept a half smile on her face, striving to look pleasant, as she continued walking.

A woman's voice shrilled through the air. "Wait. I am coming!"

Perveen stopped in her tracks and saw an elderly lady was on her tail. Well under five feet, the lady was pleasantly stout and dressed in a white sari, with a snowy mathabana scarf covering her hair. She was carrying a basket packed with white roses, and Perveen realized she'd been the shopper at the flower-seller's a few minutes' distance from the colony gate.

"Kem cho, aunty," Perveen said, preparing for an inquisition. She wished it wasn't so public.

"Aren't you Perveen Mistry?" The lady had the same bulging eyes as Freny and her father. "I know you."

Perveen was confused. "Yes. But how?"

"Your late grandfather brought you to visit here when he was adding some new buildings to the colony. In nineteen hundred, or thereabouts. And now you are trying to help our family. Freny was my granddaughter. Did your grandfather ever tell you about Bapsi Cuttingmaster?"

"He might have, but I was a very young child." Perveen bent her head slightly as she addressed the lady. "I'm so sad about Freny. I met her just once, but I could tell how much integrity and wisdom she had."

The basket of mourning flowers trembled in the woman's hands. "My son showed me the business card you gave him. He wasn't sure if he should go to see you or not, but when I saw your office was Mistry House, I told him we would be safe."

"Thank you, Bapsi-mai." Perveen was relieved that the grandmother was functioning well enough to chat, yet she didn't want to continue a courtyard discussion. She resumed walking, but slower so her companion could keep pace.

"My son and daughter-in-law live on the ground floor," Bapsi said, indicating one of the better-painted buildings. "I stay upstairs. See, Nana is looking out. She has been missing Freny."

A balcony on the upper floor apartment

was open, and a handsome white cat was peering through the bars at them. Perveen tsked, clicking her tongue against her teeth, and the cat swished her tail.

"She is my comfort now." Bapsi waved at the cat, who mewed in return. "Freny found her six years ago on the street, starved and lonely. I kept the little darling upstairs because her fur made my son sneeze. Freny would always bring meat scraps for her evening supper. I'll see her later. First we will go to my daughter-in-law."

Perveen followed Bapsi Cuttingmaster's slow steps through a wrought iron door and up a few stairs to a ground-floor apartment. The front room was a small parlor furnished by a settee covered in tweed; the chairs were covered in black velvet. A tall bookcase was filled with schoolbooks with English writing on the spines, and a number of Gujarati books as well.

As Perveen took quick measure of the surroundings, Freny's mother, Mithan, came into the room. Mithan wore plain white cotton, like her mother-in-law, and looked frail. Her face, so red with emotion the day before, now looked almost colorless.

Taking the white roses from Bapsi, Mithan murmured quick thanks. To Perveen, she said, "You were there yesterday. Did my husband go to your office?"

"Yes, this morning." She was relieved that Mithan knew he'd sought assistance.

"Is Freny released?" Mithan's voice cracked with anxiety.

Perveen explained about the inquest scheduled for the following day. She'd expected to feel like she was setting things to rights, but Mithan's anguished eyes and the mutterings of her mother-in-law made her feel as if she'd disappointed them.

"But tomorrow is too late. There will be too much deterioration. It is not safe for her soul's transition to Heaven . . ."

"I understand." Perveen sensed anxiety rising in Mithan. "But we have every reason to hope that a funeral can be held tomorrow before nightfall."

"I hope so. And that is kind of you to bring us in your car to the court tomorrow. I am very nervous about the inquest."

Perveen looked at the mother, who seemed to have shrunk into herself. "Don't worry; my father and I will help you. We can ask questions of the coroner, if you have them."

"The police came last night, wanting to look at her things." Freny's mother's voice broke, and she put a hand to her eyes before continuing. "We did not know she was in a student group that caused trouble! We can't believe it's true."

Apparently Freny had kept her involvement in the Student Union a secret from both her parents. "Your daughter didn't mention that the Student Union did anything more than talk about social change. What did the police say?"

Gently touching the roses in the basket, Mithan said, "The sergeant asked to look through her room, and we thought we had better let them because . . ."

Perveen finished the statement that hung in the air. "If you didn't, you worried they might think you were involved in antigovernment activity."

"Yes," Mithan said. "It made me angry. I asked if they had her schoolbag, because she carried it to college that morning. The detective said he didn't know."

Freny had carried her bag to college. And just as Perveen had considered it important, so did the police. "What sort of questions did they ask you?"

"It was so hard — I could hardly follow their loud and fast voices," Mithan said. "They asked about Freny's mood. I said she almost didn't go to the college that morning, because she complained of stomachache, but my husband didn't want her to miss the procession. I didn't disagree. Now

I wished I had."

"If I had heard this, I would have kept her home." Bapsi's voice was sorrowful. "I never saw her that morning because I was still sleeping upstairs."

"I'm sorry, Mamma. And it is very kind of you to bring flowers this morning. I was too upset to go out."

"Yesterday was a tragedy." Perveen wished she could say more, but she could not label Mithan's trauma.

"It started out so normally. In the morning, we left home together, riding to Charni Station and then strolling along the Sea-Face. Firdosh and I waved goodbye as Freny walked through the college gate, and then we proceeded to the Orient Club." Mithan's voice was steady. "When we returned to Woodburn a few hours later . . . you remember! She was chucked into a cart, as if she were not even human." Here, the mother's voice broke. "The girl who had argued with me in the morning would never speak again."

The front door opened, causing Perveen to look away from Mithan's quiet weeping. The woman who walked in slipped out of her shoes and nodded cautiously at her. Like Mithan, she appeared to be in her late thirties. She wore a dull brown sari draped

in the Parsi manner, and a white mathabana scarf covered her hair.

"How are you today? I have cooked your
lunch," she said, indicating the tiffin con-
tainers in her arms.

"I cannot eat now," said Mithan. "But it is
most kind of you. Maybe my husband will
eat tonight."

"Who is this?" The visitor looked directly
at Perveen.

"Mrs. Hester Kapadia is one of our neighbors," Bapsi said to Perveen. "This is Perveen Mistry. The daughter of the great
builder of our colony. She helps her father,
who is the famous lawyer Jamshedji Mistry.
They are assisting us with our troubles."

Hester's expression softened slightly.
"Miss Mistry, that is very good to know. I
had my own dreams that Freny would come
to my home one day."

Perveen wondered what this meant, but
before she could ask, Hester said, "Let me
put my food in the kitchen. Then I will
make some tea."

Hester moved briskly through the flat to
the back, where the kitchen presumably was.

Perveen did not want to get stuck at a tea
table, but she did want to see Freny's room.
In a low voice, Perveen asked Mithan, "Do
you mind if I look at Freny's bedroom?"

208

Mithan looked startled, but then nodded. "What will it change? But I can show you."

Perveen stepped into the room. Two beds were neatly made up with white quilts, and Mithan put down the flower basket on a side table, picking up a single rose.

"With whom does Freny share her room?"

"Nobody. When she was young, her brother was here."

This was the opening she needed. "Darius's death was still quite heavy on Freny's mind. She mentioned it when we spoke together. Freny was worried if she was expelled from college she would dishonor her brother."

"Yes, she would think that." Mithan pressed her lips together. "She thought his death was her fault."

"Why? Had Freny fallen ill first?" Perveen had a picture in her mind, knowing that most children's deaths in the city were due to illness.

Mithan plucked a petal from the rose, letting it drop on the bed she'd indicated was Freny's. She murmured, "It was a terrible accident."

Perveen waited as Mithan slowly shredded the rose, and then a second and third one, spreading the petals across Freny's bed. At last she sat down on the bed belonging to Darius. "Freny knew Darius wanted to play with some school friends outside the colony. Not everyone feels comfortable here."

Perveen nodded, remembering the men at the gate, and the uneasy look of the lone Hindu servant in the courtyard.

"Darius asked her not to tell us, so she simply said to me he was with a friend. She didn't say he'd left Vakil Colony and gone a mile away to a Hindu neighborhood."

A natural response for a sister to an older brother. Just hours ago, she'd let Rustom convince her not to share the story of his wild night with her father.

"The boys all played cricket there and were so hot afterward they decided to drink water from the well. This well was not a very new one, and its edge was crumbling. Darius slipped and fell in when he was trying to pull up the bucket." She swallowed, and in a harder voice said, "At first, the boys tried to get him out by themselves, because they were afraid of getting in trouble with the elders. They waited too long to get help."

Perveen felt her own eyes dampening. It was hard not to cry for this mother who had been twice robbed. "Was there an autopsy?"

Mrs. Cuttingmaster's shoulders were

slumped, and her head remained low as she answered. "Yes, they took their time with it, too. It took three days to get his body released from the coroner — which as you must know conflicts with our religion's rule to carry out rites as soon as possible. It was quite terrible for the autopsy to take so long when the policeman who came to the well declared him drowned."

"It doesn't make sense," Perveen agreed, her sorrow for the whole family rising.

"We blamed nobody for that accident — not even the boys we didn't know. But Freny took it very hard. She blamed herself for not telling us where he was going. After that, she changed."

"How so?"

"She tried to be the son we had lost — she told Firdosh she would go to college and make him proud of her. So instead of thinking of her future as a wife and mother, she began thinking of her future as something else. Maybe a teacher or doctor." Mithan looked sadly at Perveen. "And the two of us, I'm sorry to say, were often chiding her. You see, her father found her annoying. She had begun speaking only literal truths after Darius was lost. And being in college only made her more outspoken."

"To whom?" Perveen had her eyes on

Bapsi, who looked as if she wanted to say something but was holding back.

"If she went to the Hawthorn Shop to wait for my husband, she sometimes joined conversations that customers were having," Mithan said after a moment's thought. "One time she told a very good customer that he should shift to clothing made from rough locally woven cloth. And quality British imports are the basis of Mr. Hawthorn's business."

Perveen wondered if Firdosh's anger at Freny's political views was the reason he forced her to go to college that morning. "How strict was your husband with Freny?"

Mithan's eyes widened. "As strict as any good father. He expected her to behave righteously. But he never beat her or shouted at her. Even after what happened with Darius, she was not punished."

"Did he ever forbid her to participate in activities outside the home?"

"Of course. Wouldn't any father? For her safety."

"Mithan-bai, would you allow me to check inside Freny's almirah?"

"The police took all her books and papers. What else could be there?" she asked tightly.

"I don't know. I just thought . . ." Perveen trailed off. She had no good explanation for why she felt a need to look inside.

"I don't mind."

The clothing cabinet was a modern one made by the Godrej company; it was crafted from steel, a material that protected better against mildew. The top three shelves held clothes neatly folded. Perveen ran her hands through them. No schoolbag, no pieces of paper.

"It feels strange to see someone touching my daughter's things," Mithan said, as Perveen finished her inspection.

"Did Freny have any clothes that are not here?"

Mithan looked puzzled. "What do you mean?"

"She was wearing a khadi sari when we saw her yesterday," Perveen reminded her. "And you've told me she stated the virtue of homespun at the Hawthorn Shop."

"If she had such clothes, we had no idea about it. My husband has a very strong opinion against that cloth. He says we've come so far as a civilization we should not wear homespun."

If Freny had clothing of protest, she would not have stored it in the flat. It could mean there was a hiding place. Perhaps the college ladies' lounge.

Mithan gave a shuddering breath. "I

always wished she hadn't entered the college. We couldn't really afford it. Even though we had some money saved for her brother's education, it was difficult. She should have finished high school and married Hester's son."

"Hester said something just now about wishing Freny would have come to her house." Perveen spoke quietly, not wanting anyone outside the room to hear.

"Yes. The children — Darius, Freny, and Khushru — all played together when they were young. Khushru is such a nice boy and was the age just between Darius and Freny. The fathers worked together. So we had thought about getting Freny and Khushru married at the proper ages."

"Did Freny want this?"

Mithan looked sharply at her. "What did she tell you?"

Perveen shrugged. "Nothing. It did not come up in conversation."

Pressing her lips together, Mithan answered, "Once she had the chance to go to college, she thought of nothing but her work."

But Freny had seemed keen on one man. "Did she ever speak of teachers? Mr. Grady, perhaps?"

"Oh, yes." Mithan sounded more animated. "That man taught a modern history course. She was at the top of it. There was another British teacher she liked, too: a woman. Mathematics was not Freny's favorite subject, but she very much enjoyed that teacher's way. How silly — she knew these British teachers were kind, but she still wanted British out of India!"

"She had the gift of seeing people for who they are, I think."

"Perhaps. The only teacher I ever heard her complain about was Indian."

"Oh?" Perveen tried to sound noncommittal.

"Mr. Gupta. She said he was too bad-tempered to answer questions; he just told people what to do."

"Did she take a mathematics class from him as well?"

"No. But he was the Dean of Students. So everyone had to mind him."

"Who else did she know well at the college?"

"She spent some time with a Hindu girl called Lalita. I'm not sure of her surname."

"It's Acharya," Perveen said. "I gather they were fast friends."

"The girl lives near the Opera House, and she sometimes came our way so the two could walk together." Sounding reflective,

Mithan added, "Lalita is a very smart girl. Amongst the females in the college, sometimes Lalita took first place in exams, and other times Freny. My husband told Freny she must work harder to stand first in the class."

Mrs. Acharya had also referred to the competition between the two. It could be challenging to have a friendship with someone whose success meant your own parents might be angry with you. "So the friends were also rivals?"

"Both were very intelligent," Mithan said after a brief pause. "Lalita was more clever at mathematics. They were together in most classes, but this year Freny was shifted up to do some smaller classes with senior students in the subjects of history and writing."

There was a gentle tapping on the door and Hester's soft call. "Tea is ready! And my son has come."

Mithan looked dismayed. She whispered, "I only want to be alone."

"Stay a little longer, then." Perveen gave her a reassuring look and went out into the parlor.

Here, a young man of medium height dressed in a simple cotton kurta and trousers was shifting awkwardly from one foot to the other. Freny's grandmother had pulled out a chair for the shy-looking fellow, but he wouldn't sit down. He stood, holding a brass tiffin box. As Hester came forward, he put the tiffin box in her outstretched hands. Hoarsely, he said, "Mamma, I watched till the peas were soft."

"He brought the last thing I was making for you: green peas and fenugreek," Hester Kapadia said, and went into the kitchen with the dish.

"You are a good boy to help today." Bapsi favored him with a nod. To Perveen, she said, "This is Khushru, Hester's son. His father is deceased, but he was once at the same tailoring shop as Firdosh."

"Are you visiting from Gujarat?" Khushru asked. It was a natural assumption, because of the Cuttingmaster family's origins.

"No, she is no relation," Bapsi said. "She is Jamshedji Mistry's daughter and Bombay's first lady solicitor."

"Yes. My name is Perveen Mistry." Perveen wished Bapsi hadn't said quite so much about her.

"Is there some trouble?" Khushru's eyes darted from Bapsi to Mithan and then back to Perveen.

"Not at all. I am assisting the family with having Freny released for the funeral." Perveen studied Khushru's round, soft-looking face, wondering if she'd seen him before. "I was at Woodburn College in the viewing stands yesterday. I don't think you were there, were you?"

"No, I missed college yesterday because I was called to the shop." Twisting his empty hands, he mumbled, "I only learned about Freny's death from my mother last night."

Perveen could understand why the young man looked so exhausted and upset. "Mr. Cuttingmaster said the shop was looted. What happened? Were you overpowered by rioters?"

"Something like that." Khushru's face flushed.

Perveen studied Khushru, wondering how much of this was truth. Perhaps he was ashamed to admit he'd been caught in a fight, just like her brother had been.

There was a rapping at the door. "Hello, hello? I have come from Doongerwadi."

"The visitors never stop." Bapsi put a hand to her forehead, as if it hurt. "Khushru, please take care of it."

Khushru opened the front door just a crack, as if he didn't quite trust the person on the other side. The visitor was a sturdy young man with uncovered curly hair. He was dressed in a simple tan cotton jacket and trousers.

Khushru stared at him for a long moment. "Soli?"

"Yes." The young man's face broke into a tentative smile. "And it's you, Khushru Kapadia?"

"Ah, Soli, I did not recognize you. Why didn't you say something? It has been too long," Hester chimed in. "Do you remember us? How are your parents?"

"Quite well, thank you. I am the assistant manager for transportation at Doongerwadi, so that is where we are living now. Actually, I've come to see the Cuttingmaster family. I thought this was the home of Mr. Firdosh Cuttingmaster?"

Bapsi, who'd been lingering near the tea table, came forward. "I am his mother. My granddaughter is the one who has passed."

Looking somber, Soli said, "Yes, madam. I am most sorry about Freny. I met her once — she was a very kind girl. We are planning to arrive at the morgue tomorrow to bring her to our grounds."

Bapsi looked sternly at him. "Freny should have her rites here, at the house, and then go to Doongerwadi."

Biting his lip, Soli said, "It would be more expensive to have two trips. Usually our deceased family members are transported directly from the morgue to Doongerwadi."

Bapsi shook her head. "Enough! I don't want to think of money now."

"I am very sorry." Soli put the clipboard he'd been carrying behind his back. "It is only that time is short. We request permission today to reserve transport for tomorrow."

The business of death kept people busy. But this was too much for the grandmother alone. Mithan needed to aid in the decision.

Perveen went into the bedroom and found that Freny's mother was sitting in the same chair, head bent and eyes closed.

"Sorry to interrupt your rest." Perveen explained that a Doongerwadi employee had arrived and wanted to plan for the next day. "All you need to think about is where you wish to have the funeral. Your mother-in-law said she wishes everything to happen here."

Mithan's eyes widened. "That cannot be. We don't know how long the inquest will take. There may not be enough time to have the funeral here and then get to Doongerwadi before dark."

"Would you like to inform them?" Perveen offered a hand to Mithan, who held it fast as she raised herself from the chair.

When Mithan entered the parlor, Soli and Khushru bowed their heads and began murmuring condolences.

"Soli, I remember you," Mithan said softly. "I hear there is a question about Freny's funeral. My husband wishes for everything to take place at Doongerwadi."

Bapsi's eyes widened. "But our Freny should be at home one last time to say goodbye."

Mithan shook her head. "How can we do that, in this circumstance? I am so sorry, Mamma-jaan."

"You are going against my wish." Bapsi's voice trembled.

"I don't mean disrespect. But we have to think about all that's happening outside. What if goondas broke into our funeral procession?"

Bapsi's voice was sharp. "I have already been outside today to buy flowers, while you have not gone anywhere since coming home yesterday. You are worrying over nothing."

"Mamma-jaan, you haven't heard what Firdosh told me." Mithan approached Bapsi to take her hand — but her mother-in-law shook her off. Stepping back, Mithan said, "Firdosh says that one street is fine and the next has villains breaking windows and attacking our people. It's just not safe! You must know I would prefer Freny to come home again. I cried so hard about it yesterday."

"But we have not even had a visit here from any priests." Bapsi's eyes were tearing. "We must make prayers together."

"I can confirm these prayers for her are already being recited at Doongerwadi, and you are welcome to join in the service today." Soli bowed his head. "Mrs. Cuttingmaster, many of the priests at agiaries around the city are staying behind locked doors. Very few Parsis are traveling between places for fear of being attacked; I did not even wear a fetah today, to be careful. Doongerwadi, as you know, is on Malabar Hill. The police are protecting the roads there."

"Mamma-jaan, I respect you very much," Mithan said to Bapsi. "But this is what Firdosh wants."

Nodding respectfully at the grandmother, Soli said, "You and your daughter-in-law can do all the bathing and dressing at Doongerwadi. Please gather the clothing for her, and all the personal items you wish to bring for yourself. You can reside for as many days as you wish in your own bungalow at the funeral home. You will be provided all the proper meals for those observing funeral rites."

This was not a special courtesy. At Doongerwadi, a system was in place for mourning Parsi families to stay in furnished cottages and have meals provided. Freed from the daily tasks of life, the bereaved could focus on prayer and their last moments with the deceased.

"I want to pray, but I worry that Nana will be alone —" Bapsi looked woefully at the assembled women. Now that Freny was gone, the cat she'd rescued was even more precious to the poor woman.

"I'll make sure Khushru feeds your cat every morning and afternoon," said Hester Kapadia. "You must go, my dear. Everyone needs you."

"Mamma-jaan, I'm sorry," Mithan said, and the catch in her voice made Perveen feel like crying, too.

Bapsi shook her head, and tears fell fast down her cheeks.

Hester stepped closer and took the grandmother's hand. "I will spread word in the colony, both about the inquest and the funeral tomorrow. With God's grace, the roads will become safer."

Soli looked relieved that the dispute was settled. "Then I will just need her father, Mr. Cuttingmaster, to please sign the transportation order."

Mithan shook her head. "He is not here."

"I'm afraid he must sign to guarantee. There is a down payment of half the transport cost . . ."

"I have almost nothing in my purse," Mithan blurted. "The last money I had was used to pay a taxi to carry us home."

"I apologize, but the company owner insists on down payment before the hearse will come —"

Bapsi's mouth settled into a firm line. "Do not ask me to pay for something I don't believe in!"

"I can provide the down payment," Perveen said crisply. She signed the paper and counted out coins from the small beaded purse she wore on a silk cord tied around her waist.

Mithan looked gratefully at her, and Bapsi nodded curtly.

"I shall say goodbye, then," Perveen said. "But I'll be here in my car, with my father, tomorrow morning. Can you both be ready at seven-thirty?"

"I won't go," Bapsi said. "She can."

"Firdosh will surely join me," Mithan said. "Thank you for coming tomorrow."

Khushru said a quick goodbye to them and followed Perveen out the door.

As they stepped away from the apartment house, Perveen asked, "Where exactly is your family flat?"

"On the far side of the courtyard, where the bicycle is," he said, pointing to an ancient black contraption that was covered in rust.

"Your bicycle?"

"Yes. It is old, handed down from a neighbor, but the wheels still roll."

"The ladies told me that you and Freny had played together since childhood. That makes her death especially painful for you. I'm sorry."

"Yes. We even might have married, but my mother did not like her going to the same college."

"Why?"

His jaw sagged as he spoke. "Math is my subject. However, when Freny arrived the next year, she placed higher than me in the English examinations. Even though she was a year younger."

Competition reared its head again.

Gently, Perveen said, "Did you want to marry her?"

"Maybe," he said, taking time with his answer. "It was hard to think of her as a wife when she was always like a sister. I have no brothers or sisters. Darius and Freny meant everything to me."

"Did you know Freny was in the Student Union?"

He nodded. "It's a small extracurricular group. She cared more for those matters than I. And most afternoons I needed to be helping at the Hawthorn Shop. Some of the group members teased me for that."

"Dinesh?"

"Yes, and some others. Really — it doesn't matter. I don't wish to name anyone." He chewed his lip.

As they continued walking, Perveen moved fractionally closer to him. "I've got a question for you. Freny valued honesty quite highly. I'd think she would have told her parents about the Student Union, but she didn't. Do you know why?"

Stopping in his tracks, he fell silent. At last he said, "She tried to talk to them about independence, but they — her father especially — disagreed. She was very honest, so she must have kept it to herself only for the sake of not angering him more. But she was true to her belief. I would sometimes see her at college wearing a khadi cloth sari — on days that the Student Union had its meetings."

"Did you ever travel to college together?"

Khushru began walking again. "No. I go

by bicycle. If Freny's father was not able to go with her, she'd take a taxi with another girl. They met a few streets away from here."

"Lalita Acharya?" Perveen guessed.

"How do you know about her? Are you investigating this death?" Khushru's questions came rapid-fire, and his pace picked up, too.

Perveen lowered her voice. "Not at all."

They had reached the colony's gate, and the two wizened old men were looking suspiciously at her.

"Thank you for seeing me out," she said in a clear tone, so they wouldn't get the sense she'd been visiting all over the place.

On the ride home, Perveen pondered Khushru's words. He seemed riddled with misery over his failure to protect the Hawthorn Shop and to marry Freny.

If the friends' marriage had been arranged, neither Freny nor Khushru would have had higher education. Would Khushru have become a tailor, and Freny a young mother and hardworking cook and cleaner, like Bapsi and Mithan and Hester?

It would not have satisfied Freny's ambitions, yet she would still be alive.

14
A COUNTER-PROCESSION

Soli and Mithan's comments about trouble in the streets were disturbing. Perveen slumped lower in the seat as Arman drove out of the colony's gates.

Arman glanced at her and said, "Don't worry, I have my own lathi. The old men guarding Vakil Colony had one to spare."

"I would never want you to use it." As she peered out the window from her lower angle, she saw that looters were too busy loading carts with boxes and bottles to bother with looking at their car. Still, she felt fear.

Jamshedji had told her that he wanted to stop at the synagogue. How would he get home? Was he expecting Arman to come for him? Belatedly, she realized the time she'd spent in Vakil Colony might have created danger for him. But Arman reminded her that her father had not asked for a ride, and that returning to the heart of Byculla would be risky.

The ride back to the European Quarter was slow because of all the shop workers busy cleaning up the streets. Bruce Street was peaceful, the usual businesses open. Arman drew up in front of Mistry House. Before exiting to open the passenger door, he pulled a brass item from the glove box and held it aloft.

"What's that?" Perveen asked.

Grinning at her, he said, "My lucky golden egg. It protects the car. And all of us inside it."

"It's a beautiful good-luck piece."

"I didn't tell you before, because I thought you wouldn't believe it. But I'm sure it kept your brother and that American safe, too."

Mustafa opened the Mistry House door with a flourish. "Mashallah that you are returned. Your father is here."

"Wonderful!" She hurried inside. Her father was in the hallway, talking into the telephone. At the sight of her, he said a few more words and hung up.

Relief washed over her. "Pappa! How did you get home so quickly?"

"I accepted a ride from one of the district superintendents. And why were you out so long? Was there difficulty in finding a messenger for the Cuttingmasters? I was quite worried."

The only way to manage the question was to breeze through it, give him the feeling she had solved a problem rather than twisted his order. "We were quite fine. In fact, I decided to personally deliver the message to the Cuttingmaster home."

Jamshedji's eyes narrowed. "You didn't send a messenger?"

"I was the messenger!" Quickly, Perveen said, "The message was too complicated to explain on paper; and I did not know whether to do it in English or Gujarati."

"I see." He didn't sound any more believing.

"We needed an immediate answer about whether the family wanted more help, and if they would ride in our car tomorrow. I can confirm that they will. Now please don't look at me with such disapproval!"

Jamshedji looked soberly at her. "The superintendent told me that the violence is rising. That's the reason I'm concerned you went your own way without my knowing about it."

Perveen considered the constant flashes of fear she'd had while Arman was driving, especially when she couldn't see what lay around the next corner. Her father must have been imagining the worst. "I apologize,

Pappa. If the Cuttingmasters had a telephone, I would have rung Mustafa. But they don't have a telephone, and everything is set, according to Mrs. Mithan Cuttingmaster."

Perveen would have said more but there was a sudden heavy thumping on the door.

Mustafa hurried to peer through the leaded glass window beside the door. "Just the postman." Opening the door, he took a package and greeted the man. "Aadab, my friend. I hope you are keeping safe."

"Yes. This route is fine, but not so many businesses are open. If I can't put a letter through a postbox, I have to carry it back." The postman touched the heavy bag strapped across his waist. "Yazdani's is only going to be open a few more minutes. Firoze said he doesn't want to wait for trouble."

"We need to pay some bills this afternoon, and it would be sweeter to do so with pastries," Perveen said, giving her father a sidelong glance.

"A good point!" said Jamshedji, who did not like to go through his day without a few biscuits or some cake. "Mustafa, why don't you get a nice assortment for the office?"

"With pleasure," Mustafa said, heading to the back room where the cash box was kept.

After Mustafa had gone across the street, Perveen closed the door and spoke to Jamshedji. "What are our plans after we're finished with tea and bills? Perhaps home tonight?"

"Have you not heard what I've been saying about danger? We are staying at least one more night at the Taj. Not that I like it, either."

Perveen caught the bitterness in his tone. "Arman's protected our car with a lucky egg. Why don't we go back to the colony for Mamma and Gulnaz's sake?"

"They are safe and secure with Gulnaz's family." Jamshedji was toying with the notepad on the telephone table. "Truly, you are the only one giving cause for worry."

"I'm really sorry about going to the Cuttingmasters' without telling you first —"

"No!" he interrupted sharply. "It's about your behavior at the hotel. From this point on, will you please refrain from socializing with men?"

Suddenly, she felt dizzy. "What do you mean?"

He raised his head from the paper to look at her. "I've taken time to consider what I saw outside the Taj hotel this morning. The woman spending time with a European man. She was wearing a sari in just the same colors as yours."

Perveen had a sudden image in her mind of Freny sitting in the parlor listening to this hallway argument; and she knew what Freny would expect of her. "I went for a walk alone this morning and sat down to read the newspaper. I was reading the newspaper and was greeted by a business colleague. It would have been rude not to speak to him."

"He was wearing black. Is he a barrister?" Jamshedji's voice was less aggrieved.

"Actually, he's an Indian Civil Service officer. His name is Colin Wythe Sandringham. He was in a dinner suit."

"Because he just got in that morning?" Jamshedji tut-tutted.

Perveen was not going to explain about the cars coming late from Government House. Jamshedji would believe something worse. "I didn't ask. Mr. Sandringham was the assigned contact when I worked in Satapur." Perveen looked away from her father but felt herself caught by the even sterner gaze of Grandfather Mistry's portrait.

Jamshedji was still glowering. Putting his hands in his pockets, her father said, "If his work is two hundred miles away, why is he here?"

"He was ordered to accompany the prince

on his tour. I didn't talk to him extensively about it, but in general, he goes wherever the prince does."

"How ironic for you to be acquainted with such a person."

"Alice is in almost the same boat." She would have said more, but there was a hammering of fists on the door.

"Sahib! Open quickly!" Mustafa was shouting in a way she'd never heard.

Perveen rapidly unlocked the door and stepped back as Mustafa swept inside. His breathing was labored, and the red Yazdani's box was pressed flat against his chest. Immediately he locked the door and drew the two heavy bars across it.

"A large band of strangers is on their way into this neighborhood! We have to protect Mistry House!"

"As I was just saying, the city is not safe!" Jamshedji shook a finger at Perveen.

"Pappa, there's no time for scolding. Mustafa, did you see them?"

"No. They should be coming shortly," Mustafa said, his breath still fast. "As Firoze was packing up the sweets, Bernard Adenwalla shouted to him through the door. He warned that a big group of men are coming. Firoze was in such a hurry to close up the bakery, he didn't even take my payment."

Jamshedji didn't answer. His mouth had gone slack and he stared at Mustafa, as if waiting for more.

"First, the windows. They should all be closed and locked." Perveen gave the order, trying to shake her frozen father into action. Seeing him paralyzed and silent was utterly new. She continued, "Curtains drawn, as if nobody's in."

Her command worked. Jamshedji recovered himself and sped toward the parlor, while Mustafa went to the kitchen. Perveen latched the tall Gothic-arched windows in the drawing room, while the two men debated where to go.

"I will remain downstairs. If anyone comes through a window or door, I will be here with my gun." Mustafa's voice was heavy.

"A good precaution!" Jamshedji shouted across the hall. "Perveen, you should hide upstairs. Get inside an almirah without too many things in it."

Her stomach twisted as she thought about what it would be like to hide in a cupboard. She couldn't do it. "No, Pappa. We should stay on the ground floor and make a tremendous racket. If they think there's a large group inside, they will know it's too much trouble. Together, we could stand up against anyone. No need for guns!"

"Insha'Allah, there will be no bullets fired. But remember, if the situation arises, I am trained for this." Mustafa's voice was insistent.

Jamshedji sighed. "Yes, that is a comfort. Thank you."

For her father to thank his servant was remarkable; but she had no time to ponder this as a dim roar of voices came through the windows. In a firm tone she said, "I'm going to look at exactly who's coming."

"You mustn't!" Jamshedji said.

"The upstairs windows," she called back to him as she hurried up the staircase to their large shared office. Peering out, she saw nobody, but the voices were so near that the men must have been in the cross street.

She heard firm, fast footsteps on the stair, and in an instant, Mustafa was in the room.

"This is a fine vantage point for shooting," he said, lining up his rifle on the windowsill.

No person outside of the military or police had the right to fire a gun in the city. Perveen was well aware of the danger Mustafa was putting himself in. Standing at the partners' desk, on the side where her father usually worked, she tried to speak with authority to the male servant forty-odd years her senior. "Just so you are informed, if you fire upon someone in the street, it will be considered an act of aggression, not self-defense."

"Your father could argue me out of any trouble. But I need to keep him and you alive. I would fire carefully, anyhow," he said as he knelt to better position the weapon. "A warning shot."

"But a warning shot can cause panic —"

A group came around the corner. Perveen counted them quickly — ten, the majority wearing white Congress Party caps but at least four men in the leaf-green color signifying the Muslim freedom organization Khilafat.

She swallowed, trying to hold back the nausea that was rising. These looked like people whom she would have rallied with a month ago. But now they wouldn't see her as a fellow Indian freedom advocate. Anything could happen.

But they looked so . . . calm. Perveen watched four of the men on the outer ranks jog toward the buildings on the street, leaving a paper on each threshold. And now the chanting could be heard through the megaphone held by a small man in front. "No more hartal! Gandhiji's orders!"

"No fighting! No damage!" chanted the men behind him.

"No fighting! Hartal is off."

Firoze Yazdani stood in the doorway of his shop. He was holding out a red box. One of the men jogged up, made a grateful namaste with his hands, and took the box along with him.

"That is how to do things." Perveen felt her eyes filling with tears. They were tears of gratitude for being spared — and of admiration for Firoze Yazdani, who had stood openly in front of men he disagreed with and offered them sweets.

Firoze might not have believed he had anything in common with Mohandas Gandhi, but he was living the message of nonviolent resistance.

Mustafa pulled the gun inside the house and turned to Perveen. "Memsahib, I believe there is no danger."

"Yes. They are only trying to halt the violence. Perhaps they went in the group to protect themselves . . . from people like us," Perveen said.

At the far end of Bruce Street, the man spoke in the microphone again. "Strike off. Go home. Stop fighting!"

"Mashallah," Mustafa said. "God has willed it. Where is your father? I thought he was coming upstairs."

"Maybe he went back down."

They clattered downstairs, just as Jamshedji emerged from the parlor.

"What were you doing, Pappa?" Perveen asked.

"I was about to go outside," Jamshedji said. "I had a plan to speak to them. But they were through the street so quickly. We are safe."

Mustafa asked, "Sahib, did you hear all their words?"

Jamshedji shook his head. "Just a few words here and there because the windows were closed. I heard 'Gandhiji' and 'hartal' and 'fighting.'"

"We could hear clearly through the open window. The men shouted that Gandhiji wants all fighting stopped," Mustafa said. "They want everyone to resume business and life as usual."

The tight set of Jamshedji's jaw eased, and he gave Perveen a brief smile. "Let's hope others hear as clearly as Mustafa. And that the police don't go after these men for unlawful assembly."

It was like him to turn every occurrence into a legal problem — something that could be defined and defended. Perveen smiled back at him.

"Mustafa, you went to the trouble of bringing us pastries. Let's celebrate by eating them now," Jamshedji directed. "After that, Perveen and I will depart for the Taj. Even though this hartal is off, we cannot expect people around the mills to know the same until tomorrow."

An hour later, they'd been ferried to the hotel by Arman. It appeared to Perveen that vast numbers of the glamorous people who'd been at the Taj the day before were checking out. Having celebrated with the prince, they could now return home, their duty done.

"I may discuss our bill with the clerk. Go upstairs if you like," Jamshedji said, handing Perveen the key to the suite. Leaving her father in line at the front desk, she decided to take the lift. The events of the day had left her feeling too tired for the stairs.

She was sweaty, so she decided to take her things to the ladies' lounge, which contained a series of tiny rooms with sinks, toilets, and even bathtubs. A hotel maid was there to run the bath and present her with towels after she'd had a luxurious soak.

Feeling quite refreshed, Perveen dressed again in a pretty orange sari. With her hair coiled into a simple bun, she returned to the suite's sitting room, where a huge arrangement of red and pink roses graced the coffee table. It hadn't been there in the morning. Jamshedji had returned and was seated by the desk, his legs crossed and one foot anxiously tapping it.

"Is everything all right?" She glanced sideways at him from the coffee table, where she'd stopped to examine the flowers. There was no card.

He gave her a long look. "At the desk, there was something of a surprise."

"The room rate is too high?"

"That is no problem. But here is some mail for you." He held a cream-colored envelope with the crown insignia of the Taj Hotel in his hand. Her name was typed on it in capitals.

Oh, God. Maybe the reason her father was looking so coldly at her was because he'd already opened it and read the contents. If the missive was from Colin, it could undo all she'd said to make him seem unimportant to her. Could he have sent flowers? What madness would possess him to do that, when he knew she was staying with her family?

"I have not opened it," he said, as if reading her unspoken thought. "But I think, as partner in the firm with you, it is surely not restricted information."

Seeing the challenge in his eyes, Perveen ran a finger under the envelope's edge. She was so nervous she didn't feel the paper cut, but she saw the blood bubble up, as red as the flowers behind her.

Perveen pulled out the paper and shut her eyes for a moment to prepare herself. She would read it first and then give it to her father. If she didn't, he would think she was keeping secrets from him — and that he would never forgive.

Perveen looked down at the letter. The handwriting was unfamiliar.

Dear Perveen,
I went where I said I'd go this afternoon and saw something. Call me as soon as you can.

It was signed *AHJ.*

"Here you go, Pappa. As you said, my business is your business." Perveen handed him the letter. She felt giddy with relief.

As Jamshedji pulled the monocle from his vest and studied the letter, the lines of tension on his face lessened slightly. "Who is this AHJ?"

"Alice Hobson-Jones, whom you have met many times."

Jamshedji's face broke into a wide smile. "Of course, Miss Hobson-Jones! I have not seen her in weeks."

"Yes," she said. Without meaning to, Alice had saved her — but just this time. "It's not her handwriting. She must have dictated to someone."

He looked at her cryptically. "What do you think she means to say to you?"

"She was intending to go to Woodburn College today. Maybe she was so vague in the note because she wished the information to remain just between us. After all, the college is officially closed."

"If she says she saw things at the college . . ." Jamshedji tapped his fingers on the desk. "It may be important to the Cuttingmasters. As representatives for the family, we should be cognizant of everything related to the scene of the death."

Perveen looked at her watch. It was almost six. "I shall telephone her now. We never had a proper lunch. Do we have plans for dinner?"

"We can go downstairs to the dining room, or for variety, Green's Hotel. I ran into Mr. Davidar downstairs and he asked me to meet him for a few minutes. You can join us."

"Mr. Davidar was one of the people most

eager for me to leave the Government Law School," Perveen reminded her father. "I consider him an archenemy of all women professionals."

"He must be eating his hat to see you finished your studies in England," Jamshedji said. "I will drink tea with him. But you do not have to come with me if you don't wish."

"Thank you for that concession," Perveen said sarcastically. "Anyway, I shall be busy."

"With what?"

"I brought a few files with me in the car. I'm trying to prepare for the coroner's inquest."

"That is fine, but remember, this hearing is about fact-finding, not arguing guilt or innocence. Ask me more about coroner's court after I return." He pointed a finger at her. "No seaside rambling tonight."

"I will stay inside. But tomorrow, will you allow me to speak at the inquest?"

"What do you have to say?"

"I won't know until I hear what the witnesses say. But I read in one of your past cases that the mother of a victim directly asked questions of a witness in the inquest for her son's death."

"Mrs. Cuttingmaster could ask a question, if she wishes."

Earlier that day, she had thought Mistry

House was about to be attacked — and fear had surged through her. Now, she felt a return of that fear, in a subtler mode. If she asked her father for what she wanted and he declined, she could not ask again. It would be an opportunity forever gone.

She inhaled, drawing in strength and the scent of roses. "What if I handle the questions for her? I could ask any question she might have in a more composed manner. And I might hear something that she misses that could be important."

He was silent for a long while. "It is an untested process whether a female solicitor could ask a question in coroner's court. I am all for you achieving new goals. But the coroner might refuse you —"

"Which is why I like working with you," Perveen said. "If he won't listen to me, he'll hear the same question from you."

Jamshedji laughed aloud. "Is this idea of yours to help the Cuttingmasters, or is it really to advance your career?"

With a knowing smile, she said, "Is there any reason I can't do both? That is what you have been doing all your life. Ambition is not a dirty word for men."

"No. I suppose — if you did speak and what came from your mouth was sensible — I would be quite proud."

15

ORDER IN THE COURT

Perveen was finding it hard to breathe.

She couldn't decide whether the tight feeling in her body was only because she was pressed into the back seat of the Daimler with Mithan and Firdosh, the cramped quarters redolent of whiskey, as if Firdosh had drunk something that morning.

Liquid courage, some people called it. He was worried, just as she was.

She planned to speak up for the Cutting-masters; but what if the coroner ordered her to be silent? If she were to be labeled an unacceptable speaker in the court, it would set a negative precedent for the rest of her career.

She turned her head to the window to breathe the scents of the city rather than Firdosh's anxiety. She caught the smells of early morning: dirty gutter water, rotis being roasted, cow dung, and salty sea air. Bombay was the same as ever, despite the unrest.

Arman parked the car close to the coroner's court and leapt out to open the doors for the Cuttingmasters. By the time she'd followed them out, Perveen felt her breathing become more relaxed.

As they proceeded along the veranda, the grumpy clerk she'd previously spoken with pointed a finger at her. "Frances Cuttingmaster is Mr. Kelly's first inquest this morning."

"Freny." Mithan stopped walking and stared at Perveen. "Her name is not Frances. Is this even the right case?"

A first chance to advocate, and it was low stakes. Perveen took a few steps toward the man's desk. "Her name is formally spelled *F-R-E-N-Y*. Can you make the correction, please?"

Firdosh pointed an accusatory finger at the clerk. "Yes. Change it!"

The clerk delivered a poisonous glare. " 'Frances' is what I have on the paper before me, and what the coroner has in his documents. Only an amendment by the coroner can result in a name change."

"Freny Firdosh Cuttingmaster is the full given name of the deceased, and we will alert the coroner during the proceedings." Jamshedji's voice was crisp, and his expression stern. "It is the rule of law to have names recorded correctly."

"Then you request that of the coroner. Not me." The clerk turned away.

As they left the veranda and entered the courtroom, Perveen stopped to take it in. With white painted walls and a high ceiling punctuated by electric fans, it had none of the splendid woodwork and fine light fixtures present in the Bombay High Court. Yet, just like a typical courtroom, there were rows of seating for observers, a jury box, and a witness stand.

Firdosh took Mithan's hand. Softly, he said, "Just like last time."

Perveen guessed the two were remembering the inquest for their son — a nightmare revisiting them. With their son, they'd received a straightforward verdict of drowning. This inquest would probably be more complicated, and there was a chance Freny's political views, so different than those of her parents, would be exposed.

Jamshedji organized their seating by entering the second row from the front of the room, motioning for Firdosh to follow. Then Mithan shuffled in, followed by Perveen. The seating was just as it had been in the car and allowed for gender discretion — Mithan would be unhappy pressed against a man who was not her husband — but would prove challenging if Perveen and her father needed a quick word with each other.

From her position on the aisle, Perveen surveyed the crowded room. Half of the public benches appeared to be filled with Parsis. From the way they were gaping or looking sorrowful, she guessed they were friends or acquaintances. Firdosh nodded at several of the people but seemed lost in his own thoughts. Mithan sat close to him, keeping her head down, as if she didn't want to catch anyone's eye.

The press were seated together in their own bench. Some of these newsmen were looking at them; another was pointing out the college principal who, like them, was close to the front. Right next to Atherton was a very red-nosed man she recognized as Alistair Johnson, the solicitor for Woodburn College.

A third group caught her attention: four Indian constables in navy blue uniforms who sat on a bench behind two Anglo-Indian officers wearing full dress khakis. Perveen thought she recognized some faces from the college garden.

The dull roar of conversation stopped at a bailiff's order. A tall man in his forties wearing an elegant gray suit had entered the room.

"The Bombay coroner himself, Mr. King," Jamshedji said in a low voice. Perveen noted the pallor of King's face, which seemed to suggest he was often indoors. Yet his eyes were bright and his lips set in a relaxed half smile. He appeared ready to seize the day.

Firdosh nudged Mithan. "That suit is ours."

On the other side of him, Jamshedji whispered, "What do you mean?"

"Huston Mills tropical wool is sold at the Hawthorn Shop only. I recognize the color and weave. Now I am remembering Mr. King has been in the shop before. A most respectable customer." There was an approving sound to Firdosh's voice.

If this coroner was different from the gentleman involved in their past case, it might make the Cuttingmasters more relaxed. But Perveen was still on edge.

After a sharp rap of his gavel, Mr. King announced the inquest into the death of Frances Cuttingmaster on the date of Thursday, November 17. He called for the jury, and they entered through the same door he had. As they were sworn in, Perveen cataloged their appearances: one Parsi wearing a fetah cap, another man in a close-fitting cap common to Muslims, and two others with wide turbans signaling that they were Hindus of local origin. The final man, who was seated in the jury foreman chair, had a boater hat in his lap. From his olive complexion and collared shirt, she guessed he had some European heritage, and was perhaps Christian or Jewish.

"We are missing two jurors. If there is a person in the room with a summons, will you please come forward?"

Nobody did.

"Let me state for the record that two jurors, Arvind K. Mehta and Kumar L. Bhatta, did not appear and will be fined. It is essential to report for jury service." The coroner's voice was crisp, as if he relished his power.

"Does this mean the inquest is delayed?" Perveen asked her father.

"No. They can proceed with five."

Perveen wondered if the absent jurors were afraid to travel or were caught up with repairing damages. At least there was a mix of religions in the group; however, the absence of females in the jury box seemed like a form of bias in itself.

The coroner addressed the room, telling all that he and the jury had already viewed the clothed body of Frances Cuttingmaster in the presence of the police surgeon, and that now the testimony of witnesses would transpire.

"I cannot stand them looking at her," Mrs. Cuttingmaster whispered to her husband. "It's worse than with Darius."

"She will be washed clean after this. Not only from germs, but from their gaze," Mr. Cuttingmaster said fiercely.

Jamshedji stayed silent as the coroner reminded the audience that an array of witnesses would give court-ordered testimony under oath. Following each person's testimony, he would ask questions, and then he would allow questions to come from members of the public.

Perveen looked with interest at the first witness called to the stand, one Dr. Andrew McDonald, a surgeon in the Indian Medical Service who also taught anatomy at Grant Medical College. He was a broad-shouldered, confident looking man in his thirties; and judging from the depth of his tan, he was not a newcomer to India.

Despite his imposing stature, Dr. McDonald had a soft Scottish accent that was pleasant to the ear. After swearing in, he placed a small collection of papers on the lectern before him. He attested to examining an Indian female of eighteen years who showed no signs of pre-existing disease.

Dr. McDonald went on to say that he observed a mild laceration on the back of her left hand and both upper arms. The most prominent injuries to the body were a shattered skull and a broken hyoid bone.

"What bone?" Mrs. Cuttingmaster murmured to Perveen. She was taken aback, not knowing the answer, and was glad when someone from the press shouted out the same question.

"A most remarkable bone." Dr. McDonald had a hint of reverence in his tone. "I will explain more about it in due time. Firstly, the breakage pattern of the skull is consistent with a hard fall. As I previously wrote in my report to the coroner, it seems likely the body was thrown down from an elevated position."

"You said 'thrown down.' To clarify for all here," Mr. King interrupted, "are you saying that the deceased was forcibly thrown by someone, rather than jumping herself?"

"One or more persons were likely to have thrown her. Because the gallery from which she fell is not terribly far from the ground, she had to have been thrown with force to sustain such injury."

"And the fall was the cause of death?"

"Not at all." Dr. McDonald's response

was interrupted by a stirring in the court's audience.

"Order in the court, or I will have everyone removed." Mr. King shook a finger at the crowd. "Doctor, please continue."

"I mentioned the hyoid bone." Touching his own throat, Dr. McDonald said, "It is a *U*-shaped bone close to the root of the tongue and between the cartilage of the larynx. It connects to no other bone in the body, but functions as an attachment structure for the tongue and muscles in the floor of the oral cavity."

Perveen tried to picture it, realizing that this tiny bone she'd never heard of was essential for the power to speak. And in Freny's case, the power to speak truth.

"Because this bone is independent, it would simply move in a fall," the doctor continued. "The only way to break a hyoid bone is through pressure, such as when the neck is squeezed tightly. Therefore, I believe this hyoid bone was fractured because physical violence was done to the deceased."

Mithan bowed her head. "My poor girl!"

Perveen touched one of Freny's mother's tightly clenched hands. Beyond Mithan, Firdosh's face was etched in shock.

"Anything more, Dr. McDonald?" Mr. King's voice was collected.

The doctor nodded and returned to the papers on the witness stand. "Liver and spleen were examined and showed no evidence of toxic substances. Other conditions noted were reddened eyes and bruising behind the ears and on the neck, and some missing hair on the head. The deceased had a mildly swollen tongue. All of these markers, in addition to the fractured hyoid bone, cause me to declare the cause of death was strangulation."

This was a shocking, lurid death: exactly what would sell newspapers. Perveen saw furious scribbling going on among the newspapermen.

"Thank you, Doctor. Let it stand for the record that cause of death is strangulation." Mr. King pressed his hands together and faced the room. "Now we will hear testimony from Sergeant Cuthbert Miller of the Bombay Police."

A sweating, pudgy man of about thirty, who was wearing a police officer's dress khaki uniform, replaced Dr. McDonald in the witness box.

When prompted by the coroner, Cuthbert Miller spoke in the slightly Welsh sounding accent common to many Anglo-Indian families. After giving his credentials and announcing his status as the first officer to arrive, he read the police report.

"Miss Cuttingmaster was lying about five feet out from the wall of the school's building. We immediately explored the possibility she had fallen by accident or intentionally jumped, especially since there was a patch of cloth on one of the shrubs close to the building. However, the body wasn't in the bushes directly below the gallery, so the idea of a fall was ruled out. It is more likely that someone with considerable strength threw her off."

"So a scene was constructed by persons, designed to mislead police interpretation?"

The sergeant nodded. "It didn't fool me."

Appreciative laughter rippled from the press section and some parts of the room.

"You have a keen eye, Sergeant Miller. Anything else pertaining to the victim?"

The man's eyes swept over the public before he answered, as if he wanted his moment of fame to continue. "We ascertained that this piece of cloth in the bush was cut from the edge of the victim's sari. It was a fairly smooth cut, as if scissors were used. We believe the cloth was placed on the hedge by someone attempting to give the impression that the girl fell into the bushes and tore her clothing."

"Why all this fuss, do you think?" Mr.

King asked. "If there was an attempt to make the death scene appear like suicide, why wouldn't the unknown persons have laid the deceased atop these bushes?"

"Perhaps the perpetrator was forced to depart early," said Miller. "We have testimony that Principal Atherton and Dean Gupta had inspected the property ten minutes before the procession. They said they were looking for anyone still in the building to come out to see the prince, and —"

"Will you kindly list all who were interviewed for your investigation?" interrupted the coroner. "This was not mentioned earlier, and I require it for the court record."

"Yes, sir." The officer's face flushed, as if he felt reprimanded. "We interviewed all the servants inside the college that day — just three in the main building and three in the hostel. Oh, and the cook and his two assistants. All had witnesses to account for their whereabouts, and none of their fingerprints appeared in the gallery. We captured three fingerprints, but they have not yet been identified. We collected prints from all staff members on the premises."

"Faculty included?"

"No. My inspector said no reason to do so until after the inquest, as this is not yet a criminal investigation."

"Did anyone report hearing sounds of a struggle?"

"No. Besides the servants mentioned, there were two male students in the infirmary. Neither reported hearing anything, but there was a gramophone playing for them that the nurse had set up. The infirmary is on the ground floor of the hostel, which is behind the main college building. The nurse stated that nobody came or went from the infirmary all that morning."

"Very well. Are you finished?"

"We made a few more observations, sir. A constable found a piece of paper underneath the body. A typed note."

Perveen stiffened. Had there been a note with Freny all along, and she'd missed it?

The coroner looked keenly at Miller. "I request that you read it out for the court record."

Stiffly, the police officer said, "The note is in English: 'I have shamed too many people and can no longer live. Time for independence.' And the last two words are typed in phonetic Hindi . . ." the policeman added. " 'Jai Hind.' The meaning is 'Victory to India.' As I'm sure you already know, sir, that is an expression commonly employed by terrorists."

16
THE CORONER'S VERDICT

A suicide note . . . when the evidence from the doctor seemed to make it clear someone had crushed Freny's throat?

Perveen's thoughts whirled. The evidence pointed to murder. It seemed unlikely that Freny would have written such a note.

"She was not any kind of terrorist, and she would never take her life." Mr. Cuttingmaster could barely keep his voice down. "The doctor said someone broke a bone in her throat. Why is this even being presented —"

"She was happy!" Mrs. Cuttingmaster interjected. "Too happy to give up her life for any reason!"

Perveen made a hand movement urging them to lower their voices. Quietly, she asked, "When the police came to see you, did they mention any note?"

"No, nothing!" Mithan's eyes were beginning to tear.

It could be that the police had kept the information close because of suspicions the family might be involved.

Jamshedji caught Perveen's eye and inclined his head slightly to the row behind him. He was warning her that people in the rows behind them were close enough to hear. In Gujarati, she whispered to the Cuttingmasters, "I am shocked, too. But let's not talk more about it until we have seen the note."

"Can't we see it?" Mithan pleaded as the bailiff proceeded toward the jury box with the note held aloft for viewing.

"Ssh. The coroner looks like he has questions."

Clearing his throat, Mr. King asked Sergeant Miller, "Have you done any analysis on this note?"

"Yes, sir." He seemed to puff up as he continued. "Careful analysis was performed on this document. Our police analyst concluded this note was typed on the secretarial typewriter inside the administrative office. The typewriter ribbon matches the message of the note."

"Is the analyst here?" asked Mr. King.

The sergeant shook his head. "Mr. Simmons is based at central headquarters, and I believe he is occupied today with the

Prince of Wales. I brought a written report here signed by him."

The coroner took the note and read it aloud for all to hear. In addition to identifying the typewriter used for the note, Mr. Simmons had confirmed that the inked thumbprint on the typed document was consistent with the actual print pattern of Freny Cuttingmaster's left thumb. The ink on Freny's hand matched the brand in an inkpot on the secretary's desk in the Woodburn College administrative office.

Anyone could have pushed her thumb onto the paper, Perveen thought. Either before or after her death. A picture flashed into her mind of Freny under duress. It was too painful, and she shut her eyes to will it away.

She opened her eyes when the coroner called for the sergeant to step down and for Dr. McDonald to return to the witness stand. After Dr. McDonald had once again taken the oath, the coroner said, "You have explained to us about the fractured hyoid bone being a sign of strangulation. Does a possibility exist that Miss Cuttingmaster hanged herself?"

"Not in my opinion." His voice was slow and measured. "Self-strangulation necessitates the use of ropes, a belt, or similar material. Her skin shows no evidence of this, just bruising consistent with injury inflicted by two strong hands."

The coroner cleared his throat. "My questions are finished. At this point, the public is permitted to ask questions."

Perveen lifted her hand at the same time twenty other hands shot up around the courtroom. One man from the press didn't wait to be called. Instead, he shouted out his question in a brash American accent. "Do the police believe the typed note is a bluff?"

"Sergeant Miller's description of the evidence answered this." The coroner's answer was blunt. "Will all questioners please consider whether they have heard answers to the queries before raising them."

Mr. King clearly wanted to close the inquest. However, the jury had not heard a definitive opinion on the typed paper.

"Can't I see the note?" Mrs. Cuttingmaster plucked at Perveen's sleeve.

Perveen looked over the woman's head and toward Jamshedji. She whispered, "The coroner won't look at me."

She'd expected he'd raise his own hand, but instead, he made a shooing motion. "Go out into the aisle and raise your hand!"

But that was too frightening. She hadn't

seen anyone else do it. Again, she raised her arm as high as she could, but the coroner's attention remained on the press. Her father was frowning at her.

Now or never.

Perveen freed her arm from Mrs. Cuttingmaster's grip. "Come out of the row with me."

Mithan's face was shocked. "Why?"

"You wished to see the note. The coroner does not seem to notice me, so we must make ourselves visible to him."

"Is it allowed?" Mithan sounded doubtful.

"Yes, my father just suggested it. Sir, please join us?" Perveen asked Firdosh Cuttingmaster.

Mr. Cuttingmaster shook his head vehemently. "I will not make a spectacle of myself. She can go — but don't let her cry!"

Perveen whispered in Mrs. Cuttingmaster's ear, "Just come with me. I'll do the talking."

As Perveen and Mrs. Cuttingmaster stood in the aisle, rustling and whispered exclamations among the public filled the air.

The coroner scowled. "Who are you?"

"Sir, may we please approach the bench? I am Perveen Mistry, a solicitor advocating for the Cuttingmaster family. Mrs. Cuttingmaster here is feeling quite poorly," she added, hoping this would bring out some compassion. "Neither she nor her husband heard about the suicide note when the police called on them."

"Evidence cannot leave the police station!" the officer said huffily.

"Of course, it must not leave," Perveen said easily. "And the Cuttingmasters were compliant with the police when they interviewed them. Today, Mrs. Cuttingmaster only wishes to see if there's any evidence the note was written by her daughter. Her opinion might be useful for the jurors."

The coroner glowered at her. "It is a typed note, did you not hear?"

There was a slight snickering in the room after that. It was as if everyone who was waiting for a lady lawyer to say something silly had been rewarded. And she had been careless to say "written" rather than "typed."

"I understand that it is typed. But she would very much like to see the note."

"You are putting the authority of a mother over a policeman?"

"I imagine that Sergeant Miller's mother already has some authority over him," Perveen said with a smile.

A second wave of laughter rippled through the room. She hadn't expected it, but thought it was a good sign. Even the coroner chuckled. He said, "If Mrs. Cuttingmaster is willing, she may examine the note. However she must come to the witness stand."

As Mrs. Cuttingmaster went into the box, Perveen looked back to see Jamshedji frowning. What had she done wrong? Then she realized — if Mrs. Cuttingmaster was in the witness box, she could potentially be peppered with questions just like Sergeant Miller had been.

And she had not prepared Mrs. Cuttingmaster.

The witness box was actually a podium, and as the sergeant swept out, not giving either of them a look, Mrs. Cuttingmaster hesitantly went in. A bailiff came up.

Looking at Perveen, he said, "In which language shall I address her?"

"I understand English — but I would like to speak in Gujarati," she said in a low tone to Perveen.

"Is a Gujarati translator available?"

The coroner looked toward the bailiff, who shook his head.

"There should have been one. Perhaps due to the trouble —"

"I can translate for her."

Both Perveen and Mrs. Cuttingmaster were sworn in. Then the bailiff brought the paper to Mrs. Cuttingmaster. Looking over the small woman's shoulder, Perveen could see it clearly. It had been typed on ordinary white paper — what was called foolscap folio, about thirteen inches long and eight inches wide. However, the paper was folded in half, and the typed words took up a very small amount of the top half of the paper. In block letters, it read: *I SHAMED TOO MANY PEOPLE AND CAN NO LONGER LIVE. TIME FOR INDEPENDINCE. JAI HIND! FFC*

Perveen had noted immediately a misspelling in the typed word "independence," although Mrs. Cuttingmaster might not. It was highly likely the typed note was a fraud.

"Has Mrs. Cuttingmaster had enough time to examine the note?" the coroner asked Perveen.

After she translated, Mrs. Cuttingmaster said "Yes," in English.

"Do you believe the typed note could have been produced by your daughter?"

In Gujarati, Mrs. Cuttingmaster said, "She knew how to type — she told me a teacher had let her use a machine. But I don't believe she typed those words. I know she was too grateful about us paying for her to attend college to kill herself."

There were a number of people in the courtroom who understood Gujarati; a

266

murmur arose after her words.

"She is capable of typing, though?"

"Yes."

The audience rustled and chattered again, and the coroner called for silence.

Perveen cleared her throat in the same manner he had done. "Sir, speaking on behalf of the family, I have noted the word 'independence' is badly misspelled. Also, I wish to state for the record that the deceased's first name is not Frances. It is Freny, *F-R-E-N-Y*. Her middle name is Firdosh."

"Our questions are for your client," said the coroner. Turning his eyes on Mithan, he spoke slowly. "Simply answer the question yes or no, so we can proceed. Do you believe that this note was typed by your daughter?"

"No! My daughter would not misspell English. She was an excellent writer." Mithan's voice was proud. "And please make sure her name is spelled correctly in documents, sir. You are a wise man. I am sure you can do it."

This comment brought a rippling through the audience and a pinkness to the coroner's cheeks. Perveen wanted to laugh, but tugged down the edges of her mouth. The future of any woman lawyer coming after her was dependent on her professionalism.

Now the bailiff approached Mithan. Holding a paper aloft, he said, "I present a question from the jury. It reads: 'We wish to know more of the mother's opinion of the sentiment in the note. Was your daughter a protestor of British rule?' "

"Objection!" Perveen said. "This question is not germane to cause of death."

"Madam, this is not a court hearing — there are no objections." The coroner's paternalistic tone was rankling.

Perveen tried to calm herself. The coroner had prohibited questions from the journalists directed at the police. Not so for Mithan; and whatever she said here would be a matter of court record that could be used later on, in a criminal trial. Stiffly, she translated the question for Mithan, adding that whatever she said on the stand would be a matter of court record, and that she also had the right not to answer, or to say "I don't know."

This was a lot of information to take in; and when she finished, Mithan asked for the press question to be repeated. Clearing her throat, she answered, "I never saw her protest. But she told us about ideas of the other students. Her father corrected her thoughts."

Perveen felt a chill at this. How did Firdosh correct Freny? Was it a scolding, or something more extreme?

"Thank you, Miss Mistry and Mrs. Cuttingmaster. You are excused."

Perveen took Mrs. Cuttingmaster's hand as she stepped off the podium. Not only was it cold, now it was shaking. Her daughter was a murder victim — but the questions raised had made it sound as if she was a troublemaker. And surely there were several men in the jury box who were pro–British rule.

As Perveen led Mithan toward the row where they had been sitting, Mr. Cuttingmaster's eyes were fixed angrily on her. The questions just raised about Freny's activities must have embarrassed him. He probably thought the family name was ruined.

Unless he hadn't wanted to look at the note because he was involved in the killing.

Perveen thought again how quickly he'd been on the scene after Freny's death. Had he briefly left the Orient Club to kill his daughter, and then returned to be with his wife and respond to the tragedy? He had been upset, but not as distraught as his wife.

The trouble was, Firdosh was now a Mistry client. It was not her business to find out if he had an alibi for all of Thursday morning. That would be a matter for a prosecuting attorney, if he was ever charged.

The judge asked Mr. Atherton to enter the witness box. The school's lawyer came forward, too, and stood at his side, shooting an angry glare at the press section.

The principal's face glowed with sweat as the coroner began his questioning, simple as it was. He was dressed in another woolen suit. The idea that an Englishman with a prestigious job hadn't enough money to buy proper clothing for Bombay still bothered her. However, Alice had told Perveen that her teaching salary was too low to support herself. Woodburn was a missionary college — it was not like one of Bombay's newer colleges with endowments started by millionaires.

The coroner coaxed out the information that Mr. Atherton had only arrived in India one month before the current term began in October. He acknowledged he'd canceled classes on Thursday because the city had been good enough to build a viewing stand right in front of the college entrance.

"What was the day's schedule, then?" Mr. King asked.

"We began as usual at nine o'clock with prayers in the chapel led by our chaplain. Then Dean Brajesh Gupta took roll call of the students in the chapel. After that, our students went to an abbreviated homeroom meeting followed by fifteen minutes of free time, during which they were told to put away their belongings and proceed to the viewing stands."

"Was attendance taken again at the stands?" the coroner asked.

Atherton shook his head. "No, since everyone was already accounted for. However, I have asked teachers present at the viewing if they noticed any absences. Being marked for roll call meant going to the stands."

"But you did mention Freny Cuttingmaster was present at roll, and she was not in the stands," Mr. King said. "So you cannot know for certain, isn't it true?"

"That is correct," Atherton answered.

"Were you aware of any conspiracy among students to protest the visiting of Bombay by the Prince of Wales?"

Atherton shook his head firmly. "No. I'd heard nothing of the sort."

"What do you know about the Student Union?"

Why was the coroner asking questions about the Student Union, rather than staying close to the cause of death? Then Perveen remembered something she'd read in preparation for the inquest: the coroner did have it in his power to identify a culprit for further prosecution.

"This club predates my time at the college and has only met three times since the term began," said Atherton. "I understand from its faculty advisor, Mr. Terrence Grady, that the students engage in conversation about social issues and occasionally invite speakers for the student body to hear. There is also an element of charity work."

"So the organization is not devoted to dismantling the government?"

Atherton's damp face reddened. "Not at all. That would be against everything Woodburn College stands for. We are bringing the best of Britain, from spiritual to intellectual to social, to deserving young Indians."

Perveen thought his words sounded straight from an admissions brochure.

The coroner quirked an eyebrow, as if he also thought the same. "Mr. Atherton, once you reached the stands, where were you sitting?"

"The front row, center, with other faculty members." Atherton described it just as Perveen remembered.

"We heard about the roll call for students, but were any faculty members missing?"

He hesitated. "I thought we might be short one or two of the male teachers. I asked Dean Gupta to go back with me to the building to call up and down the halls for them. Everyone was supposed to be outside, representing the college."

"And did you find anyone back at the school?"

"Yes. We each inspected several floors, and while I didn't see anyone, Mr. Gupta told me that Mr. Grady was still inside his classroom. Mr. Grady explained to Gupta he had pressing work to finish. Mr. Gupta reminded him all teachers should be present. Mr. Grady did not step out with him at the moment, but did arrive a few minutes later."

Perveen remembered Atherton and Gupta seating themselves after she and Alice had arrived. Out of the crowd of teachers assembled near Freny's body, Mr. Grady was the one who volunteered to summon the police.

"Sergeant Miller, is Mr. Grady among the witnesses?" The coroner looked at the bench where the doctor, the policeman, and Mr. Atherton had waited to be called to the witness box.

The detective rose from his seat in the police contingent to answer. "No, sir. We have testimony from each and every teacher regarding Miss Cuttingmaster and the events of Thursday, and Mr. Grady's was not seen as remarkable."

Did they not think he might have been the one who harmed Freny Cuttingmaster? Perveen was aghast that the questions from the audience did not include this obvious possibility. But it was not a criminal trial — it was an investigation of cause of death.

"Mr. Atherton, are lady students safe in the college?" was asked in various ways over the next few minutes.

Mr. Alistair Johnson, the college's lawyer, went to the witness box and advocated for its long-running positive history of serving all students, regardless of gender. He pointed out that in the process of the police investigation, no fault had been found with the building or staff, and the college remained open and ready to assist with any further investigations.

"Will teachers be called to the stand?" someone who sounded American asked in a ringing voice.

In the press section, a dark-haired man had raised his hand high above the others. Perveen recognized him as J.P. Singer, who'd fought with the press attaché at the Taj Hotel. He was much closer, allowing her to see that his skin was an attractive golden color. This must have been the reason the governor's aide had called him "darkie."

Mr. Johnson's voice interrupted her covert inspection of the journalist.

"Teachers did their interviews at the college. No testimony was pertinent to cause of death, except for that of Miss Daboo. And hers was read by the coroner already." Mr. Johnson's voice was steady.

The dark American spoke again. "Could I ask Mr. Atherton what his attitude is toward the Student Union? Do you approve of it, sir?"

Johnson started to speak but Atherton spoke for himself. "That extracurricular group has only met three times this term. I am willing to treat these students as fairly as any others, but it is against school regulation for them to cause trouble in public."

"Are you referring to the action of Dinesh Apte?"

"That behavior is against the law!" Mr. Johnson cut in.

"These spurious questions do not pertain to an inquest into cause of death for Freny Cuttingmaster." The coroner's voice was sharp. "I call the matter closed. This court will adjourn briefly while I prepare my report."

Perveen looked at her watch. "It's just about nine-thirty. How long do you think he'll take?"

"I doubt it will take long. Let's stay put," Jamshedji said.

"Everyone else is going out," Perveen objected. The tension made her body feel stiff, and she wanted to move.

Jamshedji motioned for her to look toward the courtroom door, where the journalists were circling. "Those men are like flies to a pot of sweets. If we stay in our place, it is easier to defend Mrs. Cuttingmaster."

Indeed, she could see the press had lit into Mr. Atherton, whose lawyer was frantically waving them off.

Perveen sat still. So many questions had arisen in her mind; she wondered whether Mithan's testimony about the note might have any impact on the coroner's verdict.

Freny was an ordinary girl who had died; but in the gaze of the city, she was so much more. She was a tool for imperialists to use against nationalists, and a cautionary tale for city parents to use against daughters who dared to study alongside males.

Mr. King returned after just fifteen minutes, and a good portion of the people who had exited were still missing. Perveen was reminded of what it was like sometimes at Oxford, when a professor was late to a lecture and students around her went out for a cup of tea or cigarette and missed his appearance. Her father had been right to tell her to stay.

"This inquest is more troubling than many, as it involves a member of the tender sex, and has occurred in one of the most hallowed spaces in all of Bombay. This, too, at a time that the city was involved in significant unrest. Looking at evidence provided by Dr. McDonald, I concur it was death by strangulation. Therefore, I present the most obvious explanation of the tragedy; that Miss Cuttingmaster's death was a homicide committed by a person who may have believed that by making a few gestures at planting false evidence, the strangulation might be ruled a suicide. We do not know the truth about the note, but in my mind, given the medical evidence, that is irrelevant." Looking at the serious-faced men in the jury box, he added, "Gentlemen, it is now your turn."

17
Verdict and Aftermath

"My goodness." Perveen had prepared herself for an unreasonable outcome, but this was a verdict she agreed with. However, Mr. King raised the possibility that the suicide note wasn't planted evidence. He hadn't trusted Mrs. Cuttingmaster's belief, probably because he doubted her fluency in English. Now it was up to the five men who'd sequestered themselves to decide.

As the public streamed out of the room for the recess, Mithan looked sadly at Perveen. "I said that was not typed by her. He didn't tell the jury that."

"Yet he said the note wasn't important."

"You shouldn't have stood up." Mr. Cuttingmaster sunk lower in the bench. "All those questions they asked! Now Freny is getting a name for herself."

"People forget who was in court and what was said. Don't worry." Jamshedji looked fondly at Perveen, who guessed he was

278

referring to her own family law case four years ago in Calcutta.

"I am so nervous. Will you take me to the washroom?" Mrs. Cuttingmaster whispered in Perveen's ear.

"We are only going out for a minute's break," Perveen said to her father, and he didn't challenge her. She took Mithan by the elbow and down the aisle.

Fortunately, there was a facility for ladies, but it was only for one. Perveen stood guard at the doorway, watching the flow of people. One reporter in the batch was heading determinedly toward her, and Jamshedji's words of caution rang in her mind. At least Mrs. Cuttingmaster wasn't present.

"May I have a minute with you? I'm Jay Singer." As the American stretched out a hand to her, she caught a glint of silver on his right wrist that echoed the weave of his light gray suit. He was dapper, but the suit was machine-stitched. She shook herself. She was beginning to judge a man by his clothing, the way the Cuttingmasters did.

"Mr. Singer, do you write for the *San Francisco Chronicle*?"

"Don't tell me you know my byline?" His face broke into a grin, showing a set of large white teeth. "Not a lot of people outside America have heard of the newspaper."

"San Francisco is famous for gold, isn't it? I believe there are some people from India in California." She released her hand from his strong, warm grip.

"Very true," he said, plucking a pen from his breast pocket and flipping open a small spiral-topped notebook. "Immigrants of Indian extraction are mostly Punjabis who farm the land. Yet they're aware of the motherland's struggle. Ever hear of the Ghadar Party?"

Searching her memory of conversations at activist meetings, Perveen grasped onto something vague. "A group of overseas Indians wanting to aid in the freedom movement. There are many such groups in England and France . . ."

"The challenge is bringing efforts together," said Mr. Singer. "That is what I see is the difficulty in this city."

Perveen didn't want to risk being asked to give a political comment, so she changed the topic. "I know of you from my brother, Rustom Mistry. The two of you got into a fight on Thursday night."

"Not with each other," he joked. "He's quite a devil, your brother — and his assistance made it a heck of a story. But he didn't tell me his sister was a barrister."

"As I explained to Mr. King, I'm a solicitor," Perveen said, aware that he'd begun writing things down. "This means I don't argue cases; I chiefly work on contracts and such. I was advocating for the Cuttingmaster family at their request."

"Understood. The coroner is arguing homicide. And as you know, the city is in turmoil. Do they think it is likely that a rioter could have murdered Freny Cuttingmaster?" He wrote so fast, it seemed impossible the words could be legible. But he was a good foot taller than she, so she couldn't see what was going onto the pad. She had to be very careful not to say anything that could fan flames.

"They are not making any judgments without police investigation. And we are still waiting for the jury's verdict, before we know if the police will in fact be involved."

After he finished his scribbling, he looked down into her face. "I think I saw a British person in the foreman's seat. Is that what always happens?"

"No. The requirement to qualify for any jury position is that one is a respectable person." She raised her eyebrows. "How that's determined is up to the coroner and his staff. And please be careful what you write. There's a chance the man you're speaking about is not from Britain. He might be an Anglo-Indian or, as some say, 'domiciled European.' ''

Mrs. Cuttingmaster emerged from the washroom and looked questioningly at Perveen. "Is everything fine?"

"Yes, this newspaper reporter and I are just finishing up our chat." Perveen was almost sorry, because she liked hearing the blunt American questions, which were so different from the ones British journalists usually asked.

"Mrs. Cutttingmaster, I am from an American newspaper. *San Francisco Chronicle.*" J.P. Singer spoke in slow, American-sounding Hindi. "Firstly, my condolences on your daughter."

"You speak Hindi?" Mithan looked at him in amazement. "Are you Anglo-Indian?"

"He is an American!" Perveen quickly corrected.

"Just a boy from California who picked up some Hindi. I also speak Arabic and Spanish." Mr. Singer had switched back to English. "In the interest of accuracy, I'll ask if Miss Mistry shall translate for us. Ma'am, would you be gracious enough to give your opinion after the jury has delivered the verdict?"

Perveen duly translated, and before she had finished, Mrs. Cuttingmaster was shaking her head firmly. In Gujarati, she said, "Time is short. I only want to get out of here and to the dakhma before the sun sets."

Perveen translated, "She says no thank you."

"And a bit more, I suspect." He rolled his eyes heavenward. "If Mrs. Cuttingmaster changes her mind, I can be reached at the Taj Mahal Hotel. I am most interested in her story."

"Good day, sir." Perveen took hold of Mrs. Cuttingmaster's elbow. The lady flinched, as if Perveen's grasp was too fierce. Perveen let her hand drop, and the two walked side by side through the crowds to the courtroom.

Jamshedji was standing in the aisle, looking toward the door. The courtroom was mostly empty. He said, "You were away so long that I worried what happened."

"There was a reporter who asked for a short interview. I only did so because he knows Rustom."

"Oh, yes. The newsman who looks like a sardar."

Perveen corrected, "Mr. Singer is from California. It is warm and sunny there, so that must be why he's a little browner than the other foreign press."

"I believe that Singer is a German Jewish

name," Jamshedji mused. "Just like our Mayor Sassoon, his ancestors could be from another destination."

"I don't care about these people," interjected Mr. Cuttingmaster. "When will we hear about the jury verdict?"

"We will settle for a wait. Many people in the audience will go off to lunch, but one never knows when the jury will make its finding."

Time passed slowly. The heat rose in the room, which gradually filled up again with press members and the public. Perveen looked at her watch. It was almost twelve — and the proceedings had started at eight. Catching Mithan's anxious gaze, Perveen said, "There still is time."

Firdosh rose and squeezed past her father into the aisle. She had a brief moment of apprehension he was going to harass a bailiff or another court employee, but instead he walked with heavy steps to the far side of the courtroom. Facing the wall, his hands moved at his waist. Without being able to fully see, Perveen knew he was engaged in prayer, touching the kusti cord that was important in prayer to Parsis.

Perveen decided to use the quiet time to put her thoughts together. She reached into her briefcase and pulled out her notebook, opening to the scrawled pages she'd written during the proceedings. She began to re-write the notes more carefully. The conversation between Mr. Atherton and other parties had been confusing at times, especially since she'd been distracted by her own strong emotions.

"Look," Mithan said.

The coroner was coming back to his bench, and from a different door, the jury was filing in. Firdosh Cuttingmaster stepped back, clearly surprised to have his prayers interrupted. He turned to walk back toward his wife, the ends of the kusti he'd been holding still in his hand.

Now the spectators who'd gone outside rushed back into the courtroom. Mr. King's expression was irritated as people noisily re-seated themselves. He announced the rules by which the jury had deliberated and then got to business. "Have you a verdict?"

"Yes, sir," said the foreman.

The coroner's expression relaxed. "Very well. Please report to us the jury's decision."

"Mr. Coroner, three out of five are unanimous in supporting your finding of homicide. One was against, and the other one was unable to decide."

"In the case of a divided jury, we go with majority opinion," said Mr. King. "Freny

Firdosh Cuttingmaster's death is ruled homicide."

There was a rumbling in the room. Was it over the fact the decision was not unanimous? Perveen wondered whether there was such distrust of the British at the moment that two of the jury members were unwilling to believe either the doctor or police report. Or could it be that Freny had been exposed as politically active, and was therefore considered less innocent?

The coroner pointed toward the public. "Silence. May I reiterate that a coroner's inquest is not a criminal court. The Bombay Police will continue their investigation. I advise the press to speak with the office of the Bombay Police if they have further inquiries." Rapping his gavel, the coroner declared, "Court is adjourned. I am calling a five-minute recess until the next inquest, the death of Mr. Mahmoud Iqbal Khan."

Outside in the sunshine, both Cuttingmasters looked dazed. The reporters who had been interested in the case were no longer around; Perveen was relieved not to see J.P. Singer.

Sensing the parents needed reassurance, Perveen spoke as cheerfully as she could. "I don't think it will be long till she is released from the morgue to Doongerwadi."

"There is the matter of certificates," Jamshedji said. "The morgue must have the cause of death recorded and will give a certificate at the time of release."

"Not more delay!" There was a tremor in Firdosh Cuttingmaster's voice.

"Don't worry. The coroner has pronounced — it will come. As you know, the morgue is in the very same building." Jamshedji waved his arm in the general direction.

"Soon they will go to lunch. They will not care . . ."

Perveen touched her father's arm. "Wouldn't it be good for one of us to go and see about it?"

"Better that I go. They are familiar with me."

They will never know me if I don't start now, Perveen wanted to say — but she knew better than to argue with her father in front of clients. Mistry was a united team.

Jamshedji strode off and Firdosh gazed after him, shaking his head. "Everything has taken too much time."

"How can you speak of time? We have just learned someone killed our daughter," Mithan shot back at her husband. "This is something we will live with for the rest of our days."

"I am so very sorry about what happened," Perveen said, thinking of the worry that lay ahead for them. The person who'd killed Freny would be on their minds as the investigation commenced, as a suspect was apprehended, and ultimately, as a criminal trial was held.

And if nobody was arrested, they might brood on the possibilities forever.

"Let us sit in a restaurant," Perveen said. She suspected her father would likely be an hour at least, if a document had to be produced.

Firdosh sucked in his breath. "We are in mourning. We cannot partake of such luxury." Mithan nodded. "We cannot eat in public."

How could she have been so insensitive to orthodox belief? Perveen considered the other options and decided to settle them on a bench near the fountain of the healing goddesses.

As they sat down, Mithan's eyes went to the fountain. "Those are lovely figures of ladies. They are foreign, but they don't look English."

Perveen explained what she'd heard about them being goddesses of healing and added, "I wish broken hearts could heal as easily as broken bones. But I believe it will take a long time to move through grief."

"And now it is worse!" Firdosh spoke sharply from his position on the other side of Mithan. "You are endangering us."

Perveen went rigid, realizing her suspicions of his unease about bringing Mithan to look at the note were proving true. "I'm sorry. Will you please explain what you mean?"

"You and your father did nothing to defend our daughter against defamation of character!"

Carefully, she said, "I believe the coroner was only interested in knowing whether the note could have been written by her. However, I agree that many unfair and judgmental questions followed."

"That doesn't mean anything now. Our innocent daughter was murdered. Who should be charged?" Mithan's voice shook.

"The sergeant said he had questioned many people already. Surely they know." Firdosh looked at Perveen. "Instead of you, I'll have the college lawyer find out for us."

"By law he cannot respond. Woodburn College is his client, and he will be engaged only with that institution's interest." And, Perveen thought, some of that institution's faculty might be primary suspects.

"The college lawyer was not present like she was." Mrs. Cuttingmaster spoke up, surprising Perveen. "Our daughter's killer could be someone from inside the college or outside. One of the rioters, even."

Her words gave Perveen the opening to say something the couple needed to know, even if they no longer wanted to engage Mistry Law's services. "Mr. and Mrs. Cuttingmaster, I want to ensure you understand what is happening next. The police now have clear reason to pursue a homicide investigation. When they look for a suspect, they question many people. They may come to you, and it may not be apparent why they are asking you some questions. I think that it is important that you take care not to speak to them without a lawyer being present."

Firdosh looked at her with outrage. "Are you saying the Bombay Police have any reason to accuse my wife and me of murder?"

"We are learning that Freny's beliefs about India are different than ours, but we would never end her life for it!" Mithan sounded horrified.

Perveen didn't mince words. "They have interviewed you once, but they may return. During the parade you were visiting the Orient Club, which is very close to Woodburn College. They may want to know if anyone can vouch for your presence there during a certain period of time."

Mithan put a handkerchief to her eyes. "How can you continue speaking of such things at a time like this? Our daughter is not yet washed and consigned."

"I think today will be all right. I don't believe the police would be granted admission to Doongerwadi. Only Parsis can walk deep into the dakhma. The police can't reach you, as long as you are doing your mourning there."

Firdosh glowered at her. "We will remain there for at least four days; longer, if my employer allows. But when we come out, I will expect the police to have found Freny's killer."

If only it were that simple. Through the fountain's spray, she saw her father had emerged from the morgue office and was standing on the veranda.

She needed to prepare him for the Cuttingmasters' displeasure, so she excused herself and hurried toward him.

As she reached him, he gave her a smile. "All is well. The coroner's verdict reached the morgue, and Freny has already been removed to the hearse and is on her way to

Doongerwadi."

Perveen didn't think this efficiency would necessarily be met with thanks. "Oh, dear. What if the Cuttingmasters wanted to accompany the body?"

Jamshedji shook his head. "I'm sorry, but the driver did not say family was allowed. All these rules about contamination and such —"

"I hope they won't be angry. Right now they are upset at being warned to be careful if the police speak to them. I said they needed counsel present, and I don't think they want to retain us." This was a great loss — emotionally and professionally.

"What you said to them is wise, but remember that you are not a criminal lawyer. Don't let your first appearance in coroner's court go to your head!"

"You and I are their lawyers of record." Perveen looked pleadingly into her father's disapproving eyes. "We could work together in creating a strategy for a barrister to employ."

"Well, let's leave that matter to think about for later. We are bringing them the welcome news that there are no more legalities to obstruct the mourning process."

Jamshedji followed her to the fountain and explained that Freny would soon be at

Doongerwadi.

"The driver just took her away?" Mr. Cuttingmaster's voice cracked as he spoke. "That is like what they tried to do at the college."

"That hearse does not allow passengers, and it is too unsafe for a procession. I am very sorry."

Mr. Cuttingmaster's eyes narrowed as he looked from Jamshedji to Perveen. "You Mistrys ruin everything. I suppose your father also believes I killed my daughter!"

"Not at all —" began Jamshedji.

"I did not kill her." Firdosh's voice shook. "I have lost one child already, why would I wish to lose the only one left?"

"I apologize for the confusion," Perveen blurted. "I'm only advising you about the way police go about investigations. You must be very careful, Mr. Cuttingmaster."

"Please, let's not argue anymore," Mrs. Cuttingmaster said anxiously. "These lawyers warn us for our own welfare. Let's go. Time is passing. Let's go to the agiary."

Perveen felt relief to have an ally at a difficult time. Looking toward her father, she said, "We can take you directly to Doongerwadi. Our car is still here, isn't it?"

"Of course. Please do come with us," he said, bowing in the direction of the Cut-

293

tingmasters. "You have been through too much today."

Perveen pressed, "It's a good idea. Do you need anything from home?"

Mrs. Cuttingmaster shook her head. "My mother-in-law went already. She has three cases full of clothes for us — and for Freny."

Firdosh Cuttingmaster remained silent, but he stood up and followed them out across the road to the car.

Their route took them across the city, where the streets were calm but more empty than usual for a Saturday afternoon. A lack of street sellers, a lack of ladies with shopping bags, and very few children.

People did not yet trust there could be peace.

As the car climbed higher, Perveen began seeing more police and soldiers camped out along the way. For a moment she worried before remembering that the prince was staying at Government House.

It seemed ironic that Freny would be laid to rest atop a tower that was so close to the man she'd wanted to avoid. They would be linked during her body's last days of existence.

As the tall trees of the agiary's forested grounds came into sight, Mithan murmured, "It is not yet one o'clock. There is plenty of time for preparations."

Perveen was grateful to the lady for making a positive comment. "Yes, that is fortunate. After I wash up and change clothing, I would like to come to the service —"

"No!" Mr. Cuttingmaster glared at her. "I don't want to see either you or your father there. The legal work is finished. We have no more use of you."

Mrs. Cuttingmaster cringed. Softly, she said, "But they helped us."

Jamshedji turned to face the client and spoke in a gentle tone. "We shall not talk of business today. We have been off duty ever since I finished dealings at the morgue. We only wish to pay our respects."

"No," Firdosh Cuttingmaster repeated, his voice still sharp. "We only want the people with us who knew Freny."

Perveen felt dizzy with shock. "I knew Freny. She came to me —"

Jamshedji cast a warning look at Perveen. "We understand your wish for privacy. May your mourning period bring some peace."

Mistry Law's services to the Cuttingmasters appeared to be complete.

But Perveen's worries weren't over.

18
A Golden-Eared Dog

Once the Cuttingmasters had left the car, Arman closed the passenger door and Perveen settled herself in the wide space. She had felt cramped before, but now she felt lonely.

"They're angry with us," Perveen said after they'd reversed course down Malabar Hill Road. "He believes I endangered Freny's reputation and I'm casting aspersions on him."

"Do not fret overly much. He is upset in the moment. And why can't he have the right to mourn without lawyers around?"

"That's true," Perveen agreed. But she wished she could mourn with them. She had known Freny a very short time, but she would have liked to hear prayers intoned and to be in the same space with her during her last hours.

As they passed a bend in the downhill journey, a tall yellow bungalow caught her eye. "I forgot to speak with Alice today. There was no time."

"And we are approaching her home. Arman, slow down and make a stop for Perveen."

Because Saturday was a shorter college schedule, Alice might be home. "You really don't mind?"

"Calling on her will give you both comfort. And don't worry about me. I will stop for a round at the tennis club."

Perveen spoke to the chowkidar at the edge of the drive who affirmed that Miss Hobson-Jones was in. They pulled up to the grand cast-iron and glass entrance, and Perveen got out, her briefcase in one hand while she clapped the door knocker with the other.

Govind, the household's butler, opened the door and stepped away fast as a small brown dog bounded toward her and stopped right at her feet. The dog barked, but its tail wagged.

"Sorry!" Alice had appeared and scooped up the dog. "I must teach her the command 'stay.' Both in English and Hindi, don't you think?"

"Diana might understand Gujarati. Kem cho!" Perveen said, stepping closer to put out her fingers for the dog to smell.

"Why Gujarati?" Alice asked as she patted Diana's soft brown head.

"She looks to be the type of dog used for work at Parsi funerals."

"I think the same!" Govind exclaimed. "She comes from Doongerwadi, maybe."

"Just because Doongerwadi is a mile up the road doesn't mean she belongs to them." Alice's voice was defensive. "And she's not well-trained. I'm sure she's a stray."

"Memsahib, it's her face," Govind said.

Perveen nodded. "He's right about the dog's features, and I can explain a bit more, if you'd like."

"Of course." Alice sighed. "Tell me the truth!"

"Your Diana has such pretty golden ears — and she also has a white spot over one of her eyes. Parsis believe dogs are spiritual creatures, and we have a special reverence for dogs with golden ears and two spots on the forehead." As she spoke, Perveen reached over to scratch the dog's soft neck. "Dogs with these markings are brought in to view the dead. There's an ancient belief that the spots are like extra eyes. They give the dog extra sight which is needed to ensure that the person being mourned is truly gone."

"That's so macabre!" Alice looked at Diana, who was vigorously wagging her tail. "Didn't you say such dogs have two spots? Diana has just one."

"Yes. That means she isn't a sagdid dog," Perveen said. "However, she has golden ears and one notable spot. I think there's a chance she's descended from a dog with the characteristics of the others."

As if tired of the chatter about her, Diana twisted and jumped out of Alice's arms. She bolted down the long, polished marble hall toward the doors leading to the back garden.

"It's clear she doesn't want to leave," Perveen said with a laugh, as the two women followed the dog's lead toward the veranda.

"Mummy wouldn't allow it. She had a dog this size when she was a girl. She thinks that Diana is part terrier. She has slaughtered several mice and one bird already." Over her shoulder, Alice called to Govind, "Could you bring us some gin-limes, please?"

"Straight away, memsahib."

"Is your mother having her afternoon cocktail?" Perveen said, as they reached the French doors. She knew that Lady Hobson-Jones's habit was to drink casually from lunch onward.

"Not today. She went to Poona with the royal train." Alice grinned at her. "There's a full slate of activities at the Western Indian Riding Club. While she amuses herself, Father's at the Secretariat trying to figure out how to calm the city. We have privacy."

Perveen watched Diana bound away onto the lawn, her nose moving through the grass. "Pappa and I just brought Freny's parents to Doongerwadi."

"So that must mean she's been released for mourning. Will you tell me about it?"

"Yes. I hardly know where to begin." Perveen paused as Govind emerged carrying two frosty glasses decorated with mint and lime wedges. After he left, she spoke again. "It's really awful. Are you sure?"

Alice nodded. "Quite sure."

Perveen told Alice the terrible details revealed by the postmortem and summarized the trial, the verdict, and the witness accounts. Alice sat up straighter when she mentioned the Student Union.

"I've heard about that group. Boys were talking about it after class — in Marathi, so I wouldn't understand, but I got the impression this was an important club."

"The Student Union is the reason Freny came to see me in the office. She was asking about whether the students could be expelled for not attending the parade."

Alice nodded. "So that's why she wasn't

with us in the stands."

"It looks like she went to college that morning because her parents wanted her to. And then she went along with roll call, reasoning she could be marked present, but she stayed on the college grounds to make her private political statement."

"A few students were marked absent that day. I know the police came this afternoon and were in conference with Mr. Atherton — perhaps it was to see these records. Do you think a student could have done it?"

Perveen had been thinking about how much she could tell Alice. Because her friend had done some part-time work for Mistry Law, she probably couldn't be compelled to divulge things in court. At the same time, Perveen knew Mr. Atherton and others in the college might disapprove of her chatting with the legal advocate for the Cuttingmasters. "Have you ever signed papers at the college setting a guide for confidentiality?"

"I don't think so. I signed a paper saying I accepted certain work hours, holidays, and pay. But what has confidentiality to do with anything?"

"Anything you tell me you noticed at the college could be privileged information in their eyes."

"Let me get the file from inside."

Alice came back five minutes later with a folio in hand. Govind followed with a platter of fragrant fritters.

"Having missed lunch, I'm very excited about these bhajis," Perveen said, allowing Govind to place five on her own plate along with a dollop of coriander chutney.

"I have been wanting onion bhajis for days," Alice said. "Mummy abhors the smell of frying onions, so the cook doesn't make them when she is in. This is the upside to the prince being in town — she has been out almost all the time."

Perveen guessed that Lady Hobson-Jones had no fears of being attacked, since she — and the prince's party — were only perambulating in the heavily guarded European Quarter, and on the guarded royal train to Poona.

Perveen studied the short employment contract. Alice had signed away plenty of rights, including the right to ask for a higher salary, but there was no language about confidentiality on college matters except for not divulging her wages.

"This is good. You can talk to me," Perveen said, looking up at her. "And I can talk to you as long as you maintain utter confidentiality. This means not accidentally giving away what I'm telling you to Lalita, or another teacher. They can learn details allowed for public knowledge from the newspapers."

Having smelled the savory food, Diana was back, begging at Alice's feet. As she tossed down a portion, Alice said, "As ever, you can count on me."

Perveen watched the dog eat the treat with relish. "Is it wise for a dog to eat onions?"

"She is happy to eat anything. And she had potato curry with onion as part of her breakfast this morning."

"All right, then." Perveen changed the topic. "Returning to the last thing you asked me, could a student have killed her? Absolutely. So, too, could a person who taught or worked at the college, or a family member or acquaintance. Unfortunately, I offended Freny's father by saying he should retain a lawyer if the police come to question him."

"Why would he be questioned?" Alice asked.. "He was at the Orient Club when she was at the college."

"As far as we know," Perveen said. "But male relatives should usually be persons of interest. Most women are killed by men who know them. This is something my father has learned in his many years of work, and I heard the same from my professors in England."

"So this violence is everywhere." Alice's voice was heavy.

Perveen realized how hard she'd sounded. "At present, there is no reason to point a finger at Mr. Cuttingmaster. Although it is a remarkable fact that he and his wife were at the Orient Club versus another part of the parade route. That is very close to the college — not even five minutes' walk."

"Hmm," Alice said. "The college has a guard who sits in a shelter near the main gate. One would think he'd see everyone who tried to enter."

"I wonder if he missed seeing Dinesh Apte running out to the parade," Perveen said.

"In any case, he didn't stop him," Alice said. "What relevance does Dinesh have to Freny's death?"

Perveen told Alice about how Freny had raised his name at the consultation. "I think his mockery of her commitment to independence made her all the more determined to stay out of the stands. I also heard she was very dedicated to the group from another Woodburn student."

Alice's voice rose. "And who is that?"

"Khushru Kapadia. He's in his final year of studies, while she was in her second. The families know each other well, and Khushru's late father worked at the same tailoring shop with Firdosh Cuttingmaster."

Alice nodded. "Khushru Kapadia is in the same mathematics class as Freny. They sit apart, because of gender, of course, but he was one of the few boys she would speak with. She smiled at him, too."

"Smiling — as if she was in love?"

Alice looked taken aback. "I didn't think of it that way. She seemed very relaxed. Almost as if he were a brother. The girl students are loath for anyone to think they have a beau," Alice said. "Some boys do try to make conversation and recruit for their clubs. I was talking with Lalita about it a little bit."

"Lalita was in the Student Union before but dropped the group. Did she tell you that?" Perveen was curious how frank the conversation had been.

"Yes. Actually, she cried and told me she thought it was her fault that everything had happened. She thought if she'd been with Freny during the parade, nobody could have bothered her."

"She said the same to me." Perveen sensed it was time to move on to another topic. "The college principal was a witness at the inquest. He mentioned he and Mr. Gupta went into the building to look for some missing teachers, and found Grady there."

Alice pursed her lips. "I thought he was with us — yes, remember, he comforted a student when everyone was in the garden."

"That was later." Perveen told Alice about the reported testimony taken down by the police. "What is Mr. Grady like?"

Alice took a moment to answer. "He's popular with the students, but he keeps apart from the European faculty. I'm fairly certain he's doing his best to snub me."

"He sounded Irish when he spoke to me."

"He is Irish," Alice affirmed. "And if you're going to ask if he's against the British, I'll say I don't know, but it could very well be; yet he's still willing to get his bread buttered by working at a Scottish college."

"Do you think there's a chance Freny had a crush on him?" Perveen asked. "Or that he felt warmly toward her?"

Alice's eyes widened. "Lalita never said anything like that. Why do you even ask? That would be — a very serious breach of moral deportment."

"I have no evidence other than she seemed happy to speak his name," Perveen assured her. "By the way, where is his classroom?"

"He's up on the second story, close to the north stairwell. I'm on the first story, so I don't see him often."

Perveen told Alice about how she'd tried to walk along the ground-floor gallery, intending to go up the north staircase, but Mr. Grady, who'd been carrying a portmanteau, had blocked her from doing it — and then left the college himself, despite Mr. Gupta's entreaty for him to join the chapel service.

"If Mr. Grady left, that means he didn't get questioned by the police that afternoon," Alice reflected. "He must have spoken to them on Friday." Alice shook her head. "The coroner should have called him to the court — you could have questioned him then."

"Maybe I would have! At least three male faculty — Grady, Atherton, and Gupta — were inside the college grounds close to the time Freny was dying. None of them saw her, and only two of them can vouch for each other's whereabouts."

"I didn't realize that. My mind is a sieve for what happened that day." Alice put her head in her hands. "Why didn't I notice Freny was missing when we sat down and insist we look for her? Why didn't I think?"

Alice was weeping now, and her dog immediately responded by putting her paws on her shoulders and nuzzling her face. That was true love, indeed.

Perveen looked past Alice toward the thick forest in the distance. Beyond it was Doongerwadi, the Parsi funeral grounds. Most likely the women of Freny's family had washed her body and dressed her in clean white clothing. The four-eyed dog would have come and gone, and the mourners would be chanting prayers.

Before sunset, her body would be carried by two special bearers to the tower, and laid at the top, ready for the vultures to come.

In a few days, she would be nothing but bones — and those would be burned.

Govind came onto the veranda. Looking at Alice, who was wiping her eyes, he spoke softly. "Excuse me. Miss Mistry's car has come back."

Diana jumped off her lap and took off to the front door of the house.

"A belated alarm," Perveen said as Diana began barking.

Alice didn't move from the slumped position in her chair. "I do wish you could stay."

"And I'd rather be with you than at the Taj." Taking out her handkerchief, Perveen went over to her best friend. "I'm awfully sorry."

Gently, she wiped a tear from Alice's cheek. Then she hurried out, not wanting

Alice to see that she was on the verge of crying as well.

19

THE COMFORTS OF HOME

As Perveen went to the car, she forced a smile onto her face. "Back so soon from the club?"

"Yes. Mr. Tata only had time for a glass of water before going back to the courts." Jamshedji shook his head, as if this was madness. "I hope your friend had more time than that for you."

Perveen settled into the back seat and arranged the briefcase in the space between them. "Yes. The verdict of murder is hitting both of us hard. Alice was quite distraught."

"Yes, I can understand that." Jamshedji looked at her sympathetically as Arman started the car and pulled out of the bungalow driveway onto Malabar Hill Road. "By the way, I telephoned home from the club and spoke to Mamma."

"What does she report from Dadar?"

"She was quite cheerful. She said Rustom came back, and she and Gulnaz have returned to the house."

Perveen caught a bit of reserve in his tone. "Is everything all right with Gulnaz and Mamma? Was it an emergency decision for Rustom to go ahead of us?"

"No. Apparently the road was clear, without any fires or trouble. This means we can think about going home, too."

"That's good news!"

"Yes," Arman said from the front seat. "It is time to return to Dadar. I am not afraid for this journey."

At the hotel, Perveen accepted the assistance of a maid to pack up her valise. She felt distracted; as if she might forget something. Yes, she would rather be home — but it would have been ideal if she'd known about the change of plans earlier. She could have penned a goodbye note to Colin, who had no idea she was leaving. However, her father was too close by; leaving a note at the desk would be a blatant act. What would she even write? She'd told Colin that they had to remain apart. For her to reach out again would be saying something else entirely.

The Mistry home was on Dinshaw Master Road, one of the main streets in Dadar Parsi

Colony. The house itself was relatively simple: a two-story duplex painted a fresh cream color and garnished with lacy black ironwork at every window and balcony. Two shiny black doors led to the respective households; one for Jamshedji, Camellia and Perveen, and the other for Rustom and Gulnaz. The garden was shared, the grass clipped by a gardener with scissors every few days, and the roses and camellias nurtured carefully. A young mango tree was on the parents' side of the property and a guava on Rustom and Gulnaz's side. They looked like a brother and sister of different heights, both at an awkward stage of development.

Camellia Mistry must have been watching, because no sooner had the car stopped than she appeared in the doorway. As Perveen jumped out of the back seat and hastened toward her, she thought about all the chances Freny and her mother had lost.

She would not waste another moment.

Camellia's smile was as wide as her outstretched arms. "My dear! I have worried so many hours about you being in the city. All the stories we heard."

Snuggling against her mother, Perveen breathed in the familiar scent of lavender soap mixed with ginger. "There was no need for that. We were guarded like royalty in a palace."

"But during Pappa's last telephone call, he said the two of you would be in court today?"

"Coroner's inquest at the hospital," Jamshedji corrected as he came up behind Perveen. "But that is done. Arman, please remember to bring any newspapers along with the luggage."

"Yes, sir," Arman called from the boot of the car.

The second door on the duplex opened, and Gulnaz came forward with a wide smile and outstretched arms. Slightly shorter than Perveen, Gulnaz had a demure beauty that seemed especially radiant today.

"Hello, Perveen!" Gulnaz called. "Thank God you are back safely."

Her sister-in-law had always been slim, and the silk chiffon sari she wore was draped in the usual modest fashion and did not reveal much change. But when Perveen hugged her, she felt a small bulge.

As they parted, Gulnaz gave her an intimate smile. "Rustom said you know about our baby."

"Yes. Why didn't you tell me earlier?" Perveen chided. "I know that having a baby is something you've wanted ever since we were in school. You never stopped playing dolls!"

Gulnaz dimpled at her. "How I've wanted this. Mamma and Pappa thought you might feel —"

Perveen heard Gulnaz's reluctance to finish her thought. Pulling back, she said, "Jealous? I certainly am not."

Gulnaz's cheeks pinkened. "No, not at all! They are always worrying too much about you, but I know better. You will be the very best auntie. What a gift to have you living right next door. Rustom said you and Pappa were assisting a tailor's family who lost their young daughter. What was the outcome in the coroner's court?"

"Homicide. It was a very unexpected tragedy." Perveen couldn't say any more because, like Camellia, Gulnaz had no professional association with Mistry Law.

Gulnaz's smile had completely vanished. In a low voice, she said, "There is too much to be sad about these days. Now that you're back with us, you must put that incident out of your mind. Gita must drop rose petals in your bath — that is good for heartache. Then, you must lie down. I am taking many rests now. It is wonderful — I will lie down with you, if you like."

"That is hardly necessary!" Perveen knew the prospect of roses in her bath would only remind her of the rose petals strewn over Freny's empty bed.

"Gulnaz is right," Camellia said. "Both of you need plenty of rest, for different reasons."

Perveen's attention was caught by John, the family's longtime cook, who emerged from the shadow of the guava tree with a basket in hand. John DiSilva was a Catholic born in Goa with a long face and rosy complexion that hinted at his Portuguese ancestry. He had been a pastry chef at the Ripon Club until Jamshedji and Camellia had tasted his feather-light caramel custard. They had offered to double his wages if he'd come to cook for their family, which he had done since 1910. Hefting the basket so Perveen could see the plump greenish-gold fruits inside, he declared, "Good that you are home, but sorry I had no warning about it. What do you wish for supper?"

"If those guavas are ripe, can you make your special cake?" Perveen could not think of the sugar-topped confection without salivating.

"Of course." John smiled widely. "The egg man resumed his deliveries this morning."

After Jamshedji was assured that John could prepare chicken farcha for dinner, Perveen went upstairs to her room. How simple the quilted cotton bedspread looked compared to the glossy damask at the hotel. She had marveled at the Taj's sea views, but she felt restored by the sight of the garden through her own long open windows.

A squawking from the balcony alerted her that she'd been heard opening the French doors.

"All right, Lillian. Yes, I am home."

As she went out to the balcony and un-latched the brass cage, the bird exploded out toward her. Perveen saw there was a half-bitten piece of guava in the cage.

"You've been fed," Perveen said, stroking the bird's colorful wings. "Why all this complaining? I will sit with you later to-night."

But even after Perveen had soothed Lil-lian into a contented clucking, the bird would not return to her cage. Instead, she fluttered her wings and walked sedately behind Perveen into the bedroom.

Gita emerged from the bathroom, where she had started running a tub for Perveen. "No birds in the house, your mother says."

"Maybe she's come inside to make sure I'm not going away overnight again."

"Like a baby following a mother," Gita said. "And just like a baby, she will make susu on the carpet. Shoo, shoo!"

To Gita, Lillian was an oversized, glassy-eyed animal with a sharp beak. But just as Diana had taken a firm place in Alice's heart, so had Lillian in Perveen's. These pets might be the closest either of them ever had to children. And what was wrong with that?

The next morning, Perveen was not feeling so tender. Lillian had woken her with a rousing morning song: "God save the Que-Que-Queen." It was not yet seven in the morning when Lillian had started up with her primary phrase, which Grandfather Mistry had taught her back in the 1880s, when Victoria was the Queen-Empress over India.

Perveen winced at the bright daylight streaming in through the long white muslin curtains. Knowing there could be no further rest, she pulled the mosquito nets out from her bed and went barefoot onto the balcony. She opened the cage so Lillian could hop onto her shoulder, and the bird greeted her, then walked down her arm and onto the balcony railing.

Perveen watched Lillian launch into a short flight over the garden. She was met with an outpouring of protest from the wild parakeets and koels that lived in the garden and saw her as an interloper.

Lillian was too old to be easily intimidated, so she settled in one tree and screamed back at them. It was a daily disagreement that never moved to the point of danger.

Perveen relaxed, gazing into the clear early morning sky. There were no sounds of cars or hawkers yet. Most people in the colony either worked or went to school through Saturday, but Sunday was a day of rest. Today, the Prince of Wales would worship at St. Thomas Cathedral. She considered whether it was likely that Woodburn College's chaplain, Reverend Sullivan, would join the royal service. Surely Colin would be there. She assumed Colin belonged to the Church of England, although she'd never talked about spiritual matters with him. It could be an interesting conversation.

With a light tap on the door, Gita arrived bearing what everyone called "bed tea": a perfect steaming sweet-and-milky cup of Darjeeling, along with a simple biscuit on the saucer. Perveen's bed tea always arrived in her favorite Minton cup, along with a humble tin saucer of cut-up fruit meant for Lillian. The pattern was called Indian Tree, a design inspired by India, made in Staffordshire, and then returned to Bombay. And as

Perveen walked out to the balcony, her cup of tea in one hand and Lillian's saucer in the other, she pondered whether Freny had avoided drinking tea at Mistry House because the cup was British bone china.

Lillian swooped down with pleasure to her breakfast, and Perveen directed her attention to Gita. She was just a year younger than Perveen, which kept the relationship between them refreshingly informal.

"I know what good care you take of our home," Perveen said, biting into one of John's perfect nankhatai biscuits. "It must have been a frightening time, though."

"No," Gita said with a shrug. "So many police around — it was their worry, not mine. A sergeant even gifted lathis to male householders and servants."

"It sounds like the colony received special treatment from the police."

"As they should. There is no wall here, or gate that can be locked. That help was needed."

"Good morning! How lucky you are up already," said Camellia, who came out to the balcony dressed in a light cotton sleeping sari.

Perveen was surprised to see her mother awake at this hour. "And a good morning to you."

"I'm sorry to say that you've already got a visitor downstairs."

"Who?" Perveen ran a hand through her sleep-messed hair. "It's barely seven-thirty!"

"John says it's a British gentleman wishing to see both you and your father. Pappa is getting ready now, and my goodness, he is peeved about it. The English always are wanting to do business in the morning, but on a Sunday?" She put a hand to her brow.

"Mistry-sahib cannot leave his room without having bed tea. I shall bring it to him. And that gives me a chance to go downstairs and see this man." With the air of a soldier called to action, Gita departed.

"Do you know if our visitor is with the police?"

"If so, he isn't in uniform. John said he is a well-dressed Englishman, not too old, and I don't remember the surname exactly, but it was something like . . . what was it? Sanderson?"

Perveen choked and coughed as she sought to expel tea from her airway.

Camellia rushed toward her and clapped her on the back. Reassured Perveen was fine, she returned to the inquisition. "It seems you are familiar with Mr. Sanderson?"

"Not Sanderson — it must be Sandringham. Mr. Sandringham is a political agent in employ of the Kolhapur Agency, an arm of the Indian Civil Service that deals expressly with the management of princely states in western India —"

Camellia cut her off. "I know of the Kolhapur Agency. Why has this man come to us?"

"We recently had a chance meeting," Perveen said. "He is traveling with the Prince of Wales because they were at Oxford together. I happened to see Mr. Sandringham, who assisted me when I was in Satapur, when I was checking in at the Taj."

"My goodness. Maybe Mr. Sandringham has brought a special invitation to you and Pappa from the prince." Her eyes widened. "This is quite surprising. I do think that John needs to serve more than nankhatai to someone so — influential."

Perveen was relieved that her mother had not focused on the personal connection. She hurried to her almirah, looking through the stacks of fresh saris Gita had folded perfectly for her. It would take at least fifteen minutes to get dressed, even with her mother or Gita helping her. She felt bothered that Colin had come to her home after she'd explained so clearly the boundaries for maintaining her reputation. Had he gone mad and

decided this was the only way to say goodbye?

20
THE PRINCE'S EAR

A quarter of an hour turned out to be enough time for a standing bucket bath and for Gita to help her dress. Perveen chose a cherry-red silk sari with a green-and-yellow geometric border, and a white blouse with cuffs of Alencon lace. The combination suited her but was not glamorous enough to cause anyone to think she was trying to look fetching. She told Gita to coil her hair in a French twist. Even though the artistry would be covered by the sari's pallu, it made her feel more assured.

When Perveen reached the foot of the stairs, John appeared from the kitchen. Drying his hands on his apron, he said, "The Angrez is on the garden veranda, as your father wished. I have already brought out the tea. And I am making banana fritters."

Perveen reassured him he didn't need to rush and went through the house to the rear veranda. Perveen could understand why

John placed Colin there; the veranda had lovely views yet was enclosed against public sight by a high bougainvillea hedge.

But to get to the veranda, Colin would have traversed the marble hallway, passing through the heart of the home: large rooms appointed with lavish ebony, rosewood, and mahogany furniture, solemn family portraits in gilded frames, endless shiny bits of porcelain and carved jade, and a grand piano from Germany. She hoped the Western possessions wouldn't cause him to believe they had Western values.

The French doors were open and Perveen went through. Colin sat straight-backed on a small rattan settee, watching a gray monkey lope across the grass. He wore a light khaki suit with a white shirt — *ironed,* she noted with relief — and a black-and-gold Brasenose College tie.

"Good morning," Perveen said, sitting down. "This is a surprise."

"I brought a letter for you to the hotel, but the front desk clerk said your family had left." Shaking his head, he added, "What a nosy man. It's probably better that you'd cleared out."

"I'm sorry I didn't say a proper goodbye. I learned at the last minute that we were coming home, and my father wanted to drive before darkness fell." Perveen sat down across from him, noting the steamy-hot teapot and three empty cups. "Could I give you a cup?"

"If it's not too much trouble."

"We drink Darjeeling here." As Perveen poured, she began doubting her action. Pouring their guest tea before her father's arrival could make Jamshedji think the two of them were enjoying an intimate moment. However, it was good they had a few moments alone — she could prepare Colin, and quell her own secret excitement at seeing him one more time. Stirring in the milk, she said, "My father is getting ready to come down. I've spoken with my mother already, and she will speak to him. I explained to her that I know you from working in Satapur, and that you are in Bombay to be part of the royal entourage because of a past friendship with the prince. I told him something like that after he saw us talking outside the Taj on Friday morning."

Colin sucked in his breath. "He saw us?"

She nodded glumly.

"I'm only here because something worrisome has developed. It pertains to the security of your law practice."

A chill ran through her. "Did you hear there was an attack on Mistry House?"

"No. It's rather different." Looking over his shoulder, he said, "Should I wait until your father joins us?"

Maybe it was better that she heard about this first. Perhaps someone in the government decided she'd overstepped rules for women by speaking at the coroner's court. "Tell me what has happened — I can't stand to wait for it."

"All right, then." Colin lowered his voice. "As you know, we spent yesterday in Poona. The Prince of Wales dedicated some new buildings, reviewed troops, and attended the races. I was present for the dedications but passed up the horse races to proceed a few hours early to the Kirkee railway station. I was sitting inside the stationmaster's office — the space was offered as a courtesy to the few of us who were there early from the prince's party. I was grateful to have a proper desk and chair, because it gave me time to catch up on a map I'm drawing."

"Why Kirkee?" Perveen asked. "Poona Station is closer to where the prince was. And Kirkee Station is so small."

"Fewer passengers at Kirkee Station made for greater security around the royal train." Leaning forward, he said, "It was inside the station that I heard about the plot."

"What plot?" Perveen was beside herself

with concern.

"They think it's a plot — the railway officers," Colin said. "A railway worker discovered five fishplates were missing on the line of track a half mile from Kirkee Station. Fishplates are oval metal pieces that connect sections of a wooden track together."

Perveen cut him off. "I know that. So the railway people would naturally be worried the track wasn't safe for trains to travel."

"The railway police believe it was deliberate tampering because all the fishplates had vanished. And it was most likely a plan for derailment of the royal train, because ordinary passenger trains had been canceled for the day as a precaution." Colin looked down at his half-filled cup of tea, and then back at Perveen. "The prince has a military security attaché — Mortimer is his name. He generally stays close to Edward and didn't reach the station until after the races. I talked to Eddie on the train going up and apparently he decided to walk straight into the crowds at the racetrack to make unofficial greetings."

"Walking into the crowds was your suggestion?" Perveen was as stunned by this as Colin's casual use of the prince's first name.

Colin shrugged. "Not exactly. I brought up the idea of meeting people outside of the elite, but I never suggested that Eddie should go loose at the racetrack. Mr. Mortimer went with him, and was wound tighter than a clock when he arrived at the station. Mortimer had learned about nationalist paraphernalia being recovered along the rail lines about ten miles from Bombay's southeast border, and he shouted at the stationmaster about why the rails hadn't been checked before the royal train arrived."

"This is exciting gossip, but what does it have to do with Mistry Law?" Perveen worried there would be no plausible excuse for Colin's visit.

Looking intently at her, he said, "Along with the nationalist paraphernalia I mentioned, a satchel containing school materials and your business card was recovered."

She sat bolt upright. "What did the bag look like?"

"The railway police described it to Mr. Mortimer as a brown drill-cloth bag, and they believe from the name written into some book covers it belonged to Freny Cuttingmaster. Mr. Mortimer seemed almost electrified by this revelation. He ordered the bag to be brought to police headquarters in Bombay for him to inspect when he returned."

"This was the schoolbag that Freny

brought to college the day she died. There is no risk to the law firm that I can see, but it is possible evidence for the pending homicide investigation. Let's hope that the scene is fully inspected and photographs taken before Mortimer gets his hands on it."

"The bag should be in possession of city police, not the prince's retinue."

Perveen turned at the sound of her father's stern voice. He had joined them, not in a formal suit, but in his home clothes: a crisp white undershirt known as a sudreh and soft white pajama pants. Perveen guessed the intention was to communicate to their visitor that Jamshedji was a private citizen at leisure in his own home. It was an interesting move; Perveen wondered if in some small way, he was making a political statement.

Peeping out from behind Jamshedji was Gulnaz, dressed in a pink chiffon sari with Chinese embroidery of dragons and orchids. The elegant sari reminded Perveen that her sister-in-law's plan was to accompany Rustom to the Orient Club later in the day. But here she was, already dressed to the nines and beaming at Colin. "Hello, Mr. Sandringham! I don't suppose you recall our meeting in Poona?"

Colin stood and bowed. "Of course, Mrs. Mistry. You are Perveen's dearest childhood friend and sister-in-law. And you were quite helpful to the maharani."

"I was grateful you introduced me. And things are going well with her reign, aren't they?"

"Quite well. She's building three schools." Turning to Jamshedji, he put out his hand. "Sir, thank you for receiving me. I came at this early hour because of the Prince of Wales's schedule; however I wished to deliver some urgent information."

Jamshedji's face relaxed and he shook Colin's hand. What Gulnaz and Colin had said must have convinced him that Perveen had been truthful about their professional relationship. Still, it bothered Perveen that her father had doubted her.

"My goodness." Gulnaz clapped her hands together. "You are with the Prince of Wales!"

Jamshedji released Colin's hand but kept a firm gaze on him. "You spoke with my daughter a few days ago at the hotel. Are you here because you know something about the Cuttingmaster affair?"

"An affair?" Gulnaz repeated, sounding mischievous.

"Gulnaz," Perveen said, "I apologize, but there's a chance this conversation will be turning to legal business."

Sighing dramatically, Gulnaz said, "Never mind, I was only on my way to speak to John about tonight's menu. Will I see you at the Orient Club luncheon later today, Mr. Sandringham?"

Colin's eyes lit up at her words. "Yes, indeed. That will be the high point of my day. I will have long hours ahead in too many places: the Seaman's Institute, the Royal Bombay Yacht Club, and the St. Thomas Cathedral."

"But that is quite good. You will see many of Bombay's most beautiful buildings," Jamshedji said.

"Surely some of them were built by Mistry ancestors?"

"Actually — yes." Jamshedji smiled, and Perveen was glad that Colin had subtly found a way to show he'd heard of the family. "Any of those building managers could tell you."

When Gulnaz had departed, Perveen poured her father's cup of tea, adding milk and sugar as she knew he preferred. After he'd had a sip, he spoke to Perveen.

"I heard you referring to the Cuttingmaster bag. I can't imagine what Mr. Sandringham needs to know about it. As I said, it's a Bombay Police matter." His tone held faint reproof.

"Mr. Sandringham has not come to solicit information. He is giving a warning."

"Oh?" Jamshedji looked skeptically at Colin.

Colin leaned across the table toward Jamshedji. "I will tell you everything, Mr. Mistry, if you can give me ten minutes."

Jamshedji looked at his watch. "Very well. But my schedule is also busy today."

Quickly, Colin laid out the story of the damaged fishplates and Freny's schoolbag with the Mistry card inside. After he finished, Jamshedji waved a dismissive hand. "So she had our business card; we are her family's lawyer."

"Actually . . ." Perveen hesitated. "I never told anyone except the Cuttingmasters and Alice Hobson-Jones that Freny consulted me *before* her death. Now the investigators are bound to be curious."

"Mr. Mortimer described Freny as a female terrorist," Colin said. "I don't know what evidence he has to make such a statement. But a lawyer's card in her bag raised all kinds of chatter. Was she or someone close to her involved in sabotaging the rails?"

Perveen shook her head. "Freny died on Thursday, and the railway sabotage was found two days later. There is no way she could be blamed for it. And I'd go further and suggest someone might have dropped the bag intentionally. The person who killed her made all kinds of silly attempts at a suicide scene. The satchel's placement could be the work of the same actor."

"Those are good points," Colin said. "But they are not interested in Freny's murder. They're interested in any danger to the prince."

Perveen looked at her father. "If the government suspects I know a terrorist plotter, can they use special powers to demand I answer questions?"

"They could try." Jamshedji cast a sidelong look at Perveen. "We'll talk more about it later."

"I'm not reporting back to anyone," Colin said. "I came because I wanted to protect Per — both of you. But I do have one point to raise."

"You have already raised many points." Jamshedji's voice was dry. "What could be left?"

His face flushed, Colin spoke quickly. "What if, during the last few days or weeks of her life, Freny uncovered someone else's plan to cause the prince's death?" He paused to take a breath. "What if the late

Miss Cuttingmaster knew that someone connected to Woodburn College was planning to cause a train derailment? That person could have killed her — and then when fleeing Bombay, got rid of her bag along the way."

Jamshedji looked pensive. "Interesting, but why would he carry her bag out of the college? Leave evidence — don't keep it with you."

"Perhaps the bag was also used to hold whatever tools were needed to attack the fishplates," Perveen thought out loud. "Let's say the man who killed Freny still had to complete the mission of rail tampering. He threw away the bag containing the tools and everything else when he was finished. The reason the tools aren't still in the bag is because the vagrants who scavenge along train tracks day and night found them before the police did."

"It is quite a supposition. If we were to say such a thing to the police, they'd laugh at us. However, I see Mr. Sandringham's point about the business card leading police to our firm. We must prepare a strong front."

"We can't reveal we know about it. Mr. Sandringham came with confidential information. I don't want to expose him." She shot a glance at Colin, whose jaw had tensed.

"Certainly, we will not be chatting about this visit," Jamshedji said. "I had in mind that you and I would simply show our faces."

"I don't understand what you mean." Perveen looked quizzically at her father.

"I will forego my bridge game today and attend the Orient Club luncheon for the prince. And you will be with me." Taking his fingers to the outer edges of his mouth, he pulled them up. "And both our faces will be smiling. No fear. No hiding."

Perveen winced at the idea of pasting on smiles at an event celebrating colonial rule. "How can we? Reservations closed out long ago, Gulnaz told me."

"True. We know that Rustom and Gulnaz have their tickets in hand. I'm sure they won't mind giving up their seats at the luncheon for a good reason."

"I helped Gulnaz choose her sari yesterday evening. She'll hate to miss seeing her friends at this function." Perveen also expected Rustom would be disappointed, as he was the family's biggest supporter of the prince.

"Family makes sacrifices for each other." Jamshedji's stern gaze reminded her of all that had been done for her. "And today, it's important that we be seen as supporters of the Prince of Wales."

"Ah!" Perveen said. "Your hope is that somebody important in the government will notice us there."

"Finally, you understand." Sighing, Jamshedji turned from her to Colin. "Mr. Sandringham, if we notice each other at the luncheon, it would be wise not to demonstrate acquaintance. I wouldn't want you to have to explain how you and I met."

"I understand. But if there's any trouble that comes your way, please let me know. I don't mean to boast, but I do have the prince's ear."

Perveen wondered how Prince Edward was coping with the knowledge that his visit had caused so much civil unrest. "Did you tell His Royal Highness about the fishplates being damaged?"

"No. Mr. Mortimer told everyone to keep quiet about it, as it's better to have a smiling, relaxed prince than one who is filled with apprehension." Colin drained the last of his tea and stood up a bit awkwardly, as the rattan settee was low and he was quite tall. From inside the house, there was a clatter of pans, a smell of onions and ginger, and John's singing.

"Have you had breakfast, Mr. Sandringham?" Jamshedji asked abruptly.

Perveen stared hard at Colin, who had started to smile. She willed him not to accept. This type of socialization was a step too far. She imagined the questions that might come at a family breakfast, and how Colin's natural openness could cause trouble for her later.

Having glanced at her, the brightness in Colin's eyes faded. In a stiff voice, he said, "Those banana fritters were more than enough. And I'd better get on because of the visit to the Seaman's Institute. Thank you very much, though."

As Colin left the house, Perveen watched from the window. He was taking his time, looking all around before continuing down the road.

"For such a fit-looking man, he limps," Jamshedji said from behind her. "That is curious."

"Mr. Sandringham lost his foot after a poisonous snake bite a few years ago. He intervened when a child was being attacked."

"A good deed — yet he won't eat in an Indian house. Typical of those ICS types, who can't take spices and think they'll fall sick from anything more than a plate of white rice."

Perveen knew that Colin hadn't stayed because he'd read the message in her gaze. But it was better not to remind Jamshedji that their visitor had finished all the banana fritters. She'd allow her father to believe that Colin was prejudiced as long as it kept her relationship with him undiscovered.

Would Freny have thought this dishonest? Probably. But Freny had also refrained from discussing her beliefs with her father.

Perhaps all daughters did.

21
A SURPRISE INTERROGATION

"Is it a Bombay social club or Westminster Abbey?" Perveen whispered to her father.

It was just after one, and they were seated in the Orient Club at a round table surrounded by cane chairs. A red carpet divided the room, running all the way up to an elevated head table for the prince and his men.

Perveen's father didn't answer. He was looking intently at the food that had been served, but that etiquette demanded should not be touched. A footed crystal bowl of tomato aspic sat in front of each of the diners. Tomato aspic was not an Oriental food, as far as Perveen was concerned, but it was the first course of the luncheon.

So many glamorous people filled the room. Perveen's eyes had gone straight to the city's most famous barrister, Mohammed Ali Jinnah, along with his young wife, whom Perveen knew slightly. Rattanbai

Petit, known by everyone as Ruttie, was born a Parsi, the daughter of the powerful and wealthy Sir Dinshah Petit. She had converted to Islam and accepted the new name of Maryam to be in accordance with her husband, Mr. Jinnah, in a forbidden union that she had pursued against her family's wishes. It seemed that the cross-religious marriage had made her more daring: Ruttie's hair was now cut into a modish shingle, and she wore a grape-colored sari draped over a European frock. Perveen and Ruttie had played at birthday parties as children and chatted at functions as they grew older. But this time, Perveen felt too agitated for small talk, so she merely responded to Ruttie's recognizing smile with the same.

This was the first time Perveen had entered the club. She'd heard it was founded by Indians in 1905 with the intent of fostering interchange among all races. This club was an alternative to places like the Bombay Gymkhana and the Royal Bombay Yacht Club, which kept membership white-only. Along with the Willingdon Club, which was also inclusive, it occupied a very rare place in the city. She could see why Rustom had gone through the hoopla of joining it.

At precisely ten minutes after the hour, a

rat-tat-tat of military drums announced the guest of honor. Following a drumroll, the dignitaries entered the dining room. As she joined everyone in standing, Perveen was surprised to see that the prince striding up the carpet was much smaller than the men around him. He could not be much taller than five feet, seven inches, but he had a trim sportsman's figure and looked well in his impeccably cut cream-colored suit. He wore no hat, and his blond hair shone with pomade.

Eyes were the window to the soul, so she tried her best to see the prince's face, but he wasn't looking at the assembled guests. His unsmiling attention was focused straight ahead at the table where the Earl of Cromer and the club's president, Lord Jamsetjee Jeejeebhoy II, awaited.

Prince Edward took his seat at a high-backed velvet chair that Perveen guessed had a big cushion on the seat, because here he appeared almost as tall as the men sitting around him. Colin, whom she knew to be six feet tall, was a few places away at the table; men in military and police dress sat closer, including a sharp-eyed man with red hair who looked familiar. Perveen scrutinized him and wondered if he might be the man she'd seen wearing plainclothes and a bowler hat.

"Look! The Nawab of Palanpur," Jamshedji murmured, referring to the only Indian besides Lord Jeejeebhoy at the table. The nawab's turban was draped with diamonds, and Perveen would have loved a closer look at the jewelry work, for Gulnaz's sake, but there was a fine line between being seen and causing a scene.

Conversation ceased when Sir Jamsetjee rose from his place at the head table to greet everyone and start the toasts. After everyone had drunk to continued good health and well-being to the absent King-Emperor, Sir J. J. proposed a toast to the prince.

Perveen didn't say the words, although she raised her glass so she would not stand out. She told herself she was showing equal respect to the Parsi knight, who was the son of the first Sir Jamsetjee, who had founded the city's first decent hospital and medical college, the place where she'd spent so much time in the last few days. Bombay would not be as advanced without the Jeejeebhoy family — although their fortune was initially made by the patriarch's opium business, a substance that she considered a menace to all people.

The speech Sir J. J. gave welcoming the prince was a happy one. Perveen wondered if he might address the prospect of more freedom for India — after all, Sir J. J. had donated to the Congress Party — but he did not. In turn, the prince spoke about the loveliness of Bombay and the warmth of her people. He did not mention the rioting and destruction.

Perveen noted that there were few policemen in the room; just two by the door. It was reassuring not to have soldiers on the premises. The choice not to have them must have been a reflection that the terrible dangers of the past days were over.

After the toasting was done, it was time to tackle the food in front of her. She would start with the dreadful aspic.

"Don't you like the food, Miss Mistry?" inquired Mr. Hamza Shahid, a businessman who was also an orphanage founder. He probably looked askance upon the wasting of food.

"It's unique," Perveen fibbed, taking a spoonful of the slippery stuff. Examining it, she thought it was the color of congealed blood.

"Of course she is not hungry. She has been doing sad work representing the family of a young lady who perished in the recent violence," said a woman across the table. She had been introduced as Mrs.

343

Nayati Basu, the wife of Arvind Basu, the owner of several commercial buildings on Elphinstone Road.

Perveen had expected the people at their table would have known Rustom and Gulnaz. But at this table, only the Basus were their friends. Mr. Shahid explained that there had been so many luncheon cancellations that the club had reorganized seating for fewer tables, all of them filled.

There was only one Englishman at the table: Mr. Josiah Hawthorn. And he was with them because Perveen had spotted his place card on a neighboring table and moved it. She didn't know how much she would learn from him, but she felt she couldn't miss the opportunity. Her father had been speaking to someone else when she'd made the switch. Later, as introductions were made around the table, Jamshedji had looked startled, but recovered himself with a polite social smile.

Because Jamshedji did not have suits or shirts made at his shop, the two men were not acquainted. But Perveen remembered Jamshedji had said that Rustom bought shirts at the shop, so she introduced herself as his sister.

Mr. Hawthorn, a pallid man in his sixties with thinning gray hair, nodded with recognition. "Not only do I know your brother, but my head tailor showed me your business card. Firdosh was trying to decide whether to seek legal assistance last Friday, and I urged him to go straight away. I said, the work today can wait."

"That was good of you," Perveen said, remembering Firdosh's anxiety about being away from the shop.

"To think that someone would hurt that precious child." Mr. Hawthorn pushed listlessly at the potatoes on his plate. "She visited us sometimes after school, and all were fond of her, and so pleased when she started at Woodburn College."

"I knew her for a short time and also was impressed." Perveen sensed that the man was open to conversation, so she decided to push a little bit. "Does Khushru Kapadia, her neighbor and college classmate, work for you?"

Mr. Hawthorn nodded. "It is not a formal arrangement, but Khushru does assist. There was some trouble that day — he was unable to prevent the looting of the shop."

"So much trouble everywhere!" interjected Arvind Basu. "Some of our properties had smashed windows and such."

"The criminals must have started early, because Khushru said when he arrived, the damage had already been done." Mr. Hawthorn looked sadly at Jamshedji. "I wish I could have the perpetrators arrested, but I have no clue as to their identity."

Perveen flinched at the memory of the rough men, their breath on her face and their hands on her sari. Striving to sound normal, she asked, "What was the extent of the damage?"

"Firstly, the hooligans broke windows and the lock on the front door," Mr. Hawthorn said. "Then they stole the suits and threw the bolts of cloth they didn't take into disarray. They also took scissors, which might seem petty, but scissors are an expensive commodity. Not having tools is delaying our ability to resume work. There was quite an important gentleman from out of town needing alterations on an imperial uniform, and we had to send a boy to buy scissors before we could help him. Can you imagine — a haberdashery with no scissors?"

"Do you think the thieves brought the stolen suits to the bonfire?" asked Mrs. Basu.

"If they did, it will surely make me weep. The work that my tailors put into those clothes. I even grieve for the weavers of the woolens." Mr. Hawthorn looked morosely at the diners at the table, who all murmured or shook their heads in shared sympathy.

Perveen wondered if the men she'd seen smashing the shop window in the early afternoon had been the same people who'd stolen the suits. Twelve o'clock was too late to show up at the bonfire. The rioting had started after people left the bonfire and met with people departing the parade.

Should she tell him?

Looking at Jamshedji sitting so close to her, she decided against it, for the same reason she hadn't told her father earlier. She said to the haberdasher, "I am so very sorry about it. I believe the attacks on foreign textiles are intended to protest taxes Indians are being made to pay."

"Aren't they mad? As a Bombay citizen, I pay the same government taxes." He raised his hands in an expression of disbelief. "And the clothes we sew aren't sinful! All of the gentlemen in this room, excepting a few nawabs, are wearing European suits. How can Indians rise in business and civic life without tailors who can stitch them proper clothing?"

Perveen had no retort for this, and she did not want trouble at the table. So she merely nodded and felt grateful for her father's sudden return to the conversation.

"Mr. Hawthorn, you are part and parcel

of the city, no matter your origins. We are all Bombay." At Jamshedji's declaration, the table's occupants smiled. "We can reassure ourselves that rooms like this exist to bring Indians and Europeans together. We make friendships that do not rise and fall with political opinions."

"Frankly, Mr. Mistry, we are here meeting together — different faces and races — because we can afford the club membership and monthly dining charges," Mr. Shahid said soberly. "We have a special advantage."

"Yes." Mr. Hawthorn nodded at him. "The reason the freedom movement was nonviolent in past years was the decisions were being made by men like us who were literate and considerate of legal procedures. When one encourages the uneducated to join in, they will not make change in a civil fashion. Those types only want to fight."

Mr. Hawthorn had ignored the self-critical message within Mr. Shahid's words, and in response, the philanthropist shook his head. As if to break the awkward moment, Jamshedji proposed a toast to continued peace.

After all of the table finished their goblets of champagne or guava juice, Jamshedji said, "This is a most cordial gathering, but I spy a past client across the room. I beg your pardon while Perveen and I go to pay our respects."

"Enjoy yourselves. But you must return before pudding is served!" Mrs. Basu advised. "Blancmange!"

"What is this about?" Perveen asked when they were away from the table.

"We are making a small, friendly promenade. There are the ones who must see us." He inclined his head toward a cluster of gentlemen who had also left their tables and were smoking in a corner.

"Isn't the tall gentleman with the heavy mustache the commissioner of Bombay Police?" Perveen asked him.

"Yes, it makes sense that Mr. Fisher accompanied the prince to this luncheon. Let's go forward to say hello. Then I'll introduce you, and you can make a few friendly remarks before we leave."

Perveen and her father threaded their way through the tables, smiling and saying hello to those they recognized. By the time they reached the group of officials, Perveen felt a surge of nerves. She did not like the set of Mr. Fisher's face — it looked tense and unwelcoming. And one of the men who'd had his back toward them turned around, and she recognized him as the man she'd seen at the head table. who had badgered her at Woodburn College: Mr. Mortimer, the

349

prince's intelligence officer.

Perveen nodded in greeting, and after Mr. Fisher had greeted her father.

Colin had spoken of Mr. Mortimer's being involved with the prince at the race track in Poona, but she would not divulge that. From the tension in her father's posture, she could tell he remembered this fact as well.

"Good afternoon, Mr. Fisher," Jamshedji said at last. "Isn't it a delightful luncheon?"

"Very nice." The commissioner did not make any effort to divert his cigar, which was blowing straight into their faces. To his companions, he said, "Mistry is a solicitor with a solo practice on Bruce Street."

"Actually, I'm planning to alter the practice name to Mistry and Mistry." Jamshedji smiled briefly at Perveen. "My daughter Perveen is also a solicitor. She has closed more than a hundred cases in the year she's worked with me, and I am thinking of making her partner."

This was the first Perveen had heard of becoming partner, and the moment would have been joyous if she hadn't felt the chilly gaze of Mr. Mortimer upon her.

"Congratulations, Miss Mistry," said the commissioner. "My men said you spoke in the coroner's court yesterday."

"Yes, I did some work advocating for a family."

Mr. Fisher's eyebrows went up. "I did not know women lawyers were permitted to speak in the court. Isn't there a prohibition on the books?"

Perveen's heart fluttered at the challenge. "The only court that has made a stand about discriminating against women lawyers is the Bombay High Court."

Instead of responding to this, Commissioner Fisher looked searchingly at her father. "Mr. Mistry, is your involvement with the Cuttingmasters continuing?"

Jamshedji shrugged. "One never knows. But the family is satisfied with the coroner's verdict. And we are most grateful to the coroner for being willing to hold the inquisition in a timely manner, so funeral rites could go forward."

"Do you know where your daughter was on Friday?" Mortimer asked Jamshedji.

Perveen bristled because he had no reason not to ask her directly.

"Friday?" Scratching his chin, Jamshedji said, "We had breakfast at the Taj dining room, and after that, arrived together at our chambers after ten-thirty, and went out to the coroner's court around eleven. After that we had various appointments — why do you ask?"

"You were at the court on Saturday, not Friday, sir," Mortimer said sharply. "I saw you."

"We also went on Friday to ascertain when the inquest might be held." Jamshedji's answer was crisp.

"There would not be a formal record of your appearance, then, would there?" Mortimer looked at Fisher. "How does this court operate? Is there a record taken of visitors?"

"No. There aren't records of persons without particular business inside the court." With narrowed eyes, the commissioner studied Perveen and her father.

Perveen glanced at her father, who was looking unsettled, and then thought of something to say. "While I was there on Friday, I had a conversation with a clerk, and I spoke with a student named Miss Lalita Acharya just after you saw her, Mr. Mortimer."

Mortimer flinched, and the commissioner looked directly at him. "Why were you involved?"

"I'm not," he retorted. "I am with the prince always. This woman is mistaken."

Perveen's already quickened heart was now pounding. She could have made a mistake, but Lalita's description had caused her to assume it was him. If Mr. Mortimer was lying, Perveen wondered if he wasn't supposed to have been there.

"Let's return to your afternoon movements," Mortimer said to Perveen.

"On what grounds is this a matter of interest?" Jamshedji asked.

"Nobody is impugning your character," Commissioner Fisher said. "But Mr. Mortimer here protects the prince, and it is in the interest of the safety of our future monarch that your daughter answers him."

So Perveen was under suspicion, not her father. Perhaps it was because she'd been spotted at independence discussions, where you never knew who might be a police informant.

Or, as Colin had said, because her name was on a business card in the recovered satchel belonging to a student who'd been labeled a terrorist.

Perveen looked to her father, whose expression was tense. He nodded. "You have nothing to hide."

"Directly after the court, I went in our car to see our client Mithan Cuttingmaster at her home in Vakil Colony."

"And you were with her also?" Mr. Mortimer looked at Jamshedji.

"No. I had business with another client close to the hospital."

Mortimer asked, "And how many hours until the two of you were together again?"

Was Mortimer exploring whether she had opportunity to travel to Kirkee and back?

"Two," Jamshedji said. "We met at the office and then retired to the Taj Hotel."

"Why do you live in a hotel?"

Before Jamshedji could answer, Perveen spoke up. "Mr. Mortimer, we live quite a distance from our office, in Dadar Parsi Colony. Because our colony is a half hour north of central Bombay, we chose to stay in a hotel for safety. We didn't return home until yesterday evening."

The commissioner was looking uncomfortable, and Perveen was thoroughly soaked in sweat. It had become clear that she and her father were persons of interest to Mr. Mortimer, even though he had no grounds to suspect them of any danger to the prince. She and her father needed protection. The conversation should not continue without a lawyer's presence, she realized. But she didn't want to say that. "Dessert is being served. I would not wish any of us to miss the Orient Club's famous blancmange."

"Good day, gentlemen." Jamshedji put a hand on Perveen's elbow and continued in a circular route around the room's tables. In an undertone, he said to her, "I cannot believe what transpired. You should have alerted me to that man before we approached. Why is he your enemy?"

Perveen felt helpless with frustration. "How could I have identified him to you when his back was turned? He was present at the scene of Freny's death and ordered me to leave. And he's the one who was on the scene in Kirkee when Freny's satchel was discovered."

As they walked, they came parallel to the head table, and she could not help but cast a glance toward the end with the men in uniform. To her surprise, Colin's chair was empty. As she scanned the line, she saw him sitting next to the Prince of Wales.

Very likely Colin had shifted seats because Mr. Mortimer had temporarily left the head table to talk with the commissioner. She studied Colin and the prince, who had their heads close together, as if sharing a confidence they didn't want others to hear. She remembered how Colin had spoken casually of Eddie and knew it might be a true friendship.

She had not realized that she had stopped until her father touched her arm. "Come. This is not a viewing stand."

But Colin had seen her. He was looking at her, and as if catching the shift in attention, the Prince of Wales was peering out in the crowd, looking all around to see who had caught Colin's eye.

Perveen was not the only Indian woman in the room — at least twenty percent of the tables were taken by ladies — but she was the only one standing. And she caught the prince's gaze, seeing him look her up and down.

Surely Colin hadn't said they were friends. Or was it that Mortimer had pointed her out earlier as a woman of suspicion? The prince's eyes were appraising — rude, she would have thought, but in context, she realized that he might feel she was somehow notorious.

When they returned to the table, Jamshedji pulled out Perveen's chair with a flourish.

"Just a minute, madam."

The club's maître d' was standing stiffly with two waiters posted behind him.

"Yes, I do want dessert, thank you," she said, noting the courses had changed.

"I cannot bring you pudding, madam. I have learned the two of you took seats reserved for other guests: Mr. and Mrs. Rustom Mistry."

Perveen flinched. It was embarrassing to be singled out in front of the table like this. But the place cards did have Rustom and Gulnaz's names on them.

Jamshedji opened his mouth, and it was clear from the gleam in his eyes he was ready to read out the intrusive maître d'.

Before her father could started spewing, Mr. Basu spoke up in an authoritative tone.

"Let me explain, please. This gentleman and lady are Mr. Rustom Mistry's father and sister. I can vouch for them."

"Mr. Basu, this was a reservation-only, ticketed meal. Just one hundred fifty seats available to see the prince." The haughty maître d turned to regard Jamshedji. "Only persons who are club members are entitled to enter the club whilst the prince is here."

"My son gave the tickets to us because he could not attend," Jamshedji said with a smile. "You see, his wife has been blessed with impending good fortune, and she was not feeling well enough today."

This was halfway true. Perveen noticed some people around the table had started to smile, but Mrs. Basu looked nervous. Sharing news of an impending baby was sometimes seen as risky.

"Sir, you are not a club member," the maître d repeated sternly.

"I am the member's father and his guest!" Jamshedji's eyes had narrowed, as if he was spoiling for a long argument.

The club's host shook his head. "I do not wish to cause offense to anyone, but for the prince's security, we are following strict regulations of only allowing ticketed luncheon guests who are members to be present."

"There was no ticket needed to enter," Jamshedji argued back.

Perveen turned her head to look where Mr. Fisher and Mr. Mortimer had stood. They were both seated at the head table in close proximity to the prince. The police superintendent was chatting with the man to his left, but Mr. Mortimer was staring straight at them. "Let's not cause a scene, Pappa. We should go home. After all, Gulnaz is in a delicate condition. I would rather check on her than get into an argument here."

From the moment the maître d' had started speaking, the others at the table had fallen silent. As Perveen turned to leave, she thought she heard Mr. Hawthorn say, "Sorry, Old Boy."

"This is mortifying!" Jamshedji hissed as the two of them crossed the room.

Only the guests at their table knew about

their removal, but Perveen imagined gossip would spread. And if Colin happened to see her being thrown out, he would be concerned. She prayed he'd have the good sense not to follow.

22
SUNDAY STROLLING

"The Orient Club's action toward us was outrageous and uncalled for! It could be the basis of a civil suit," Jamshedji huffed at her as they left the ballroom.

Perveen said what she had been thinking for the last few minutes. "Surely Mr. Mortimer caused our expulsion. He wields incredible power because he's responsible for the prince's security."

"But once he heard that you were the city's sole woman solicitor, he should have treated you with respect. And me as well."

"Let's kill all the lawyers, Shakespeare said." The brash voice behind her was familiar.

Perveen spun around to glare at J.P. Singer. "I didn't know you were eavesdropping. You'll get no comment from us."

He laughed, straight white teeth flashing against his tanned skin. "I only had the chance to join you because I was also thrown out. Tell me, where is your brother? I was looking forward to seeing him here today."

"He is home." Jamshedji tilted his head to look the tall American up and down. "You look familiar, but I can't place you."

"J.P. Singer, a foreign correspondent with the *San Francisco Chronicle,*" said the reporter, holding out a hand.

Jamshedji didn't take the hand, but pointed a finger at him. "You're the madman who fought an Englishman inside the Taj Hotel. I suppose you were up to the same tricks here?"

Perveen was surprised at her father's aggressive tone; he must have been carrying over the anger from his own humiliation.

"Sorry to disappoint." Singer gave him an easy smile. "I got kicked out! The maître d' accused me of violating rules when I approached the head table. They wanted all reporters to stay at a table in the back and just scribble down the pretty speeches. I had a different story in mind and hoped for a quote from the prince."

Almost imperceptibly, Jamshedji had moved closer to Singer. "I'm interested to hear the focus of your story."

Mr. Singer brushed back a wavy lock that had fallen across his forehead, revealing a handsome, rounded brow. "I am describing the prince's journey through India, emphasizing the reactions of Indians. I wanted to find out if he'd spoken with any Indian who wasn't royalty or a robber baron."

"That is — admirable," Jamshedji said, after a pause. "I sorely wish I had the chance to read such a story, but American newspapers are not sold in the newsstands."

"Yeah. After all, the British Empire would prefer to sell British papers, or papers printed in India with British editorial control. But I did bring some papers along with me. I'll give you one when we see each other again."

This was quite an assumption on the reporter's part, but Jamshedji was smiling and nodding. It worried Perveen to see how easily her father had been charmed. She asked, "Mr. Singer, I'm curious about the fight my father mentioned. How did it happen?"

In an instant, the easy smile on his face had been replaced by a hard expression. "The press liaison was telling me I couldn't go with the others to see the prince on his daily activities because I wasn't registered early enough or some such nonsense. It's discrimination, pure and simple. The English and Australian and Canadian reporters all have access. So I told him what I thought of that."

"You are quite a warrior." Perveen remembered the mixture of excitement and horror she'd felt at the confrontation she'd seen at the Taj.

Singer shrugged. "I suppose it's in my blood."

She thought of J.P. Singer's mysterious origins — the brown skin that led Daventry to call him "darkie" and the name that her father told her was Jewish. She resolved not to ask the man about his race and religion; all of that was his own personal business and had no bearing on how she should treat him.

"Tell me more about this discrimination." Jamshedji's voice was open and easy, as if he were interviewing a prospective client.

"There is a hierarchy amongst the press — one might call it a caste system," Singer added ruefully. "The newsmen coming from the Empire's various colonies and dominions take precedence. The rest of us come later. For instance, I could not get into the evening parties at Government House, but I did get a spot at this event, and my guess is because it was a lesser draw. The only silver lining to the exclusion from parties was that I was literally in the streets at the start of the unrest. I could report on it, though it was a dangerous few days. Your son was generous and offered me a ride to a police station when there were no taxis on Thursday evening."

"Ah, the truth comes out. Thanks to you, he was where he shouldn't have been!" Jamshedji shook his head.

Perveen was surprised how well her father was taking this revelation, and how casually J.P. Singer could say things about himself that most young Indian men would never share with an elder. "You know, Mr. Mistry, I offered to pay for the windshield and any other damage that night, but Rustom refused. In the spirit of international friendship, I hope you'll take this toward the damage." Reaching into the inner pocket of his jacket, J.P. Singer removed a wallet and slipped out a crisp note printed with green ink. "This is ten dollars. I hope that is enough."

Jamshedji waved it away. "No need for that. Our driver, Arman, already arranged the repair at a far smaller amount. And while the damage was unfortunate, window glass is easier to fix than broken bodies. More than fifty citizens have died in rioting and there are thousands in prison, waiting for trials that this government can purposely delay for months."

Singer had produced a notebook and was writing in a swift shorthand. "More than fifty have died . . . how do you know this? The police department has reported a lower number."

Jamshedji gave him a knowing look. "You cannot argue with the accuracy of a morgue logbook."

"Ah! And where are these morgues?"

"The biggest one is at Sir J. J. Hospital."

Singer swung his attention from Jamshedji back to Perveen. "Where we all were just yesterday. Now that your father knows me, why keep playing the no-comment game?"

"There's nothing more to say." But Perveen could not help smiling at Mr. Singer. He was both handsome and wild — a combination that she had always found irresistible.

Singer's eyes were glowing. "Mr. Mistry, you're helping me to make lemonade from lemons."

"And how is that?" Jamshedji asked.

"Just a few minutes ago, I was miffed to be thrown out of the club. That was the sour part of the day. Yet I ran into you both and now have a tip on how to get better numbers for my story. It's Sunday. Does that mean the morgue is closed?"

"No! It's operational seven days a week, and I saw many taxis today. You will easily find a ride." Perveen was determined not to let him request another ride from Arman, who had been glancing warily at him from their car during the conversation.

Singer returned his notebook to his jacket's inner pocket and grinned. "I'm on my way. Nobody's going to break this story before I do."

Jamshedji held out his card to him. "Before you leave Bombay, you must come to see us at home. Any friend of my son's is welcome for a meal. We usually eat at nine."

"Many thanks, sir. I'll trade you an American newspaper for a home-cooked Indian meal." Singer flashed Perveen a warm smile. She got the meaning. It was not just Rustom he wished to see again.

As the newsman disappeared toward a waiting taxi on the beach side of the road, Perveen said, "He is fiendishly skilled at charming people. First Rustom, now you!"

"The press is a necessary weapon in a lawyer's arsenal. When he visits us, you should watch how I speak to him. 'No comment' should not be an automatic answer," Jamshedji said in a lecturing voice. "He has made his admiration of you clear. For Singer to write a story that mentions our name could put us in the ranks of internationally respected lawyers."

"But nobody reads the *San Francisco Chronicle* in Bombay," she said shortly.

Jamshedji chuckled. "He is on your side, politically. I am surprised at your attitude."

She could not put into words why she felt uncomfortable with Mr. Singer. He had so many questions for everyone, and clearly was in favor of bringing light to India's struggle. Perhaps it was that he seemed to have made several inroads into their family. That, and the way he'd been so forward with her.

Just then a familiar dark blue car pulled up alongside them.

"Alice!" Perveen said with surprise. Her friend was in the front seat next to her driver, Sirjit, which was unusual. The back seat held two young Parsi men dressed in formal white suits.

"My father received a telegram. We're dropping it to him before going on to the college." As Alice elaborated on her father's busy schedule, Sirjit slipped out of the car, telegram in hand.

"I hope the club admits him," Perveen said, watching him head to the club's servant entrance.

"Of course, they will. But I hope it's not

over — is that why you're outside?"

"No," Jamshedji said. "We are leaving early. And I did spy your father at the head table."

"If you're finished, might Perveen come out with me for a little bit?" Alice asked.

"I have no objections — although I see your car is full." From the way he glanced at the two young men, it was clear he wouldn't approve of Perveen squeezing into the back seat with them.

"The boys are my students, Mr. Mistry. I saw them walking along Ridge Road — they'd been at memorial prayers at Doongerwadi. I'm dropping them at the college."

Perveen looked at the young men more closely and recognized the soft features of Khushru Kapadia, Freny's neighbor. The taller boy at his side was aiming his camera at the Orient Club. In an instant, she'd placed him, too: Naval Hotelwala, the student photographer.

"Hello," Perveen said, dismissing all thoughts of Mr. Singer. "It was a gracious act for you two to pray for Freny. I didn't know you were friends."

"Ever since our first day!" Naval said cheerfully. "Khushru wished to go to Doongerwadi to mourn, and I went with him. I'm worried about his mental state. He should not be alone."

Perveen took a second look at Khushru. He had seemed more vital on Friday, but that could have been because the reality of Freny's death hadn't fully sunk in. Now his face was slack, and he did not acknowledge her presence.

"I'm so glad that I saw them," Alice said. "Even though it's Sunday, they've decided to go to a mathematics study group. It will be good for them to have something else to think about, for at least an hour or two."

"Yes. The logical mind takes over and makes the emotions easier to bear," Jamshedji said.

Perveen nodded. After her marriage had broken up, she had thrown herself into legal studies. She had come away with a profession and a much stronger mindset. Perhaps she could console Khushru. Looking toward her father, she said, "I'd like to go with them."

"Can she, please? I'll drop Perveen home before dark," Alice entreated.

"It's a little crowded." Frowning, Jamshedji looked at the car's rear seat. There was no way around it — Perveen would have to sit with at least one side of her pressed against a young man, and that was unacceptable.

"Sir, do not worry about us!" Naval opened the door and jumped out, giving a slight bow. "We are so close to college that we will walk the rest of the way. Nothing is nicer than strolling on Sunday."

Perveen appreciated Naval's swift understanding of her father's unspoken anxiety. Nodding at him, she said, "If Alice and my father don't mind, we could all stroll together to the college instead of sitting in a car."

"Yes, you must have been sitting in deadly boredom inside that club," Alice said sympathetically. "Walking is a grand idea."

"I shall not stop anyone from a Sunday stroll. Enjoy yourselves!" Jamshedji waved as he headed to the Daimler.

Perveen and Alice exchanged a brief smile of success as Sirjit reappeared from the club, telling Alice that her father's telegram was delivered. Alice explained they would walk to the college.

Sirjit nodded. "Don't worry, madam. I will park in the usual spot. I'll see you when you are finished."

"May I carry the folios for you, ma'am?" Naval volunteered.

"Yes — but don't you dare look inside. I'm bringing in next week's quiz!" Alice said, handing over the tan folios.

This brought laughter from Naval, and a half smile from Khushru.

Alice strode along, swinging her arms in a carefree manner.

"I think you're a very dedicated professor to come in on a Sunday," Perveen said.

"I can hardly get anything done at home with Diana constantly demanding my lap." At the boys' confused expressions, Alice explained, "Diana is my new pet dog. I love her dearly, but she's more work than the lot of you put together."

"You are so kind, madam, to everyone. You should be named one of the permanent professors." Khushru had finally spoken, but his voice was hoarse.

"Yes," Naval enthused. "Miss Hobson-Jones, you are far sharper than Mr. Gupta. And he is an honors Bombay graduate."

Alice shot Perveen a significant look.

"What are you thinking, ma'am?" Naval asked.

"That the college one attends does not define intelligence or ability. Miss Mistry can vouchsafe that some very lazy students have graduated from Oxford." With a mischievous smile, she added, "One of the most itinerant is inside the Orient Club right now."

371

Naval hooted. "You are afraid of no one, Miss Hobson-Jones!"

"She is too funny by half," Perveen said. As they crossed the street, she asked, "Naval, what is your field of study?"

"I study commerce," said Naval. "I'll take my diploma next summer and join my father in our hotel business. Khushru will have a fourth year of study somewhere else, because he is reading mathematics."

Naval's habit of speaking for Khushru was slightly annoying. Perveen looked directly at the smaller student, whose pace was slower than hers, so he was slightly trailing. "Khushru, what will you do with your degree?"

"I used to want to pursue higher studies at University of Bombay." He was panting slightly, as if the walk was exhausting. "But I'm not sure anymore."

Naval threw up his hands. "You have nothing to worry about, my friend. Though you really should have done the accounting course or commerce, like me. Then you would never need to worry about money again."

"Is it really so easy?" Perveen prodded.

"My grandparents came with just a small bit of gold sewn into their clothing. Now they have Victoria Hotel in Poona. My grandparents run the original property, Hotel Spenta, outside town. It's a very cozy place. If you ever go, tell them I sent you. And try the Dar Ni Pori at breakfast. It's ever so tasty."

"What is Dar Ni Pori?" Alice liked to know everything about food.

Naval grinned at Perveen. "Being a Parsi lady, you can tell her."

"Not every lady is handy with recipes," Perveen admitted, not having heard of it.

"Dar Ni Pori is a wheat bread with nuts and dal and raisins inside." Naval's eyes glowed as he spoke. "My grandmother still insists on making it for the guests. And for me — whenever I want."

"How divine it must be! And so is your marketing," Alice said with an easy smile. "Is the hotel business the reason your family has its surname?"

"It certainly is." As a balloon seller approached them, he waved the man away. "However, when I have a son, he shall choose his own path. Maybe he will be a photographer or even a cricketer."

"That reminds me of what we were talking about earlier," Alice said, returning her attention to the quieter student. "Khushru, your future plan sounds like it will suit you. And remember that mathematics leads society's progress. There would be no houses built or streets or dams laid out without mathematics."

Naval laughed and then clapped his hand to his mouth. "Very true! I did not mean insult, madam."

"It is true that an accountant might receive a steady wage and have the opportunity to build a business," Alice said. "But when we work with numbers and abstract reasoning, the benefit to our society is infinite."

They had reached the college's fence, and Perveen wished she had more time to understand the two boys, who seemed rather mismatched. "What benefit do you think the freedom movement has for society?"

Naval looked startled, and she realized the change of topic was abrupt. "We were in the Student Union for a few months last year. Dreadful!"

Perveen kept her tone light. "What was wrong with the group?"

He wrinkled up his handsome nose. "Those chukoos did nothing! Always so much planning and gup-shup gossip. I told Khushru here this was no place for us."

"And what do *you* think?" Perveen asked Khushru directly.

"I used to hope for freedom. It is not possible for me anymore." Khushru had looked downcast in the car, but now his face was positively miserable.

"Why is that?" Alice's voice was empathetic.

Naval put a hand on his friend's shoulder. "He's a bit too upset about it to talk. On Friday, he was at the tailoring shop, and some hellions showed up. He repelled them but it was frightening —"

"Please don't talk about it. You weren't there!" Khushru pleaded.

Ignoring him, Naval said, "With the bravery Khushru has shown, he could be a policeman — better yet, an inspector. But then why go to the expense of a college degree?"

Perveen asked Khushru, "Did you tell Mr. Hawthorn about the fight?"

Shaking his head, he muttered, "No. I don't make excuses."

As they drew close to the college's gate, Perveen noticed a man ahead of them. He was a European, with golden-blond hair that shone under the midday sun. He had stopped at the guard booth and was leaning in to converse with the chowkidar. He pulled something small from his pocket and gave it to the chowkidar as he passed through, swinging a portmanteau from his right hand.

With a sense of alarm, Perveen nudged Alice. "Did the gentleman just pay baksheesh to get inside the college?"

"What?" Alice followed her gaze. "No, that's only Terrence Grady from the history department."

Grady, the Irish teacher leading the Student Union; the one who'd refused to go to chapel with the rest of the school and left the campus carrying the same portmanteau he was carrying today. She hadn't recognized him in the moment because she hadn't seen his face.

"There's no reason for a teacher to give baksheesh. He has every right to enter the college."

Naval's voice carried, and Mr. Grady, who'd been walking, turned around to look at the four of them. He gave a half wave to Alice, then proceeded onward.

"Oh, dear," Alice said. "I hope he doesn't think we were talking about him."

"We were," Perveen said. "But perhaps there is a reasonable explanation for giving the guard money. Perhaps he knew the man had a financial hardship."

Naval had hurried ahead to the guard booth and was waving them on. "Miss Mistry, please come up. You must examine the logbook."

Perveen did so. Looking down in the faculty book, she saw Mr. Atherton's name, but no other teacher's.

Naval raised his eyebrows. "You may have been right!"

As Alice signed in, she looked from the book to Perveen and shook her head. Then she addressed the guard. "Grady-sahib was just here. But where is his name?"

The guard blinked rapidly. "Who, mem-sahib?"

"Mr. Grady," Khushru said. "He gave you baksheesh, didn't he?"

"No, nothing." The guard's face was like stone.

23
SURPRISE ON THE STAIRS

No matter how sweetly Alice questioned the man, he held to his story. Perveen told Alice, "That's enough. It's surely no consequence."

Alice signed the faculty book, adding Perveen as her guest, and the boys signed their names in the student log.

"Like you said, maybe he gave the guard some money out of charity," Alice said after they'd gone through. "I'm sure the guard lost salary for the day the college was closed — the teachers did."

"I'm beginning to think Mr. Grady is the untrustworthy type," Naval said as the group passed into the garden.

Perveen glanced at Naval, sensing he knew a lot more. "I do wonder why he carries such a heavy portmanteau."

Naval shrugged, and it was Khushru who answered. "I think it's a lot of newspapers. He thinks newspapers can be as good for learning as books."

"I'd rather read newspapers than write papers," Naval commented as the group walked along the ground-floor gallery. "He assigns such complicated papers that cannot easily be completed. He told us to interview a person between the ages of fifty and one hundred. Then we were supposed to describe an experience of their life journey and relate it to a situation in history."

"What an unusual assignment," Perveen said, intrigued by its freewheeling nature. "Did you seek out city leaders to talk about milestone events in Bombay?"

"No. He encouraged us to find an ordinary person from our community or the college," Khushru said.

"I couldn't think of anyone and it was getting late, so I interviewed my grandmother, the one who came from Persia and helped my grandfather set up the hotel. Khushru, who did you interview? I forgot."

"One of the tailors in the Hawthorn Shop. He comes from Calcutta and remembered when England split up Bengal in 1905. It was a deadly mistake." Khushru's grim expression caused Naval to roll his eyes.

"Mr. Grady tried to sponsor a weekly student newspaper, but the administration didn't approve. A semi-annual magazine called the *Woodburnian* already exists." Naval said as they approached the foot of the stairs. "Mr. Grady wrote for the *Bombay Chronicle,* but said he resigned when the paper's editor was sent out of India. Personally, I think he was sacked by the next editor and won't admit it."

Perveen guessed that Naval was speaking of Benjamin Horniman, a firebrand Englishman sympathetic to Gandhi and the freedom movement. Because Horniman kept writing strong editorials in support of Indian independence, he had been deported back to England. The newspaper had endured but was far less exciting. A picture of Mr. Grady was coming together in her mind: a man who could no longer write words of protest for the public to read, but who intended to teach students to do exactly that kind of work — all within the boundaries of a Scottish mission college.

Naval offered Alice her folios. "We are headed for the hostel now. That's where the mathematics crew is meeting."

"Odd that the meeting isn't inside the library," Alice said, watching the boys walk all the way down the hall and out to the back garden. "Perveen, do you think they are fibbing?"

"I can't tell. Naval has a very charming and forceful personality. But perhaps he's what Khushru needs — someone to keep him moving during a time of grief."

Alice's classroom was of good size and packed with symmetrically spaced eight-foot-wide desks, each with a long bench tucked neatly underneath. It reminded Perveen of her own school days at the Petit School, with Gulnaz at the desk behind her, giggling.

"How many students sit at each desk?" Perveen asked.

Alice was rummaging in her own desk and looked up to answer. "Normally four. There's just one desk allotted to the girls, so they crowd in as need be."

"Windows on both sides. That must be good cross-ventilation when the sea winds are blowing." Perveen looked out the windows on the east side and could see the inner courtyard and the hostel buildings just beyond. It made her think about whether anyone could have entered the building unseen, through open windows on this side of the building.

Alice pulled out the chair behind her desk and seated herself. She made a regretful face. "Perveen, like I said, I have a bit of grading. After I'm done Sirjit can take us somewhere."

Perveen decided to give Alice room, and perhaps satisfy more of her own curiosity. "Do you think anyone would mind if I take a walk along the hall?"

"Not likely. Atherton is a floor below, and Mr. Grady's just above. But if there's any trouble, just give me a shout."

There shouldn't be trouble, not with the gentle hum of student voices coming from the library nearby, and the occasional passage of servants or students along the gallery. She walked slowly, noting that the open space provided a clear view of the front gardens, Kennedy Sea-Face, and Chowpatty Beach.

To drop a dead body straight down the building's façade was bold — but the guard couldn't see anything, because the booth where he sat faced the college's gate, not the college itself.

Perveen considered the stone half wall that formed the boundary along the gallery. The wall reached just a bit higher than her waist, a decent height to protect anyone from being accidentally knocked over. The gray and gold Kurla stones from which the wall was built were masked by a black fingerprinting powder. The largest concentration was smack in the middle of the gallery, which overlooked the spot on the hard path where Freny's body had landed.

Turning around, she saw a wide doorway in the hall marked OFFICE. The black fingerprinting powder stained the doorknob and doorframe; the door was closed, and, she imagined, locked fast.

She walked the hallway a few more times, seeing nothing significant, and then Alice came out. "I'm taking a break. Are you deadly bored?"

"No. But I've a question. You said the principal's office is on the ground floor. Who works in this other office?"

"It's for administration. The secretary and the comptroller and registrar all have their offices within the space." Alice looked at the doorknob. "It looks dirty."

"Fingerprinting powder. I see a worker trying to get rid of the mess the police made."

Alice followed her gaze to the far end of the hallway, where a young man dressed in a vest and lungi was scrubbing the black fingerprinting powder off a patch on the floor. "That's Rahul. He's one of the regular cleaning boys."

"I wonder what he told the police," Perveen said.

Looking sideways at her, Alice said, "I can

easily start a conversation, but as we were saying, I've got the problem of being British. But I can introduce you, if you want to chat in Marathi."

"That's an idea." Perveen imagined a servant might have observed many things beyond what the police asked.

The women approached, and Rahul stopped wiping the corridor but did not look up.

"He must be anxious," Alice whispered to Perveen. In loud, slow Marathi, she said, "This woman is my friend."

"My name is Perveen Mistry. I was visiting the college the day of Freny Cuttingmaster's death. I knew her and am very sad about it."

"Yes, memsahib." His voice was barely audible.

Perveen moved to get a look at the young man. Rahul's hunched shoulders and downcast expression made him look as if he anticipated a scolding. "The police were rude to everyone that day. Even me! It must have been especially awful for you."

He nodded.

"What did they ask you?"

He took a long moment deciding whether to answer. When he did, his voice was barely audible. "They asked, did we see the memsahib in the building that morning. We did not. All students were together watching the prince."

"I know you told the truth about that," Perveen assured him. "And did you see any other persons in the building?"

He shook his head, but not so quickly.

Remembering the guard who'd been paid off by Grady, she asked, "Did someone tell you not to mention they were in the building? Perhaps gave you baksheesh for it?"

"Nobody did that. Please, memsahib, I must work."

She tried another tactic. "Did you hear any voices?"

"No. We were in the library cleaning the books." Rahul's shoulders were tense. After a moment, he said, "I did not hear voices."

In Bombay, no place was completely quiet. Was he withholding something? "Did you hear anything else?"

Looking down, he said, "I heard the door to the library open twice. The police did not ask."

This could be gold. "Did someone come inside the library?"

"I don't know. I was staying in my place, dusting books. But I heard breathing."

"What was the breathing like? Fast, slow, heavy?"

"Very slow breathing," Rahul said.

A chill ran through her. "Can you make the same sound for me?"

He sucked air through his nose and let it out slowly. It reminded her of someone's breathing in deep sleep, and also, when she had seen people meditating.

It could have been Freny hiding. "That is very helpful for us to know, Rahul. How long did the breathing last?"

"Only a minute or two. It was all done by ten-forty-two."

The specificity seemed odd. "How do you know?"

He looked affronted. "There is a tall clock inside the library. We were told to have all the books dusted that day, and I was checking so we did not go too slowly in each section."

"Do you clean the books every Thursday at this time?"

"No. Our boss told Vivek and me to clean the library because the students would not use it at all that day. Principal-sahib complained of mildew on books and wanted everything cleaned up."

Perveen nodded. "What is the name of your boss?"

"Bilal." Rahul's face flushed. "He might not like that I was speaking to you."

"I don't need to speak to him, but why is that?"

"He was not in the college on Thursday. There were many other servants missing, too."

"He was observing the hartal?"

Rahul nodded. "Yes. A few others were gone as well. But I did not want to lose a day's wage, and Bilal said a few people must work that day or the sahibs would get angry."

The ones who had stayed out lost money, but they also escaped suspicion.

"What else did the police ask you?"

"They asked if we killed the girl. We said in the name of Shiva we had not done it, and they searched the quarters where we sleep, tossing everything about. They broke the picture I have of my mother, but they found nothing."

"I'm very sorry." A picture behind glass was a real treasure; how could he replace it, on such low wages?

Rahul's voice lowered. "But Grady-sahib helped us. He came to our side when the constable was pushing us to say we hurt that poor girl. Grady-sahib said he wouldn't stand for it. So they stopped."

Another check in Mr. Grady's column. Perveen glanced at Alice, who had a questioning look in her eyes. She guessed that Alice could make out just a bit of the conversation and was surprised to hear Mr. Grady mentioned.

The sound of brisk footsteps coming down the stair from the floor above caught their attention. Rahul jumped up, dust cloth in hand, and headed down to the opposite end of the gallery.

"Let's go," Alice said, and the two of them rapidly headed for her classroom.

"Excuse me, madam. Weren't you here the day of the procession?"

Hearing a familiar Irish accent, Perveen turned to see Terrence Grady glaring at her. There had been no need for Rahul to flee; but he didn't return.

Alice drew herself up in the same manner as when she'd addressed the police on Perveen's behalf. "May I present my dear friend Perveen Mistry? Of course she was on campus. She helped with the emergency."

Snidely, he said, "The last I heard, there were no women officers in the Bombay Police."

"If you were to read the *Bombay Chronicle*'s current edition, you might find mention of my name," Perveen said, striving to sound unannoyed. "I'm a solicitor who advocated for Freny's family at the coroner's court yesterday."

He paused, as if to reconsider her; and when he spoke again, his voice was more respectful. "I wanted to be at the inquest, but Atherton said the police were satisfied with my written testimony and I needed to teach. I wanted to know how it happened."

"We can talk about that, if you like." Perveen made the invitation, hoping Alice wouldn't mind.

"Very well. Please join me in my classroom, Miss Mistry. As long as you are able to climb another flight of stairs?" He looked pointedly at Perveen's sari, suggesting that it might cause her to fall.

And that made her straighten up, more determined than ever to get the interview.

24
THE TEACHER'S TALE

Terrence Grady's classroom was a similar size to Alice's, although it had a much more cluttered atmosphere. Perveen's attention was drawn to framed pictures of Swami Vivekananda, Madame Bhikaji Cama, and Rabindranath Tagore. Glass-fronted bookcases were packed to overflowing with books: encyclopedias, geographic surveys, histories, biographies, and novels in rows, with more books perched sideways atop these rows. One bookcase was almost completely filled with dog-eared newspapers: peering in, she saw the *International Herald Tribune,* the *Manchester Guardian,* the *New York Times,* and even J.P. Singer's paper, the *San Francisco Chronicle.*

"It's like a bookshop!" Alice said, her voice delighted.

Perveen nodded, feeling glad that Alice had left off grading to accompany her. "It must be quite a feat to buy all these papers not usually sold in Bombay."

Lowering his voice conspiratorially, Grady answered, "I'm allowed to take copies from a few social clubs after they are done with them. They're quite tattered, usually."

Perveen asked, "Do you pick up papers at the Orient Club?"

His open expression seemed to close. "Who told you I did?"

"Nobody!" she said hastily. "It's awfully close to the college."

"Yes, they know me there," Mr. Grady said. "Other teachers bring me papers from their clubs. Overseas papers are an important way for Indian students to know what's going on in the world without the usual government filters."

"I'm going to the Yacht Club later today. I'll see what papers I can find for you," offered Alice, who was continuing to browse.

"As long as asking doesn't tear you away from your duties toward the prince," Terrence Grady said in an arch tone. "There is a fancy tea for him today, I heard."

"Yes. I have no official duties at the tea. But it would be rude not to attend."

Sneering slightly, Grady said, "If it weren't for your being a councilor's daughter, you would not have official duties here."

Perveen noticed that Alice had crossed her

arms tightly, a sign of nerves. Perveen said, "I'm surprised you don't know that Alice was hired because of her accomplishments at Oxford and previous teaching experience at a school in an impoverished borough of London. However, we are not here to chat about anyone's credentials. You asked about the coroner's finding."

Grady moved to his desk and sat down. It was a bold breach, because gentlemen were not supposed to sit when ladies stood. "That's right. The *Times of India* said the coroner's verdict was homicide by strangulation. Was there real evidence for this?"

Perveen relayed all the details that were now public record.

Grady steepled his hands and leaned forward. "So somebody constructed a false scene to make it look like an activist student had thrown herself from the college in order to protest the prince. That's disgusting."

"They also talked a bit about your behavior," Perveen said. "Mr. Atherton testified that he and Mr. Gupta went looking for you. Mr. Atherton said you heard nothing unusual whilst in your room, and you came out to the stands shortly after Mr. Gupta knocked on your door. But not immediately, for some reason."

"Because I was writing." Running a hand

through his fine golden hair, he said, "Well, it sounds as if the testimony resembles what I said, more or less."

"Yes. It is never guaranteed that one's words are quoted correctly. I'm sure you know, as a former newspaper reporter."

"Who told you?" He looked accusingly from her to Alice.

"Students. If you told them, it's hardly a secret," Perveen retorted.

"It's quite an ordinary story," he said with a shrug. "I arrived from Ireland six years ago and was hired as an investigative reporter at the *Bombay Chronicle.* When Mr. Horniman was forced out of India, I had to find another way to live. I thought, why not work with India's young people?"

"That actually is hardly ordinary," Perveen said with a smile. "You also supervise student clubs, don't you?"

Grady had opened his central desk drawer and answered without looking up. "Just one."

"The Student Union, isn't it?" Without giving him time to react, she asked, "What do you think about Dinesh Apte running out to disrupt the prince's parade?"

His head jerked back; he hadn't expected this. "I was shocked. I had no idea he would perform such a risky protest. The only silver lining is the military didn't kill him."

"Do you know where he's being held?" Alice asked.

"In a cell at Gamdevi Police Station." Sounding bitter, he added, "I wasn't allowed to see him even though I left the college immediately and had bail prepared."

If his story was true, his swiftly leaving the college made sense. Perveen asked, "Is trying for bail the reason you wouldn't go to the chapel assembly?"

Looking at Alice, he said, "Is this going to the administration?"

She shook her head. "Why should it?"

"I wanted to help Dinesh. Too many students have died for the sake of freedom. And I'm not the type to mourn in a place where meaningless prayers are being said." Giving them a cool stare, he added, "I was born Catholic, but I consider myself an atheist. Does that shock you?"

Alice beat Perveen to the answer. "Not at all. It only tells me you don't believe the perpetrator of Freny Cuttingmaster's murder will suffer in hell."

Alice could be socially awkward, and she'd directed him to the homicide in a more aggressive fashion than Perveen would have done.

Grady's face had flushed red. In a tight

voice, he said, "No. I don't think he will suffer at all."

"You say he." Perveen tried to play on his vanity. "As a former investigative reporter, which direction do you think the police should pursue?"

"I have no idea of the person's identity — but I would hardly think any one of the teachers or students here would hurt another." Having taken out a pen, he closed the desk's drawer with a soft thud.

"Two of the senior students said you've been giving them very creative assignments that show an intersection between historic events and everyday people." Alice's tone was mild.

Mr. Grady gave a faint smile, as if her compliment had pleased him. "That is why I was so busy in my room that morning. The essays were longer and more intriguing than I expected."

Seizing the moment, Perveen asked, "Did Miss Cuttingmaster write an essay?"

Alice interrupted. "Freny was a year younger than Naval and Khushru. She wouldn't be in the same class."

"That's not true!" Grady said sharply. Turning back to Perveen, he said, "She enrolled in my course because Miss Daboo recommended she take an advanced course in the humanities this year. And while she was a good student, at times she appeared somewhat overwhelmed. Not turning in the essay on time, for example. I would have expected it of some of the others — Naval Hotelwala and George Joseph, say, but not her."

"I know those students," Alice said, nodding.

"Did she say anything about the nature of the historical topic of her paper?" Perveen asked.

"You do have a lot of questions." Mr. Grady took the cap off his pen and picked up a pad of paper. *Oh, dear.* The former reporter might be reporting on her.

"Her paper related to the freedom movement. She wanted to interview Mr. Gupta, but he was reticent. I told her to look up the things she still wished to know. The Asiatic Society keeps newspapers going back for decades."

Perveen could guess why Freny wanted to question Mr. Gupta. He was older than most of the faculty and would have the benefit of remembering nineteenth-century political struggles. Keeping her eyes on the teacher, she asked, "What's your impression of Mr. Gupta?"

Mr. Grady was indeed writing down her

questions. Without looking at her, he said, "Brajesh Gupta thinks I don't run a properly maintained classroom. I think he shouts too much. Likely he is jealous of me. I came in just two years ago and my world history class has become one the most requested."

"How is Mr. Gupta's behavior with women?" Alice asked.

His brow creased. "I don't know what you are asking."

In a tight voice, Alice said, "Does he speak negatively about women in teacher meetings or the lounge?"

It could only mean that Alice had heard something that hurt her.

Mr. Grady laid down his pen. "There is harmless joking done by almost everyone. Regardless of what the chaplain wants, the college itself does not operate like a Presbyterian chapel."

Perveen asked, "How do you think female students are treated in the school?"

"Quite well. After all, they are granted degrees. We can't say the same for Oxford and Cambridge."

"Do you think Miss Cuttingmaster believed she had to prove herself to the Student Union?" Perveen noted that he'd made an unsubtle dig at the two of them with their prestigious educations in England but no degrees to show for it.

"I imagine that was the case. She shouldn't have — but she did worry." He fell silent, as if he was thinking of something that had happened.

Perveen wanted to prod the teacher about it, but she knew he was on edge. Gently, she said, "I met Freny Cuttingmaster a few days before she died. She said you were a good teacher. She also said that some of the male students — Dinesh Apte, specifically — doubted her loyalty to the cause."

"They may have said things to each other that I didn't hear — or understand. My Marathi is not as strong as I'd like." Grady looked past Perveen and out the window, where a crow was perched, looking in at them. "The only instance I can think of was a few months ago, when the first bonfire of European clothing was held."

"Yes. That was also at the mills," Perveen said.

"Dinesh suggested everyone go together to take part in stoking the bonfire with clothing, but the female members said they didn't wish to participate. That was when the talk about girls being frightened and Parsis not being good nationalists started." Grady's voice was bitter. "It was wrong, and perhaps I should have said something, but I did not want to appear like a controlling Britisher."

Perveen understood what he meant. And he'd used Dinesh's first name, as if he was less formal with him than others. Casually, she asked, "By the way, do you have a list of the Student Union members?"

He did not write this down. Looking at her with a grimace, he said, "I promised the students I won't hand over information about them."

"Is that because it's a secret society?"

Grady rose from his seat and walked around the desk to glower down at Perveen. "No! They have a right to share and organize as they wish. Yes, I am their advisor, but that does not mean I tell tales on them. As a solicitor, do you have a similar agreement?"

Almost unconsciously, she found herself backing up. "I do indeed — for my clients. I won't ask any more about your students. But don't you wonder about the behavior of your colleagues? They are quite different than you, with their academic backgrounds."

"And don't they think a degree makes them better writers!" he said sarcastically.

If she played her cards right, he'd probably answer a few more questions about the teachers. "Ridiculous, isn't it? At the inquest, Mr. Atherton said that Mr. Gupta went alone to speak to you at your door. Is that correct? What did he say?"

"There was a knock on my door and Gupta called my name. I answered I would be coming out shortly." His words were straightforward, but he was shifting his weight from one leg to the other.

"But he didn't open your door to speak with you?" Alice pressed.

Grady shook his head. "No. He rattled the doorknob and called out. Why?"

There. He'd said something of value that hadn't been mentioned at the inquest. Perveen blurted, "A doorknob usually rattles if it is locked."

"Yes, I locked my door." He stepped away from them and moved toward the bookcase by the door. Shifting through the newspapers on top of it, he asked, "What are you doing, running your own murder investigation? You should come over here and find a lurid example, if you like."

"I don't want to look at your newspaper collection." Perveen was trying hard to keep him speaking about the matter at hand. "I came to talk with you because you wished to know what happened in court yesterday. As you know, any bit of information that could help the Cuttingmasters is important to reveal. Just to clarify: Miss Cuttingmaster was a student in your world history class that meets on Tuesday and Friday mornings?"

"You already know that!" he grumbled.

"I'd like to know when she talked to you about the paper being late."

"I told her to go to the Asiatic Library on Monday, I think. What does it matter? After the shock of Dinesh's imprisonment and Freny's death, it's hard to remember what else happened in the week."

"And she still didn't turn it in after going there." Perveen kept her eyes on him as she continued. "Perhaps Freny spoke to you about her progress with the essay on Thursday morning. After all, you both were in the building when everyone else was gone."

Mr. Grady's face reddened, and he did not answer.

Alice spoke up. "I know how these students are. They are mortified of being teased so they ask for extensions and help when others aren't around. It would be a good thing if this college had regular office hours for faculty, not just classroom time."

"Yes," Grady acknowledged. "But that is not how our days are organized. We spend all day lecturing."

Perveen took up the story again. "So Miss Cuttingmaster came to see you in your room when everyone else was going to the stands. And if your door was closed — locked, even — she might have asked if she could stay put, working on her paper, until the prince had passed."

Grady whirled about to face them. In a tight voice, he said, "I'm under no obligation to answer questions of anyone but the police. And they were satisfied with my answers. As I said to the detective: I never heard anything happening outside my door. And that's all."

Perveen shot back, "The police wouldn't likely ask a British teacher whether he'd had an Indian female with him in a locked room!"

"I did not harm a hair on her head," he said, raking his hand through his own hair. "She only wanted to be out of view of everyone. She sat at her usual place and did some writing. When Gupta came calling, she could have said something, but she went dead quiet. I told him I would come out in a moment. After that — I don't know. I assumed she would make a decision about whether to stay or go on her own. I am not responsible for her conduct. But I am horrified about what happened to her. That person deserves hanging."

He had admitted the truth — perhaps a partial truth, but more than they'd had at the start of the conversation. Softly, she said, "I'm grateful for your honesty."

The tension in his face eased. "And I do acknowledge that you're helping her family. But nobody should be worried about me. I'll tell you where you should be looking."

"I'm very interested to hear," Perveen said.

"Let me explain it this way." Looking past her through the window that opened to the back courtyard, he said, "All the college's hostel residents are males. Every night, at least one or two boys climb the college's fence on Babulnath Road to gain access to the college grounds after hours."

"Is that to avoid being caught for breaking curfew?" Alice asked.

"Yes. Everyone knows the fence can be climbed. And during the procession, a lot of locals were perched on the street side of the fence. It was all for a better view of the parade, because they wouldn't have been allowed in the stands alongside the college folk."

"Do you think someone from the outside climbed over the fence to come in and kill Freny?" Perveen asked.

"I think it's a strong possibility. And as we know, not everybody in Bombay likes Parsis."

Perveen chose not to respond to this. She had something else on her mind. "You said you could see these fence-sitters from where you were during the parade. You told us you came out, but I don't recall seeing you join us in the stands."

"I didn't sit down. I stayed on my feet, so I was not part of the adulating mass."

The Irish were as angry about British rule as many Indians were; they had even mounted their own freedom movement, a so-called Irish Republican Army. Could Mr. Grady actually be the terrorist Mr. Mortimer was looking for?

He had left college with a portmanteau on Thursday. There was no college on Friday. There was ample opportunity for him to travel to Poona or hand off whatever he had to an accomplice.

"How close were you to the parade route itself?" Perveen asked.

"So close that I was the first person from college to try to assist Dinesh. But it was hopeless. The police had more than their usual lathis — there were bayonets and rifles and pistols, and what looked like three dozen of them converged on Dinesh. He could have been killed."

Alice had been quiet, but now she spoke. "The police force would never shoot an Indian in front of a large international press corps. It would create a very poor image for the Empire worldwide."

Mr. Grady's response was sharp and immediate. "Is that really so? Perhaps you sit at the governor's knee to hear such things."

"That rudeness is uncalled for," Alice said hotly.

"Some say women shouldn't be in colleges because they cannot restrain themselves from policing others." Grady's tone was mocking. "In fact, one could argue that coeducation is the death knell of social intercourse."

Grady had been both helpful and evasive, but Perveen doubted they'd get more of use. She worried about the rising color in Alice's cheeks and didn't want her friend to inadvertently say something that could be carried back to Mr. Atherton. Sweetly, she delivered her own bon mot. "Mr. Grady, did you just tell us you support intercourse at college?"

His face flushed. "What are you implying, Miss Mistry?"

With a rush of bravado, she added, "What an interesting choice of noun. It means many things."

"Get out right now before I —"

"Throttle you?" Alice said, her eyes full of fire.

His hands were clenched, and his eyes full of rage. After a quick exhalation, he threw open the door.

Perveen went, Alice right behind her.

25
A SECRET OFFER

As they climbed down a flight and then toward Alice's classroom on the first floor gallery, both women were silent. Perveen had plenty to say to Alice in private. However, as Alice turned the knob of the mathematics classroom door, a rustling sound came from within.

Alice hesitated, as if she'd heard the sound, too; but she still went forward, opening the door all the way.

Horace Atherton was near Alice's desk — not touching anything, but close enough to see the opened folios. Instead of appearing startled, he looked unsmilingly at the two of them.

"Mr. Atherton. This is a surprise." Alice's eyes flickered to her desk.

Perveen was uneasy. If the principal was inspecting Alice's desk, he probably was trying to uncover more than the content of the mathematics quizzes.

Atherton did not move from his position. "I've been waiting to speak with you. It's not a good idea to leave a forthcoming test unattended. Students can't be trusted."

"True," Alice said. "How did you know I was coming today?"

"You are signed into the college logbook today, just as you were on Friday, when college was closed."

"I am teaching many classes. Those folios on my desk contain sixty tests that need to be graded."

Perveen admired the steadiness of Alice's voice, and Atherton's expression seemed to relax slightly. "You are one of the hardworking ones. But why is this lady with you so often?"

Before Perveen could explain herself, Alice said, "We were going about town this afternoon, and I only stopped to finish marking a few papers. It's terribly distracting at home these days!"

"Miss Hobson-Jones, I don't doubt you are a diligent teacher, but you must be aware the person with you is the legal representative for the Cuttingmaster family. I saw her speaking on behalf of the mother in the coroner's court."

"Sir, the Cuttingmasters wanted help getting their daughter's case through the coroner's inquest. That matter is finished." Perveen wasn't telling the whole truth of her continued interest; but to share that would be to put Alice at risk.

Pointing a bony finger at her, he ordered, "You must leave. I need to speak with Miss Hobson-Jones."

Perveen looked at Alice, trying to read from her friend's chastened expression if she wanted Perveen's help.

"I'll meet you at the car." Alice's voice was strong, and she gave her a warm smile. "I won't be more than a few minutes, I'm sure."

"Very well. I'll be with Sirjit." Perveen used the driver's name to ensure Atherton knew she wouldn't be alone. If Alice didn't come out within a quarter of an hour, she would return to the college to make sure she was safe.

Perveen had the sense that Atherton might be prepared to sack Alice. Why else would he be skulking around her room? Trying not to panic, she proceeded through the garden and past the guard at the main gate.

Alice's family's Crossley wasn't parked in front of the college as she'd expected it would be. Feeling anxious, she hastened around the corner to Babulnath Road. The elegant blue car was parked in the shade of a massive banyan. In the back seat, Sirjit napped with his mouth slightly open, his chest under the white uniform shirt rising and falling. When Perveen said his name, he jerked awake.

Sliding out of the car, he dusted the seat where he'd been with a clean handkerchief. "Memsahib, am I taking you back home already?"

"No. Miss Hobson-Jones is speaking with the college principal. Most likely she will be with us in ten or fifteen minutes. Will she guess that you're parked here?"

"No need for guessing. This is our usual place."

Sirjit had one of the car's rear doors, but she shook her head. She wanted to walk along the black fence separating the college's garden from the road. Nobody was climbing it, nor sitting on it, but she saw bits of litter along the bottom: twists of newspaper, metal bottle caps, and the like.

None of these fragments meant anything to her; she hoped the police had searched the area on Thursday and taken items of relevance then. This gave her an idea. "Since this is your usual place, were you parked here during the prince's procession?"

"Yes." Sirjit scratched his cheek. "It was supposed to be a half day for Miss Hobson-

Jones, but it took much longer, because of the tragedy and the police speaking to the teachers."

"While you were parked, did you see anyone going into the college, perhaps over the fence? Either before the parade, or afterward."

"No. I'm sorry, I wasn't looking in that direction. I wanted to see the prince, just like everyone else."

She thought about his words. "Do you mean that some people were standing along this road?"

"Yes, of course. They wouldn't be welcomed in the college's stands."

Just as Mr. Grady had said. "Did they only stand along the road?"

"Some did. Others were on the college fence — the young men climbed high, so they could get a view over the others' heads."

"About how many people were on the fence during the morning of the procession?"

He looked at the fence, eyes narrowed. "At least fifteen. But I was not looking at them. Are you asking because the police are seeking someone who was there?"

"I don't know what the police are looking for." Perveen approached the cast-iron fence, which was about five feet high with decorative spikes on top. Plenty of property walls in the city had spikes of glass embedded in the top, which were even more of a threat to thieves than these spikes were. Yet break-ins continued. The city was not as safe as when Perveen was a child, and she imagined that the situation would continue to worsen as the population expanded.

Her watch said ten minutes had passed. Returning to the car, she was about to tell Sirjit they would need to go into the college together. But as she looked in the other direction of the Sea-Face Road, she saw Alice approaching.

"There she is!" Sirjit's voice was cheerful, and he bounded out of his seat in the car to open the door for Alice.

"Sorry about that, Perveen. I'll finish the grading at home, and I've got a copy of the *Woodburnian* for you. I realized the club photographs were inside, so we might be able to find information Mr. Grady wouldn't give us about the Student Union."

"Thank you!" Perveen looked closely at Alice, and saw that her blue eyes were bright with excitement. "What happened with Mr. Atherton?"

Alice raised her eyebrows and laughed. "I have some news. Actually, there's loads to discuss, and I'd rather not go home immediately. Where can we have a good heart-to-heart?"

"Memsahib, her father is expecting her home in one hour's time," Sirjit said primly.

Perveen thought quickly. "Why don't we go to Five Gardens Park, which is so close to my house? A kulfi-wallah comes there on Sundays."

"Ah," Alice sighed with satisfaction. "A pistachio ice is just what I'd like."

Five Gardens Park was a small and lovely park nestled between the Parsi colony and a Hindu colony. It was full of people strolling and playing cricket. Because it was outside the European Quarter, there was nobody who might know Alice, or care that she and Perveen were sitting on a bench together. But before the friends settled on a wrought-iron bench with distance from others, they stopped to buy their kulfi. Alice took pistachio, and Perveen had plain cardamom. There was a brief squabble about paying the vendor, which Perveen won.

The cold, sweet ice cream was a most comforting taste after all the tension of the day.

Some distance from them, a cricket game was being set up. Boys from the Hindu colony and the Parsi colony were facing off. It was a game, not a fight, the way things were supposed to be. Looking at Alice, Perveen said, "Tell me about it."

"My encounter with Mr. Atherton was rather strange. Not what I expected." Alice licked her ice-cream cone.

"I was worried you might not get out alive!" Perveen confessed.

Alice shook her head. "I didn't like that he was waiting inside my room, but he told me he was worried. He said women's security is his utmost priority. Parents are trying to get school fees returned and keep their daughters home. He was concerned that the female lecturers would leave as well."

"Because Freny's death was found to be homicide." Perveen thought it over. "And if many of the girls resigned from college, it would be a disaster."

"Yes. And he told me something else." Alice finished her lick of ice cream. "Apparently a burglary occurred inside the college, perhaps on the same day that Freny was killed. He said he told me because I happened to be in the college today, but he's going to announce it to everyone — staff and students — tomorrow."

"The police didn't mention a burglary in court," Perveen said. "How could they not?"

"It wasn't discovered until yesterday. Quite a lot was taken from the bursar's cashbox: five hundred and twenty rupees! Last Wednesday was the deadline for students to pay all their fees for the term. Fees were due before October, but the college's charter allows for a grace period meant to accommodate the students with existing hardship."

If the thief was part of the college, he or she would have known the procession would provide a perfect opportunity to take money from the office. The other possibility was that the theft was by police during the search of the office, or perhaps on Friday, when the campus was officially closed.

"Mr. Atherton normally pays teachers' salaries on Friday, but school was canceled that day due to the rioting. On Saturday, he should have paid us, but he had no money on hand because of the theft." Alice gave her a significant look.

"And why didn't Mr. Atherton say anything to all of you about the theft on Saturday, if it had been discovered then? Were the police called?"

Alice wiped her mouth with her handkerchief. "He said to me he wanted to speak with the board of trustees before anyone else. He wanted an idea of how to resolve the situation and find money for paying faculty and staff. When they met earlier today, they authorized his using funds from a special account. We will all be paid tomorrow. And he told me that he's got me in mind to become Dean of Students. He really wants me to stay."

Perveen thought Alice should have been elated about the news, but her expression was morose. To clarify, she asked, "Would it mean becoming a permanent lecturer?"

"Yes. But a gentleman many years older than I has that position right now — Mr. Gupta — and he and the other Indian faculty could become furious if I get it. Just think of Miss Daboo, who cannot seem to rise in the English department! And who am I to discipline students?"

Perveen considered Alice's casual ways with both female and male students. "Actually, you might do better with your natural good cheer than Mr. Gupta does by shouting and Miss Daboo by reproving. You've got a different perspective."

"It's not all smiles," Alice said. "Take Naval. Despite all his fawning and jokes today, he's been a churl when I've taken off points for his often-late homework. It drives me mad! The boys living in the hostel have more spare time than the students who commute. Naval should not have the privilege of an hour's time to crib answers from his desk-mate before he turns in his work."

"Are you sure Naval's copying his friend's homework? Cheating is quite an accusation." But as she spoke, Perveen wondered if this was the reason for the unusual friendship between Naval and Khushru.

"I'm pretty confident that I'm right." Alice outlined the points. "Naval's homework problems are usually solved identically to Khushru's. Yet their test results differ, with Khushru usually scoring twenty to thirty points higher than his friend."

"I understand your suspicion." Perveen thought more about the social behavior she'd seen between the friends. "Khushru might feel unable to refuse him. Getting back to the matter at hand, do you think Mr. Grady might have been the thief?"

Catching a dripping rivulet of kulfi, Alice savored it before answering. "Terrence Grady had the opportunity to take money from the college. And he certainly could have used it in his attempt to pay bail. Although that portmanteau is large enough to house something else, like Freny's satchel."

"Freny's satchel was recovered by the police." Perveen told Alice what Colin had shared. "You can't repeat this because it could compromise the investigation."

"I understand," Alice assured her. "So it is sounding as if Freny's killer could have traveled outside of Bombay. He could be gone for good."

"Or, if the killer is attached to the college, he could have dropped the evidence to create the illusion of escape. It's about three hours' ride there, and trains are frequent," Perveen mused. "Alice, would you mind if I told my father about the burglary? I'll make sure he keeps it between us."

"Go ahead. Mr. Atherton is keeping the news from the students, but he said he will tell the other faculty tomorrow, anyway. But why do you want to tell your father?"

After a moment's hesitation, Perveen said, "I worry that the police might suggest Freny committed the burglary."

Alice pursed her lips. "That's implausible. No money was found near her body."

"Police don't know where she was in the building. They might conclude she always intended to take money from the cashbox when everyone was out."

"You and I both know that could never be true!" Alice blurted.

"It could come out that she had a partial scholarship and was worried about the remaining cost of college to her parents," Perveen said, watching Alice's expression grow even more horrified. "A prosecutor could bring it up, if they can't find a living person to hang the robbery on. They could say that someone caught her taking the money and killed her."

"Or the other way around," Alice said. "Someone could have had the money in hand and killed her for seeing them with it."

Perveen's eye was caught by an errant cricket ball flying in their direction. "And we also can't ignore Mr. Gupta, who did not want Freny interviewing him. The police might question him, though I'm sure Mr. Atherton will come to his defense."

Alice balled up her soiled handkerchief and began to clench and unclench it. "I don't know what to think about our principal. This afternoon, he handed me the chance to become a dean. It would be a dream come true — but it's too early! It doesn't feel right."

26
A FAMILY FIGHT

Perveen thought about Alice's suspicions as she walked the short distance from Five Gardens Park to her home. With each footstep, she felt a growing dread. Not only did she have Freny's death, possible corruption at the college, and suspicious government agents swirling in her head, she also had a difficult conversation ahead with Gulnaz and Rustom about the debacle at the Orient Club.

She had to tell them what had happened, unless her father had already done it. As she entered the household, she decided to delay the difficult deed by stopping in a place of comfort.

Peering through the open door to the neat black-and-white tiled kitchen, where dishes were cluttered near the sink, she saw John was bent over a double boiler at the hob.

The sweet smell of sugar and milk wafted toward her, making her sigh. "Hello, John.

What are you cooking?"

"Custard." Keeping an intent gaze on the pot, he said, "What else do you want?"

Taken aback by the man's shortness, she said, "I was hoping for some chai."

"I'll make it," said Camellia Mistry, bustling into the room. "I won't have John ruining the custard for the sake of a cup of tea. What are those white smudges, Perveen? Were you drinking milk?"

Feeling infantile, Perveen wiped her mouth. "I had some kulfi in the park with Alice."

"Ah. I'll make your tea."

There was a rhythm to the process. First, a pot of equal parts water and milk was put on the hob. To this, Camellia added a few spoons of Assamese tea, two slices of ginger, and a fistful of fresh lemongrass leaves and mint. After arriving at a gentle boil, a tablespoon of sugar went in, and the brew cooked for five minutes.

Perveen had seen this process so many times that she could have made the tea herself, but she didn't want Camellia to become as disagreeable as John seemed to be.

"Thank you," Perveen said, taking the steaming cup that her mother handed her.

"You are most welcome." As Camellia

smiled at her, Perveen realized she probably had heard nothing about the club debacle.

The two women proceeded upstairs and through Perveen's tidy room to the veranda. Putting down the cup on a rattan table, she opened the cage for Lillian, who hopped out and snuggled into her shoulder.

As Camellia took a chair across from the swing, Lillian delivered her full vocabulary rapid-fire. "God save the Queen! Vande Matheram! God save the Queen!"

"Good afternoon, Lillian." Shaking her head at Perveen, Camellia said, "I believe that bird is your best friend."

"Alice would take issue with that." Reluctantly, she told her mother what happened. "I'm worried that Rustom and Gulnaz will be embarrassed if they hear — but the more serious trouble is whether we've put the law firm in a precarious position."

"Surely that can't be," Camellia reassured her. "Drink your tea and just forget about it."

Perveen shook her head. "I have so many things in my background that could lead to the government thinking I'm an agitator. I signed a letter that went to the governor protesting unethical treatment toward our province's political prisoners. The government has probably recorded my attendance at the most recent lectures by Mr. Gandhi."

As Perveen shook Lillian off her arm to take a sip of tea, the parrot proceeded toward Camellia. Shooing the bird into the air, Camellia said, "But you always knew that your behaviors could start a police file. Pappa warned you the moment you returned from England and began going to Mr. Gandhi's meetings. We could have stopped you, but we did not."

The sweet tea seemed to sour on her tongue. "I didn't think I was setting myself up for trouble. I only wanted to be part of a groundswell that couldn't be ignored."

Camellia permitted Lillian to settle on the arm of her chair. Looking back at Perveen, she gently shook her head. "What happened today is not going to change anything for you. And please don't believe you and Pappa were the only ones excluded at the Orient Club. The international journalist J.P. Singer also was expelled."

Perveen was surprised to hear her mother speak knowingly of the man. "What did Pappa tell you about him?"

"Mr. Singer appeared about an hour and a half ago wishing to see you and Pappa. Rustom and Gulnaz were home, so they invited him to come in. I told John to quickly bake something." Camellia drank a bit more tea, as if she was enjoying being the one to give Perveen a surprise. "We gave Mr. Singer his first taste of nankhatai, which he thoroughly enjoyed. He said there is a similar biscuit in his country, but he called it shortbread."

"No wonder John was so cross with me! He had to make snacks for a surprise visitor who arrived before breakfast time, and a second uninvited person at tea time."

"And in between our visitors, John made a special lunch. I asked him for shahi mutton pulao to make up for Rustom and Gulnaz missing the Orient Club luncheon." Camellia's voice softened. "Poor John. So much work today."

Perveen was still thinking about the journalist's arrival. "Mr. Singer must have moved fast this afternoon to do his reporting work and then come for tea. When did he leave?"

"He was here about an hour and left thirty minutes ago. He kindly brought several copies of his newspaper. He showed us some articles he'd written about city politics and a most heinous murder. The papers should still be on their veranda."

Her mother's words rekindled the dread of telling Gulnaz and Rustom about the brouhaha at the club. "Perhaps I'll look later."

"Gulnaz asked what his initials stand for, and he told her to call him Jay." Camellia gave a hearty chuckle. "She was rather shocked by his forwardness, but I believe that is likely the way that Americans are — much more casual than the British. We had some trouble understanding all his words. Mr. Singer said that in his country, citizens speak with dozens of accents."

As if tiring of the conversation, Lillian gave a giant squawk and, with a beating of wings, flew into the garden. Watching her fly off, Perveen said, "Mr. Singer is a bit of a noisy bird, isn't he?"

Camellia regarded her with incredulity. "Not at all! I found him dashing. He reminds me of the dark-eyed Arabic hero of the picture we saw last year: *The Sheikh.*"

"Rudolph Valentino is really an Italian." Perveen was dismayed her mother could so easily be captivated. "Did Mr. Singer ask you a lot of questions?"

"A little bit. He talked quite a bit about what the Americans think of the freedom movement and showed us a brochure of an American group who are aiding in independence. He wanted to know our opinion about the prince's visit, and with the three of us there, Gulnaz, Rustom, and me, he had three different opinions."

This surprised Perveen. "How did you respond?"

"I told him that a year ago, I was most comfortable with the movement. Intelligent, well-meaning people from good families were involved in those meetings. But now, every lad from the street is shouting against England. There is a roughness now — a danger." Camellia lowered her voice. "And what about the things that have happened to Parsi women in the riots?"

Perveen was startled. "I don't know what things you mean."

"Two ladies were walking in the city on Friday, and some men warned them they were in danger from a supposed mob on the next block. Instead of saving them, they took them to a house, where they were thoroughly abused." Camellia's voice shook with outrage. "I am amazed the men did not kill them at the end. This wretched attack is why Gandhiji called off his strike so quickly and went on the hunger strike."

Perveen shut her eyes, wishing she'd never heard. The attack on her was nothing compared to this. "Did Mr. Singer say how he learned about this?"

"He said one of the injured ladies wrote

to Gandhiji to explain it. Mr. Singer asked Gulnaz and me our opinions, as representatives of the female gender. I sent Gulnaz out, because it is unhealthy for her to have anxiety, especially in her condition. And then I told him I did not think revenge was the answer. Catching the perpetrators of such a heinous attack is the police's job — and the men deserve a day in court." Camellia put down her cup gently, and she looked seriously at Perveen. "His information has only made me wary of going back into town. This afternoon, Pappa said you were with Alice and her driver, but I still was quite worried until you came through the door."

"I was perfectly safe. And as you know, I wound up eating kulfi, watching Hindu and Parsi boys playing cricket together in Five Gardens Park. That game can only be a good sign."

"Yes." Camellia waved her hands at Lillian. "Go on now. Fly free."

Perveen still felt unsettled that her family members had spoken to the journalist without her being present. "I wonder if your words will be quoted along with your name in his next article."

Camellia shook her head. "Our names will not be there. Rustom told him all we said has to be off the record, because of possible controversies with his clients. Mr. Singer said he understood."

Perveen should have felt relieved, but she did not trust the man. She sat silently, watching Lillian flit from tree to tree.

"Mr. Singer said his favorite stop on the ship before India was Cairo, but he also adored Italy," her mother chattered. "He is truly on a whirlwind adventure around the world. It is fortunate he is a bachelor, because it is too difficult on a family to have a husband so far away."

She hadn't thought about whether J.P. Singer was a husband or a bachelor, but perhaps being unencumbered led him to be a bit more daring — to practically get into a fistfight in the Taj. As Perveen kept her eyes on Lillian's explorations, she thought about how life for unmarried men was so very different from her own. Although most Indian bachelors lived in their parents' homes, they didn't face curfews or restrictions on movement. And British bachelors had the most freedom of all. The East India Company and the British Army believed it was advantageous for young men to start their careers free of wives and children: being single would encourage the men to serve longer tours in remote locations. But since the mid-1800s, moral leaders had pushed the virtues of marriage to British women, in order to prevent the bachelors from taking up with Indian women, which had been the inevitable result of the earlier policy.

She considered Terrence Grady. Might a bachelor who taught female students every day develop a passion for one of them? And if that student rejected overtures from him, would her elimination be necessary to keep his action from being exposed to the public?

"May I join you?" Gulnaz had appeared at the door.

Gulnaz's habit was not to ask permission to join conversations. However, Perveen had banished her from the conversation with Colin Sandringham earlier that day. She'd made her sister-in-law feel like an outsider.

"Please do." Feeling guilty for more than one offense, Perveen moved to the side of the swing. But her sister-in-law disregarded the offering and determinedly settled herself in an empty chair near Camellia.

Perveen could smell that the Limoges cup Gulnaz had carried up was filled with hot milk and turmeric. This was a good drink for someone expecting a baby. Gulnaz sipped, and Perveen hoped this meant she was intent on relaxing.

Setting her cup closely to Camellia's,

Gulnaz spoke. "Rustom and I enjoyed seeing Mr. Singer. He said he was also booted from the Orient Club. But he was not a member like Rustom. He won't suffer a loss of money and reputation."

Perveen felt her breath heavy in her chest. "I'm dreadfully sorry, Gulnaz. We should never have gone."

"Gulnaz, why so worried?" Camellia asked lightly. "You weren't this way earlier."

"A note from the club president arrived an hour ago." Her voice was heavy. "He's told Rustom to resign his club membership for violating the guest policy."

Perveen felt like the family had been slapped. "But Gulnaz! That isn't fair."

"Especially since my husband didn't break any rules," Gulnaz said bitterly.

"Dearest Gulnaz, don't get upset," Camellia beseeched. "It's too much for you and the baby."

"Never mind." Folding her arms, Gulnaz looked away from them and toward the garden. "I liked that club very much. In the club's wives' group, two others were expecting. We had joked about all staying in the maternity hospital at the same time."

Perveen heard the pain in Gulnaz's voice. "Gulnaz, I'm really sorry. But all is not lost!

If those are true friends, they won't desert you."

"We shall see." Gulnaz shot her a scathing look. "Anyway, now that we've been booted out of the Orient Club, we could join the Willingdon Club. The grounds are so beautiful there, and the club has many more amenities. Because my father's a member, he can gather the necessary nominations."

Beneath the casual words, Gulnaz was clearly furious at both her and Jamshedji. As a daughter-in-law, she could not outrightly complain. But after Perveen's parents passed away, Gulnaz would become the matriarch in charge of the house. And if she had a son, she might prefer him and his wife to live in the side of the duplex where Perveen did now.

Would she still have a home, then?

27

A MARKET FOR BLAME

On the ride to the office the next morning, Perveen tried to box away the memory of the friction with Gulnaz. She paged through the June issue of the *Woodburnian* that Alice had borrowed from the library. In addition to essays, there were photographs of clubs, including the Student Union. Lalita and Freny stood close together on the edge of the first row. On Freny's other side were Khushru and Naval Hotelwala. In the row behind, she identified Dinesh Apte. Everyone looked serious, as was the custom for posing in official photographs.

"You are quiet today," Jamshedji said. "What is it you're reading?"

"A college magazine called the *Woodburnian*. Alice got hold of a copy for me."

He leaned closer to the magazine. "Is Dinesh Apte in this picture?"

Perveen pointed to him. "That's Dinesh."

"The radical is one of the shortest. How

typical!" Jamshedji said.

"Don't tell me there's a scientific correlation."

"Small men throw themselves on the public stage to gain stature. They might even become larger than life."

"What does that say about you, then?" Perveen teased.

"At five feet seven inches, I am neither tall nor small as compared to my countrymen. I pose no threat, nor can I be diminished. It is a comfortable place to stand." Tapping the magazine, he added, "Enough of idle browsing. I must prepare you for today. It's the first real day of business as usual since the riots, and I predict we'll have many inquiries from businessmen wishing to lay blame on someone for their losses. The challenge will be sorting out which blamers have any proof to use. Judges won't want their time wasted."

"I will keep that in mind. My schedule is quite open to see clients until two-thirty. I have a meeting with the trustees at the Asiatic Society at three, just assisting with some paperwork for the next vice president and some other incoming officers."

"The Asiatic is one of our best clients." Jamshedji nodded. "Go there as usual. I'm sure it won't take more than an hour."

Her father had predicted correctly about a rush of business in the morning. A line of men, some familiar and others unknown, started on Bruce Street and continued up the steps leading to the portico over the front door.

Perveen had never seen visitors queued up at Mistry House. As she and Jamshedji exited the car and tried to get up the steps, someone shouted, "Get in line like the rest of us!"

"Good morning, gentlemen. This is our firm!" Perveen held up the tiffin box, for nobody except a business owner would bring lunch into Mistry House. "Please let us go inside, and we can open our office to see you."

"Good morning!" Jamshedji smiled widely at the queuing people. "We will be filling our pens with ink and laying out paper for contracts!"

The two of them proceeded up the steps and into the door that Mustafa swiftly opened for them.

"What a day, what a day," Jamshedji said as he handed his fetah to Mustafa to put away. Glancing along the hallway, Perveen saw two well-dressed ladies through the open door of the parlor.

"Someone's already here!" She looked inquiringly at Mustafa, who beckoned them to follow into the dining room.

"So many people are wishing to see you today. I only let the ladies inside, because I feared they would not wish to stand like commoners. Both of them are mothers with relatives in custody."

"They must be most anxious. Please take care of them right away," Jamshedji said to Perveen. "And Mustafa, please arrange for several messengers to help us today. We need to book up criminal defense barristers before they're all taken."

"Certainly, sahib. I will take care of it." Mustafa opened the dining-room door, ready to go out.

Perveen could still hear the rumble of voices, and she imagined the trouble that a mixed crowd could bring. "We can shorten the line by immediately giving the men appointments for various times today, rather than dealing with each man at length."

Jamshedji nodded. "A good idea. It will be better if you book all of them in order of arrival. But do speak with the ladies first."

It was just after nine o'clock that Perveen began with the ladies, taking each one upstairs to her office for a private chat. The first lady was a Hindu who tearfully described her twenty-year-old son arrested for looting and destruction — just because he was wearing Congress Party white and was seen running on the same street as a damaged toddy shop.

The other client was a Muslim woman fully clad in burka. In an unsteady voice, she told Perveen her husband had been jailed on accusation of assault. The police arrested him around the corner from where a Parsi man lay bleeding. She told Perveen, "My husband was at the butcher shop earlier. I'm sure that's why his kurta had blood on it."

After the women had signed retainers and left Mistry Law through a back door so as not to be near the waiting men, Perveen went through the front door and moved along the line to set up appointment times. More than half were shopkeepers wishing to charge someone for building damage or merchandise theft. Others were men facing charges of theft, battery, and vandalism; they had already been bailed out by family, and knew they needed help on specific court dates.

As she looked into the face of each potential client, she felt like a hunter. The memory of the men who'd attacked her was sharp and painful. But she didn't see anyone she recognized from that dreadful five minutes on Thursday.

When she had finished booking everyone, many of the waiting people dispersed. The strategy worked: there was a steady flow of clients until the half hour she'd kept free for lunch.

"Your father is still with one of his clients," Mustafa said, pulling out her usual chair at the long mahogany table in the dining room.

"Oh, dear. I hope he has a chance to eat." John had sent lamb mulligatawny in the tiffin container, along with rice, dal, and rotis.

"He forgets his stomach when he is busy," Mustafa said, ladling the savory stew into a soup plate. "You must eat well, though. It will be hard weeks ahead for both of you."

After lunch, Perveen was set to interview three prospective clients between one and two-thirty. But Mustafa popped in just as the second client was finishing his papers. He announced, "Someone arrived who isn't on today's calendar. A Britisher."

Perveen's back went up. Could it be the caller was someone in plainclothes from the police or even Imperial security? Unless he was Colin. "I have my list of clients already scheduled."

"Your two o'clock is not here yet. And this fellow told me he is on a most tight schedule. He did give his card." Mustafa handed her a cream card very much like Alice's.

The name on it was Horace Virgil Atherton.

"Why didn't you say who it was straightaway?" Perveen wasn't pleased to hear who her visitor was, but Mr. Mortimer would have been even worse.

"Because you are in conference." Mustafa inclined his head in the direction of the man sitting on the other side of the desk.

She'd been taken off guard and had almost violated client privacy. Now she smiled at the new client and accepted the papers he'd just signed, along with five rupees for the retainer. "Thank you, Mr. Mehta. I will get to work."

After the man left the office, Mustafa asked, "What else for today?"

With resignation, she said, "I'll see Mr. Atherton. But if he's still here by two-thirty, please come into the parlor and remind me of my next appointment. I won't keep the Asiatic Society waiting for the sake of a surprise British visitor."

28
A GENEROUS OFFER

"Good afternoon, Miss Mistry."

Mr. Atherton spoke before she could greet him. Wearing the same suit as the day of the procession, he stood ramrod straight in the parlor where she'd met the ladies earlier.

"Good afternoon. Won't you sit down?" She gestured toward the wingback chairs, hoping he wouldn't notice the loose piping Freny had.

Taking a few steps toward the chair, he waved at the framed degrees on the wall. "You studied in Oxford. And it says you clerked for a law firm in London, too."

"Yes, Mr. Atherton," she said as she took the other wing chair. "Did Miss Hobson-Jones mention that we were at St. Hilda's College together?"

"No, she only said you were friends. So you have studied *English* law?"

"Yes," she said, noting how he'd stressed the word. "British civil law as well as Hindu,

Muslim, and Parsi law. I see the tea is already here. May I pour you some?"

Without waiting for an answer, Perveen tipped the Sèvres teapot and poured a stream of golden-brown Darjeeling into the thin cup. Mustafa had prepared warm milk separately, because most British preferred it that way. But before pouring, she asked, "Milk as well?"

He regarded the milk pitcher with an anxious look.

"Yes, it is boiled," Perveen said.

Exhaling, he murmured, "That is good, thank you."

While she fixed her own cup, her thoughts raced. Woodburn College had its own legal counsel; he had no obvious reason to seek her out for work. He could only be attempting to get information from her.

Her suspicions were proved right when his next question came. Clearing his throat first, he asked, "How are Freny Cuttingmaster's parents faring?"

She wouldn't say anything revelatory. "I haven't seen them since we left the coroner's court. At that time, their mood was understandably somber."

"She was their only child." He swallowed. "I am a bachelor; I have no children of my own. But I can imagine what the loss must be."

Perveen studied the gentleman she'd immediately judged an adversary. He had come to India by himself in his fifties, an age that most British civil servants were retiring. Why had he taken the assignment?

"The college's board of trustees is deeply saddened by what happened. We received news of the coroner's verdict yesterday afternoon and met to discuss what we might do for the family." Reaching into his breast pocket, he pulled out a fat cream envelope. "We wish to present a condolence gift of five hundred rupees. I hope you can convey it to them — along with a letter from me."

Perveen wasn't sure she'd heard right. "But five hundred rupees is many times more than the cost of a year's tuition."

"Yes. We want them to know how sorry we are for the loss of their daughter."

"It is most generous. But why would you ask me to give it?" Perveen stared into his face, wondering what else was behind this. Did the college have a fear of culpability? Maybe he was as suspicious of Mr. Grady as she was.

"We cannot trust a sum like this to a peon. If I traveled myself to their home, which I've been told is in the Indian quarter, it could be difficult." Atherton set the envelope down on the tea tray between them. "You are their advocate — and, as Miss Hobson-Jones said, a lawyer with a reputation for honesty."

Although she wasn't the family advocate any longer, that didn't mean she couldn't bring the Cuttingmasters the letter. She could also let them know they had the option of refusing the money. There were good reasons for caution, when a homicide investigation was just starting. "I'll bring it to them, but I cannot guarantee they will accept the money. They might assume the college is buying their silence about something."

"That is not the case." Although he shook his head, he was twisting his hands, and the smell of sweat seemed to rise.

Pointedly, she remarked, "I'm surprised your lawyer, Mr. Johnson, isn't here."

"Miss Hobson-Jones spoke very highly of you," he said, shifting anxiously in his seat. "That is why I came."

Perveen wondered if he thought it would be easier to pull wool over a lady's eyes than a gentleman's. And then a second thought came to her: What if this payment wasn't even a board decision? Perhaps that was why no lawyer had come along with the principal, and why he appeared so nervous.

If it was Mr. Atherton's own idea to offer it, he'd have needed to raise the money privately. Five hundred and twenty rupees had been stolen a few days earlier. She and Alice had assumed it happened the day of Freny's death — but it could have been later, sometime between Thursday night and Saturday morning.

Perveen affected an expression of concern. "I wish Mr. Gupta had accompanied you. It must have been difficult to find our office by yourself."

"Gupta has nothing to do with the board. Why would you speak of him? Did Miss Hobson-Jones say something?" He looked pointedly at her.

Alice had said Atherton wanted her to replace Gupta in the role of Dean of Students. But Perveen couldn't let on, nor could she allow him to know she'd heard about the stolen money. "It's only that he seems to have been so helpful to you."

"He's teaching, as is everyone else." Atherton indicated the envelope still lying on the table. "Open it up. Make sure I counted right. Indian money is still confusing to me."

Perveen opened the envelope. She did not read the folded letter within, just took out the bills, mostly ten- and twenty-rupee notes. The total was just as he'd said.

"Yes, I can do this favor for the college board." Perveen realized he hadn't spoken of paying her, and she felt too awkward to bring it up. But she would have to record doing this, for the sake of the homicide investigation. "I'll just put away the money and give you your receipt."

Quickly, she exited to go to her upstairs office. She retrieved the receipt book and returned to the parlor, where she proceeded to write out a receipt for five hundred rupees.

"Really, the receipt is not necessary. I trust you." He looked solemnly at her.

She suspected he was more worried about leaving a record. Firmly, she said, "Any monies received by Mistry Law must have a receipt. My father treats the practice like a bank."

Reluctantly, he took the thin paper she handed him and stuffed it into his pocket. "Very well. Please give the parents my condolences and best wishes for their future."

As Mr. Atherton walked out the door, Perveen lingered at the window, watching him.

Neither of them had been forthright with

the other. But at least she wasn't breaking any laws.

29

Upstairs at
the Asiatic Society

The two o'clock client had arrived twenty
minutes late and was full of apologies. She
decided to take him, as it was a simple case
of filing a claim for damages with his insurance company. After talking with him and
reviewing his paperwork, she finished at ten
minutes to three. Ordinarily she would have
walked to the Asiatic Society, but with such
tight timing, she was glad that Arman could
drive her.

"It is a busy day for you," Arman said, as
they pulled away from Mistry House. "New
clients are coming like bees to jasmine."

"Yes. Let's hope we aren't stung with too
many unworkable cases." She had remembered her father's earlier warning about the
necessity of evidence for judges to even hear
the arguments.

Arman stopped in front of the grand flight
of stairs leading up to the monumental
Town Hall, a gracious neoclassical building

that housed the Asiatic Society of Bombay. This was one of the city's most historic colonial buildings, the place where Lord Elphinstone once read aloud Queen Victoria's 1857 proclamation that the East India Company would become part of the Crown. In the old days, the library building was an important civic meeting place; but in modern times, members enjoyed its vast library of rare books, ordinary books, artworks, and coins.

Mistry family history credited Perveen's great-great grandfather as being one of the stone masons responsible for the fine flight of 132 marble steps in front of the building, which was set high up over the street both for prestige and protection from monsoon rains.

As Perveen walked through a set of louvred doors into the society's spacious foyer, she noticed a gilt stand holding a typed announcement. THE THINKERS PRESENT: MAPPING SOCIAL GEOGRAPHY, AN ILLUSTRATED LECTURE, would take place at six o'clock that Friday evening. The list of speakers included Mr. J. C. Varma, the society's curator of maps, Professor I. M. Baskar from the University of Bombay's department of geography, and C. W. Sandringham, ICS.

She read the sign again. This was the event that Colin had casually mentioned. And she had said she couldn't go. Now she regretted it.

From the ground floor, Perveen took the spiral staircase down to the library's lower level, where one of the trustees and his organization's secretary awaited her in a handsomely appointed office. As tea was poured for all, Perveen explained the revisions she'd made to their agreement.

Mr. Varma chuckled after her presentation. "Miss Mistry, you have done your homework. But these are all good men coming in," he said. "I have no worries."

"I am glad to hear the new officers have good character, but what is this about a housing promise?" She looked inquiringly at Mr. Varma. "Who suggested this change to the standard agreement?"

"One of the incoming vice presidents doesn't reside in the city. As you know, city rents are high. A society member is offering him housing at one of his properties, so I wanted to make this clear."

"It's a risk to mention it. What if the offer becomes known to one of the other vice presidents, who might feel slighted?"

Perveen convinced the trustees to eliminate the housing promise in favor of having the benefactor make a private real estate arrangement with the new vice president. As she readied herself to leave, she mentioned the sign she'd seen upstairs. "That lecture on Friday evening sounds interesting. I never heard of social geography."

"I don't know what it means, either," said Mr. Varma with a chuckle. "The whole event is quite impromptu, but the speakers are sure to explain every bit of it to us. May I reserve a seat for you?"

Intent on hedging her bets, she said, "It's a busy week at the office. I'll send a note that morning if I can attend."

Back upstairs, she paused outside the society's grand lecture hall, looking at the sea of chairs already set up. Surely it would be a dry discussion and only a fraction of the chairs would be filled. Nobody in her family would want to go; the only person she thought could possibly follow such a talk and have a challenging question at the end was Alice.

But before Perveen invited anyone, she would have to ask herself why she wanted to attend the lecture — and that was the problem she couldn't address.

As she passed the newspaper reading room, she recalled that Mr. Grady said he'd recommended to Freny on Monday that she use the Asiatic Society's newspaper library. This meant she'd possibly come to this very room after seeing Perveen, or on Tuesday or Wednesday.

The newspaper room was dim, lit only by green-shaded lamps placed here and there on a long, scratched table. Scholars ranging from college-age into their eighties were bent over the tables, perusing books and newspapers.

A white-haired man was sitting at a small desk with a nameplate on it, conferring with another man. He might be the librarian. As she waited for the men to finish, she sat at a reading table near a mostly empty rack of current local papers. As an elderly gentleman returned the *Times of India* to hang near the others, she decided to pick it up.

The lead story was about the prince's successful visit to Poona. But lower on the same page was an article about "Street Violence Tragedies" that contained the coroner's verdicts for suspicious deaths occurring since the prince's arrival.

Advertisements around the articles took up most of the broadsheet's space. There were offers for sea tickets to London, and the Wellington Bakery was selling a confection called Bombay Prince Cake. But it was a small advertisement for lodgings that made her pause.

Victoria Hotel, in Poona's finest neighbor-hood. Hotel Spenta, only ten minutes' walk from Kirkee Station. Family owned and operated with finest food and sanitation at frugal prices.

Hotel Spenta was Naval's grandparents' hotel. She hadn't known it was so close to Kirkee Station, where the royal train had stopped.

Glancing up, she saw the librarian was no longer busy. As she laid down her paper and proceeded toward him, she noted the name-plate on his handsome mahogany desk.

"Mr. Nambudripad, my name is Perveen Mistry. I believe that last week a student came to look at back issues of some local newspapers. I'm trying to discover which papers she searched."

Giving her an annoyed look, Mr. Nam-budripad said, "Simply ask the student. I am not needing my time to be wasted."

"I cannot ask because she's deceased. Her name was Freny Cuttingmaster." Even though she had her back to the silent room, she felt its energetic appraisal.

"We have both females and males study-ing here. They usually come in the afternoon after college. But I can't say yes or no on this person."

"Isn't there a paper record of users? Perhaps a logbook?"

Tilting his head to the side, he considered her questions. "No need for such, because the library's guard registers those who enter."

"Does it ever happen that someone asks for several different newspapers to be brought out to them?" As he shrugged, she asked, "How does the librarian remember which ones to bring?"

"For that they fill out a chit."

"With a name?"

"Yes. But we don't keep the chits — they are disposed of afterward. Promptly. There are gentlemen waiting. I must ask you to step aside."

Knowing she'd reached an impasse, she said a quiet thank-you and slowly left the room. She knew there was little to be gained, even if she had found the papers Freny had asked for. Perhaps Freny hadn't even come to the library.

Suddenly, there was a rapid tapping behind her. She twisted her head around to see a tiny old man pursuing her, leaning heavily on a cane. She recognized that he'd been the one to return the daily paper that she'd taken up to read.

"Do you have a moment, Miss Mistry?"

Obviously, the gentleman had been listening to her conversation with the librarian. Looking down into his deeply lined face, she acknowledged him with an honorific. "Yes, Babu-ji?"

"My name is Dass. I read here every afternoon until closing. I knew the young Parsi lady you spoke of. It was just today — reading the newspaper — that I learned of her demise. It saddens me greatly." He touched his chest. "She was intelligent and honest. She came once every few weeks, and I had spoken with her twice."

"Mr. Dass, thank you." She was touched to know Freny had been remembered by someone outside of the school and her family. "I am very grateful for this. Did you see her at all last week?"

"Yes. Tuesday, it was. She asked for a number of newspapers and she was told to fill out a chit. While she was waiting, I asked her about what she was researching. She wished to know more about a political case in which two young men killed a senior official. Both men were executed, and many of their followers who protested this were caught up and punished as well. When she told me the year, I asked her if she was studying the incident that led to Bal Gangadhar Tilak's arrest. She appeared very pleased and told me what I already knew: that he was imprisoned for six years in Mandalay for deploring the executions."

"Thank you. I am glad at least to know what she was going to write about."

"Also, I can tell you this." The old man's voice was emphatic. "It's true that librarians throw away the chits in small bins near their desks. After the library closes to the public, when cleaning is done, someone sorts through discarded papers in these bins. So much can be used again, so the cleaners like to sell these papers. They are often used as packing material by merchants."

"It's clear that you know more about the library's operations than some who are paid to work here! Everything you've said makes perfect sense, but it seems like any evidence of Miss Cuttingmaster's search is gone."

Holding up a gnarled finger, Mr. Dass intoned, "Only chits with writing on both sides are allowed to be taken out by the cleaners. Any chits with a blank side are given for reuse near the card catalogs."

Perveen had believed she was done with the Asiatic Society, but his words had generated one last hope. "I see. Where are these card catalogs?"

"The nearest ones are in the literature reading room across the hall, and also in

454

another map room upstairs. It would be my pleasure to bring you there, Miss Mistry." As he finished his invitation, he resumed walking briskly, the cane hammering across the marble floor. As she followed in the gentleman's wake, Perveen tried to learn more about him. "Mr. Dass, are you a teacher, or perhaps a scholar?"

"No. I am retired from the post office for the last ten years. Most afternoons, it is my daily routine to arrive at three and leave at six."

"Your routine seems very pleasant." Perveen imagined what her life might be like when she was alone and in her seventies.

"Many men feel it is important to read news first thing in the morning. But the news is often terrible. I would rather read late in the day, so as not to spoil my mood. It will take me a long time to mourn this poor child."

The card catalogs in the reading room had tin boxes full of small paper pieces just as Mr. Dass had said. One side of each was unmarked, but the other had names and requests for books and newspapers on it. There were many names, but none that were Cuttingmaster. She took care to look for the papers dated 1908 and 1909 — the years of the political crisis — but saw none.

As she sorted through a stack, Mr. Dass took the other half. Some of the chits had names on them; others didn't. The search seemed even more futile than before.

"You are very good at making sense of the librarian's handwriting," she said, looking at the swiftness with which he read.

"At the post office, it was my mission to read bad handwriting." He stopped short, looking at a large paper scrap. "This is a search for 1908, for the *Bombay Chronicle, Mahratta* and the *Times of India.* But the name is not hers. It is Singer."

"I might know this person," Perveen said as she took the scrap into her own hand. Judging from Sunday's date, she realized J.P. Singer must have come to the library as her father had suggested to him.

The old man looked sidelong at her. "I did not know you were interested in this name as well. Is there a relation between the two?"

"I don't know." But if she saw Singer again, she'd ask what he was looking for in the Asiatic Society library.

"I am finished with my chits and have nothing more to show. Now, I can see if any used chits were placed in the other reading rooms."

"I'd like to continue, but I don't wish to

take you away from your scheduled reading." She worried that he might not be able to manage the stairs but didn't want to offend him.

"It is an interesting break from the mundane. Come, let's go to the map room."

Perveen felt touched as he led her upstairs, walking slowly and holding fast to the railing of the spiral staircase. She must speak to the society's secretary about the possibility of an elevator.

Inside the maps room, there was another poster about the forthcoming speech on Friday. This probably was Colin's favorite part of the building, she thought wistfully as she followed her guide to the massive mahogany card catalog in the room's center.

Small stacks of chits sat in wooden trays on top, with tiny pencils alongside. With Mr. Dass's fingers sorting the chits and handing over each one he'd examined, they could double-check each other's reading.

"Hai Ram!" Mr. Daas exclaimed so loudly that others sitting at a distance looked up.

Freny's neatly printed name was written atop a battered chit. Underneath, she'd requested several papers from the year 1908: *Bombay Chronicle*, *Jam-e-Jamshed*, *Mahratta*, *Kesari*, and the *Times of India*.

The year of Bal Gangadhar Tilak's conviction and banishment, 1908, was also the year Perveen had turned ten and her father began inviting her to accompany him to court. She could remember what it felt like to sit on a bench next to her father, watching the barrister he had hired argue the case. As she'd watched and learned, she felt a breathlessness inside her, both eagerness and fear.

She had a similar feeling of suspense as she studied the chit. "This is exactly the card I need. Thank you so much for bringing me here."

Rising slowly from his chair, he smiled. "It was my pleasure. Give that chit to Mr. Nambudripad and he can fetch the same newspapers. Just cross out 'Cuttingmaster' and use your name."

"I shall fill out a new request to see the same materials. I'd rather keep this one just the way it is," Perveen said, sliding the chit into her briefcase.

30
AFTER DUSK CONFESSIONS

Two hours later, Perveen had gone through the English papers from 1908 that Freny had read. Her eyes were blurred from reading so many tiny words on newspaper that was deteriorating. Aside from the name Bal Gangadhar Tilak, she had not found any other mentions that struck a chord: not Grady, Gupta, or even Atherton.

A bell rang, making her jump. The library was closing.

"Do you wish the papers saved for you at this table tomorrow?" asked Mr. Dass, who had remained at her side. "I'll request it of Mr. Nambudripad."

"I have too many appointments tomorrow. I doubt I can return for a while." Slowly refolding the newspaper, she added, "I know better than to expect Freny found anything here that is significant."

"You did not even start reading the *Mahratta*. I shall come earlier tomorrow, so I can read the rest of these papers for you, as well as my own."

She was not a swift Marathi reader, so this would be excellent. "You would do such a thing for me? Why?"

The librarian interrupted sternly, "Time to go, everyone must go!"

Looking reprovingly at the librarian, who was strolling the room, urging the readers to depart, Mr. Dass muttered to Perveen, "It is not you I am helping. It is every student who comes here, asks a question. They do not know this place like I do. This is my home."

"In that case, I gratefully accept your help. Keep an eye out for these names, please. And anything about Woodburn College." She opened her legal notebook and wrote down: *Brajesh Gupta, Horace V. Atherton,* and *Terrence Grady.*

Perveen gave Mr. Dass her card and insisted that they walk out of the library together, because it was after six now, and the sky was dark and the flight of steps so vast.

He consented to take her arm as they proceeded down the steps, and on the pavement, Mr. Dass promised to write to her about anything he uncovered. He proceeded around the corner, and then she started to walk along the road, looking for the family car.

"Miss Mistry?"

She recognized the sound of Colin's voice, and then his familiar uneven footsteps.

It couldn't be — but it was!

Colin had wanted her to visit the Bombay Asiatic Society with him. She'd refused, yet it had still brought them together. Happily, she answered, "How did you know I was here?"

"I had no idea. However, I saw you with your client and decided to wait for the chance to offer a quick greeting."

Awkwardly, she said, "He is what I'd call a helper, rather than a client."

"I see. It turned out that I just finished a quick meeting in the building myself."

She wanted to hear more, but the exterior of the Asiatic Society was the equivalent of a theater stage in the city's center. Everyone passing by looked up at it. Edging away so they didn't look like a couple, she said, "I saw the signs about your talk on Friday. It looks very intriguing."

Colin shook his head. "The prince's schedule has changed, so I can't be in Bombay on Friday. In fact, the royal train departs for Baroda tonight. I may not be back at all."

So this was not really a brief greeting: it was meant to be a final goodbye. It was good of Colin to wait for her. And she knew, with a rush of emotion, that she didn't want to say goodbye.

She just needed to keep talking. "The princely state of Baroda is the perfect place for the prince to continue his polo games. And there's very little likelihood of political protest there. The maharajas keep a very powerful hold over peasants."

"He will see non-British India, though," Colin pointed out. "Outside of the palace grounds, it will be very different from Bombay. And that could bring some surprises."

Perveen tilted her head, imagining Colin and the prince in their own compartment, two young men chatting and looking out the window as the land flashed by. "Wouldn't it be amusing if you and the prince called for random stops? That way you could visit real villages and small towns."

Colin's eyes had sharpened. "Are there any places you'd recommend?"

"You'll pass Kirkee on your way out of Bombay presidency. A student from Woodburn College — Naval Hotelwala is his name — boasted that his grandparents have a small, old-fashioned hotel in Kirkee called Hotel Spenta. They are famous for homely breakfast dishes. Imagine His Royal Highness eating a Parsi breakfast." She winked, willing him to laugh along with her, but he didn't.

"You wouldn't let me eat a Parsi breakfast yesterday," Colin said. "But you'd wish it for the prince?"

"I'm sorry. I felt I couldn't trust you with my father and brother. They would have had you drawn and quartered before you realized it."

"Quite doubtful." His voice was tight.

The conversation wasn't going well. Perveen glanced west and saw where Arman had parked the Daimler. She knew that Arman had not seen her, because he hadn't come out and opened the door. This meant she still had time. She asked Colin, "Have you ever walked through Elphinstone Circle Gardens?"

"No. Is it a botanical garden?"

Pointing at the fenced circular park located across the street, she said, "Hardly! It's a park surrounded by roadway. It used to be grazing land for cows in the area. The East India Company men converted it into a park about seventy years ago. One of Bombay's largest banyan trees is still standing there." She hesitated, then took the plunge. "Won't you let me show it to you?"

"I can think of nothing better."

Perveen waited for a few cars and carts to pass, and then led the way across the street. Inside Elphinstone Park, the only people were perhaps a dozen young men with books on their laps, all set up on benches under the park's gaslights.

"That's unusual park behavior, isn't it?" Colin commented from his position a few steps behind her.

"This park has light to read and write by, so the students living in homes where oil is scarce come here to study after dark."

They passed the banyan, and Perveen described what her grandfather had told her about cotton merchants meeting underneath and pledging to share funds to build a Native Stock Exchange, later named the Bombay Stock Exchange.

"So a grand tree is the root — or I should say roots — of growing industry," Colin mused.

"You're right. And that banyan is so old, its hanging roots must number in the hundreds."

Perveen spied an unoccupied bench distant from the students. She could see why nobody was there — the gas streetlight nearby was out. She sat down on one end and beckoned to him.

Colin stayed where he was. "There is no other bench. We cannot play spies here."

With a rush of bravery, she said, "I don't mind if you sit with me. The lamp's out, and it's growing dark. If anyone hears our conversation, they'll think it's two English people."

He sat down, but not close. There were probably forty inches between them.

From somewhere nearby, there was a sound similar to a spinning coin. Colin laughed. "Imagine. An Indian nightjar in the midst of all of this."

"A what?" Perveen was amused.

"It's a bird that becomes an active hunter of flying insects at night. I can't recall the Latin name."

"Which is hardly important in India," she joked.

After they'd both laughed, they stayed in companionable silence until she felt brave enough to speak. "Colin." It felt daring to use his first name again. "I apologize for my terrible manners during this visit. But there is so much difficulty here. The prince's schedule. The safety of everyone in Bombay.

And I mourn Freny Cuttingmaster every day."

"Yes, I can understand that is heavy on your mind. And you haven't even mentioned what happened at the Orient Club. I wanted so badly to speak up for you, but I remembered your father's admonition."

"I saw you at the head table," Perveen said. "You even moved to a chair right beside Prince Edward, so you could talk like old friends. You like him, don't you?"

Colin shifted his right leg to a more comfortable angle. "I don't agree with a lot of Eddie's thoughts, but yes — I'd say it's easy to get along with him. You probably don't know why you were sent out."

"It was because of Mr. Mortimer's suspicions."

Colin lowered his voice. "Actually, it was because Eddie wanted to meet you. He'd heard just a bit from me, so he was curious. And that placed Mr. Mortimer in a quandary. He didn't want to allow it."

Perveen put a hand to her mouth, imagining it. "My father would have been so pleased, but truly, it might not have gone so well."

"At least the Mr. Mortimer and his ilk won't dominate India forever. I fervently hope that India will be independent by 1930 at the latest." Flinging out one arm theatrically, he added, "A new world with new laws! And I wonder how your situation might be different."

"My situation? I'd hope that Oxford will have formally recognized all the women's colleges, so I'd have the degree I'm still waiting to hang. And I dream of lunching with other women lawyers at the Ripon Club."

"You only speak of work." Colin lowered his voice. "What if India were to have a single legal code that allowed for personal freedoms such as no-fault divorce?"

"I can't even imagine that." Shrugging, she added, "What would altered laws in India mean for us? When my country is independent, the Indian Civil Service will not be run by Englishmen."

"But what if I'm not in the civil service?" Colin paused, as if he expected her to answer. When she did not, he continued. "Has my arrival in Bombay ruined everything for you?"

"I like knowing you're here," she said after a pause. "But it's not your natural habitat. You prefer to live deep in nature, where there are no Mortimers peeking out from the trees."

"Satapur is beautiful — but it's sometimes

lonely." He draped his arm along the back of the bench — not touching her, but close enough to make her think about what it would feel like. "I have so many internal questions these days. What if I worked in Bombay, rather than Satapur? And what if you had never married Cyrus Sodawalla?"

Heart beating fast, she struggled to answer. "If I hadn't met him, I'd have obeyed my parents and finished studying at the Government Law School. I might be a law clerk, if not a solicitor. And my parents would handpick a promising solicitor or barrister with perfect Parsi heritage to be my husband. Then there might be an extra name on our letterhead, although I am sure the building would forever be known as Mistry House." She did not add that once she had children, she would no longer be working at Mistry House. That was the kind of fact everyone understood.

"How pragmatic." Colin tapped his finger on the edge of the bench, an anxious staccato rhythm. "Such an arranged marriage will probably be Prince Edward's lot, despite his wishes."

Colin's gossip about the prince surprised her. "What are his wishes?"

"I don't know if I should tell you."

"Please! You know that lawyers are the

best at keeping confidences."

Colin slid close enough to whisper in her ear. "He is in love with a married woman named Freda Dudley Ward. Eddie wishes her husband, who is a Liberal member of Parliament, would find grounds to divorce her. But even if that were to be, our future King-Emperor cannot marry a divorcee."

"So they are also star-crossed lovers!" As the words burst from her, she belatedly realized she'd given herself away.

"It is like I was saying. The prince and I are not intimate friends. But we are honest enough with each other to know we both share a similar emotional torment."

Colin's head was bent, as if he were waiting for her to lash out and tell him he had done wrong: the message she had given almost continuously since his arrival.

Perveen couldn't repeat her script tonight. Taking a deep breath, she adjusted herself to close the remaining inches between them, and she put her palms on Colin's face.

His skin was warm, with a very light stubble on his cheeks. She moved her hands, exploring up to his cheekbones and eyes. It was as if she were blind — but what she was doing for herself was mapping him, because she knew this might be the last time they were ever so physically near.

It was impossible to tell who started the kiss. No blame could be assigned, she thought, as the kiss moved from a soft exploration to something deeper. She removed her hands from his face as he pulled her into an embrace. She tasted tea and mint, and it brought her back to the mountains, where her feelings had begun.

Their feelings. Colin's mouth moved from her mouth to her hair. She heard him whispering something in her ear but willed herself not to decipher the words. Too many boundaries could not be crossed in one night.

At last, she remembered who she was, and that she was kissing a man in the middle of Elphinstone Circle. Even though the streetlight was out, they could not guarantee that a constable wouldn't appear with a torch in hand.

She pulled away from the warmth of Colin and steadied her breath before speaking again. "I — I don't know why I did that. It was imprudent."

"It was reckless for both of us," he admitted. "But it was right. I don't feel twisted with worry anymore. However, there is something else I need to confess to you."

"Oh?" She had a feeling of dread.

"It's my work. I may be leaving my current position."

This was why he'd talked about cities. He was likely being sent somewhere prestigious. His association with the prince and viceroy would make New Delhi a possibility. She could not bear to hear that he would be completely leaving her, so she cut him off. "I'm sorry to hear about that. But we can't talk details now. I don't mind if you write to me, but it's a risk to both of us to stay out any longer."

"You thought nobody was looking at us in this little park," he objected.

"But I've realized how much time has passed. It's almost half-past seven, and I have someone waiting for me."

"Who's that?" He sounded tense.

"Arman, our family driver. His car is parked near the Asiatic Society building." She heard the catch in her voice. "I'm sorry, but I don't think I can offer you a ride. He might give away something to my father —"

"Don't worry about that. Of course you must go, Perveen. And it's an easy walk to the hotel. And I think I will feel like I'm fly-ing."

She was suddenly anxious, even though they were in the European Quarter, and the riots were over. He could become lost. "Do you absolutely know the way?"

"I draw maps, darling."

Darling. She felt the endearment in her chest. "When exactly are you leaving for Baroda?"

"I've got to pack and meet the royal train at Victoria Terminus before eleven. My time here was quite short." In a rush, he added, "I might still give the lecture. One never knows."

"Maybe I'll be there."

"Goodbye, Perveen." He paused. "I feel strange saying this, but what happened tonight — it's made me happier than I ever could have believed. No matter what might never happen for us, I can carry this with me."

Was she happy? She considered the question as she laid her hand on his for a moment before standing up to walk away toward the lights.

No. Happiness was for those who saw possibilities in the future.

All she could foresee was pain.

31
A TURN FOR THE WORSE

The memory of Perveen's secret meeting made her behave virtuously the following morning. Instead of lazing on her balcony with Lillian she searched for the earrings she'd borrowed from Gulnaz and returned them, with apologies. And now she was handing her father his briefcase as they prepared to leave the house for work.

"Much to do," Jamshedji said as they climbed into the car, which was shining clean from Arman's early morning washing. "We have a full raft of people wishing to file civil suits against their neighbors, and you say you want to call on the Cuttingmasters."

In the car, Perveen explained about the burglary at the college, and Mr. Atherton's gift of five hundred rupees to the Cutting-masters. He agreed with her that the money needed to stay in the safe until they'd agreed to accept it. He also advised against presenting the college's offer to the mourning parents at Doongerwadi. "It's bad form to speak of a financial offer inside a place of mourning. You should go to their home instead."

"Then I could visit them later in the week," she suggested. "I have appointments every hour today, don't I?"

"You do — but lunch hour is free. You can use that time to quickly travel to the colony. If they haven't yet returned from the dakhma, you can leave Mr. Atherton's letter along with a cover letter from us."

Perveen didn't push Jamshedji to explain why he felt so strongly she deliver the letter that day. She suspected it was because the firm needed to make an immediate, earnest attempt at communication with the Cuttingmasters.

Therefore, at one o'clock, Perveen rode with Arman to Vakil Colony.

The two old sentries were still chatting to each other in their chairs next to the closed gate. This time, they gave smiles of recognition and opened the gate quickly so that Arman could drive inside.

She gave them the ostensible parking money again, and wondered if the residents watching from windows might judge her to be corrupt, the way she had when Mr.

Grady gave money to the college guard. She hadn't had the chance to ask him why.

As she walked through the faded colony, something bright caught her eye. A shiny blue Raleigh bicycle was leaning against the same wall where Khushru's battered black bicycle had rested a few days earlier. Probably a friend had come to see him — most likely Naval.

Then she stopped, thinking about it. It was one-thirty on a school day. Why would he be home? Especially since his own bicycle was absent.

The Cuttingmasters' lace curtains were drawn. When she knocked on the door, there was silence. After waiting a few minutes, she knocked again. Nothing.

"What is it?"

Hearing a familiar voice, Perveen looked up and recognized Freny's grandmother, Bapsi.

"Perveen! Why are you back again?"

Bapsi's sharp tone suggested she still resented Perveen's involvement in the decision not to bring Freny's body home. And she might have heard from someone that Perveen had brought embarrassment to the family by bringing Mithan to the stand.

"Hello, Bapsi-mai. I was hoping to speak with your son and his wife, but they must

475

still be at Doongerwadi."

"They will return before supper tonight. I came home early."

Perveen wondered if she could trust Bapsi to give Atherton's letter to them without opening it. An alternative would be to put the letter directly into the slot of the Cuttingmasters' flat, but she was almost certain that Bapsi would have the key. There was no point in covert action.

"You have come so far," Bapsi called down. "At least have a cup of tea with me."

Perveen was surprised at this offer, but it was a good opening. She climbed the stairs to the first floor and, as the old lady held open a door for her, the cat called Nana emerged.

"I returned last night because I was worried about Nana," Bapsi said as Perveen stroked the cat. "Khushru said he would feed her, but she seemed starved when I arrived."

Just like the flat downstairs, the grandmother's home was filled with practical old Victorian furniture, but she had many more photographs, paintings, and calendars on her walls. Perveen settled into an easy chair with elaborate doilies on the arms while Bapsi went into her kitchen to put water on the hob. On a silver table, Freny's portrait

476

was draped with a fresh jasmine garland. On the side table was a cluster of other framed pictures, including one of a boy in his early teens. He had the same eyes as Freny, but was gifted with a wide, cheeky smile. It was unusual to smile for a professional photograph — how indulgent the family had been to allow it.

"Is that Darius?" Perveen asked Bapsi when she returned carrying a tray with two cups on it.

The woman put down the tray and followed Perveen's gaze to the table. "Yes. Just a year before the accident. We all mourned him so much — not just because he was the only son, but because he was such a fun-loving, joyful boy. Freny never stopped feeling she was at fault for him going to that colony. She said she'd never hold secrets again."

"Yet she joined the Student Union without telling her parents."

"But she told me." Bapsi had pride in her voice. "So there was no secret — she was honest with the one she trusted most."

Perveen stayed quiet, hoping the grandmother would reveal more.

"She was very excited to be in this group. She admired so many of the young men. She thought one might be the next Bal Gangadhar Tilak." Bapsi smiled sadly. "She could only think of the others rising high, because for her to speak out would destroy her father. And she'd never do such a thing."

Most women born in the mid-nineteenth century would disapprove of their granddaughters socializing with males — but Bapsi was different. It was most likely because when Freny had spoken openly to her, she'd really listened.

"Bapsi-mai, did Freny say which boy was like Bal Gangadhar Tilak?"

Bapsi shook her head. "No, and I'm sure it wasn't Khushru. Such a soft rabbit, that boy. He was only in the group because his friend wanted company there — but they both quit it."

Perveen checked her watch. It was still almost a quarter hour until Arman would return with the car. "I'd like to speak with Khushru's mother. Where is their home?"

"They stay in the flat on the second floor of building B. There is a blue bicycle outside; it belongs to Khushru. Would you please take something back for me? I have cleaned the bowls they brought me."

"Yes," Perveen said, glad for the excuse Bapsi was giving her. "And before I forget, I've come with a letter for your son and daughter-in-law from the principal of the

478

college. After they read it, they may want to speak with me."

Bapsi gingerly took the letter. "My son is wishing nothing more to do with the law."

"It's not about a court case. It's from the college."

"That's fine, then."

Perveen's arms were laden with crockery as she walked across the courtyard a few minutes later to the building with the bicycle. As she looked at it, she remembered speaking about a looted sporting-gear shop with a client. What if Khushru had been late to his part-time job because he'd stolen a bicycle — and the reason she hadn't seen it earlier was because he was hiding it until the riots were over?

The thought made her anxious, because if she were to learn anything indicating the bicycle was from Vargas Sporting Goods, she'd need to use the information for her client's case.

There was no sales sticker on the bicycle that she could see. Feeling worried, she climbed the stairs to the Kapadias' apartment. Breathing heavily, she could understand why Bapsi had asked for her help.

"Hello?" she called at the doorway, from which a rich aroma of ginger and onion wafted. "Mrs. Kapadia, are you in?"

There was a clattering of pans in the kitchen and in a moment, Hester was at the door, wiping her hands on her apron. She looked at Perveen in surprise. "You carried my bowls! You are the Cuttingmasters' solicitor. You should not do the work of a maid."

Perveen smiled at her. "It's good for me to exert myself — and please call me Perveen. Bapsi-mai sends her thanks to you."

Hester's face relaxed. "I am already working on more dishes because Mithan and Firdosh return home tonight. They will be able to eat meat again, so I am making dhansak."

Dhansak was the special meal served to comfort after the first stage of mourning had passed. It was said that the variety of spices — more than thirty, depending on the cook — nourished the body in a particular way, and the meat provided strength to go out in the world again. There was a whole process of remembrance that would last a year, with special meetings of relatives and prayers of different kinds. Maybe by the next year, the Cuttingmasters would relent and allow Perveen to mourn alongside them.

"Did Khushru go to college today?"

"No, he is not well. He is in bed today, as

he has been since Sunday evening." The confident lilt in Hester's voice was gone.

"Oh, dear." Perveen remembered the listlessness she'd attributed to grief. "What kind of illness?"

Hester raised her hands. "Who knows? He has a weak stomach. I have brought him soup, tea and water, but he refuses all. He could not fall sick at a worse time, because mid-term examinations are coming."

"He was walking about on Sunday. Perhaps he caught something at Doongerwadi or later at the college."

"Yes, he spent all day with Naval." Sighing, she said, "I hope he is well enough for college tomorrow. He must get out of bed and go because there will be a mathematics examination."

"Is that shiny blue bicycle his?" Perveen remembered what she'd seen against the wall.

"Yes, indeed. A gift from Naval. Who ever thought my son would have a school friend as kind to him as a wealthy uncle?" Hester looked expectantly at her.

"It's quite a grand bicycle." Perveen forced herself to speak in a light tone. "I wonder where Naval got it."

"Army Navy Store. The very best, he said."

The department store was inside Fort, so if it had been looted, she would have heard about it. The bicycle probably wasn't stolen; but it still was a curious gift for one student to bestow upon another. "Has Naval always given Khushru such large gifts?"

"No, this is the first time. He said it was to cheer him after the tragedy. So tomorrow, Khushru can ride it to college."

"He might not be well enough to go, Hester-bai. Surely he can take the examinations later."

"This is Khushru's final year. These marks are very important if he is to get a scholarship to the University of Bombay." Stirring the pot of dhansak, she added, "He deserved a full scholarship to Woodburn, but they only discounted half. The rest he paid for all by himself. He would not let me put my needlework money toward anything except food and housing."

Perveen felt she'd learned everything she could from the mother. "Please tell Khushru I hope he feels better soon."

"Wait, Perveen-bai. Would you please go in to see him?" Hester put down her spoon and looked pleadingly at her. "You are a professional. So tell him, even if he is feeling weak, it is better to show his face in school, just as you do your work without complaint."

"Of course I'll see him."

Hester showed Perveen to the closed bedroom door, but the sound of water boiling over on the stove sent the mother hurrying back to the kitchen.

Perveen knocked, but when there was no reply, she opened the bedroom door. The pleasant kitchen smells were suddenly replaced with the stench of vomit. Evidence of Khushru's illness was all over the bed and pooled on the floor.

"Khushru! What is this?" she exclaimed, looking desperately for a cloth, and finally settling on a worn towel she saw in the room's corner.

The student was curled in a ball, facing the wall. He didn't look at Perveen, just breathed fast.

Perveen was shocked that Hester thought he could possibly resume his studies the next day. Perhaps the vomiting had just happened. "You are clearly very ill. How long have you been vomiting?"

Instead of answering her question, he muttered, "Leave me. I deserve this."

When she'd talked with Khushru during the brief walk to the college, she had noticed he was more subdued than his friend Naval. She had chalked it up to personality differences. But now she sensed the boy was depressed as well as seriously ill.

Noticing a pitcher next to the bed and a glass still half-full of water, she said, "Please, drink a little water."

When he didn't respond, she pulled him away from the wall and shifted his position so he was sitting upright against a pillow. She held the drinking glass to his mouth at a slight angle, and from the movement of his lips, she saw he was trying to oblige. Yet a few seconds later, the water burbled up and over his lips.

Perveen put down the glass. If he could not even swallow, he was seriously compromised. "Khushru, when did you last drink water?"

He remained mute.

"Did you eat something that perhaps made you ill?"

The young man groaned as Perveen laid a hand on his forehead. It felt cold, not warm with fever. What was this illness that had gripped him?

"Don't lie down again," she told Khushru, and went out into the other room.

"Is he any better?" Hester asked.

"He vomited all over his bed! He needs to go to see a physician."

"I don't know." She shook her head, making it clear that his needs were taking a toll on her. "It has only been a day and a half he's been like this. He's feeling more poorly today than yesterday, but surely he will be better soon."

Perveen was shocked by the mother's reluctance to act. "Have you seen him in the last few hours?"

"Not since eight o'clock, when I brought him water, tea, and a breakfast he didn't eat." Frowning, she said, "I can't keep running to check on him when I have to make dhansak. And don't you get your hands dirty, Perveen-bai."

"I don't think we should wait." Perveen spoke bluntly. "My driver can bring him to hospital. I think Sir J. J. might be best."

"But that hospital charges fees." Hester had alarm in her eyes. "Parsi General will not charge us."

"Sir J. J. is much closer — and it's connected with the Grant Medical College, so the doctors can test for a wide variety of illnesses and substances." She did not want to say "poisoning," in case she was wrong. But that was what she suspected. "You speak of money being important; but you cannot afford to delay treatment for Khushru. You could lose him just as the Cuttingmasters lost their children."

32
A NAMED SUSPECT

At Sir J. J. Hospital, Perveen jumped out of the Daimler and went into the lobby to summon assistance. Khushru was lying across the back seat with a lap robe over him and Hester at his side. Finally accepting the seriousness of Khushru's condition, his mother had wept the whole journey to the hospital.

Three orderlies followed Perveen with the gurney and reached the car. The one closest to the front spoke. "Are both of them ill?"

"No, just the young man. Please tell his doctor he might have been poisoned. He has been vomiting for days and cannot even swallow water." It was important to tell the orderlies what Hester might forget.

"All right," the orderly interrupted. "The boy's mother can stay with him. Go on your way. The doctors do not want too much crowding."

■ ■ ■ ■

Perveen got into the car, still feeling rattled. She'd worried that Khushru might expire on the car ride. The orderly's curt instructions made her wonder if she'd been overbearing. It was true that blood relatives should take responsibility for a patient's situation. However, Hester Kapadia had seemed more concerned for her son's mathematics exam than his health.

By the time the car pulled up to Mistry House on Bruce Street, it was three-thirty. She had clients stacked up waiting: two complaints of property destruction, and a mother seeking assistance with her Congress Party–member son's arrest. There was also a message from Alice that Mustafa had taken.

Miss H-J will be home after five o'clock. Please call.

Perveen frowned. "Did Miss H-J give any reason why?"

"No, madam. She rang just one hour ago."

"I wonder if she was calling from the college," Perveen said, although there was no possible way to speak with her now. The best thing would be to get through the day's work. That evening, perhaps the two of them could visit Khushru in the hospital.

"Your father wanted you to see this." Mustafa handed her that day's *Times of India.*

It had been folded in quarters to show an article on the front page.

POLICE NAME SUSPECT IN COLLEGE GIRL MURDER

The Bombay Police announced the identification of a suspect in the homicide of Freny Firdosh Cuttingmaster. Dinesh Apte, 19, a former student at Woodburn College, has been charged. Apte was already in police custody at Gamdevi Police Station on charges of disturbance of the peace, attempted assassination and inciting sedition during His Majesty the Prince of Wales's arrival. Police accuse Dinesh Apte of strangling Miss Cuttingmaster before rushing into the parade, where he pursued the prince's carriage until military and police captured him. The accused's lawyer, the Hon. Mr. Mohammed Ali Jinnah, refutes this accusation. Mr. H. V. Atherton, principal of Woodburn College, announced that, as of last Friday, Mr. Apte was expelled.

Shaking her head, Perveen read the article

again. Freny had told Perveen that Dinesh was unkind to her. There certainly had been time for Dinesh to attack before running out to the parade. Yet she had stronger suspicions about Mr. Grady and Mr. Gupta; and now, since she'd seen Khushru's condition, she was considering Naval.

Dinesh Apte's advocate, Mohammed Ali Jinnah, would almost certainly refuse her access to him. Then her connection with the lawyer's wife, Ruttie, came to mind. Perhaps she could use their childhood alliance to see if he'd allow her to speak to Dinesh. But for that, Mr. Jinnah would expect some benefit to their case. And would that be ethical?

Arman came down the hall, his face shining clean from the scrubbing he'd given it in the washroom. He had cleaned up head to toe after having carried Khushru into the car, a heroic act which Perveen would relay to Jamshedji. Arman had done far beyond the usual since the prince's arrival; he deserved a bonus.

"Mustafa's kurta looks fine on you," she said, looking at the fresh, starched shirt that had replaced his soiled one. "I'm grateful for what you did and glad to see you looking fresh again."

Arman cocked his head appraisingly. "And

489

you are looking too anxious! You must not worry about that boy in the hospital. You said to his mother, the doctors are very wise about every kind of illness. They will try every medicine to cure him."

"I hope so." Looking into Arman's earnest face, she realized that she, too, would have to try what seemed impossible. "I have a favor to ask. Whilst I'm here seeing clients, could you please bring a letter to a barrister's chambers within the High Court?"

Looking quizzically at her, he said, "That's a very simple favor. Of course!"

Perveen sped past the waiting clients to go upstairs to her office, where she quickly handwrote a letter to Mr. Jinnah. Her note opened with her pleasure at seeing her childhood friend Ruttie with him at the Orient Club. She next wrote that she might have information of interest pertaining to Dinesh Apte and begged a chance to speak with both of them. The letter said she'd be waiting at Gamdevi Police Station at five-thirty, and signed the letter.

Once again in the hall, she handed the letter to Arman. After reading who it was addressed to, he raised his eyebrows. "Big man in the courts. I know where his chamber is. I won't leave until I have an answer for you."

■ ■ ■ ■

Now, for the work at hand. Fixing a smile on her face, Perveen stepped into her parlor and addressed the Parsi liquor-store owner wanting to sue Mr. Gandhi. Explaining why this was an impossibility took more than a quarter hour and did not result in gaining a client.

Equally complicated stories unfolded as the afternoon continued. Some complainants could identify who had smashed their windows and had eyewitnesses, but about half of them weren't sure if the perpetrator was a personal enemy or simply a representative of the Congress Party, or "those Hindus and Muslims."

And this was where the tiny seed of hate began and would grow a sturdy trunk that forked many branches. Like these lawsuits.

As Perveen's last visitor signed the retainer, she went to the parlor window. The Daimler was not there. Perhaps it meant that Arman was still at the High Court. It put her plan of going to Gamdevi Station into question.

Perveen headed upstairs to see her father. She had a lot of difficult things to say.

Jamshedji Mistry was at the partners'

desk, bent over a stack of papers. Without looking up, he said, "Such a busy day — I've hardly seen you."

"Yes. Busy for both of us." She felt it important to acknowledge the long hours he'd spent.

Still reading the paper in front of him, he spoke. "Arman said that at Vakil Colony, you discovered Khushru Kapadia was ill. You think it may not be natural causes."

"I suspect poisoning. We took him to Sir J. J. Hospital. I am hoping for a quick diagnosis."

"And I hear that you sent Arman out on an errand to the High Court?"

"Yes. That's what I came to talk with you about." Perveen explained her desire to interview Dinesh Apte and her proposed meeting with his advocate at Gamdevi Station.

Finally, he looked up. "You are asking *the* Mohammed Ali Jinnah to be at your beck and call?"

"Yes," she said, striving to appear as if this were a normal request. "You know him, don't you?"

Shaking his head, he said, "What you asked him for is very much against legal etiquette. And why would you ask to meet with Mr. Jinnah at a police station rather than his chambers?"

In a steady voice, she said, "I must speak to Dinesh. I really don't believe it's possible for him to have accomplished the murder. He might be scapegoated because he knew Freny, he's already in custody, and the police have no idea of how to locate the perpetrator."

"You cannot defend Dinesh Apte." Jamshedji's voice was stern. "He already has the best criminal barrister in Bombay. Not to mention you're not a barrister at all."

Perveen was frustrated her father was fixated on the obvious. "I don't intend to defend him. But Dinesh was very involved in the Student Union. He may know something that could definitively identify Freny's murderer."

"Jinnah will of course ask him that when creating the defense. It's not something you're bringing to him that could bolster the case."

"We never know what will come out in an interview — and Mr. Jinnah very likely has many cases going. And I need this information now — not when the trial commences in the distant future. Khushru's life may be hanging in the balance." Shaking her head, she told him, "I wasn't able to prevent Freny's death. I will tell Mr. Jinnnah what that feels like."

"A veteran barrister has surely felt that kind of pain before. It might work." Jamshedji tapped his pen against the desk.

Then Perveen had another idea. "And what about what Mr. Sandringham told us? If there's an ongoing plot to murder the Prince of Wales, and anyone from the college is definitively involved, the police must be informed. A life is a life, regardless of where one lies on the political spectrum."

"Correct," Jamshedji said. "But we shall not try to cross that bridge before we come to it."

The sound of an engine rose up from underneath the window. Jamshedji glanced out. "Arman has returned. Go as quickly as you can, and don't be too disappointed if Mr. Jinnah isn't there."

Arman started speaking even before she got into the car. "I gave the note to a junior advocate, who said Mr. Jinnah was in court. I'm afraid I don't have the answer to it."

"Never mind." Perveen steeled herself for failure. "My father said we can travel to Gamdevi. Let's go."

Perveen had been to the handsome graystone station many times before; however, she'd never had such a complicated reason for showing up. She ran through the explanation in her mind as she entered the building.

The desk sergeant at the front counter barely looked up at her when she asked if Mr. Jinnah had arrived. Shaking his head, he said, "No more press."

"I'm not press. I'm a solicitor waiting to meet him."

He didn't answer.

A short row of wooden seats was filled with a sad-looking assortment of civilians and legal professionals, and very likely a few reporters. None were female. Mindful of her father's dislike of her sitting next to men, she stayed standing. Nobody would be able to carry tales about Bombay's first woman lawyer behaving without etiquette.

She waited, eyes on the door, as the crowd waxed and waned. There was a hallway leading to the cells. Somewhere in those depths Dinesh was being held. Had he been beaten, or forced to confess to something he hadn't done?

An officer of higher rank, judging from his badges, strode in from the hallway and caught sight of her. Immediately, he barked, "Madam, what is your business?"

"I'm waiting for Dinesh Apte's lawyer." She felt shy to say "Mr. Jinnah" again, because the sergeant might join the conversation and suggest she be thrown out.

"Mr. Murthy is with him now. He should be coming up shortly."

"Who is that?"

"Dinesh Apte's counsel."

If only she'd thought about this earlier. After all, Arman had spoken of an associate getting the letter. Now she understood she'd have to deal with someone else; someone who wouldn't care that she knew Ruttie Jinnah, or that she was her father's daughter.

Five minutes later, a young man in a suit emerged from the hallway connected to the lockup.

"Hello, are you Mr. Murthy?" Perveen guessed.

The young man turned immediately. "Yes, madam. And you?"

Courtesy was a good start. "My name is Perveen Mistry."

"Yes. The lawyer who sent the letter."

"Mr. Murthy, could we please speak for a few minutes?"

Looking at his watch, he said, "Yes. But let's go outside."

The sky was darkening, so they stood under a streetlight. Perveen could see Arman watching with interest from the car, twenty feet away.

Patting his breast pocket, he said, "I read your letter. I am Mr. Jinnah's junior associate and have taken over for him on Dinesh's case."

"Do you mean that you're assisting Mr. Jinnah?"

Puffing out his chest, he said, "Not any longer. He has delegated everything to me."

She had a suspicion that Mr. Murthy had misunderstood his role. "Will you be representing Dinesh in court, then?"

"Yes, I think so." He smiled nervously. "It will be my third case."

"Third case?" She needed clarification.

"Third case as a barrister in court. I graduated the Government Law School this spring with honors. Now, you wrote that you have information about the case that could be beneficial to my client. Tell me what you have for us." His tone was patronizing.

This young man would not be able to understand about the lives at risk. She had to be strategic. "You went to see Dinesh just now. How is he coping with being in detention?"

Murthy blinked, as if the question was surprising. "Naturally, he is most upset. He came in for one crime and now he's being charged for more, of which he is completely innocent."

"Does he know that I wanted to speak with him?"

"Yes, I told him about the letter, and that you might have helpful information. He already knew your name. I was surprised, but he had heard of you from another student at the college."

"Did he say who told him about me?"

"No, and I didn't ask. We had too much to talk about. However, he wanted to see you."

"Really?" This was what she'd wanted. "I am grateful for your time and am ready to speak with him now. I have only a few questions —"

"The thing is, I am quite busy. I must get back to my chambers immediately."

She felt deflated. "So, I can't meet him, then?"

"No. I am saying go inside and speak to him." He waved his hands in exasperation. "You are taking too much of my time. But I want to hear the information you have for us not later than twelve noon tomorrow. Can you promise me that?"

"Of course. Thank you." Perveen struggled to hide her shock. Was Mr. Murthy so green as to let a client speak unguarded to a different lawyer? Clearly, he did not know she had a prior relationship with the Cutting-masters.

There was nothing else to do at the moment but take the surprise blessing he'd given and go back inside Gamdevi to see Dinesh.

33

INSIDE THE CELL

Once Perveen explained what Mr. Murthy had said to the desk sergeant, he told her to sign in on the record of visitors to detainees. However, she had to wait ten minutes for a guard to emerge and escort her to the quarters where prisoners were held.

While Gamdevi Station was a shining example of modernity in its public areas, the cellblock was dank and dirty. The fact that it was evening only made the cellblock more forbidding. The guard preceded her, carrying his lantern along a corridor lit only by a few hall lamps. As the guard and Perveen approached, prisoners rattled the bars and called out weak requests for food and water. She kept her head down because as they sighted her, a chorus of calls came: sister, mother, darling, lover.

They all wanted to be saved.

At last, the guard opened a padlocked cell door and waved to her. "This is Apte's cell.

While you are inside, I will keep the door locked. Call down the hall when you want to leave."

Dinesh must not have shown himself as visibly dangerous, or the guard wouldn't lock her in. But she realized it was still a risk, and her heart thudded with anxiety. "Mr. Apte. It's Perveen Mistry. Your lawyer said I could come to speak with you. Is that all right?"

A shape in the back corner shifted and slowly unfolded, as if in some sort of physical distress. Then Dinesh slowly got to his feet, holding onto the cell's bars for support.

In the weak light coming from the corridor, he looked frightened and somewhat aged — not old, she realized, but with skin that looked parched. His young face was now covered in a beard, and he wore a striped prisoner's uniform.

"Miss Mistry." His voice came slowly, and was hoarse, reminding her of Khushru. "I am thankful."

"I am, too, for the chance to speak." She hoped he hadn't been so deprived that his mind was not clear. "Are you thirsty?"

"Yes. No water since yesterday."

In a modern station like Gamdevi, this was unthinkable. Turning back to the hallway bars, Perveen called out, "Sir, could you please bring him a cup of water?" Along the cellblock more inmates began their own calls for water, while rattling the bars.

"No. I cannot leave you alone. That is another man's job." The guard's voice was terse.

Dinesh's voice was low. "Will you be my new lawyer?"

She wanted to get information from him, but she couldn't give him false hope. "I don't work for Mr. Jinnah's firm, sorry. I am a solicitor with my father at Mistry Law. I am here because I wanted to ask you a few questions."

"Will you tell the police?"

This was tricky to answer. "I don't work for the police. However, if you tell me something Mr. Murthy doesn't already know, I'll explain to him how important it is to ask you more about it. We have an appointment tomorrow." Gaining confidence, she added, "I'm here because I don't believe you are guilty, and I think there's a strong chance you have information that could lead to the arrest of the guilty individual. Still, we are not in a formal lawyer-client relationship, which would ensure total confidentiality. I could be subject to police questioning."

"I want the world to know the truth of who killed her. Ask me anything."

Perveen had never been more conscious of listening ears nearby, so she lowered her voice and switched to English. "I want to know more about your actions that morning, and who else you might have seen or heard. Could you tell me about where you were waiting before you ran out into the street?"

"Inside the college." Bitterly, he added, "Freny could have told you, if she were still alive."

"You disliked her, didn't you?" Perveen pulled a notebook out of her briefcase and felt around for a pencil.

"Dislike her?" There was a catch in his voice. "No. It was the opposite."

For the first time since they'd been together, she felt disbelief. After all, Freny had told her about his personal disparagements. "Please tell me more."

"She was so brave." He was silent for a while, and then spoke again. "Not only brave — intelligent, honest, and beautiful. From her soul to her face. But she was Parsi."

"Meaning, Parsis cannot ever be trusted?" Perveen remembered what Freny had said.

"No. I am Hindu. I couldn't risk being

close to her, because" — his voice dipped, as if he was afraid for even her to hear — "because of what might happen."

He'd had a crush on her. Or maybe more. As Perveen realized all this, she heard a scuttling sound in the corner.

"Is someone else in here?" The noise had put her on edge.

"Mice." Sighing, he said, "I behaved rudely to her so she would avoid me. Somehow, she guessed that I was going to do something of my own planning at the procession. She passed a note to me that I should meet her on the second-floor gallery on Thursday morning."

"What time was the meeting supposed to be?"

"Ten-thirty. She must have known it would be after the roll call and before the prince actually arrived. Unfortunately, I had the note inside the pocket of my kurta when I was arrested. That is the evidence the police are using to say I killed her."

"What happened at your meeting?"

"She came late — at ten-forty. I think it was to ruin my plan of interrupting the prince. Anyway, I waited for her, and she let me have it. She spoke of Bal Gangadhar Tilak and said that I should not repeat his mistakes. This was not the first time she'd told me what she thought I should do."

"Did anyone you know follow the prince's itinerary beyond the procession?"

"What do you mean?"

"The prince traveled to Poona a few days ago." She could not say what had happened with the railway.

"I don't know about that. I've been inside this place for days. Let him enjoy India, while I lose my future in this country."

She could think of someone who was very tied to current affairs — who might have taken pains to learn the prince's schedule. "What did Mr. Grady know about your plan to interrupt the parade?"

"I told nobody, so I don't see how he knew anything. Although Freny was suspicious I had something planned. When she met me, she said she feared that I had a gun or knife and would assassinate the prince. She had been reading too much history of the movement. I explained that my body was the only weapon needed to cause disruption, but she still didn't want me to go. She announced that she would sit out the parade with me in one of the classrooms. This was the Student Union's original plan. I said I wouldn't do that."

Perveen was scribbling his words down in the dark, hoping she'd be able to read them later. "Yet you knowingly would put yourself at risk for arrest?"

"Yes. There are too many people who stop listening to the voice of truth because they value their associations with this college."

She wondered if this was a reference to his fellow students, Brajesh Gupta, or Terrence Grady. "Freny was writing a paper about Mr. Gupta for Mr. Grady's class. Did she ever say anything about either of these lecturers to you?"

"Oh, yes!" His voice warmed, as if he was eager to talk. "Dean Gupta had been a freedom fighter in Bal Gangadhar Tilak's group. She wanted to ask him about their past activities and what it was like when Bal was arrested. But he refused to discuss it."

This was the reason for Freny's search at the Asiatic Society library. She wanted an inside story about nationalist activity; however, Mr. Gupta might not have wanted anyone at the college to know about his past. He had a motive to keep Freny silent. "Did you see Dean Gupta in the building that morning?"

He was silent for a long moment, and then shook his head. "No. Was he missing from the college stands?"

"For a little bit," Perveen said. "Mr. Atherton said he and Dean Gupta went into the building to look for anyone who might not have come out to the stands."

"Ah!" Dinesh's exclamation cut through the dank air. "When I was arguing with Freny, I heard footsteps coming up the south stair. There were voices. It must have been them."

"How did you respond?"

"I told Freny we'd better go off separately. I thought of running down the north stair, but I didn't know who might be below there, so I went into the library for a bit."

She remembered what Rahul had said about hearing someone come in, breathing heavily. "And what happened with Freny?"

"I told her to go into one of the rooms and hide herself until they'd gone."

"Do you know which room she went into?"

"The administrative office. I thought she was slightly mad to take such a risk — but it was the closest doorway, and it was un-locked."

"And then?" Perveen felt she was on the verge of understanding what had happened.

"I waited inside the library five minutes or so. When I opened the library door, I could hear that the parade was in full swing. I made my run."

And that was why he'd arrived just a bit

too late for the prince to see him. She said, "Then you were arrested. It must have been terrifying."

"No," he said firmly. "I felt such a relief that I had done it and would no longer have to call myself a coward."

"Did you expect a lot of people would hear about what you'd done?"

Nodding, he said, "Yes, I did. But now, my good name is ruined. The police say I'm a murderer. Just like those men who were fighting and killing in the street. They also have bloodied our cause beyond recognition."

"How long ago did you hear about Freny's death?"

"I heard from Mr. Grady when he came to the station after my arrest. He was the one who tried to post bail for me. I saw him at the hearing and he told me what happened to her. He was quite shaken."

"How high was the bail demand?" Perveen asked, thinking about the money that had gone missing.

"There was no bail granted. He took whatever money he had and gave it to Mr. Jinnah as a deposit. But now Mr. Jinnah is very busy because of people arrested during the riots. He sent the younger lawyer, Mr. Murthy, instead."

Perhaps because Mr. Jinnah thought Dinesh's case had shifted from being that of a valiant freedom fighter to a murderer — bad publicity for the freedom movement. "Who else did you see or hear in the building?"

"I believe somebody else was in the library, but I did not look around to see. I was trying not to be found."

"Excepting your time in the library, did you stay on the first floor gallery?"

"Yes. Miss Hobson-Jones was gone, so I stayed in her room."

"And what did you do all that time?"

He was silent for a moment. "I had nothing to read there — it wasn't interesting like Mr. Grady's room. All I could do was look out the back window to the college garden. I watched some birds to calm myself."

"Calm yourself for . . ."

"For running out into the procession. I knew when I did it, I would never be admitted back to this college. The only thing I regretted was what it would do to my parents; but in the end, my name would go across the country. Sometime later, they might be proud."

His mention of the garden made her think of the fence along the side, and the men who'd supposedly climbed up for a view.

"Did you see anyone walking about the college garden?"

"Not walking about . . ." He paused. "I mean, I saw some boys crossing the grass from the hostel toward the college building."

"College boys? Could you identify them?"

"No. Only that they wore those hats that are like pillboxes on their heads." He held his hands upright, spread about ten inches apart. "What do you call them?"

"A fetah." Her mind was reeling. Woodburn College had a sizeable Parsi population — she knew from looking at the names and faces in the *Woodburnian*. But who would the two Parsi boys be, coming late from the hostel? Not Khushru, who was a commuting student. However, Naval had attended college that day, and he'd come late to the stands with his camera. "Did you see these two go to the front of the school?"

"I couldn't. From the classroom, my view was only of the back courtyard. They came along the north side, walking fast, so I would think they were going that way."

"How long were you in the library before you saw the boys?"

"Five minutes." His voice was sure.

The same amount of time he said he'd spent inside the library. She wondered

510

about the accuracy. "How do you know?"

"I was watching the clock on the wall for the projected time of the prince reaching the road near the college. We knew about timings because Principal Atherton was concerned about having enough time for activities in the chapel. I realized he'd come when the applause and cheers began."

"Did you pass the guard box when you went out?"

"No. I had thought about it earlier and knew the guard might run after me. I went out of the college and over the fence on the north side. There were some men hanging on the fence, but they gave way." He paused. "Do you think they could be found and speak as my witnesses?"

"Possibly." Perveen wanted to get back to the issue of the Parsi students, but she heard a scraping sound behind her. The guard was back.

"The sergeant says enough visiting time for you."

Perveen nodded to the guard. "Thank you for bringing me here. And Dinesh, keep your courage up. I will speak to Mr. Murthy tomorrow."

She paused at the desk to tell the sergeant the detainees were desperate for water. "It's important that people are treated as humans. As you know, if someone dies here, there will be an inquest."

"There are many reasons men die in detention." He spoke tightly, but as she exited, she heard him mutter to another guard about water.

It was just after seven and fully dark. Perveen was glad to see Arman waiting close to the station. He was not in the car but outside, his eyes on the station door.

"You were there a long time, Perveen-bai. I was worried you might have been arrested yourself!"

"Very funny," she said, getting into the car's back seat. She couldn't talk to Arman yet — she needed to take notes about all she'd heard. Some months ago, Colin had gifted her a small battery torch — and she pulled it out of her briefcase now and used it to illuminate the notebook where she wrote down what Dinesh had said.

The driving route brought them back along the Kennedy Sea-Face. As they approached Chowpatty Beach, Arman's voice cut through her concentration. "Look. Someone's climbing over the fence."

Perveen jerked her attention away from the notebook and to the direction he was pointing. Nobody was left on the fence, but she did see someone in trousers loping away from them.

"Is that him?" she asked.

"I hope it's only a student and not a troublemaker!" Arman turned his head and looked earnestly into her face. "We could follow?"

"Yes!"

However, by the time Arman had turned the car around and they'd driven several blocks into Babulnath Road, they could only find an aged accountant, who had said several men had passed to and fro, but none whose description he could remember.

"We did our best," Perveen consoled Arman, who had seemed ready to drive for hours. "If we learn that anything criminal happened at the college, you could tell the police what you saw. But let's get on to Mistry House so I can tell my father what I learned at Gamdevi Station. He was almost certain Dinesh's lawyer would deny me access. But I got to speak to Dinesh alone."

Arman put the car in gear and turned back into the Sea-Face Road. "Is this lawyer the same man I observed you talking with on the street?"

"Yes, Mr. Murthy. He permitted me to see Dinesh alone because he had to urgently return to his chambers."

Arman snorted. "Urgent? I doubt it."

Perveen heard the smugness in his voice. "Why do you say this?"

"After you went back inside the station, Mr. Murthy stepped into a hotel. He came shortly thereafter with a police inspector. They shook hands before parting ways."

"That's strange." She considered the situation. Jamshedji had cordial relations with some police, but this was after years of interactions in court and police stations. She wondered if this inspector was taking advantage of Murthy's naivete to gain information that could be used by the police in their investigation of Dinesh.

This was a troubling development, especially since she'd promised to speak with Murthy about what was said in her interview the next day.

At Mistry House, Mustafa opened the door straight away. "Welcome back. Your father is out."

She was startled. "Is there some trouble?"

"Not at all," he said, closing the door behind her and Arman. "Mr. Wadia invited him to the Ripon Club. They are celebrating the good that has come out of the worst of times."

Nawaz Wadia, the solicitor who'd given her a lift the previous Thursday afternoon, was surely also busy with extra clients. "I imagine they'll eat dinner."

"Yes. Arman, you are asked to fetch him there at ten," Mustafa instructed.

Perveen thought about the timing. "I'd rather not interrupt them by going to the club now. And it is too tiring for Arman to wait outside."

"I wait all day." Arman yawned. "It is the safest part of my job."

Mustafa gestured toward the parlor. "Rest yourself, Perveen-memsahib. I'll make you tea. A telegram came and some other mail you might want to read."

Two hours was easily enough time to pay a visit to Khushru in the hospital. Shaking her head, she said, "That's a kind offer, but I have an idea where Arman can take me for a short visit. But first, I need to telephone Alice. After that, we will be on our way."

34
The Final Visiting Hour

The phone rang many times at Alice's home before Govind answered.

"Not back yet?" Perveen was exasperated. It was eight o'clock, and Alice had planned to be home at five. "Is she still at the college?"

"Yes," the butler answered. "She rang to tell me that she is continuing grading."

Remembering the figure she'd seen climb over the fence, Perveen felt a flash of fear for Alice. "Is Sirjit there at the college?"

"Yes, of course."

Perveen thought back to what she'd seen around the college. No cars had been parked, nor had she seen a lit window. Either Alice was somewhere else entirely, or on her way home. "Please tell her I'm on my way to Sir J. J. Hospital to see Khushru Kapadia. He's being treated there. It's a serious situation and we must talk by telephone tonight."

"Of course, Miss Mistry." Govind's voice was sympathetic. "Do not worry at all."

As she put down the phone, Mustafa cleared his throat. "As I mentioned, there is a telegram. It came twenty minutes after you left for the police station."

"I hope it's not bad news." Perveen opened the envelope and removed the pale yellow paper. She read the typed words several times to make sure she understood. VISITED HOTEL SPENTA AND LEARNED NAVAL STAYED OVER THURSDAY NIGHT STOP MORE EXPLANATIONS WHEN I HAVE ACCESS TO TELEPHONE STOP AS EVER COLIN SANDRINGHAM STOP.

It seemed that Colin had done as she'd suggested but never thought possible; he'd brought Prince Edward to an ordinary Indian hotel. And somehow, he'd gathered the information that Naval had been there.

"Who sent the telegram?" Mustafa was all but peering over her shoulder. "Do you have a client out of town, or is it a relative?"

"Neither. I'd say he's more of an — informant. He's named Colin Sandringham. If he should telephone when I'm consulting with clients tomorrow, will you come to the door and tell me?"

"Of course. I shall take it as duty." Mustafa put his hand on his heart. "Be quick now, so you can return from your hospital visit in good time for your father."

As she settled inside the Daimler, Perveen thought about the way so many people seemed pulled by duty. She'd felt responsible for not gathering a full accounting of Freny's worries.

Both Freny and Khushru had felt responsible for Darius Cuttingmaster's drowning. Lalita was sorry she hadn't stuck with Freny. Mithan and Firdosh Cuttingmaster mourned their action of sending Freny to Woodburn College. Dinesh faulted himself for suggesting Freny hide apart from him. Even Mr. Atherton felt the college owed the Cuttingmasters money.

Those who committed crimes often regretted it. In this situation, though, might someone who hadn't disclosed guilty feelings be the actual criminal?

"There he is again." Arman's voice brought her back to the present.

"What?"

"I noticed a Rolls when we were leaving Bruce Street."

Perveen turned her head to look at the car behind them.

"Some rich people driving at night," Arman continued. "But it is strange they are no longer in the European Quarter."

"If that car doesn't belong to a maharaja, it might be someone high up in government," Perveen said.

"Shall I try to evade them? Surely I know the streets better than they do."

"No. If someone is following me, they know where I live and work, so I will see them again. And we are going to Sir J. J. Hospital. Park under the lights, right up front, and if they come behind us there, we will see who they are."

Perveen had spoken matter-of-factly, but she did not feel that way. She remembered what Arman had said about Dinesh's counsel, Mr. Murthy, coming out of a hotel with a police officer. That person could have notified Mr. Mortimer.

As they pulled up the driveway and parked at the entrance, Perveen looked behind her. The car that had followed them continued on a nearby road until it was gone. They could be waiting on the far side of the building, she imagined, or they could have passed on. In any case, they did not want to be identified.

A young nurse in the central lobby downstairs said that Khushru Sohrab Kapadia was upstairs in the general men's ward and visiting hours would be over in a half hour.

As Perveen signed in, the woman added, "Your brother already went up."

Perveen was startled. "My brother Rustom?"

Taking the logbook from Perveen, the nurse indicated a scrawled line just above hers. "No. Farrokh."

"Farrokh Kapadia," Perveen read aloud, then shook her head. She didn't know who it was. As she walked up the stairs to the ward, Perveen remembered the outline of the man Arman had seen climbing over Woodburn College's fence an hour earlier. Perhaps this was the person who'd come to the hospital and signed in as Farrokh Kapadia. It was a Parsi name that meant nothing to her, unless it was an alias for Naval Hotelwala.

Naval had been there for Khushru when Hester hadn't. But was Naval's constant companionship more harmful than healing?

Perveen headed to the men's ward. The door was open, and she peered into the dimly lit room filled with rows of cots. It took a few minutes before a weary-looking nurse came out with a clipboard and answered Perveen's question.

"Yes, Khushru Kapadia is an inpatient here, but he is not presently in the ward."

"Have the doctors taken him for a procedure?"

"No. His visiting brother took him in a wheelchair to get fresh air."

Out in the dark. This was alarming. "Did the doctor have a diagnosis for Khushru yet?"

A man's voice called out, "Bedpan, please!"

The nurse looked toward the room and then back at Perveen. "I'm sorry, I must tend to the patients. I believe the doctor treated Mr. Kapadia with charcoal. Poisoning is suspected — but the pathology result is not here yet."

So her suspicion was right. "Very well; I'll look for them in the garden. And if they come back before I do, please tell them that I'd like to speak with them."

If they came back. As she rode down on the lift, she thought about where the supposed Farrokh Kapadia might be taking Khushru. The hospital was surrounded by many gardens; it was Sir J. J.'s idea that a place where the ill and injured came should not be dank and dreary. He surely hadn't intended the vast gardens to be a place that someone could use as a murdering ground.

She doubted that Khushru's visitor knew

521

the hospital layout any better than she did. The best she could do was find witnesses to their expedition.

The durwan on duty at the hospital entrance listened to her query about a twenty-year-old male patient in a wheelchair accompanied by another young man.

"Are these Parsi boys?" he asked. When Perveen nodded, he said, "The patient's relative asked about where to get fresh air. I told them I did not think it a good idea to go far, especially with visiting hours ending shortly."

"So did they stay inside?" Out of the corner of her eye, Perveen could see Arman in the parked Daimler. He was looking expectantly at her. She shook her head, silently telling him she wasn't ready to go.

"No." The durwan pointed into the darkness. "They went along that path."

Because Khushru was in a wheelchair, they would not be able to easily traverse lawns. And following paths would keep her from getting lost. Perveen walked past Arman in the car, murmuring to him she would be back soon.

"I'll come!" Arman said.

"No cars left unattended!" the durwan called out. "Hospital rule."

"Sorry, Arman. Just stay where you are,"

Perveen said, hiding her unease. "We don't have time to argue with the man."

"But where are you going?"

"After a pair of young men. Did you see anyone pushing a wheelchair?"

"Yes. They went along that way," he said, pointing in the same direction that the durwan had. "Who are they?"

"Khushru Kapadia is the patient. The young man who's with him has an unclear identity. Please keep watch if they return before I do."

35

AT THE FOUNTAIN'S EDGE

Perveen picked up the edge of her sari so she could walk rapidly. She felt grateful for the tall gas lamps that glowed every so often along the path, and also for the presence of a few young doctors and nurses coming and going from hospital duty.

Her pace was quick, and soon she was breathing fast, both from exertion and fear. Where had Naval taken Khushru? Her mind raced with thoughts of whether the students had veered from the paths toward various small buildings — or even gone outside of the hospital grounds.

The movements of Dinesh, Freny, the faculty, and the unknown killer felt like a five-hundred-piece puzzle. She'd fitted together many of the pieces, but the most important ones weren't there. She felt now that it was Naval and Khushru who held them.

Dinesh Apte said he'd observed two Parsi

boys crossing the back courtyard after Freny and Dinesh had heard the teachers' voices and gone into hiding. Earlier, she'd ruled out the possibility that one of the two boys could have been Khushru. But now, she wasn't so sure.

Khushru was not recorded as being at roll call on Thursday morning. However, he hadn't been at the Hawthorn Shop at that time, either. Where had he been?

Khushru could have entered the college grounds over the fence after everyone was in chapel, or in the stands. Once on campus, he could have lingered close to the hostel to wait for Naval.

But what was this about? This was the piece that felt frustratingly elusive.

Passing one of the clinic buildings, she considered what she knew about Naval. His family based in Poona was well-off. There was no obvious reason to steal from the college office. Yet his good friend Khushru had trouble paying. He was working part time to save money for advanced studies at Bombay University.

After the procession, Naval had gone to spend the night in Kirkee with his grandparents, not his own parents. No school was held on Friday. His absence wouldn't have been noted. He'd come back over the weekend, spent time with Khushru and the math study group, and on Monday, brought a bicycle to him.

Had the bicycle been bought with ill-gotten gains? And had Khushru refused to ride it — and then been poisoned by Naval, who realized his friend was too big a risk for confessing?

And Freny's satchel had been discovered on the train tracks southeast of Bombay on the way to Poona — near the Kirkee station.

Perveen had to find the boys. She could create a commotion. If Naval meant Khushru harm, he would run. On the other hand, if he was a true friend, he would stay.

She heard the familiar splashing sound of the fountain ahead. The fountain with merciful ladies, so close to the morgue. She knew this place.

As she drew closer, she saw the outline of the coroner's court and morgue buildings. Windows in the morgue glowed yellow, and she imagined a handful of men working inside, masks on their faces and gloves on their hands, deciphering causes of death.

She was now thirty feet from the fountain and heard the conversation.

"Don't be so foolish. You have everything now!" Naval's voice was almost wheedling.

"No. There is nothing for me anymore. I cannot go on." Khushru's weak reply was followed by a bout of coughing.

"Nobody is looking around anymore. They've hung everything on Dinesh."

"That's wrong. Just leave me here," Khushru groaned. "I want this to end. I cannot stand another minute with Freny haunting me."

"You and that talk of ghosts. It is not real," Naval said.

"I saw her in the colony courtyard, and in my own bedroom. She appears, then vanishes. And there — can't you see her? She is there!" Khushru gestured toward Perveen, and she quickly stepped back behind the fountain. She hadn't realized the light had illuminated her.

"Those are the delusions of illness. You took poison, remember?"

A door creaked somewhere along the coroner's court and morgue complex. Perhaps a police surgeon or morgue worker was taking a welcome breath of fresh air. *Good,* Perveen thought. She had intended to cause a commotion, but she didn't know how she would manage it. All she knew was that she didn't want to be alone.

Quietly, she edged around the fountain, trying to catch sight of the newcomer to the scene. But there was nobody — not until she turned her head and saw the outline of a tall man just a few feet behind her.

Her first thought was that the coroner had come out. But as he drew close enough to touch her shoulder roughly, she realized the man was Naval.

"I came — I came looking for the two of you, on the nursing sister's advice." She was stumbling over her words.

"No. You were spying. Just like her." Naval's words were sharp.

Perveen was chilled; every hair on her body had gone on alert. In a flash, she'd gone to stand protectively behind Khushru, who was cringing low in the wheelchair. Willing her voice to cooperate, she said, "Good evening, Khushru. I've been worrying ever since we brought you here in the morning. The nurse said it was poison — just as I'd thought."

Khushru's only answer was a faint groan.

"Don't blame me! I had nothing to do with it." From the other side of the fountain, Naval's voice rang defiantly.

Perveen looked through the darkness toward where she thought Naval was still standing. Not seeing him made her uneasy. "Sunday afternoon, did you eat anything at the college?"

"I don't deserve life." Khushru's words were halting. "I took the rat poison my mother keeps in a jar in the kitchen. It was supposed to kill me straight away. But I failed at it, just as I fail at everything."

"You are hardly a failure. You are a very strong student, Miss Hobson-Jones was saying —"

"Yes, yes," chimed in Naval, emerging from the shadows to approach them. "Just two days ago, we were talking about you going to the University of Bombay. You have everything to live for."

Everything was starting to come together. Khushru's lack of money, the endless jobs he did to make the tuition payment — he had shirked college and his job to steal alongside Naval. The simple plan had failed because Freny was hiding in the office and had either confronted them or been caught by them. But how could she say this without enraging Naval, who must have been the mastermind? Slowly, Perveen said, "Khushru, I know that you didn't want to kill Freny."

Khushru inhaled, and then coughed hard before the words eventually came. "I didn't want it. But I watched it happen. I didn't know what to do."

"Hush, now." Naval had his hands on the

wheelchair and gave it a shake. "You're dreaming things. It is the medicine, Miss Mistry. Don't let him confuse you."

Perveen bent to look closely at Khushru's tear-stained face. Softly, she said, "I don't believe you are alone in this."

"I am not." Drawing gasping breaths, Khushru continued, "Naval also should confess. That is what I was saying ever since we walked to the funeral."

"What a fool I was to befriend you." Naval's voice was low and furious. "I am the only one who could show you the way to success. And now you are telling lies, just to clear yourself."

"Let's see if I understand what happened on that very difficult day." Perveen was playing for time, hoping that someone inside the mortuary would emerge. "Khushru didn't arrive at the Hawthorn Shop until late, because he'd agreed to meet you, Naval, at the college."

"Not true. He was marked absent!" Naval said.

"The two of you knew that the remaining tuition payments had been submitted the previous afternoon." Turning briefly to Khushru, she asked, "Were you able to pay? Your mother thought so."

His head dipped even lower as he mumbled his reply. "Just part. And the college had said I couldn't get more scholarship funds."

"Naval," Perveen said, looking back at the stone-faced young man in charge of the chair, "Was it like this? Your good friend was desperate to finish the year with his bachelor's degree. You knew that if you were to raid the admin office at a time the college was unlocked, yet everyone in the viewing stands, you could cover this handily."

"What a ridiculous idea. Tuition was due days earlier, and he had paid. That's right, Khushru, isn't it?"

Khushru closed his eyes and didn't answer. Perveen thought about how he shared his test answers with Naval, and a possible puzzle piece slipped into her hand. "Naval, you are well-off. You could have advanced the money to Khushru and told him he needed to steal it back, along with the rest, from the college on Thursday."

Naval's voice wavered. "How can you accuse us of touching that cashbox? You saw me in the stands, Miss Mistry. And Khushru was not at college. Don't make this poor boy suffer any more than he has already with these slurs on his character!"

The theft had never been announced to students. Yet Naval had revealed the money was taken from a cashbox: an object that was hidden from view because it was kept inside a desk.

She saw Khushru pull himself higher in the chair. He whispered, "Freny must have told her the truth. She can still hear Freny's voice, just like I do."

"She will always speak to me." As Perveen looked into Khushru's sorrowful face, she knew she did not believe in ghosts. But Freny had changed her, guiding her to look for truth in ways that were far from obvious. "Tell me, Khushru, did you find Freny in the office, or did she confront you?"

"Both," Khushru said unsteadily. "She was underneath the secretary's desk. When we were counting out the money, she stood up and told us to return everything or she'd expose us as thieves. I begged her not to say anything, that we would put it back right away."

"What was her response to that?" Perveen asked.

"She could not speak, because Naval had — he had fallen upon her."

Naval shook the wheelchair so hard that Khushru almost fell out. "You were just as much a part of her death! You watched, and you typed the note."

Somewhere, a clock was pealing. Nine

o'clock. The final visiting hour was over. She wondered if the main hospital door would remain open. But she couldn't leave Khushru alone. Naval would not leave a talkative witness alive.

"Khushru, what happened to Freny's schoolbag?"

"I took it to the Hawthorn Shop."

"But that's not where it was found. I think Naval told you to bring it with you, because it was an easy way to carry the money. He met you later and gave you whatever share he thought was fair."

"Ridiculous!" Naval's voice rose in anger.

Ignoring him, she said, "Then Naval fled the city, carrying the bag with him. He must have hidden the money at his grandparents' and disposed of the bag later, along the track, to make it look like her killer had left town. This was insurance, as the faked suicide note might not be believed."

"Who are you to say these things when the police have evidence it was Dinesh Apte? You're harassing us. We have worked hard and will graduate this year. We have nothing to do with that stupid girl —"

"What you say is very different from what Khushru has confessed." Perveen stared at Naval. "What did it feel like, going to the funeral? When your lips were moving in prayer, was it for her, or were you calling on Ahriman?"

She was speaking of the devil, language that Freny's father would have used. She was so focused on her vision of Naval that she reacted too late to his attack. One moment he was ten feet away — the next his breath was on her face. Before she could fight back, he'd pushed her hard on the shoulder, yanking down the gauzy length of sari covering her hair.

The physical touch was shocking in itself; and in the next instant, he had grabbed her hair. She shrieked at the pain as he used her unwound braids like ropes to drag her backward.

At the edge of her vision, Khushru was struggling out of his chair, but he only made one step before collapsing.

Naval was as strong as she'd imagined. Intermingled with her terror, though, was her own anger. She stumbled in the direction he pulled her, unable to escape his grip, but she screamed.

The first cry was weak, but the second time was louder. She screamed and screamed again, until he smashed a rough hand over her mouth.

Now her body was against his, and she felt, with horror, that he was aroused. Had he felt this way when he killed Freny? Was it exciting to destroy a woman?

Her back was slammed against something hard, and suddenly her feet were in the air.

Naval's hand came away from her mouth to twist her head, while his other hand remained on her shoulder. He'd managed to tip her over the fountain's hard stone rim. She felt water pulling at her hair as Naval wrenched her face into the basin.

The water came up around her so suddenly she was too late to keep it out of her mouth. She was on her way to drowning, despite the fountain's shallowness.

Fight! There was a voice shouting in her head, not her own, but high-pitched. It was Freny's voice.

If only she could fight the weight pressing down on her shoulder and head. If only she had held her breath instead of swallowing. If only —

In the next instant, she felt the weight lift, just as a shower of something warm and damp covered her back. Naval screamed. And just as suddenly as she'd hit the fountain, she was being pulled out of it. Strong hands were on her shoulders, gently assisting her to sit on the fountain's edge. After she'd coughed out most of the fountain water, she looked up into the very blurry face of J.P. Singer.

"Miss Mistry, what did that sunnabitch do?"

She shook her head, not quite understanding the American slang. "Where is Naval?"

"Taken care of." Singer's voice was hard.

Perveen wiped her mouth with the back of her hand, and as her breathing slowed, her vision stabilized. Perveen followed his gaze to see Naval sprawled on the grass, a dark stain on the back of his shirt. Then she touched the dark wetness on her sari pallu.

"It's Naval's blood, isn't it?" As she spoke, she realized the great difficulty J.P. Singer now faced. The foreign journalist had stabbed a wealthy Indian citizen in the back.

"I don't know who he is. Never saw him in my life. I was only coming out of the morgue and heard screaming. Do you know this bastard?"

"Naval Hotelwala is a student at Woodburn College. He killed Freny Cuttingmaster just as surely as you have saved me." Perveen kept her eyes on Naval, but he did not move. "We need help immediately. There are doctors inside the morgue —"

"Hold on. What about him?" J.P. Singer's gaze swung around to Khushru collapsed in front of the wheelchair.

"He's no danger to anyone," Perveen said

536

quickly. "Khushru Kapadia was being treated at the hospital for poisoning. I think Naval brought him to this fountain to drown him." Perveen took a deep breath, rejoicing in her clear lungs. "I can't thank you enough for coming out of the morgue, Mr. Singer. Your action saved my life. My father and I will do anything to assist you as needed —"

Ignoring her, J.P. Singer had moved to the fountain and was swishing something in the water. When he turned back to her, she saw him slide a narrow silver knife back into a sheath under his clothes — a specific kind of knife that she had only seen once before in her life, during a Sikh cultural demonstration. She asked, "Is that a kirpan?"

"Yes. I wear it always. We don't start fights — but God expects us to defend others and ourselves."

He must have been a Sikh. Had he changed his name from Singh, as all Sikh men were named, to Singer? Was it for assimilation or another purpose? This was not the time to ask. Her gaze slid to Khushru, who was struggling to get up into the wheelchair again. J.P. Singer walked over to him and gently lifted him back into the chair. Khushru's head went back, and he looked at the journalist with wide eyes. "It is my turn. I accept my death."

"No," Singer to Perveen. "I won't touch anyone who's not a threat. Are you strong enough to get back to the hospital on your own?"

"Yes." Her back hurt, and the back of her head throbbed. She touched her head and felt a raw space where Naval had pulled so hard that hair was gone. "I can call for help. We could knock at the morgue's door to alert anyone who might be inside. I will most certainly vouch for your saving my life, and they will do what's necessary to take care of Naval —"

"He's gone. I don't take shortcuts."

"What are you saying?" Perveen looked into J.P. Singer's impassive face.

"He's dead, Miss Mistry."

"Dead?" Perveen echoed, looking at the still form.

"You said you were willing to help me."

"Yes." Perveen was relieved that he understood he'd need legal assistance.

"Listen." Singer's voice was low as he walked slowly toward her. "Can you give me five minutes to leave this area before you go to the hospital for help?"

"Don't leave. You're a journalist!" Perveen protested. "This is your story, and there are legal repercussions if you aren't here to give an account to the police."

"I can't stay. For so many reasons."

"You don't understand. You really need a lawyer's help!" As Perveen stared at him, he moved toward her, and bent his head. His lips touched her cheek, and then were gone. "I wish things could have been different."

What did he mean by that? Perveen stood and gripped the handles of Khushru's wheelchair, watching their savior vanish into darkness.

He had only asked for five minutes.

J.P. Singer had saved her life. She would allow his escape.

36
SOCIAL GEOGRAPHY

The Bombay Coroner's inquiry into Naval Hotelwala's death by unnatural causes occurred three days later.

J.P. Singer was not present at the coroner's inquest. He'd vanished like smoke in the warm autumn air, leaving possessions in his room at the Taj Hotel that included one American passport issued in the United States for Jai Preet Singh, and a second passport issued by the US Consulate General Naples, for Jay Peter Singer. The Bombay Police sought information about the man from his newspaper in San Francisco, but nothing had arrived by the time of the inquest.

Perveen wondered how much truth lay in the government's assertion that the man who'd saved her life was actually a foreign agent who'd arrived with the hopes of killing the Prince of Wales. The stub of a train ticket to Poona on the day the railway was tampered with was also found in his room, as well as many more Ghadar Party pamphlets and drafts of essays about the inhumanity of British rule.

Naturally, Perveen was called as a witness at the inquest. In the witness box, she'd had to steady herself to replay the terrifying memories of the incident by the fountain. Her voice was shaky as she narrated how the journalist had heard her screaming and come out in time to interrupt a homicide by drowning. Khushru had relayed most of the same details, although he had not heard everything Naval had said.

Khushru had never been the chief actor in Freny's death, but because Naval was not alive, it looked as if he'd bear the responsibility.

It was a difficult situation. Although Perveen wanted justice for Freny, she felt in her bones that Khushru should not hang for it. He was an accessory to murder, not a murderer. But his trial was many months away. All she needed to worry about was the outcome of the inquest into Naval's death.

The coroner spent two hours laying out, in grisly detail, the nature of Naval's fatal stabbing, and why it should be considered homicide, a deliberate act of violence, based on the behavior of Singer and his background. Yet after an hour's deliberation, the jury came back with a verdict of death by knife wound; there had not been enough votes to rule the death a homicide.

As Perveen exited the courtroom, she was rushed by reporters.

She was glad that J.P. Singer would not face a charge of homicide. Yet she knew he was still being searched for on suspicion of terrorism. Therefore, she had to choose her words carefully. If she appeared to be supporting a suspicious foreigner on the lam, she could be labeled a seditionist.

She made her statement, over and over again.

"The jury did the best they could with limited information. Mr. Singer's swift action was in defense of me and Mr. Kapadia when we were in mortal danger. And furthermore, based on what Naval Hotelwala admitted before his death, I believe the murder of Freny Cuttingmaster last week was perpetrated by Mr. Hotelwala, not Dinesh Apte, nor Khushru Kapadia. It is thanks to J.P. Singer that I am alive today and continuing my legal work on behalf of Bombay's people."

"You will not refer to your rescuer as Mr. Jai Preet Singh, then?" asked someone from the *Times of India.*

"I don't believe I have the right to do that," Perveen said easily. "Two passports with different names were found in the hotel room, yes, but there are also numerous published articles using the name J.P. Singer. Because the gentleman is a citizen of the United States, it would be wise to gather information from that country's government. In any case, this inquest is solely about the cause of death for Naval Hotelwala — not to debate the identity of J.P. Singer."

The Hotelwala family had been in the courtroom, just as Freny's had been for her inquest. Perveen had noticed the somber-looking middle-aged Parsi man and woman, with an elderly lady wearing a white sari. They sat in a row near the front with space on either side of them.

She knew they were very likely suffering the same strong emotions that Freny's family had: desperation to have their child released to be buried privately, and a mixture of horror and sorrow at the violence of the death. Very likely they regretted sending Naval to live apart from them, just as the Cuttingmasters mourned enrolling Freny in college. They were likely horrified and ashamed to hear their beloved child's reputation destroyed in public, and remorseful for the murder he had committed and the suffering he had caused.

All these things, on top of losing a precious child who had once been their angel; their great hope for building the family hotel business.

As Perveen stepped out of the coroner's court onto the crowded veranda, she had a straight view to the fountain where she'd almost lost her life. Feeling her throat close, she whispered to Jamshedji, "Let's not go that way."

He put a hand on her elbow. "Very well. Let's exit on the other side, toward the hospital."

A tall blonde woman in a knee-length frock was striding toward them, seemingly oblivious to heads turning in her wake. Perveen's brief anxiety was replaced with joy. "Hello, Alice! What a surprise."

"I had class this morning, so I'm sorry I couldn't be in the court itself. What happened?" Her eyes fixed on the press and police still assembled on the court's veranda.

"The jury agreed that Naval's cause of death was stabbing. They also had a chance to indict Mr. Singer on homicide, but they declined." Perveen added, "Good luck to

Mr. Mortimer and the Imperial Police, who are hell-bent on arresting him for terrorism."

"But no longer looking at you," Alice pointed out. "Which is a good thing. And we cannot assume that Singer is still in India. He could have sailed off from the Bombay docks in a fishing boat, or hopped on a north-bound train and trekked over the mountains to Afghanistan or even China! There is no telling what someone so strong and clever would do. I only wish I'd had the chance to get a better look at him when he was chatting with you outside the Orient Club."

"The drawings in the newspaper don't do him justice," Perveen said, recalling his rugged handsomeness. Was it the way he looked, or his exotic accent and slang that had made him so appealing? "I suspect that wherever he lands, nobody will ever catch him."

Jamshedji cleared his throat. "If you must gossip, do it over a quick lunch. But I must remind Perveen she has a client at two o'clock."

"She won't be late, Mr. Mistry. My driver's nearby." Alice waved as Jamshedji departed, swinging his Swaine and Adeney briefcase in a jaunty manner.

After the ladies made their way off the hospital campus and through the door of a Muslim biryani and kebab restaurant, Perveen asked for a table in the back that faced the door. She intended to make an exit if the wrong kind of press appeared. In the meantime, they studied menus, debating the virtues of the various kebabs. After they'd placed their order, Perveen asked Alice about college reactions to the news about Naval's death.

"In the college, sympathies are running high for Khushru," Alice said. "Other students felt that Naval was always a bad influence. I've heard more than one student say they believe Naval was the mastermind who bullied Khushru into everything. There is sympathy for Dinesh as well."

As she'd promised, Perveen had gone to see Mr. Murthy the day after she'd met with Dinesh. Mr. Jinnah had joined their meeting, and after Murthy admitted that he'd answered some police questions about Dinesh, he'd been taken off the case. Despite the compromising behavior of Murthy, after Perveen's information, Mr. Jinnah was almost certain the murder charge against his client would be dismissed.

Across the restaurant, Perveen recognized a Parsi couple standing by the curtains at the door, looking around. She whispered to Alice, "Look. Freny's parents are here."

Alice followed her gaze. "Why? Does this mean they were attending the inquest for Naval's death?"

"Maybe they were. But I'm surprised they would enter a restaurant during the mourning period."

The Cuttingmasters had stopped looking around and were heading directly for her.

"I know what it is!" Perveen put a hand to her mouth. "I forgot to follow up on whether they wanted the college's financial gift. They must have spotted us leaving the coroner's court and want a word with me."

Alice raised her eyebrows. "Well, now's the time to go. Shall I slip out of the café to give you privacy?"

Reaching across the table, Perveen gripped her hand. "Please don't leave just yet. If anything, they would be reassured to meet a lecturer from the college."

As the Cuttingmasters arrived, both Perveen and Alice rose to their feet.

Alice spoke first.

"Please excuse me, Mr. and Mrs. Cuttingmaster. I am Alice Hobson-Jones, a lecturer in the Woodburn College mathematics department. Please know that your Freny was one of the most wonderful students to ever be in my classroom. She was such a smart and lovely young woman. I can't begin to imagine how much you miss her."

Perveen was warm with pride for Alice. Her friend was often physically clumsy, but she'd said just the right thing. Mithan was smiling softly, and Firdosh had stretched out his hand.

"Miss Hobson-Jones." Firdosh Cutting-master spoke without any of the anger that Perveen was familiar with. "Thank you for your kind condolences. You were one of our daughter's favorite lecturers. We are honored to meet you."

"I will never forget her." Alice's eyes were shining with tears.

Perveen could hardly follow up Alice's heartfelt condolences. So she said softly, "Hello. I hope that you are well."

As the group stood awkwardly, two waiters hurried up, each holding a chair. Mithan nodded at her husband, and they both sat down.

"We are not eating," Firdosh said. "Mourning is still on. But we wish to speak with Miss Mistry."

"I'm glad to hear this," Perveen said. "I very much need to apologize. I left an important letter for both of you with your mother and did not return to get your answer."

"You have been very busy," Mithan said, her gaze serious. "You were looking high and low for the correct person to be charged."

"Yes. And you came close to losing your life." Firdosh cleared his throat, as if he was uncomfortable. "I give thanks to God your father was spared such a loss. Now, about the letter."

Alice hopped up, murmuring, "Perveen, please excuse me for a few minutes."

They all watched Alice travel the short distance to the sweet counter. Then Perveen spoke again. "I didn't read the letter because it was addressed to you. But Mr. Atherton told me there was an offer of money. That sum is in a safe. I didn't want to bring it through the city to your place when you were away from home."

"It was quite surprising." Firdosh looked toward Alice's back. "I truly don't mind if she returns. It could be helpful."

Perveen waved for Alice to return, which she did.

"Mr. Atherton sent me a letter on behalf of the college's board of trustees." Firdosh explained that the college's board had met and given personal donations expressing their sorrow over the loss of Freny. "Quite a bit of money — five hundred rupees."

Alice's eyes widened. "Quite a packet!"

"He said they were all personal donations?" Perveen asked.

"Yes, from ten board members, some of whom must be quite wealthy."

So this was the reason Atherton had brought her cash, rather than a check — and had not felt that a receipt to the college was necessary.

Firdosh continued, "What can Mithan and I do with such a load of money? We have a home with very low rent that is comfortable for us. I am well-employed and wish to continue my work."

"As you should." Mithan patted his arm. "Some say you're the best tailor in the city."

Firdosh Cuttingmaster smiled back at his wife. "We have plenty. And yet both our children are gone. Many times, we have asked ourselves: Did God allow this travesty because of something we've done? That was why I was so angry with you, Miss Mistry. I wanted nothing to do with finding the truth of something I feared would make me face all of my faults."

"Your daughter's death was not your fault," Perveen said. "It had nothing to do with political differences."

"You helped me understand that." Firdosh leaned toward Perveen. "It seems to us that there are many young people in Bombay Presidency who would like to attend college but cannot pay for it. We wish to use the money to create a scholarship in Freny's name for students who need extra assistance to attend Woodburn and other colleges in Bombay. We will cover the remainder of the tuition that their colleges cannot give as scholarship."

Perveen was astonished by his suggestion. Half-choked, she said, "This is an act of such compassion. I imagine that the college trustees will be stunned at your selflessness."

"It is a complicated matter to make a scholarship. And we do not wish to be involved in choosing from amongst the applicants." Looking across the table at Alice, Firdosh continued, "Perhaps you could do this for me, Miss Hobson-Jones? You are connected to the college so you understand its workings."

"I could certainly do that," Alice said. "And your money could be the seed of something larger. Perhaps I can coax my mother and her friends into adding to the pot."

Savoring the taste of the malva cake in

her mouth, Perveen thought a bit further. "Five hundred rupees could be used up in less than five years, unless it was put into some kind of interest-bearing account. Some banks make special provisions for charities. I'd be able to help you set up a charitable foundation, if you'd like. There are steps to register it with the city."

"It shall be the Freny Cuttingmaster Triple H Foundation." There was pride in Firdosh Cuttingmaster's voice.

"Yes. When people write her name, and say it aloud, she lives on," Mithan Cuttingmaster said softly.

"What's Triple H?" Alice asked as she picked up a sugar bun.

"Humata, Hukhta, Hvarshta," Mithan said. "It means good thoughts, good words, and good deeds. We think about this every day; it is a tenet of our faith."

The pleasant planning session with the Cuttingmasters ended at one-thirty. Perveen rode in Alice's car back to her tasks at Mistry House, and Alice returned to the college.

Six o'clock came too fast. After an afternoon filled with legal writing and client consultation, Perveen readied herself for the lecture at the Asiatic Society. She was dressed in the same blue sari that she had worn to court, but she slipped the pallu away from her head to look at her hair.

It wasn't surprising that the Cuttingmasters thought she looked different. Because she had lost such a big chunk of hair during Naval's attack, she'd been forced to try a new style. Her shoulder-length bob wasn't quite as daring as Ruttie Jinnah's shingle, but it was a shocking length to her family, even after it had been styled in a most attractive manner at the Taj Hotel's salon.

Her head felt slightly lighter. It was easier to keep her chin up, as the British liked to say. With a sari draped overhead, the public would not even know she had a modern hairstyle. *Unless she wanted to reveal it,* the stylist had added with a wink.

Where would that be? Certainly not at the Asiatic Society of Bombay.

After Arman stopped the car, she climbed up the long flight of stairs, remembering how she'd slowly walked down them with Mr. Dass and then met up with Colin. She had not seen him since that night, though she had sent him a letter of thanks for his telegram. The simple question he'd asked when visiting Hotel Spenta provided the last clue to her understanding of Naval. It also had led the police to find the college's stolen money hidden in an empty rice jar at Hotel Spenta.

The companions she'd drafted to join her at the lecture, Alice and Gulnaz, were seated in the second row with an empty chair saved for her. Alice had changed from her dark cotton teaching frock into a bright blue chiffon, and Gulnaz was looking lovely in lime green, the bulge of her baby seeming slightly bigger than the week earlier. Perveen spotted Mr. Dass along the row and greeted him.

The old man blinked and then smiled in recognition. "Miss Mistry, I've read about your adventures. I have copied the text of several newspaper articles. I can give them to you after the talk."

Perveen offered her gratitude and moved along to take the seat between Gulnaz and Alice. There was no time for chatting because Mr. Joshi, the club's president, came onto the wide podium at the front of the room. He was followed by Colin, who was wearing a finely tailored tan suit and crisp white shirt. Colin's eyes scanned the crowd, and she saw him give quick smiles to several people. He hadn't seen her yet.

"A sincere welcome to all, and may I express my delight at this heartening participation. Much has happened in our city that is far from civil; I venture we are all grateful for a return to regular office and school schedules and safety. From its earliest days, the Bombay branch of the Royal Asiatic Society has been the essence of civility, a place where any man or woman can share in enjoyment of knowledge and beauty.

"Tonight, we will begin with a special guest, Mr. Colin Sandringham, one of the co-founders of The Thinkers, an organization that fosters relaxed and open conversation about India's past, present, and future. Mr. Sandringham has not been with us regularly, due to his former responsibilities as an ICS political officer with the Kolhapur Agency."

Former responsibilities. Her stomach dropped. Had Colin been sacked because he'd made the bold move to stop the royal train in Kirkee, in order to visit the Hotel Spenta?

"Indeed," the trustee continued, "We're almost as grateful for this change in station as we are for the fresh thinking Mr. Sandringham has brought to the society. It's no wonder that he was elected unanimously by our members as a vice president."

The rest of Mr. Joshi's remarks were hard to remember, because Perveen was lost in her own thoughts. She'd worried Colin had lost his position; but it turned out he'd been trying to tell her he might come to Bombay. And on Monday, she'd looked at a sample contract meant for him and rewritten a section in order to limit his housing benefit. If he ever heard this, he'd have a good laugh.

The applause had finished, and Colin was shaking hands with Mr. Joshi, who left the podium.

Taking his place at the lectern, Colin spoke to the assembly. "It is very difficult to express my gratitude at being given a chance to become deeply involved in an organization like no other in this city: a group of people dedicated to the preservation and appreciation of many of the world's greatest manuscripts, artworks, coins, and books. Trustees have assured me that I'll learn as I go along — and this house of knowledge is filled with brilliant teachers, whether they are readers sitting at the table, librarians, or the custodians of art work. This building is Bombay personified; and as I learn it, I will learn the city's heritage."

Colin was a wonderful speaker. The awkwardness she had seen in the beginning had faded; his face was no longer flushed, and he spoke with a natural warmth. He rested easily with his arms on the lectern, regarding the diverse group of Indians and Europeans who had come together for the lecture.

Perveen caught his eye, and as he looked at her, the corners of his mouth tilted upward. He was clearly glad that she'd come. Everything was bound to change — and while she felt fear, there was also a rush of relief that she'd never again feel that he was missing from her life.

Perveen would tell him this later. For now she gave him the smallest of smiles, hoping that Alice and Gulnaz wouldn't notice.

Taking his spectacles out of his jacket pocket, Colin directed his attention to a sheaf of papers on the lectern. "My topic this evening is social mapping. What is social mapping, you may ask? How is it different than the mapping of mountains and rivers, or buildings and towns?

"I will begin with the marvelous city in which I am an unabashed, enthusiastic new resident, gathering insights from local friends and colleagues. The British have always held that the founding of Bombay came with Fort, the bustling and important administrative neighborhood around us. Yet as we know from history, before the East India Company built Fort, this was a military safe hold held by the Portuguese. For many years prior to the Portuguese, this area belonged to the great Marathas, who might have named it Bomba, although we are not entirely certain. Why was this place where we are so highly coveted? I am interested in the people who were here, and how the places were changed by them. For instance: How did a temple give way to a railway station, and grazing ground for cows transform into a social hub for textile traders? These are just a few of the stories we will discuss tonight . . ."

"I hope he finishes before my water breaks!" Gulnaz whispered.

"Shush, dear." Perveen patted her sister-in-law's hand.

She was ready to hear all of it.

GLOSSARY

Aadab: polite phrase and gesture of greeting among Muslims

Agiary: worship place for Zoroastrians

Ahriman: destructive spirit who is Ahura Mazda's antagonist in Zoroastrianism

Ahura Mazda: name of God, the highest deity in Zoroastrianism

Alhamdulillah: Praise be to Allah

Almirah: freestanding cupboard

Angrez: English-origin person

Anna: small unit of money equal to four paise or one-sixteenth of one rupee

Asha: righteousness or truth

Ashem Vohu: important prayer mantra in Avestan, the original Zoroastrian language

Ayah: maidservant tending to a woman or child

Babu-ji: respectful term for addressing a Hindu man

Badmash: bad guy

Baksheesh: tip, charitable gift or bribe

Bandhej: also known as Bandhani, a tie-dying textile art

Bombay Presidency: a large administrative subdivision of British India that had Bombay as its headquarters

Baug: separate neighborhood often called a colony

Bhakra: Parsi fried doughnut

Challo: let's go

Chukoo: silly show-off

Chutiya: vulgar term used to insult a person meaning female genitalia

Dakhma: a Tower of Silence where the Zoroastrian deceased are laid to decompose, usually in an agiary

Dar Ni Pori: Parsi bread stuffed with sweet, spiced lentils

Dhansak: famous Parsi curry made with spices, dal and meat, often eaten after the first period of mourning is complete

Dhobi: washer of clothes

Doongerwadi: historic funeral grounds in Malabar Hill including dakhma, worship halls, and shelter for mourning families

Durwan: a guardsman for home or business

Farcha: Parsi style fried chicken

Fetah: tall, stiff hat worn by Parsi men

Gandhiji: respectful term for Modandas Gandhi

Goonda: gangster

Gup-shup: gossip

Gymkhana: field day for sports or sports arena club

Hai Ram: Hindu exclamation meaning "Oh God" that can be used in religious and secular life

Hartal: planned work stoppage as form of protest

Humata, Hukhta, and Huvarshta: Divine thoughts, divine words, and divine deeds; a cornerstone of Zoroastrianism

Insha'Allah: If Allah wills it to be

Kem Cho: How are you? in Gujarati

Kolhapur Agency: the British colonial government's grouping of 26 princely states in Western India that later became known as the Deccan States Agency

Kusti: Zoroastrian sacred cord worn around waist

Kurta: collarless tunic

Lathi: stick used for fighting

Lungi: short loincloth

Maharaja: Hindu ruler of a Princely State

Maharani: mother or wife or daughter of a ruler

Maratha: name describing the people of Western India's descended from warrior clans

Marathi: language spoken in Maratha-dominated areas, including Bombay

Mathabana: thin white cloth tightly wrapped to cover a Parsi woman's hair

Memsahib: obsequious term of address for a superior woman

Namaste: Sanskrit/Hindu salutation of greeting or goodbye that means "I bow to you"

Nankhatai: sweet Parsi shortbread biscuit

Nawab: a Muslim ruler of a Princely State

Paithani: tapestry weave textile handloomed in an area of Maharashtra

Pallu: the hanging end of a sari

Parsi: Indian-born member of the Zoroastrian faith

Poona: important business and military town in Bombay Presidency

Sagdid: purification ritual before a body is carried away to the dakhma

Sahib: obsequious term of respect for upper class man, European or Indian

Shahi Mutton Pulao: spicy lamb and rice dish

Shukriya: thank you

Sudra/sudreh: light white undershirt worn by Zoroastrian men

Susu: childish Hindi word for urine

Vakil: advocate who can be a person's public pleader, lawyer or agent

Vande Mataram: "Hail to Mother India": an 1875 Sanskrit poem by Bankim Chandra

Chatterjee in 1875 that became a nationalist anthem

ACKNOWLEDGMENTS

The Bombay Prince was inspired by the 1921-22 tour of the Indian subcontinent by Prince Edward VIII. The prince's daily schedule mentioned in this novel is based on British government records, and information about the days of unrest following his procession came from newspapers of the era. Specific events that happening at fictitious Woodburn College and on the railway are imagined.

I was fortunate to have had the help of so many wonderful, knowledgeable people during my writing process. Historian Dr. Dinyar Patel generously answered my questions about Bombay's early 20th century unrest. Parinaz Madan, a solicitor and writer practicing in Mumbai, kindly read my manuscript and helped me fine-tune details relating to history and Parsi culture.

I offer my gratitude to Mumbai solicitor Mehernaaz Wadia, and in the US, Dr. Mitra

Sharafi of the University of Wisconsin
School of Law.

Deepak Rao, a police historian in Mumbai, had the answer to seemingly every question about early 20th century police life. I also appreciated the thoughts of longtime Mumbai resident and author Rinki Roy Bhattacharya. Dr. Usha Thakkar, a history professor and director of Mani Bhavan, the Mohandas Gandhi museum, continues to be an important mentor to me. Dr. Yogesh Kande, a board member at the Asiatic Society of Mumbai, graciously brought me behind the scenes of the grand institution.

I'm grateful to my cousin Sonal Parekh's knowledge of all things Mumbai: from telephones to tea and tableware. Dr. Michelle Philip at Wilson College graciously assisted my research on the early 20th century college experience. At the Taj Mahal Palace Hotel, I enjoyed Taj marketing executive Nisha Dhage's behind-the-curtains tour of old-fashioned guest rooms and halls. Also in Mumbai, I'm indebted to Jehangir Patel, editor of *Parsiana* magazine, and Dr. Simin Patel, a historian and photographer of Indian cities, who has much for the historical traveler at her website and archive, bombaywalla.org.

To my Soho Press friends, Bronwen

Hruska, Juliet Grames, Rachel Kowal, Paul Oliver, Rudy Martinez, Steven Tran, and Alexa Wejko: many thanks to all of you for believing in Perveen Mistry and building out the series with such success. And I'm similarly thrilled by the longtime dedication of my agent, Vicky Bijur, who continues to open doors for Perveen in many countries.

I'm blessed by many relatives in the Banerjee, Parikh, Parekh, and Massey clans rich in wisdom and love. My stepmother, Dr. Manju Parikh, shared her long-ago master's thesis, which was a launching point into my understanding of class conflict amongst freedom activists. And to Tony, Pia, and Neel: thank you for giving me a full, far-from-solitary life.

ABOUT THE AUTHOR

Sujata Massey was born in England to parents from India and Germany, grew up in St. Paul, Minnesota, and lives in Baltimore, Maryland. She was a features reporter for the *Baltimore Evening Sun* before becoming a full-time novelist. The first Perveen Mistry novel, *The Widows of Malabar Hill,* was an international bestseller and won the Agatha, Macavity, and Mary Higgins Clark Awards. Visit her website at sujatamassey .com.

The employees of Thorndike Press hope you have enjoyed this Large Print book. All our Thorndike, Wheeler, and Kennebec Large Print titles are designed for easy reading, and all our books are made to last. Other Thorndike Press Large Print books are available at your library, through selected bookstores, or directly from us.

For information about titles, please call:
(800) 223-1244

or visit our website at:
gale.com/thorndike

To share your comments, please write:
Publisher
Thorndike Press
10 Water St., Suite 310
Waterville, ME 04901